EVERLASTING LOVE

"You want me to pose as your bride?" Meagan could read his thoughts. "All right, technically I suppose that's what I am. But I'll never pull off acting like an eighteenth-century woman."

"My people believe you're from Ireland. They'll not question what you do. And remember they've seen you already. In the kirk and when you ran outside."

"But what about the way I speak?"

This set him to thinking.

"I'll say that deafness till the age of twelve left you with impediments. You've only to still your clackiting tongue as best you can and the ruse will succeed."

Clackiting tongue indeed. She was one of the most soft-spoken women she knew. It was obvious clashes between them loomed ahead. For so many reasons, this was impossible, preposterous, absurd. And yet....

Her eyes met his.

"Would another kiss help you decide?" he asked.

The memory of his lips on hers took her breath. Robert Cameron was a truly dangerous man.

EVELYN ROGERS

THE FOREVER BRIDE

LEISURE BOOKS **NEW YORK CITY**

*This book is lovingly dedicated
to the memory of
EMMA FRANCES MERRITT
teacher, writer, friend.*

A LEISURE BOOK®

February 1997

Published by

Dorchester Publishing Co., Inc.
276 Fifth Avenue
New York, NY 10001

Printed in the United States of America.

THE
FOREVER
BRIDE

The Legend of the Forever Bride

Once upon a time in the misty long-ago, a Scottish lass, the last of her clan, dwelt in solitude in a castle deep in the Highland hills. Legend says she spent the days toiling for her keep, and the nights dreaming of a true and lasting love.

Time drifted onward, each year more lonely than the last, with only the echo of her step on the cold stone floor and the beat of her heart to break the stillness of the slowly passing hours. Springtime struck with special cruelty, the hills bursting in the glory of new life, a mockery to her own barren state.

One evening in the month that would come to be called May, a storm of great fury rent the heavens, threatening to bring down the solid walls of the castle. Unable to sleep, bereft of her dreams, she huddled before the hearth, seeking warmth and light in a world gone wild.

A knock at the door sounded above the rolling thunder. Fearing naught but loneliness, she opened her home to the stranger who strode in from the night, a young and stalwart man whose every aspect

7

seemed untouched by the storm. She offered him food and drink, then sat before the hearth to stare in wonder at his face and form, his strength, his even features, the kind and steady look in his eyes. He was, in truth, more perfect than she had ever dared to dream.

Knowing herself to be plain, she felt beautiful under the tenderness of his regard.

"Why are you here?" she asked.

"You called," he answered.

Understanding that he spoke the only truth that mattered between them, she could not hold back another question: "Will you stay?"

"My curse says nay, though you are what I've searched for through the years."

Great sadness darkened his words, yet she heard, too, the clear, sweet light of joyful peace. She knew not whether it was the heat from the flames or from his presence that warmed her, but for the first time in remembrance she felt the chill of her existence leave her heart, and when their eyes met she knew that she was loved.

As though she had willed it, when the mantel clock struck midnight, the storm lifted and they made their way to the chapel to declare themselves husband and wife in the old way of marriage by consent, a bond that joined them together forever in the sight of man and God. Moonlight bright as the rays of the sun spilled through the high open windows onto the pair as they swore their devotion, one for the other.

A ghràidh mo chridhe . . . love of my heart.

The ancient chant they spoke in unison once, twice, thrice.

As the words spilled from their lips, a bell pealed, echoing through a chapel that had no bell, and from a land that had known only roe deer and bear, the *people came, filling the kirk with their glad tidings, smiling them on their way to their marriage bed.*

Through the hours of darkness they made such sweet love as might make the angels gaze in envy. At dawn the lass awoke to find her true love gone. She grieved, but the people stayed to comfort her. Though the trees wept their leaves in sorrow and the wind cried across the storm-tossed land, she accepted peace in her heart because no longer did she dwell in solitude.

The legend says that on the anniversary of her wedding day she stole once again to the chapel to whisper the ancient chant. A ghràidh mo chridhe, she offered three times to the solemn stillness. And once again her husband, her one and only love, returned to take her in his arms, to carry her to the castle, and to their marriage bed.

In the morning he was gone, but each year on the same May evening she hurried to the chapel, and each year he appeared at her side. Time passed; she grew old, yet once a year, as she lay in her husband's arms, she was young and beautiful.

He called her his forever bride, the love of his heart, and she knew he spoke the truth.

Chapter One

One man, one night a year.

Would such a marriage work?

Meagan Butler stroked *The Forever Bride*'s leather binding. She'd never analyzed her favorite story before, but today seemed an appropriate time. Appropriate, too, was the place where she was reading—the small Scottish kirk pictured in the book's lavish illustrations.

One man, one night. Never one for prolonged, unbridled passion, Meagan saw the possibilities. It depended on the man . . . and the night.

Staring into the kirk's musty air, she considered the fantasy figure who made the anniversary visit, wafting his wife to her youth, thrilling her with hours of lovemaking, then disappearing, leaving her to pass another year as she chose.

A ghràidh mo chridhe. Love of my heart.

It was a beautiful incantation. What exactly did this love of her heart do to the woman? ". . . sweet love as might make the angels gaze in envy" might do for old-time readers, but it was far too vague for a woman who'd read Jacqueline Susann.

Meagan threw herself into the speculation. He had to be kind and gentle, of course, and totally absorbed in making the woman happy. His touch would be like warm silk caressing her body, sending her senses soaring.

Meagan doubted she was far wrong, especially about the silk. If only the story went into more detail.

She shook herself. What a silly dreamer she was, entranced by a brief, bittersweet legend. Why it was her favorite love story, she had no idea, nor did she know why she carried the small volume with her. Most perplexing of all, why did it stir some unnamed longing deep in her heart? She truly did not know. But here she was, in the Highland kirk where the legend's vows had supposedly been made, prepared to make vows of her own.

Today was her wedding day, a fact that should supersede all other considerations, all other speculations. She and William would be together the rest of their lives. From her days as a sickly child, she had found comfort in love stories, from the well-known classics to obscure legends like *The Forever Bride*. It was time for a love story of her own.

Sitting straight in the kirk's uncushioned pew, absentmindedly stroking the diamond of her engagement ring, she figured quickly. Tomorrow she would be thirty—an involuntary shudder ran through her—and William was thirty-eight. With modern life expectancy being what it was, especially for fitness freaks like the two of them, they faced forty or fifty years of married happiness. Average that out to forty-five, multiply times three hundred and sixty-five, minus two weeks each

Evelyn Rogers

year for separate business trips, and that left . . .

Fifteen thousand, seven hundred and ninety-five days together. And the same number of nights.

Meagan had always been good with numbers. This one ought to send blissful thrills down her spine. Her fiancé was, as the legend said, the love of her heart. Attorney, only heir to old New York money, tall, handsome, devoted, eager as she to start a family. He even shared her temperament—slow to anger, shy in crowds, most definitely ambitious. And he respected her privacy as she did his.

Best of all, while she couldn't exactly manipulate him, manipulation not being her strong suit, neither would he do or say anything to which she strongly objected. A dependable, uncomplicated man, that was her husband-to-be. What wasn't there to love?

Maybe his name. William Sturgeon. Correction. William Stuveysant Sturgeon IV. Meagan Sturgeon. It didn't exactly flow from the lips.

"Meg the Fish," a smart aleck at the ad agency had said.

"Meg who's reeled in a big catch," she'd flipped back, bothered only slightly at how mercenary she sounded. William *was* a catch, and she would be unrealistic not to admit it.

Her problem was that, as a copywriter, she cared too much about the sound of words. If the name Sturgeon had been good enough for five generations of stalwart New Yorkers, successful professional men with their hardy, civic-minded wives, it ought to be good enough for a postal worker's daughter from Hoboken, New Jersey.

Even one who wasn't a beauty.

In the matter of her looks, Meagan was a total

12

realist. She had movie-star coloring—black hair, violet eyes, and smooth, tawny skin—but her features were not so kind. Lips too full, chin too strong, eyes too wide apart. She knew her faults.

She had a weight problem, too, but that she had licked by regular exercise and watching every bite she took. She couldn't remember eating something that wasn't fat-free.

She was especially proud of her thighs. Morning workouts on the step machine—the Stair Monster, she called it—had left her legs tight and gently curved, so much so they barely jiggled on her daily jog.

"Pardon the interruption, lass, but is anything amiss?"

The question startled Meagan from thoughts of her thighs. She smiled up at the keeper of the Scottish castle where she and William would be staying for the night.

Thistledown Castle, sitting high on a promontory overlooking the northern edge of Loch Lochy, was the stronghold depicted in the legend's illustrations, the home of the almost-abandoned bride. William had reluctantly agreed to their wedding in its kirk. He could hardly refuse Meagan's hesitantly put request, since he had a very important meeting in Glasgow, less than two hours' drive away. He could combine his business with the wedding trip.

Also, even more reluctantly, he'd agreed to a honeymoon motor trip through both England and Scotland. For that she had taken off two weeks from her job. He would, however, have to check in from time to time with his partners in New York.

She would rather he forsake all thoughts of work, but that would have been asking too much of him, and asking too much of her to argue over the point. He would be driving in before long. She must be content.

"Miss Butler," the housekeeper said, "'tis growing late."

Meagan struggled to remember the woman's name. Ah, yes, Janet Forbes. Fiftyish, tall and sturdily built, and with the strong, craggy features of her Highlander ancestors, Miss Forbes seemed as formidable as the castle where she was employed.

"I'm sorry," Meagan replied, suitably chastised. "Of course it is."

She took one quick glance at the church interior, at the light filtering through the high, clear windows, at the rough stone walls, at the oak pews and pulpit, at the checkered marble floor. The kirk's only decoration was a series of paintings in the barrel-vaulted ceiling—the four seasons, signs of the zodiac, biblical scenes. Faded now, they hinted of an old grandeur, especially when they captured the incoming light.

Meagan felt moved by the atmosphere, by the awe and reverence the musty interior instilled. Like other kirks built in the Middle Ages, this one was shaped like the letter *T*, with the canopied pulpit placed in the center of the axis, pews to either side. The long perpendicular aisle to her back had once been used by the laird and his family, but it was now curtained off for repairs by the National Trust of Scotland, which had acquired and currently maintained the castle and its environs.

No trace of the laird or his family remained.

Miss Forbes cleared her throat. Meekly Meagan followed her out the door, her precious book forgotten on the pew as she pulled her daily list of things to do from her blue jeans pocket. The list was short:

Tour the castle
Pick up plaid
Marry William

She'd done everything but the last.

A chill shivered through her as she followed Miss Forbes along the shrub-lined path leading to the castle. The Scottish wind, she told herself, coming off the lake, biting even in May.

Certainly she had no doubts about the last item on her list.

"We've not had a wedding here in fifty years or more," Miss Forbes said as she led Meagan across a courtyard and into the main entrance, up a winding staircase to the third floor, and into the room which she had secured for her wedding night.

Her bridal attire was spread out on the high feather bed—a coarsely woven black dirndl skirt and white blouse, dark stockings, heelless slippers, and the red-and-green Cameron plaid that would serve as head covering and veil.

Not exactly white satin and lace, but it was in keeping with the setting. Miss Forbes had suggested it in place of the tailored cream suit she had brought, and Meagan had readily agreed. She hadn't bothered to arrange a kilt and accompanying paraphernalia for William. He wouldn't have put on the costume, wisely perhaps, since he did not have particularly attractive knees.

"Have ye no family to be here for the ceremony?" Miss Forbes asked.

"My parents are both gone. There's no one else."

The simple words stirred an inordinate pain in her breast, even after a year of being alone. She knew both her mother and father were watching this day with pleasure. She'd promised them she would marry William before she was thirty. She would do it, too.

Thanking Miss Forbes for her assistance, assuring her she would be at the chapel promptly at three, she prepared a hot bath in the adjoining bathroom's luxurious tub. Most of Thistledown had been kept rustic for authenticity's sake, but someone at the National Trust had been wise enough to know that tourists would not be thrilled by authentic plumbing as well.

Her one disappointment in the setting was that, unlike the kirk, the castle was not the original one. After the infamous Battle of Culloden of 1746, in which the Jacobite forces were soundly defeated by the British and their Scottish supporters, Thistledown Castle had been sacked by the vengeful Duke of Cumberland.

A late-eighteenth-century laird, a Highlander named Robert Cameron, had begun its restoration, and quite a restoration it had been, with a repaired quadrangle added to what was then the only structure remaining intact, Thistledown Keep. He'd taken care to include the castle's many corbeled and gargoyled turrets, the dormer windows, and gables that seemed to burst from every outer wall.

She would have liked to see his picture hanging in one of the castle's corridors.

"He was a simple man, and single-minded," Miss Forbes had explained when she expressed her disappointment. "The laird had no time for aught but tending his home and people."

"You sound as if you knew him personally."

"And how could that be, lass? 'Twould be something out of a fairy story if 'twere true."

Caught up in Thistledown's spell, Meagan almost believed such a thing really could be. Here was a fairy-tale setting to go with her favorite fairy tale. William had to be pleased.

He didn't seem especially so when she obeyed his summons to meet him on the ground floor. What was he doing here an hour early? She was still wearing her jeans, still getting ready for her bath.

His welcoming smile did not come quickly enough to cover the first look of disappointment that flashed in his eyes.

"You're not ready," he said.

"You're early," she said.

It was hardly a romantic greeting for a bride and groom an hour before they wed.

She grimaced; William did likewise, as if they had reached the conclusion simultaneously.

He kissed her; she tried to be encouraged, and returned the kiss with more than usual energy.

His gray-blue eyes registered approval.

"I thought we might move up the ceremony a bit," he said, backing away and taking her hand.

Was William impulsively eager to get to the marriage bed? It seemed unlikely. They hadn't slept together in the month since they'd finally set the wedding date. The temporary celibacy had been Meagan's idea; he had reluctantly agreed, but until this moment she had seen no signs of stressful sexual deprivation on his part.

In truth, he hadn't been overly zealous about their times together. Not cold, either, just quick and efficient as he was in most things. She would never compare his touch to warm silk, the way she had with her legendary hero; William was more like cotton, of the very finest grade.

She supposed that at their best, all men were like him. Silk was for legends and for dreams.

17

Meagan's experiences before William had been limited to a college affair and a disastrous mating with an actor she'd met on a blind date soon after moving to the city. In both cases she'd become engaged and in both cases had soon begged off.

William was fiancé number three, the man she would finally wed. Of course she would. He was on her list.

And there was, of course, that promise to Mom and Dad.

Besides, he loved her and seemed even more determined than she that they wed.

"We're not getting any younger," he'd told her more than once. Her bones creaked each time he said the words.

He wanted to get married as soon as possible, did he? So did she.

"I can be ready soon," she said with a smile. "I'm not sure about the minister."

"Don't worry. I've already arranged for his presence."

"I should have known."

"You don't sound pleased."

"Oh, William, of course I am."

She stared at his Brooks Brothers pin-striped suit, at his straight-arrow carriage, at his shoulders enhanced to wideness by his tailor, at his square chin. Six feet tall, a touch of gray at the temples of his dark hair to give him an air of distinction, a readiness for children and the ability to provide for them far beyond anything she had known as a child, he was indeed a catch. She had to reel him in fast.

A group of tourists passed behind them, led by one of the Scottish docents. Included in the group was a far-too-attractive redhead who noticed William more than the paintings on the walls.

Reel him in fast, Meagan reminded herself.

"Give me fifteen minutes," she said. She thought of the hot tub. "Make that twenty. I'll meet you in the kirk." He frowned, and she amended, "The church."

A peck on the cheek and she hurried up the winding stairs, threw off her clothes, and allowed herself five glorious minutes in the bath, splashed on the expensive perfume William had given her, and dressed in her Scottish attire. True, the items were reproductions of centuries-old wear, but they looked authentic and they felt authentic and they made her feel like a Scottish forever bride.

The only concessions to the twentieth century didn't show: white lace panties and bra and matching garters to hold up the dark stockings, and her mother's hand-embroidered handkerchief folded in one of the skirt's deep pockets. William had wanted her to wear his paternal grandmother's traditional gown, but she'd convinced him it might be damaged in transit.

When his mother agreed, she knew she had won. Mrs. William Sturgeon III, Hortencia Sturgeon, her mother-in-law-to-be, already showed little enthusiasm for the marriage; her only son was not inclined to give her further reason for disliking his bride.

Thank goodness her father-in-law-to-be showed more willingness to accept her into the family, albeit in his typically detached way.

It was Hortencia's idea for them to draw up a premarital agreement. Meagan had felt insulted, but under the woman's steady stare, she'd signed without protest.

She really wasn't after William's money, except for the security it gave their offspring. She fully intended to make her own as the most successful advertising agent in the business. Because of the campaign she'd created, one based on famous love stories, her lone client, a fledgling cosmetics firm, was already showing signs of steady growth.

Meagan studied herself in the mirror. Had she strayed too far from convention? Most important of all, would William approve? The skirt and blouse seemed much too plain for the newest Sturgeon, in sharp contrast to the heavy perfume she wore. Maybe she needed some of her client's products artfully applied to her face. She wore makeup at the office as part of her professional armor, but her tawny complexion kept her from wearing it now.

Her lone indulgence in artificial enhancement was acrylic nails. As healthy as she was, she couldn't grow her own, a condition she attributed to her frailty as a child.

She draped the length of plaid over her shoulder-length hair and let it fall across her breasts. The softly woven woolen cloth came practically to the hem of her ankle-length skirt. She felt immediately transformed. Why, even Robert Cameron himself, savior of Thistledown Castle, would take her for a Highland lass.

Unless, of course, he saw the diamond rock on her hand. Two carats, set in a crown of gold, it had set William back a ton of money. And it looked out of place with the plaid.

With only a twinge of conscience, she wrapped it in the embroidered handkerchief and stuck it firmly in the bottom of her pocket, where she figured it would be safe. Exiting her room, she was surprised to see Miss Forbes watching her in the hall. More surprising was the look of approval on her face.

"Ye'll do, lass. Ye'll do just fine," she said.

Do for what? Meagan had no time to ask.

She hurried to the kirk. William met her at the side entrance. With a sinking heart she took in the contrast between her plaid and her groom's pin-stripes. He scarcely gave a glance to what she wore.

"You're not supposed to see me until I enter for the ceremony," she said.

"My conscience bothered me. I wanted you to know the truth. Sybil is inside."

"Sybil? Your secretary?"

"She rode up with me from Glasgow."

"To go over business, I suppose."

"I hated to waste the two hours," her bride-groom explained.

As if getting to his wedding were wasting time.

"She'll serve as your attendant and witness," he added, making matters worse.

"I'd made arrangements for the minister to provide a witness."

"But that would be a stranger. Now you have someone you know."

The someone being a stern-faced woman who had served the Sturgeons for at least three decades, someone who could report back to Hortencia just how the wedding had gone.

She ought to put her foot down right now. She had the right to pick her own attendant, even if it was someone she'd never met. A tough modern woman, demanding her rights, that was Meagan Butler. Or so she told herself, and so she presented herself.

It wasn't true. Privately she questioned everything she did. Such as starting her marriage with a fight. Her wimpdom side, she called it. It was taking over now.

"All right," she said, sighing. "Let's go on in."

William hesitated, which wasn't like him.

"There's more," she said with dejected certainty.

"We need to return to Glasgow as soon as it's done."

"It?"

"The ceremony, I mean. I'm truly sorry, Meagan. I know how much staying here meant to you, but business matters are more complicated than I anticipated. I had to leave the negotiations at a very delicate juncture."

Delicate juncture? Wasn't there another delicate juncture he ought to have in mind? Meagan wanted to kick him in the shins, but her soft shoes would injure only her.

Besides, he looked so apologetic, so truly regretful. The cad. And he had agreed to this isolated wedding when his mother had wanted a social affair at the Fifth Avenue Presbyterian Church in the heart of Manhattan. But that would have involved crowds and strangers, anathema to them both; it was to William's credit that he had stood up to his mother and sided with his bride.

It was, however, much to his discredit that he preferred seeing to business before getting that same bride alone.

Maybe here was where she should protest. If she threw a big enough fit, he would probably agree to stay at Thistledown. But he wouldn't like it. Somehow he'd make her feel the same.

"And the honeymoon trip?" she asked, knowing the answer already. As far as bad news went, she was on a roll.

"In the fall, perhaps. I promise we will return."

She looked past him to the high turrets of the castle. The gargoyles sneered back with disturbing insolence. The cold wind picked up, swirling around her, whipping her skirt, practically tearing

22

the plaid from her grasp. She held on tight and tried to remember the legend's Gaelic incantation; for the life of her, it wouldn't come to mind.

Her head reeled from the effort, or maybe it was just the terrible turn of events. Right now William Sturgeon IV was a husband she could well do without, except perhaps for that fantasy visit each year.

The first one being tonight at Thistledown Castle, no matter what his business demands might be, a night during which he could start giving her the babies she craved, then leave her so she could raise them in the same love she'd known as a child.

The dizziness stayed with her as she led him into the church. With only a civil nod to Sybil, she took her place before the minister. An uninvited guest sat in one of the pews. It was Janet Forbes. Somehow she wasn't surprised; indeed, she found the woman's presence oddly comforting, as if she were the only one on the bride's side.

William took his place beside her. She caught him glancing at his watch. His Rolex, naturally. With that glance, the last shreds of the magic she'd wanted for this day disappeared. The dizziness became overwhelming. She felt as if she might faint.

"Give me a moment," she whispered, then stepped backward through the curtain blocking off the laird's aisle.

Confused and hurt, her doubts feeding a rising panic, she sat heavily on the nearest pew and saw her precious book beside her. She touched it and the incantation returned, the only coherent thought in her jumbled mind.

A ghràidh mo chridhe.

She whispered the words three times, and felt a

23

warmth encircle her, soothing her troubled thoughts.

As if by a miracle, the magic of the day returned; she scarcely minded even the light-headedness, so wrapped was she in a strange blanket of peace. She felt an urge to stand and return to her place in front of the pulpit. Eyes downcast, she pulled the plaid close over her face. If the wonderment she felt showed in her expression, she didn't want William to see. He'd think she was coming down with some obscure Scottish disease.

She moved forward, her step so light she seemed to pass through the curtain as though it wasn't there. Right away she felt a difference in the chapel. With the minister droning on, she heard no more than the name *Meagan* as she closed her eyes and concentrated on what that difference might be. It was the smell of the place. No longer musty, the air held the scent of heather and wild green grasses, as if someone had filled the place with potpourri. But this scent was cleaner and fresher and sweeter than any potpourri she'd ever smelled.

Suddenly she was aware of the quiet.

"I do," she said, hoping that was the right thing to say.

"Then I pronounce ye man and wife," the minister said in a brogue so thick she could barely make out his words.

She opened her downcast eyes, expecting to see William's handmade Italian shoes. Instead she viewed a pair of sturdy, low-cut boots and, of all things, argyle socks covering a pair of extraordinarily muscular calves.

When had William changed attire?

She looked at the knees. Handsome they were,

as well formed as the calves. They were definitely not William's knees.

Nor was the kilt anything he would wear, the sporran, the dark green jacket, the tartan pinned by a wooden brooch at a very wide shoulder.

It wasn't his mouth moving in on hers.

And it certainly wasn't William's kiss. This one swept her up like the wild Scottish wind, demanding, promising, arousing erotic desires. She felt his touch all the way to her toes, robbing her of breath, frightening her as much as it thrilled.

When her bridegroom lifted his head, she stared at a face she had never before seen, a visage of coppery skin and strong features and brown eyes as deep as infinity.

She promptly fainted in a heap beside his boots.

Chapter Two

Despite her obvious charms, Robert Cameron's new bride fell short of expectations.

For one thing she seemed a sickly sort, fainting as she had when he claimed his husbandly kiss. Having lost one wife to frailty, he'd not want to lose another, but he would face hell's fires before leading a celibate life.

Especially with a mate who looked like this one.

He contemplated her appearance on the marital bed, where she reclined in unconsciousness like a virginal sacrifice, toes up, black hair spread across the white coverlet. Only the gentle rise and fall of her breasts gave proof she was alive.

Almost as bad as her feebleness, she was older than he had been told. Comely she might be, with thick lashes resting against golden cheeks, but she would never see seventeen again. He should have gotten a look at her before the ceremony, if only to ward off all surprise.

Never trust an Irishman, his late, beloved father had always said. His father had been right.

How his people must be chortling now, especially his cousin Colin Cameron, his best and closest help. Under Colin's bemused stare, he'd
carried his new lady from the kirk, across the
crowded, festive grounds of the keep, and, with a
cheer echoing at his back, up to his chamber.

Here she was, still lost to consciousness, and all
from a simple kiss, while his people continued to
celebrate below. Let them laugh and draw what
amusement they could from his situation. In re-
cent years they'd had little cause to laugh.

No more had he, their hapless laird. Was his
countenance so grim he'd put his bride to the
swoon? Not so, thought more than one fair maid
of Thistledown. And he'd pleased his first and
dearly beloved wife, may her young soul rest in
peace, though it was true her glances had been
colored by love.

He would take a Scottish lass's approving smile
over an Irish stranger's seizure any day.

Unfastening his brooch, he tossed tartan and
jacket aside, removed the furry white sporran at
his waist, and sat on the bed to doff his boots and
socks. He'd best consummate the marriage fast,
lest the feeble woman wake and change her mind
concerning the matter. He needed her dowry far
too much to allow such a catastrophe. In truth,
he'd find it impossible to return.

But even in the raging hungers of his youth, his
lasses had shown signs of cooperation. Robert
cursed his conscience. He'd not take a sleeping
woman, no matter his rights.

She stirred as his boots hit the floor. Encouraged, he tugged his shirt free of the kilt and
worked quickly at the buttons, then decided not
to undress all the way. She was the one who ought
to be naked. He should take a look at what he'd

got, then motivate her to wakefulness with a well-placed touch.

No hint of conscience pricked following this new decision. Like all the Camerons he was a practical man, else he would not now be wed.

He removed her plaid and stroked her thick black hair. Though too short by far, coming scarcely to her shoulders, it had a pleasing raven's-wing shine to its blackness. And he remembered eyes the color of darkest purple heather, just before she'd fainted at his feet.

He especially liked the full lips that hinted of a passionate nature. Her breasts were a mite small for his taste, but they'd swell under his massage. And after bearing a dozen bairns, she would plump to more than adequacy.

Slipping her shoes from her feet, he lifted her skirt. She made no move to stop him, nor to urge him on. The black stockings he was familiar with, having lifted many a Highland skirt in his thirty-five years. The garters were something else. Lacy white, they seemed to do their job despite their insubstantial appearance.

Good legs, he noted, not in the least bowed, though he would have preferred more substantial thighs.

He folded the skirt higher. What was this slip of silken nothing that covered her maidenly prize? Right indecent it was, no more than a triangle the size of his palm. Robert stopped himself. Since when had he been averse to a little indecency? Especially in the seclusion of his marital chamber.

His kilt shifted from his sudden erection. Something other than his bride had been awakened by his exploration.

Best discover how this bit of silk had been constructed. It had no fastenings that he could see.

He pulled at the garment; it stretched like the neck of a goose, then snapped back in place when he let it go. He pulled once more, strictly in the interests of scientific investigation, as he'd been taught at the university, taking gentlemanly care not to peek at the part of his bride he most eagerly wished to see.

Appetite always improved the taste of a meal.

Here was something to make him voracious, especially the glimpses he got of black hair tightly curled at the juncture of her thighs. He snapped the curious garment once more, then again it was pull, release, snap. He'd seen naught like it, not in Holland, nor Edinburgh, nor even the fleshpots of London town. Right away he liked the easy access it provided. The Irish might not be so simpleminded after all.

And the Scots were not so crude as their repute. For all it felt fine to indulge in a rare moment of play, he'd best approach his marriage with the solemnity it deserved. He wasn't supposed to enjoy his bride except in the usual way of a man. He must bed her so that he could keep her gold.

With a grimace of reluctance, he lowered his bride's skirt, smoothing it over her legs, dropping the hem at her ankles while he thought of all that the cloth concealed.

"What are you doing?"

His bride's voice came out loud and clear, despite a curious manner of speech. He looked up into a pair of startled violet eyes. "Learning the ways of your people. And bringing you back to the land of the living."

He reached out to touch her face, to bring her gently around. "Happen I've done a fair job."

She slapped his hand and sat up straight in the bed. In an instant her hands flew to her head and,

Evelyn Rogers

in a tone not nearly so sharp, she whispered an agonized "Oh."

Could she have indulged in a nip or two to give herself bottle courage? Was she now paying the price?

He could little criticize, since he'd done it once or twice through the years.

"Take care, Meagan-Anne," he said. "You've had a terrible fright, seeing your mate for the first time."

Her fingers pressed against her temples and she closed her lids over those magnificent violet eyes. "Meagan," she said. "Not Meagan-Anne."

Another Irish lie, thought Robert, though why her father should have bothered with anything but honesty concerning her name, he couldn't say. The woman's particulars had meant little once the money was sent.

Still, life would be simpler if they got on one with the other. And that meant always telling the truth. Well, perhaps not always, at least for him. A man must keep his options open.

He propped the pillow at her back against the carved headboard. "Rest, Meagan, not Meagan-Anne. We've all the time in the world to do what we must."

Her eyes flew open. "What did you say?"

"We've all the time—"

"No, before. About seeing my mate."

A little slow, was she, besides being a tippler? A pity when, despite her age, she bore a bonnie look. Pitiful, too, was the strange way of her speaking. In his worldly travels he'd heard naught like it anywhere.

"Your mate," he said with great patience. "Your husband, the man this very day you vowed to love

30

and obey until the end of time. I'm Robert Cameron—"

"Ha!" she said in scorn, but Robert plowed on.

"—laird of Thistledown Keep, sometime scholar, onetime passable soldier for the famous Fraser himself, gamesman, lover and pursuer of good and prosperous times. And, of course, cousin of a cousin to Seamus MacSorley, a name you'll not be denying."

"I most certainly do deny it."

She edged as far from him as she could manage, her bent knees clasped to her breast, then eyed him with vexed suspicion. "Is this some kind of joke? It's not like William to set up something so"—she considered his kilt and his naked calves—"so involved, and certainly not with someone so . . . physical. I see his mother's influence in this. They're both trying to get back at me for the wedding arrangements."

Robert felt a heaviness in his heart, and a bitterness that he never quite got used to, though it came upon him far too often these days. Daft the woman was, knowing not her name nor that of her father, or so she claimed, speaking so strangely he could scarce understand her, and now mentioning another man when their wedding vows must still be echoing in the kirk's close air.

"If you're trying to get out of the marriage, lass, you're too late. A hundred good and true people of Thistledown heard you swear to love me and to obey. Now I'll admit the loving part—"

"Sybil!" His bride's eyes lit. "She's behind this, isn't she? Hortencia's emissary. No wonder she rode up from Glasgow with William. She wanted to see the results of her handiwork in person."

She studied the wide, high-ceilinged marital

31

chamber. The room gave Robert pride, with its oak furniture carved by the craftsmen on his land, including the high feather bed, and its white wool coverlet woven by the nimble fingers of Ermengarde Drummond.

Best not dwell on Ermengarde, or her fingers. Both were a part of his dissolute past.

His wife's gaze skittered over the room's finery and settled on the draperied window. "Come on out, Sybil. You've had your little joke." Her sidewise glance took in the clothing he'd tossed aside, as well as his person. "Whoever he is, he looks and sounds the part very well."

Definitely daft.

"There's no one here but the two of us, certainly no witch or prophetess."

"What witch?"

"The sibyl you've summoned."

He'd barely got the words out when, quick as a vixen, she jumped from the bed and dashed to the window. For a bride, she seemed uncommonly distressed to find no one behind the heavy draperies.

"Let's remain in solitude, wife," Robert said with what he thought was admirable calm. "'Tis more suitable for the task at hand. And dinna look so alarmed. You know the marriage must be consummated. You've reached an age to understand what goes on between a husband and his bride. Indeed, considering your advanced state, I'll understand if I'm no' the first."

"Cut it out, Mr. Cameron. If that's your name. You're not my husband!"

With that absurd declaration, she commenced to pace back and forth across the room, her skirt whirling with each turn. For all her lunacy, she had a grace to her movements that appealed and a teasing curve to her calves. Once again thinking of the strange undergarment beneath the heavy skirt, Robert remembered the business at hand. More than one man had made do with a crazy wife, and most not nearly so fair; he'd give the challenge a try.

"Aye, Meagan, not Meagan-Anne, I'm your husband for life."

She ran a hand through her hair. "No, you're not," she said, proving herself as stubborn as he.

"We sound like a pair of squabbling bairns."

Robert kept his calm as he spoke, but a fearful temper began to simmer behind his forced smile. He'd been through too much, bore the bitter memory of too many tragic times to endure the lass's nonsense for long.

The English with their cruel laws had not defeated him, nor the French on the killing fields of Quebec, not even the betrayal of his fellow Scots nor the vicious twistings of fate.

He would not be defeated now, not in his own bedchamber, not by a looby wife.

"Deny me all you will," he said, "I've a hundred witnesses to claim we're wed."

She came to a halt before him, hands on nicely rounded hips. "So produce them. And don't look so obstinate. There's nothing else going to take place in this room, and you full well know it. Oh, Sybil has outdone herself this time, and while she may well be a witch, she's also very much a real person."

"But one you little care for, it would seem," he put in, but she paid him no mind.

"I can't believe William went along with her elaborate scheme, especially since it takes time from his work. He must have wanted to scare me back to civilization. Well, I've got news for him.

33

I'm not frightened, just mad."

Mad indeed. Another consideration struck him, and his voice rose. "Do you speak of William Ogilvy? Has the man been playing you false? It scarce seems likely, since you're newly arrived, but the rascal has a reputation for the lasses. And who be this Sybil, if not a witch? 'Tis a name I dinna ken."

"Sybil is William's secretary. And it's William Sturgeon, not Ogilvy, as you full well know."

He watched in bemusement as she dropped to her knees and lifted the coverlet to glance under the bed. Reaching into the darkness, she pulled out a chamber pot, wrinkled her nose, then pushed the pot back out of sight.

"Sturgeon's a fish," he said, trying to act as though nothing she did was out of the ordinary when in truth she'd done nothing right.

With a perplexed glance toward the bed, she stood to face him. "It's also my fiancé's name."

"Fiancé be damned," Robert snapped, then doused his anger with a splash of sensibility. "Hie to my arms, Meagan, where I can stroke another kind of madness on you. I'm your betrothed and your husband in one, and I've a need to make you mine."

This time when she ran a hand through her hair, he noticed a soft pink tint to her nails. He'd never seen the like; somehow the tinting went with her underdrawers.

She took time in her rantings to give him a thorough inspection. Mostly she divided her attention between the expanse of his shoulders and his knees, as though she'd never seen such portions of a man's anatomy before. She did not appear dismayed by what she saw, nor, he had to admit, did she seem particularly eager to caress anything.

"Do you like the kilt, lass? I risked flogging to wear it for the nuptials. I'd be glad to remove it if it gives offense."

The interest in her eyes turned once more to puzzlement. "Why would you be flogged?"

"Have you never heard of the Diskilting Act? Since Culloden it's been considered an act of treason to wear the clothes of the Highlanders. We've a high sheriff hereabouts with an eagerness to see the law enforced."

"But that battle was two hundred and fifty years ago."

"Coming upon twenty," he said, then attempted a note of charity. "You've erred in your math, that's all."

"Math is not where I make my mistakes. And quit the act, Mr. Cameron. This is not the eighteenth century, no matter how much you look the part."

"And what century would it be?"

"The twentieth, drawing very close to the twenty-first."

Robert shook his head, all patience fled. "Daft as the widow Knox's duck. No wonder your father was eager to pay such a kingly sum to get you out of his hair."

He lunged for her, but she was quick on her feet. Before he could catch her she threw open the door and dashed into the hall, coming to a halt so quickly he almost crashed into her.

She was looking straight ahead through the window to the grounds that held the ruins of the once grand Thistledown Castle. Broken stones and jagged, half-formed walls stared mutely back. From this height the separations of once proud rooms were faintly visible. The sight seemed to pain her as much as it always pained him.

"Where am I?"

The lost expression on her face softened Robert's ire. She could not help being what she was. Nor could he save himself from himself. He had taken her money; now, without grousing, he must pay the price.

Besides, his luck wasn't all bad. She could have looked like the widow's demented duck as well as having its intellect.

"We're high in Thistledown Keep. Your new home. And I truly am your husband, for better or worse. Come to my arms, lass, and let me show you it will no' be so bad."

His offer was tempting. Ever since William had shown up early, bearing little else but bad news, Meagan had not been herself. Whoever the man was, he was a handsome hulk, all coppery skin and dark copper hair, brown eyes as inviting as limpid pools. She'd read that exact expression more than once in her books; she now understood what it meant, especially if *limpid* could also include a wicked glint.

Never had William looked at her with such unsettling sympathy. If she were the clinging sort she would fall into this Robert Cameron's very strong arms and lean against his manly chest.

Meagan caught herself. She definitely had been reading too many love stories. The man was either crazy or a consummate actor. Either way she must escape.

"These witnesses you mentioned. Where are they?"

"About the grounds. On such a fine day we chose to keep the celebration out-of-doors." He gestured down the hall. "You'll find the people you seek this way. But beware. They'll no' let you get away, nay more than I."

She started. Could he read her mind? Without a backward glance, she put her jogging muscles into play and dashed down the two flights of stairs, then out into a blinding sun. Shading her eyes, she studied the waiting scene.

A phalanx of strangers stared back, frozen in their pursuits by her sudden appearance—hairy, rough-clad men, most of them burly as weight lifters, women dressed much as she was, except that their feet were bare, half-naked children scampering in their midst. Those who weren't holding tankards were caught at games of shot put or hammer toss.

The men came right out of the Highland Games demonstration she'd seen in Glasgow two days before, except that those players had worn an air of *Here we go, performing for the tourists again.* These people seemed pleased with what they were about, as much as they were surprised by the sight of her.

Something else about them—the hairiness, the hardness, she knew not what—gave them an authentic air. And not one of them wore a kilt. Fearful of a sheriff's wrath perhaps? Impossible.

The curious intelligence in their eyes disturbed her as much as anything, with the possible exception of Robert Cameron's knees. She felt a familiar constriction in her chest at the sight of so many strangers. Now was not the time to hyperventilate.

"Did he frighten ye from yer bed, Lady Cameron?" one of the men yelled, and the others whooped with laughter.

"Our laird must learn gentler ways now that he's

a married man," another added, and she was pelted with suggestions about what this laird of theirs might do.

She looked past them to where, no more than an hour ago, the castle had stood, but she saw only jagged walls that ended far too soon. All around the ruins lay piles of tumbled stones, and where the gargoyles should be glaring down, her eyes met nothing but wide blue sky.

Beyond the ruins a high stone wall encircled everything, locking her in with these strangers, locking out the world that she knew.

A chill gripped her, and a feeling that she was no longer sane. So stunned was she, she barely took note of the woman who sidled close.

"Our Robert kens the way of gentleness, for certain. 'Tis meet, though, that he be inspired."

Meagan forced herself to consider the voluptuous beauty with her mane of wild red hair. Something about her looked decidedly familiar. She thought hard. Here was the predator from the group of tourists, the one who'd stared with such obvious interest at William.

"Thank goodness," she said with a sigh of relief. "Where did the guide go, and all the others? And who are these people?"

The woman smirked. "Poor Robert. He's wed to a looby wi' a mouth full o' mush."

Meagan might not know what was going on, but she knew an insult when she heard it. It mattered little that the woman could be right.

Before she could defend herself, another of the women spoke.

"Hie away wi' ye, Ermengarde. Our laird's took."

Took he wasn't, at least by her, but she didn't think these people would listen to her story any more than her ersatz husband had done.

38

A new thought occurred. Was this a demonstration of virtual reality? Other than the rudiments of word processing, Meagan knew little about computers, but she'd read about such a thing. No, she realized with a sinking heart. This strange world into which she had awakened was far too complex. No programmer could come up with the smell of that all-too-real chamber pot. It had been empty, but it had definitely been used.

Numb with fear, she turned in search of a way to run, but her path was blocked in all directions. She whirled back toward the keep and looked directly into another familiar face, one she could put a name to.

"Miss Forbes. At last." In desperation she grabbed the woman's sleeve. "Please tell me what is going on. Have the managers set up some kind of nightmarish game? If so, it's definitely not amusing."

Another thought struck. "I know. This is a movie set, isn't it? The real Thistledown is just over the hill."

The suggestion was met with a pitying expression. "There's nary a castle beyond what ye see, lass." Prying Meagan's hand loose, the woman took her by the arm. "Leave us go inside. The sun's confused ye, 'tis all that's wrong."

Panic welled inside her. She tried to jerk away, but her captor possessed a wrestler's grip, and Meagan allowed herself to be led back into the keep. Out of sight of witnesses, Miss Forbes released her with a look both stubborn and regretful.

"Whatever passes here, whate'er has gone afore, ye're now the lady of the keep. And so must ye remain, until our laird says otherwise."

Meagan wanted to scream out in protest, to

beg for help, but she saw in the woman's eyes a determination as unyielding as the surrounding stone walls.

Knowing she would find no answers down here, she made what she hoped was the right decision. Drawing a deep breath, donning her tough outer shell, she ran back up the stairs.

Robert met her in the upstairs hall. She backed him into the bedroom and slammed the door.

"All right," she said, steadying her breath, regaining her control. "Out with it. What the hell is going on?"

His features tightened into a harsh, bleak look that stopped anything else she might say. For a moment she forgot herself and thought of him. Robert Cameron was a very complicated man, someone who'd known hard times, someone who didn't like being crossed.

"You've a raw tongue on you, woman. I've already said what's supposed to be going on. Since you've returned to me, you must be willing. Get in the bed."

His order killed all sympathy. "I most certainly will not."

"You like the rug then? A fine new wool it is, woven on Cameron land, but 'tis no' so fine as feathers."

Meagan stamped her foot in exasperation. "I'm sure it's a perfectly good rug, but quit changing the subject. What year is it?" She made a fist. "And if you don't tell me the truth, so help me, I'll—"

Robert Cameron put up his hands in defense— broad, callused hands that could have crushed her in an instant, but she was too upset to worry about her safety.

"I've told naught else but what is so. If you've a

mind to consider the century altered, there's little I can do to change your belief except to wait until the spell has passed."

"The year."

"Seventeen hundred and sixty-five."

Fear shivered through her, and her heart thrummed heavily in her breast. She'd been so brave because she thought the whole scene was a sham. She didn't feel the least bit brave now.

"I thought you'd say something like that," she said in little more than a whisper.

"At last some sense. Can I hope there's more to come?"

"This is much too serious for sarcasm." Too serious, and too insane. Like Alice, one of her favorite characters, she must have tumbled through the looking glass.

She closed her eyes for a second, then opened them wide. Whatever fate awaited her, she would not go into it blind. Now was the time for sacrifice and courage, for taking incredible risks.

"I would very much appreciate your kissing me," she said.

Her tormentor grinned. The effect on her senses was devastating, and her distress increased in a totally different direction. Here was every hero she'd ever read about, a handsome hulk with a decidedly shrewd air about him, a charmer who could put two words together without saying *you know*, and in a brogue right out of a Scottish film. He had a lost look to him, too, at times, as though he'd suffered greatly in his life.

A cross between Sean Connery and Conan the Barbarian, that's what he was, intimidating while he intrigued, the glint in his eye hinting of an urgency he barely contained. If she were a different sort of person, she might just say to heck with her

41

fiancé and fall into his arms.

But, despite her bouts of dreaming, Meagan was realistic enough to know she must be stern. Otherwise she'd be a wimp.

When he moved close she stiffened her spine. Much to her regret her heart refused to go along with her determination. It pounded in a way she'd never known.

"The only reason I'm doing this," she said, as much to herself as to him, "is because this started with a kiss, and I thought—"

His lips touched hers with the gentleness mentioned by the voluptuous Ermengarde, and she swallowed the rest of her words. The ceiling could have fallen around Meagan and she would not have moved.

His hands rested on her shoulders, and his fingers kneaded her back. "You're a fine-looking woman, wife, and you wear a heady scent. I should have bedded you when I had the chance." Again came the devastating grin. "Foolish man that I am, I knew not to expect passion so soon, and instead chose consciousness. Will you give yourself to me, lass, now that you're awake?"

Meagan stared up at the determination in his shadowed brown eyes, at his strong features, at his bristled cheeks. He was incredibly real to her, no matter the impossibility of their meeting, all man, and much too overpowering for any experimentation on her part.

She started to say she'd changed her mind, but he gave her no chance to speak. When his mouth claimed hers once again, there was nothing of the gentleness that had been in his first kiss, and everything of demanding desire. The power of his touch went through her like an electric shock. Here was no caress of warm silk, or even high-grade cotton. Like his tartan plaid, Robert Cameron was pure wool, hot and rough.

His virility filled her senses, frightening her as it had in the kirk, but she refused a second swoon. If she were to make this a real test, she must do it right, and she kissed him back as thoroughly as she could.

Chapter Three

Robert was beginning a genuine involvement in the kiss when his bride pounded against his chest.

She was not, he decided, asking for more.

With a willpower that surprised him, he abandoned her sweet lips, but he kept her in his embrace.

"I was ready to put some tongue in it, lass. You've ended the matter too soon."

The agitation in her eyes gave no hint as to whether she agreed.

"No one has ever—" She caught her breath and continued on. "No one has ever kissed me like that."

"And have there been many before me?"

She made as if to speak, then stopped herself, and he let her squirm from his embrace. He'd already found out what he needed to know. Daft or not, she had embers within her that had not yet been stoked to flames.

Robert was ready to start the stoking. Not a stupid man, he saw the need for humoring her, then claiming what was his. She just might be a genuine prize after all.

She looked around the room. "I'm still here."

Patience, mon. "Aye. In seventeen sixty-five."

Her sigh was enough to break another man's heart. Not Robert's, not with other parts of him making stronger appeals.

"So the kiss didn't work," she said.

"You disappoint me, wife, or could it be I disappointed you? What did you expect the kiss to do?"

Her eyes met his. Deeply wounded, they were, yet warmed with traces of passion. Robert felt an unexpected jolt. 'Twas certain she had a way about her. If he could overlook a quirk or two, the matter might yet turn out right.

She stroked her arms as if she had a chill. "I thought it might send me home."

"To this twentieth century you spoke of?"

She nodded.

"I'll admit to a modest proficiency in my mating, but I've yet to send a lass hurtling through time. Besides, Thistledown Keep *is* your home now. You've left Ireland behind."

"I've left the United States behind."

"'Tis a place I know not."

She graced him with a long and searching look, only this time she glanced not at his knees, but remained with his eyes.

"You really don't know about it, do you? Not if this is the year you claim."

The tremor in his wife's strange, soft voice inspired Robert to abandon the sharp retort he wanted to give. Instead he kept his silence. Ofttimes with a woman it was the better way.

"I've read so many stories about tripping

45

through time, but I thought they were simply fantasies. And now . . .''

She moved to the window, staring long and hard at the lake. At last she turned to face him. "Who do you think I am?"

Robert thought a long time before answering, then settled on the truth.

"Meagan-Anne MacSorley, daughter of Seamus MacSorley, cousin to a sept of the Cameron clan, a lass long betrothed to me, and on this very day my wife, according to the vows we exchanged in Thistledown kirk. Which part disturbs you?"

"All of it," she said, her voice small. Robert watched as she hugged herself, stilling her trembling hands against her sleeves. An unexpected sympathy rose in him; he thrust it ruthlessly aside.

"I heard you say in your strange way of speaking the words that bound us together for life. Others heard as well."

"Oh, I'm not denying that. But I was confused."

"'Tis unlikely the church or the state will consider confusion as cause for severing our union. In any case, you're mine and that's the end of that."

"Had you never met your bride?"

"You know full well you arrived last evening from Ireland, under the escort of your brother. Two days late to be sure, but here nevertheless."

"Call this brother, then. He'll say he never saw me before."

"The rascal took off for a hunt before dawn, declaring his duty was done."

Robert had been vexed over the desertion, but now he saw its point. The man had been less than eager to turn over in person his demented kin.

"Someone must have seen this Meagan-Anne when she got here."

"Janet Forbes took you under her care until the ceremony."

"Weren't you even curious to see what your bride looked like?"

You could have been plain as Mackenzie's goat and I would have taken you for my bride.

In this case, Robert softened honesty. "Family honor made your appearance of little import. We've long been betrothed." He could not restrain himself from adding, "Though I did believe you were more in your youth."

"I'm not a child, if that's what you're getting at, but I'm hardly in my dotage."

"No offense intended, wife."

She did not appear appeased.

"My age is beside the point. We'd best get un-betrothed and unwed or else this honor you speak of will be poorly served. I'm Meagan Butler of New York City, New York, in the United States of America, and the only betrothal I have is to William Sturgeon."

She gasped, and her hand flew to her lips. "William! I forgot all about him. He must think I abandoned him at the church."

"William the Fish."

His bride ignored him, choosing instead to renew her bothersome pacing, adding to it a mutter or two about a watch and light-headedness and an incantation from a story she had read.

"*A ghràidh mo chridhe,*" she said.

"Love of my heart," he translated.

She halted. "You know the legend."

"Nay, but I understand the old language well enough. There are many in these parts who speak it still, though, in response to their laird's request, they try to change their outdated ways."

She seemed scarcely to be listening. "I stepped

away from the pulpit, whispered those words three times, and when I stepped back—"

She snapped her fingers. He hadn't seen her so enlivened since she leaped from their marriage bed.

"That's it! The incantation must have done the trick. All I need do is return to the church and repeat it, and I'll be back where I'm supposed to be."

She appeared too joyous by far at the idea. Ridiculous as her claims were, Robert was not about to let her put them to the test.

"Back to William the Fish."

"If you must have it that way."

"And to his cold kisses."

"How do you know they're cold?"

"How else could a sturgeon kiss? To another sturgeon it might satisfy, but no' to a woman like yourself."

The joy died in her eyes. Robert was not the least bit sorry to see it go.

"His kisses will do," she said, with more determination than conviction. "After all, once the ceremony is done I'll be a Sturgeon, too."

"Och, what a waste that would be."

He smiled at her, thinking he spoke no more than the truth. How much he wanted to hold her again, to kiss her, to pluck at those magnificent underdrawers. His loins were on fire from no more than the thoughts in his mind.

How fine it was to hunger for something that was also the right and necessary thing to do.

Impatience tore at him, worse than his temper had done. Couldn't the woman see the movement beneath his kilt?

"I've a notion," he said. "Let's summon Janet and learn what she has to say about Meagan-

Anne. If she claims you were the one delivered by the brother, then you must agree to stay. If she says otherwise, I'll give you the chance to go."

"How do I know she'll tell the truth? Downstairs she told me no matter what happens here, I'm to remain your wife."

"If I ask her to speak the truth, she will. Have you always possessed a suspicious nature?"

"It comes with living in New York."

"Now there's a place I've heard of, when I was in Quebec."

"So you've been to America."

"I've been to the colonies, if that's what you mean."

I've been to hell, he could have said, but his experiences in the Highland regiment were not for idle conversation, even to win himself a necessary wife.

He turned abruptly and opened the bedroom door. A single bellow down the stairs brought Janet Forbes on the run. She was one of the few servants he'd allowed himself since his return to Thistledown, and a more loyal, hardworking sort he'd never seen.

When she appeared in the doorway, breathing evenly, looking calm as you please, Robert suspected she'd been hovering close by. She certainly bore scant resemblance to anyone dashing up a flight or two of stairs.

"I've a request, Janet, and I want you to fulfill it with complete honesty."

"Since when have I done otherwise?"

"I mean you no insult. You and your family before you have served the Camerons with honor as far back as I can remember."

"And even further forward," said his bride. "Unless Miss Forbes is a time-traveler like me, she's got a relative working here several centuries from now."

Without a change in expression, the woman said, "'Tis Mrs. Forbes, a widow these past ten years. Mother of a fine lad, who boasts two fine lads o' his own. Make your request, laird."

"Did you greet my betrothed when she arrived last night?"

"Aye. And her brother." She scowled. "That one was no' a lad to be trusted. He could scarce wait to leave his sister, without so much as a fare-thee-well."

"'Tis the sister I'm most concerned about. Describe her."

"Michty," she exclaimed, her dark eyes widening, "can you no' see your bride afore you?"

"The question is whether she is the woman you saw last night."

A mulish expression stole across the woman's strong features. "'Twas dark."

"And you took her to her tower room without so much as a candle to light the way?"

"Aye, I had the taper, but she followed ahint."

Robert cared little for the way the conversation was going. Nor did he like the look of satisfaction on his wife's face.

"Describe her, Janet," he said, not unkindly, though his heart felt heavy in his breast. "Was she anything like the woman who married me this day?"

The woman stared at her laird's bride for a long, long while, then turned sad eyes on him. "Nay, this one is taller and darker and older by at least ten years. Whoever stands afore me now, she is no' the lass who stood afore me last night."

*   *   *

Meagan should have been elated at the pronouncement—overlooking the comment about age—but one look at Robert Cameron's stricken face made her feel unexpectedly disappointed because she was not the woman he wanted her to be.

What kind of spell was he putting her under, with his kiss and his touch and the lost look he buried between devastating grins?

"So why did you no' stop the ceremony and fetch the right bride?" said Robert. Meagan thought that for a proud man proved wrong, he was taking the news very well.

"She's disappeared," Janet said. "I went to the kirk to tell ye, but here was this woman, so wrapped up I couldna be sure she wasn't the right bride, and then when she swooned the way she did, I saw it was too late. Why she'd said her vow, I dinna understand, but she was yours and, seeing as how you needed a bride, I kept to my silence."

"Have you no notion where the other one has gone? Speak freely. I've heard the worst."

"I made inquiries, no' using her name, ye ken. A lass was seen skulking around the change-house this very day, someone unknown in these parts. When she arrived at Thistledown yestereve, arguing with her brother, she had seemed little taken with the idea of the marriage. She must have run away."

"Aye," he said, his gaze shifting to the open window, holding there for a long while. Meagan tried to read his mind, to sense his mood, but she saw only that he was deep in thought, and he kept his thoughts to himself.

At last he returned to Mrs. Forbes. "You'll no' be telling this about, until I've decided how to proceed."

The housekeeper drew herself up to a proud height. "Nay, I've kept the news to meself thus far; I'll continue to do so until my laird instructs otherwise." She hesitated. "Though I feel the need to offer a word of advice. Ye'd best keep her quiet, else all will know she canna be from Ireland."

She left, closing the door behind her, but Meagan was not the least inclined to say *I told you so*.

When Robert took up the pacing she had begun, she scrambled away from his long stride. Gradually the thoughtful look left his eyes, and when he halted to stare at her, a nervous shiver shot through her. Whatever decision he had reached, she doubted she would approve.

"Because of you, I've lost valuable time in searching for my true betrothed."

"Unfair," she said in righteous indignation. "I didn't ask to drop in at your side."

"Did you no'? What was the purpose of the incantation, repeated three times, by your own admission, if not to summon the love of your heart? 'Tis clear this William you speak of is no' the one."

Meagan wanted to protest, truly she did, but for some unfathomable reason she felt bound by the honesty to which he had bound Janet Forbes.

Instead of defending her love for her fiancé, she changed the subject.

"So what do you plan to do?"

"Search for the lass, and pray word doesna spread about her running away."

"Would that be bad? Surely the family honor is not at stake here."

"In a way it is. As is yours." He sat on the bed and patted the spot beside him. "Sit, Meagan. I've a proposition to put to you."

"I'd rather take it standing."

His eyes glinted. "There are those that like it so,

52

but I thought you preferred the rug."

She shook her head in exasperation. "Have you only one thing on your mind?"

"With you standing there looking as ripe as MacFerron's figs, it's never far from my thoughts. For all the good it does. Until you admit to your own hunger, I've only words to put to you, and no' what I'd like—"

He stopped himself, but she could guess what provoking, sexual remark he'd been about to make. MacFerron's figs, indeed.

"Sit, lass. We'll both be at ease. I promise to keep my hands to myself."

She did as he asked, as far from him as she could manage without tumbling onto the floor.

"Have you a need to return so soon to this time you claim as yours?" he asked.

"You still don't believe me."

"I'm trying, lass, but 'tis more than a simple man like me can comprehend on such a momentous day."

"You're about as simple as a microchip. And don't ask for an explanation. You wouldn't believe me if I told you. To answer your question, yes, there's a need to return right away. I left my husband-to-be standing in front of a preacher without a bride."

"Will he be deeply wounded?"

"Of course he will," she snapped, but in her heart she wasn't really sure. How long would he search for her until returning to his business in Glasgow? Had he already left Thistledown? The thought did her ego little good.

"Besides," she went on, "before my parents died I promised them I would marry by the time I turned thirty. And that's tomorrow."

His thick brows lifted. "Thirty?"

"In my time it's a perfectly respectable age, although I suppose in yours it's considered over-the-hill."

"A curious expression, this 'over-the-hill.'"

He took a long while to look her over with a thoroughness that sizzled her nerves. Never one to blush, she felt her cheeks burn, and she fought the urge to hug herself in self-defense.

"I'll say this for you, Meagan," he said in a rich, deep voice as unnerving as his gaze, "like a smokehouse ham, you're well preserved."

"Thanks loads."

He shrugged, making her all too aware of his wide shoulders. "As you observed yourself, this matter is too serious for sarcasm. How can you be turning thirty if you're centuries away from being born?"

"I'm obviously born."

"And grown up nicely, but this is a strange turn of events, lass. We dinna ken the rules. 'Tis possible you'll little age, going backward in time. What if you grow younger day by day?"

The idea was certainly intriguing, like the man who suggested it. She'd accepted the forever bride's passage through time, forgetting while she read that the story was fiction. And here she was, all too real, all too alive, caught in a situation equally impossible. Torn between fear and anticipation, she asked herself a question she would never have thought of in New York.

What if the line between fact and fantasy really could be blurred?

Balderdash, as one of her historical heroines might have said. She shook her head to clear it.

"You're trying to confuse me."

"And you've no' done the same to me?"

He had a point. Meagan renewed her resolve.

"I'm not going to be here day by day. I'm returning this afternoon."

She meant it. All she had to do was go to the chapel and say—

A daunting thought stopped her. What if the incantation didn't work? Panic set in. After all, she didn't have the book with her. What if repeating the phrase wasn't enough? She'd been telling herself that returning would be a simple process, but what if the phrase had nothing to do with her situation?

What if—

She caught his thoughtful stare. Dark eyes pinned her to the bed. So this was how a trapped animal felt. She rubbed damp palms against her skirt, unwilling to let him know how close she was to absolute terror. Invincible as he seemed, somehow he would seize upon her weakness, and she'd be lost in time.

"I'm returning this afternoon," she repeated, for herself as much as for him.

"Leaving me to ruin."

"How is that?"

"When word spreads of my bride's abandonment, I'll have to return her dowry."

"Who will make you? Her brother's gone, isn't he? Write her father saying all is well."

"We've a sheriff here who'd have another mind. An evil man, to be sure, with a stink about him that comes from a fetid soul."

"He's the one who would fine you for wearing the kilt."

"Put me under the whip, more than like. If he had the courage to try."

"I take it you two don't get along."

"If you mean we care naught for one another, you've got the matter right. He would take great delight in seeing that all knew of my plight. Before the next full moon, MacSorley would hear the truth and I'd find myself in bankruptcy court."

"Have you already received the dowry?"

"It lies in wait for me here at the keep, locked away where none but the laird can find it."

"Are you so in debt you can't send it back?"

"'Tis owed to the Glasgow bank that holds a wadset on Thistledown. A good man, the banker, who knew my father and trusted his son. But he'll no' trust me when payment comes due and I face him empty-handed."

"I take it this wadset is some kind of mortgage. Has the loan already been spent?"

Robert let out a long, slow, very audible breath. "Aye, on Cameron people and Cameron land. But dinna fret; 'tis no' your problem. Hie back to your time and your place."

His sigh might have been convincing if she hadn't caught him studying its effect on her from the corner of his eye. She must remember always that Robert Cameron was a calculating man.

"You don't believe me, do you?" she said. "About the twentieth century, I mean."

"I've no time to sort out the truth of you just now. 'Tis bad enough you're no' MacSorley's kin."

Once again she caught the edge of bleakness in him that he tried so hard to hide. He suffered as much as she.

So what if he didn't believe her story? Knowing it to be true, she scarcely believed it herself.

Meagan let out a sigh to match his. She'd always believed in fate. Was it her destiny to remain with him for a while? So many coincidences said it was so—the similarity of her name to that of his intended wife, the descendant of Mrs. Forbes helping arrange her wedding to William, the flirt in the touring group having a double in this early time.

Did these coincidences have a meaning she couldn't see?

Something, certainly, was keeping her in this room, something deep inside her that she didn't understand. Sympathy? Curiosity? Wimpdom? It couldn't be Robert Cameron's masculine appeal. She was practically married to someone else.

Perhaps it was her love of a good story. She'd never read a better one than this.

The answer seemed far too simple for a situation this complex, but she clung to it because it was all she had. All, that is, if she didn't consider her fears about the chant not sending her home.

"So what is it you want me to do?" she asked, biding her time, gathering her facts the way any modern woman would.

"No more than gi'e me the searching time lost from believing you were the Meagan I was promised. Meagan the Younger, that is. She's scarce turned seventeen."

"Which makes me Meagan the Elder, I suppose."

"You said it, no' I, but it has an apt ring to it, dinna you believe?"

She refused to dignify the name with an answer.

"Tell me one thing if you can," he said, unperturbed by her silence. "Why did you choose my kirk to be wed in?"

"I—"

Meagan didn't know how to go on. Should she tell him about her fascination with the legend? About the glorious illustrations picturing a restored Thistledown? About her dreams of a fantasy lover with warm-silk hands?

He wouldn't understand much better than she.

For a woman who tried always to know her own

mind, she was distressingly confused.

"William had business in Glasgow, and I thought this would be a wonderful place for our wedding."

"He journeyed here for business and no' for love?"

"Both. Surely in your position you can understand that."

"The fish is about to lose his land?"

"Of course not. He just wants"—she floundered for how to go on—"more, I suppose."

"I've many a countryman who would understand. Mayhap destiny has brought us together, lass, at least for a while. How sad you've no' the imagination to accept it."

How similar his thoughts were to hers, except for his last observation. The one thing Meagan had in oversupply was imagination. Staying here for a while . . . giving him the time to look for his real bride . . . experiencing another century, another people . . . why, she could use the information she gathered in one of her ad campaigns. Maybe fate really had—

Oh God, what was she thinking? This was the eighteenth century, for heaven's sake, a time of hardship and deprivation and little personal freedom, especially for women. Once she got out of here—*if* she got out—she would never, ever, ever complain about William again. In the meantime she would learn what she could while she had the chance.

And she would grow tougher in the process. To stay took more courage than to go.

"You want me to pose as your bride?" She could read his thoughts. "All right, technically I suppose that's what I am. But I'll never pull off acting like an eighteenth-century woman."

"My people believe you're from Ireland. They'll not question what you do. And remember they've seen you already. In the kirk and when you ran outside."

"But what about the way I speak?"

This set him to thinking.

"I'll say that deafness till the age of twelve left you with impediments. You've only to still your clackiting tongue as best you can and the ruse will succeed."

The close-to-accurate story startled her. She *had* been ill until about that age. But her illness had been due to an inadequate immune system that left her susceptible to most any disease.

Clackiting tongue indeed. She was one of the most soft-spoken women she knew. It was obvious clashes between them loomed ahead. For so many reasons this was impossible, preposterous, absurd. And yet . . .

Her eyes met his.

"Would another kiss help you decide?" he asked.

The memory of his lips on hers took her breath. Robert Cameron was a truly dangerous man.

Jumping from the bed, she hurried to the window and gazed onto Loch Lochy, the afternoon sun sparkling like jewels on its surface, and to the wild Highland hills on the far side. What a breathtakingly beautiful land this was. Could it be her destiny to stay here a day or two? Certainly not forever. She had plans for her life . . . a happy marriage, a successful career, a family. In twentieth-century parlance, she wanted to have it all.

Which left little room in her life for an overpowering laird who thought matters could be settled with a kiss.

Suddenly he was behind her, his presence a mighty force.

Using all her modern-woman strength, she turned to face him. "Maybe I do owe you something. After all, in my time the castle has been restored, and the credit goes to you. It's clear you can't face ruin and at the same time meet this destiny you speak of. And get that glint out of your eye. I mean the restoration of your home."

"Your answer is aye?"

"As long as you understand two things. I don't meet people very well, so I'm not likely to be the lady of the keep that you want and undoubtedly deserve. And the second is that you'll not kiss me or in any way make husbandly overtures. I'm your bride in name only. Is that clear?"

He stepped close, and his nearness wrapped around her like hot, rough wool.

"If all were right and just in the world, Meagan the Elder, you're the lady I would choose, tocherless or no'. I've little use for a child."

"Tocherless?" she managed, wondering what a tocher could be and where she might get one.

"Alack, you have no dowry. 'Tis a flaw I canna overlook, having other considerations to keep in mind. For the present, that is. Difficult though it may be, I'll keep my hands to myself."

He sounded so regretful Meagan's knees weakened, and her resolve almost followed. But she did not pull away, and she did not blink. If he had other considerations, so did she.

"Good," she managed. "And don't think I'll change my mind about sleeping with you, no matter how romantic I find this land of yours."

He grinned. Her stomach turned somersaults.

"If you're expecting me to be sensible, wife, you're going the wrong way about it, staying so close and keeping your scent in my nostrils."

"Then I'll wash it off. And don't look so hopeful.

I don't mean now. I'm serious, Robert. My staying is for Scotland, and not for a particular Scot."

Proud of her declaration, she stepped away and turned before he could read in her eyes the doubt she felt in her wildly pounding heart.

Chapter Four

"Tully MacSorley, get your arse out here."

Annie hid in a shadowy grove near the change-house where her brother was ensconced, wishing he could hear her muted command. If only she had nerve enough to stride inside and fetch the rascal, but too many others consorted with him, drunken, wild-eyed Scots who no doubt claimed friendship with Robert Cameron.

The very name made her shudder. Who would have thought that Meagan-Anne MacSorley, Annie to her friends and Brat to blood kin, should come to such a pass? If she'd obeyed Papa's orders, she would be wed to that Cameron ogre at this very minute, a love prisoner to his cruel lust.

She'd heard stories about the Scots and women, stories that should not come to the ears of an innocent maid. Well, maybe not so innocent as she ought to be, but not nearly so experienced as she wanted.

If only Liam weren't so upright and moral. But he was, and worse, he dwelled hundreds of miles away, across a cold, cold sea.

Annie sighed. She'd escaped her marital fate not a minute too soon, just as that sour-faced housekeeper came looking for the laird's sacrificial bride. Slipping out of the keep, she'd successfully tracked her brother to the nearest change-house. Here, more's the pity, her dash for freedom had come to a halt. She'd been waiting hours for his appearance, but she saw not his arse, nor his nose, nor one portion of his anatomy edging through the front door.

Night was coming. Annie held little affection for being out and about in the dark. Staring at Tully's fine MacSorley mare tied no more than a dozen yards away, she considered her options.

She could wait for him to stagger outside and demand he take her back to Ireland.

She could go in and get him.

She could return to that loathsome Thistledown where she was supposed to spend the rest of her days, and declare the wedding plans had been a terrible mistake.

That she could convince Tully to help her was a given; she'd always been able to talk him into what she wished. That he would leave the squat, shabby inn before dawn was open to debate. The lad liked his whiskey far more than he cared for his kin; he'd not be leaving while he could still lift a cup.

So go inside and get him, she told herself.

The loud laughter and chorus of coarse song that shook the inn's turf and stone walls kept even Brat Annie in the gathering dark.

Returning to Thistledown was scarcely an option; she included it only as personal proof that she was thinking things through.

Which was something Papa and her brothers said she never did.

"Think Things Through," her harried father was wont to shout when she'd been caught out in another escapade.

She always had a perfectly sensible explanation for what she did—hadn't taking Gill Dillon's litter of piglets been done to show him the penalty for mistreating his sow?—but Seamus was not one to listen to a stripling of a daughter. He preferred to marry her off.

Annie shuddered. She hadn't gotten a look at Robert Cameron, but she'd heard the wild celebrating of his clan through the night. Knowing their laird was in his dotage, she imagined how their wedding night would be—him bent and gray, drool bubbling at the corner of his toothless mouth, his gnarled fingers groping under her skirt as she lay stoically and stiffly in bed.

Wed such a man, when she had Liam O'Toole waiting for her at home? She'd throw herself into Loch Lochy first.

"Tully, get your arse out here," she whispered again, stamping her foot in impatience, trying to sound brave and older than her seventeen years. But with night coming on, a cold wind whipped through the trees and dark clouds drifted over the moon. Annie was afraid of nothing—except the hideous hobgoblins that howled with the wind.

She pulled her wool mantle close to her shivering body, and she thought things through.

She studied the horse. Riding was something she did very well—out of necessity, to keep up with the MacSorley men. Being the lone female in a house of seven males—her mother having died when she was three—toughened a lass.

Annie looked across the bare ground separating

the woods from the inn. She stepped from the protection of the trees.

"What the devil do you think you're doing?"

"Aiii!" she yipped and jumped back into the shadows, forcing her eyes to the dark figure looming close to her side.

"Surely you're nay daft enough to go inside."

She swallowed her fright. Whoever he was, he sounded little older than she, and from what she could tell by the sight of him, of little more heft.

Without thinking she hit him in the arm. The firmness of him gave her reassurance, since clearly 'twas not a night creature threatening harm. More lad than man, he appeared, and she could handle any lad when the need arose.

He rubbed the sleeve of his coat. "What drove you to such a thing?"

"You startled a year's breath from me, that's what. And hush. They'll hear you."

"From the sound of 'em, they'd no' hear the skirl of a score of bagpipes in the road. Now answer my question. This is no place for a lass. What brings you here?"

Ah, yes, he sounded very young. Annie smiled in calculated shyness, draped the hood of her mantle over her head to give her a more pitiful look, and dropped her gaze to the ground. "I've come to fetch me brother home. He drinks, ye ken."

She let her voice trail off, as if the admission pained her. In truth, she knew Tully drank no more than most in his acquaintance, and even then mostly to show that at twenty he was truly a man.

"And where might your home be?" her inquisitor asked. "No' in these parts, I'll be bound."

"Ireland," she said with bold pride.

"Your brother's come a long way for a nip."

"He's run away, you see. I followed to fetch him home."

"You followed him from Ireland."

"Aye," she said, cursing herself for coming up with such a weak tale. She hoped the quaver in her voice gave it piteous strength. "We've our invalid father to care for, the two of us, and I cannot manage alone."

"Your invalid father."

"Aye." She warmed to her plight. "He broke his leg chasing the thieves who stole our sheep. And then the potatoes rotted in the field, and—"

She would have gone on, but the wind chose that moment to blow the clouds from the moon and she got a good look at her inquisitor. He appeared older than his voice, but still no more than twenty, with even features, brown hair and matching eyes, and a decided grin on his face. A handsome young man, if undistinguished, stockier than she'd thought, and decidedly rude.

But of course he was a Scot; like his countrymen, he'd no doubt learned his manners from wild boars.

She raised a fist.

"I'd rather you no' hit me again," he said. "I might have to hit you back."

"You wouldn't."

He thought a moment. "Nay, but I'd want to."

"At least you're honest," she said, letting the hood slip from her head.

"And you've a great deal of red hair."

Annie brushed it from her face. "I plan to cut it off."

"Don't."

The urgency in his voice flustered her. Too, it gave her hope. If he cared about her hair, he might care about her safety. And if he was as simple-minded as Tully, she could get him to do her will.

She stuck out her hand. He hesitated for a moment, then shook it. She felt no calluses on his palm.

"I'm Annie. Also known as Brat."

"'Tis no surprise. I'm Fitzroy Sutherland. Also known as Fitz."

"You live near here?"

He hesitated longer than he had with the handshake. "Nay."

Annie was not so easily put off.

"Where then? Not Ireland, I'll be bound."

"Farther to the north. I'm staying with my uncle in town."

Annie looked around at the flat-roofed tavern, at the dark, forbidding woods. "There be actual towns in this godforsaken land?"

"None so grand as you have in Ireland, you'd be claiming, but a town nevertheless."

Annie ignored the teasing tone of his words.

"Might I find lodging there?"

"Nay, no' a lone lass like yourself."

Her lower lip trembled. The ploy never worked with Papa, nor with her older brothers, and even Tully was beginning to catch on.

It was time to test the charity of this newfound Fitz.

"I've got to find a place to hide. A barn, a shed. Anything will do."

He stared at her with warm concern.

"Mayhap you're in danger? Is it your brother you fear?"

Annie shook her head. "He does only what he is told. Are you by way of knowing a man called Robert Cameron?"

"'Tis a name I ken, but little more."

An edge to his voice encouraged her to go on.

"I was to wed him today, despite the fact I've sworn allegiance to another. Last night I saw the brute by the fire, drunk and slovenly, bragging to his friends how he would train his Irish bride with a stick." She grabbed Fitz's sleeve. "I had to run. I had no choice."

For all she knew, she spoke the truth, considering the stories she'd heard, and her voice held all the weight of real fear.

"And this brother you seek?"

"He delivered me to the Camerons, then was ordered away. He's weak, you see. He must do as my father commands."

"Your father the invalid."

"You've found me out," she said, sounding lost and forlorn. "Me father can walk. He did break his leg once, but two years have gone past since the healing. Caution drove me to the lie; for all I knew, you could be the kin of my betrothed."

Fitz shifted his weight and glanced toward the change-house, as if fearful of being overheard. "I know him only by what my uncle says."

"He speaks badly of him?"

"Aye." Fitz looked as though he wanted to say more, but he held his silence.

Encouraged, Annie plunged on. "When you appeared at me side, frightening me to numbness, you asked what I was doing. The truth is I was about to borrow my brother's horse for a ride deeper into the woods. I have a need for time to think things through."

Annie rather liked that last touch. Her father would approve such prudence, and besides, it was the truth.

"How do I know the horse belongs to your brother?"

"Watch." Annie whistled between her teeth. The horse's head bobbed. "Gertie," she called out. The head bobbed twice, freeing the loosely bound reins.

"'Tis no' right—"

She stamped her foot in vexation. "Do I look like someone who would steal someone's horse?"

"I've no idea. In truth, I've never met a lass like you."

Annie wasn't sure he intended a compliment.

The door to the change-house opened, spilling light into the dusk. A short, slight figure filled the doorway. Tully! He turned to say something to his drinking companions, swaying as he hitched up his breeches.

Suddenly she hated the idea of asking his help. He wouldn't give it, either, not until he sobered up and listened to reason. In the meantime he could cause her grief, lecturing the way Papa did, raising a ruckus that would echo back to Thistledown.

He moved away from them, into the trees at the far side of the tavern to relieve himself, singing one of his bawdy songs in an off-key tenor.

When he returned would he mount the horse and ride off, or would he return to his ale? With Tully there was no predicting. She had to act fast. Before Fitz could question her further she made a dash for the mare, moving swiftly and quietly across the hard-packed dirt. Hiking her skirts, summoning all the agility of her desperate youth, she grabbed the dangling reins as she scrambled into the saddle.

Fitz was close on her heels, hoarsely whispering something about his uncle, but she paid him no mind. He threatened to block her way. Tully would return at any minute. She extended a hand. Her slight build notwithstanding, she helped the lad jump onto the mare behind her. Her heels urged Gertie into a gallop. Fitz grabbed her waist to keep from falling off.

They were barely within the curtain of trees when Tully came thrashing after them, yelling, "Stop, thief!"

Little chance, she thought, grateful he hadn't been able to identify her in the dimness. She gave Gertie her head, letting the mare's instincts guide them through the dark.

A noise akin to thunder exploded in the night. With a start she realized someone was shooting at them. Annie's heart pounded in her throat, and she dug her heels hard into Gertie's flanks.

"That must be my uncle," Fitz said into her ear, his arms taking a decidedly proprietary hold on her.

"He'd shoot us?" she asked, keeping low, her eye on the winding path Gertie chose for escape.

"He'd think 'tis his duty. Trying to frighten us, more than like. He's no' much of a marksman, I fear."

"Why would it be his duty?"

"I neglected to mention who he is. He's high sheriff of the county. Sheriff Edgar Gunn."

Chapter Five

William Stuyvesant Sturgeon IV could not believe he'd been abandoned at the altar. And a stark, plain altar, at that, out in the middle of nowhere, available to only the most intrepid of tourists, which he certainly was not.

He couldn't get over it, couldn't accept it, couldn't let it go. One minute Meagan was standing beside him in that ridiculous garb she'd chosen for the ceremony; the next minute she had disappeared behind a curtain. Gone. Poof. Like a cheap magician's trick.

Like a magician's cheap trick, that is. William liked to get his words right, even in times of greatest stress. It was the mark of a good attorney, and the mark of every Sturgeon he'd ever met.

This was the most stressful time he could remember, worse than when he'd taken the bar exam. His almost-wife, upright, honorable, conservative, the woman he'd chosen to bear his children, had disappeared practically from his arms;

despite frantic efforts to find her, six hours later she had not reappeared.

And here he was, William Sturgeon, for God's sake, returned in the last light of day to the scene of the crime—the kirk—to figure out what to do.

Stunned, he could think of only one thing. Why was she gone?

He pulled out the wedding band he'd thought to place on her finger, narrow so that it would not overwhelm the grandeur and width of the engagement ring.

I thought she loved me.

No, that wasn't true. He'd *known* she loved him, the way he loved her.

He twirled the band between manicured fingers. She'd never been cruel. So why go away?

The unthinkable occurred to him. Perhaps she'd fallen out of love. But she was so practical. Would she really break their engagement this way?

Not my Meagan.

For she was his. God in heaven, they had plans. If that didn't make someone belong to another, he didn't know what would.

He'd been such a good sport, too, coming to this run-down old place for the ceremony. Surely she understood he'd hated the idea.

Was she trying to pay him back for asking that they return to Glasgow for the wedding night? And for postponing the honeymoon?

Sybil thought so.

"You were marrying beneath you," she'd said by way of consolation when it became apparent the wedding was off.

The housekeeper from the castle—Fobs or Forbes or something like that—had offered to serve them tea.

He had declined and she'd upped the offer to

whiskey. Normally he wasn't a drinking man, but this time he agreed.

He'd searched the grounds, the castle, even the road leading back to Glasgow, but in vain. Sybil had helped, and the Thistledown guards, along with police from Fort William, the nearest town, but the only evidence they'd come up with was the foolish book Meagan had left on one of the pews.

The woman read too much fiction; that was her trouble. Fiction gave her ideas.

But she'd never been cruel, a fact he kept coming back to. Leaving him this way, without explanation, was cruel indeed. He hadn't talked to Hortencia yet—Sybil had taken care of that chore—but he would have to before long. That would be the cruelest part of all.

While his father had given tacit approval to the wedding, his mother hadn't cared for his choice of bride. On that point William refused to worry. He and Meagan were too much alike to listen to advice about how they should wait until they knew one another better.

They'd known each other for two years. And they weren't getting any younger, not if they planned to start a family soon.

Which they did.

William tapped the book. He'd tried to skim it, something about a forever bride, but to him it was no more than drivel and he'd set it aside.

Nice illustrations, though. Like one of the illuminated manuscripts at the J. Pierpont Morgan Library in New York. It might be worth some money. He should take it with him when he left.

Which led him to another quandary. When to leave? He'd already canceled his afternoon meeting with the law firm in Glasgow. They had assumed it was because he was eager to start his already-too-short honeymoon.

And he would be, if he could only find his bride.

The forever bride? Bah. The never bride, it would seem.

He ran a hand through his hair, mussing its neatness. Wait until word of this spread around New York. He'd be the butt of jokes in every attorney's office in town.

"I thought I'd find you out here."

He looked up to see Sybil's familiar figure walking into the kirk. Pencil thin in her black suit, gray hair pulled back so tight her narrow lips flattened, she raised her eyebrows. For the first time he noticed they were blackened with some kind of cosmetic pencil. How strange to notice the artificial lines now.

It was as if, since he couldn't learn any details about his absent bride, he must observe everyone else.

William didn't like getting off task.

"I thought maybe—"

"She might return?" Sybil sat beside him on the pew and patted his hand. "I don't think that's being realistic, do you?"

"Nothing about this situation is realistic."

"Pardon me for saying so, Mr. Sturgeon, but I've always thought Miss Butler—that is, your mother thought she was not quite stable. All those fanciful stories, you know, and the advertising she wrote gave ample proof that she was capable of almost anything."

But not running away. Of that William was certain. Every word of criticism offered by Sybil drove him to his fiancée's defense.

True to his profession, he took an adversarial position. Something had happened to her. She'd been kidnapped by some wild-eyed Scot, or else she'd suffered a mental breakdown. The excitement of the wedding and all, the idea of becoming a Sturgeon, of taking her place at his side, could have addled her brain.

Or maybe it was simply the enormity of the occasion. She'd been sickly as a child, he recalled. Perhaps her lapse had been both mental and physical, and from wherever she'd gone she couldn't return no matter how hard she tried.

All speculation. He despised such a thing. Everything spelled out, written down, communicated, no misunderstandings—that was how he conducted business, and how he conducted his life.

Resolution filled him like Scotch in a glass. Meagan Butler might not be a Sturgeon, but he was, and Sturgeons did not give up. He still had their room reserved in the castle; he would extend his stay until he knew exactly what was going on.

Instinct told him Meagan remained close by. Normally one to scorn instinct, he drew comfort from it now.

He tapped *The Forever Bride* against his knee. "I'm not leaving here until I've found her. When you talk to Mother, please make clear exactly how I feel."

"I don't understand. Surely—"

"Sybil, please do what I say. Tell Mother I still intend to marry Meagan. If I can find her, that is. I'm not giving up so easily."

He stood, the slender book still in his hand.

"Mother will understand. She knows that no matter the difficulty facing them, Sturgeons do not quit."

Chapter Six

Meagan would have given a year of ad-agency commissions for the sweats and running shoes back in her Manhattan apartment closet.

Or was it forward in Manhattan?

What a dumb thought. She'd better concentrate on keeping up with Robert as he maneuvered down the hill.

She fought back a sigh. He must have covered a hundred such inclines over the past half hour, the dying day growing dimmer with each one. She'd made it up and down all of them, usually with her skirt tangled between her legs. When the plaid she wore around her shoulders caught on a thorn-covered bush, she jerked free and muttered an exasperated, "Damn."

"You shoulda remained at Thistledown," Robert said over his shoulder, his long stride holding steady as he reached the base of the slope.

"I should have remained in New York."

He halted so suddenly she crashed into his back. His very broad and solid back. The strength of

him was both a comfort and a disturbance here
in the shadowy woods through which the trail
took them.

"Take care," he warned, turning to face her.

"Get your taillights fixed," she muttered, more
shaken by the contact than made good sense. She
tucked her hair behind her ears. Isolated as they
were in the twilight wilderness, they might as well
be the last two people on earth.

"My tail should have lights?" His gaze was a
glint in the gray light. "You come from a curious
time."

She shrugged in answer, fighting to appear
calm. Curious time? Most certainly, but it was *her*
time. She doubted she would ever draw an even
breath in 1765.

Right now, for instance, with Robert's shadow-
brown eyes looking her over and his strong mouth
twitching at the edge of a smile, she could no more
fill her lungs than she could fly over the surrounding pines. It didn't help that in his forest-green
coat and open-throated white shirt, with his hair
unkempt and dark as his eyes and his trim trousers tight against his muscled frame, he was the
most romantic figure she'd ever seen.

Romantic and provocative. How he delighted in
teasing her. She knew he doubted everything
she'd said.

And why shouldn't he? She herself was having
trouble adjusting to what had come to pass. The
only thing she knew for sure was that, having
given her word to help him, she had to keep moving, keep active, do whatever she could to forget
the emptiness inside her, and the terrible, lost
feeling of being truly alone.

If that meant being stubborn and out of sorts,
that was what she would have to be. Stubborn and

irritable beat hysterical any day, no matter what century it was.

The attitudes were certainly understandable, considering he'd chosen a cross-country trek rather than the more civilized road she suspected ran nearby.

But then, educated though he appeared to be, he did not seem the kind to choose civilization when he could take a wilder way.

Knowing how he could turn her bones to butter, she forced herself to look at him carefully, at his strength and sureness as he studied the stillness of the woods. Despite his precarious finances and some obviously haunting memories, he harbored no doubts about his goals or his situation in life. He wanted his land to prosper, and for that he needed the right wife.

Love was a luxury in his eighteenth-century world. And in her own century? Was her need for marriage any different from his?

Tears burned her eyes. Blinking them away, she stared at the ground until she got control. Where had they come from? And why now? She should have cried the moment she realized her situation, not in her present circumstances, not when she needed to be tough.

Feeling his gaze settle on her, she looked into his eyes. Robert was not a man to suffer weakness silently. She must not let him know of her trembling inside.

"This is no place for a woman, out and about roaming the hills in the darkening."

She could have predicted he'd say something like that. She welcomed his autocratic manner; he didn't look so romantic with a scowl on his face. And she didn't feel half so vulnerable.

"You said that before."

"You dinna listen well."

"I heard you say it would be a quick journey to this change-house, whatever that is, to see if your bride still lurked about." As she spoke she stood straight, proud that at five-foot-five she was several inches taller than the Scottish women she'd seen. "Quick it's not, but do I seem out of breath?"

He stared at her breasts. She covered her blouse more tightly with the plaid.

"You've shown no signs. But I'd feared your legs could no' stand up to the demands of the path."

"I have good legs," she said, stung. And then, "What makes you doubt my legs?"

"I did some investigating afore you woke. 'Twas the thighs that had me most concerned."

"There's nothing wrong with my thighs."

"Excepting they're a wee bit on the thin side. No' so terrible, you ken, that I wasn't willing to overlook them, for the sake of marital bliss."

Chauvinist pig, she thought, then wondered what else he had inspected. And what he had thought.

She blushed when she considered the possibilities. She also felt a sudden heat surging through her veins, settling in the area between her suspect thighs.

"Don't worry about me," she said, as always fighting his effect on her. "I told you I'm a jogger."

"A curious word."

"You think everything about me is curious."

The look he gave her sizzled the soles of her shoes. "No' everything." The air around them grew amazingly tropical for a Highland May twilight, as warm as her fast-flowing blood. She couldn't swallow, couldn't breathe. And then he smiled, breaking the tension. "I could say *intriguing* if you've a mind for a different manner of speaking.

79

Or baiting, enticing, more than aught else tempting."

He rolled the words out in a deep cadence; they touched her like a caress. She found herself actually swaying toward him. He saw it, too, and he winked.

The rakehell, she thought, dredging up a word from one of her books.

Somehow she found her voice and her resolution. "What I've a mind for is to find your Meagan the Younger and leave."

His smile died, and for some unfathomable reason she regretted her brusqueness.

"There, my almost-bride, I agree. We'd best get to the change-house to pick up her scent."

Her scent. As if she were an animal meant to satisfy his hunger. Which she was, in a way.

"'Tis possible," he went on, "she's caught the post south to Glasgow, or north, mayhap, to Inverness."

He seemed to be covering all possibilities. Meagan almost felt sorry for the girl, who must have understood her role in this marriage. She'd taken the unexpected course; she'd rebelled and run away. And here her unwitting replacement was, planning to help drag her back.

Robert plunged onward through the evening shade. Forgetting everything but her own plight, Meagan hurried to keep up. Since they'd set out on this journey, not once had she complained, and she would not begin now.

But, oh, she would have paid much for those sweats and running shoes.

So caught up was she in proving herself, she barely heard the gunshot reverberating through the trees. She had no idea the direction it came from, nor the distance it traveled, but Robert seemed more sure of himself, breaking into a run that tested her endurance, slowing only when they heard loud voices directly ahead. They came to a clearing, at the center of which was a low, thatch-roofed structure made of rough stone. Near the front door, a half dozen men stood arguing, speaking so fast she couldn't make out what they said.

Twenty yards away she spied a gravel road that wound its way into the growing dark. It was the civilized route Robert had forsworn, the route of the post, a way out of this wilderness for everyone but her.

Robert came to an abrupt halt in the shadows. Meagan narrowly avoided running into him again.

He muttered something unintelligible. Considering the tone of his voice, she took it to be a Gaelic curse.

"What's wrong?" she whispered.

"Gunn," he said.

She looked over the gathering. In the dimness she could make out nothing other than the obvious agitation of the men.

"You want to shoot someone?" she asked.

"The fox-face at the center."

Squinting, Meagan could only guess which one he meant. "Tall, thin?"

"Aye. No flesh nor heart to him. That's Sheriff Edgar Gunn."

"The one who is not to know your bride has absconded."

"The same. The bastard beside him is no' much better. Bailie Fergus Munro, Gunn's lackey. 'Tis glad I am he has the brains of a trout."

Gradually Meagan's eyes adjusted to the dark and she saw more clearly the Mutt-and-Jeff pair who were Robert's enemies. Where Gunn was tall and thin, Munro was squat and square, Gunn gaunt of features, Munro flat faced, as though he'd been run over by a truck.

"There's none amongst them I could call friend," Robert said, "more's the pity."

She heard no fear in his voice, but she was frightened enough for the two of them.

"What do we do now?" she asked.

He motioned her away. She stepped backward. A twig snapped.

"Who goes there?" the sheriff barked as he lifted his pistol in their direction.

Again came the muttered Gaelic curse, but when Robert stepped into the clearing, it was with a smile on his face. Guiltily, Meagan forced herself to follow.

"Take care, Edgar. You'll be shooting an innocent man."

"Cameron." The sheriff spat out the name.

"Aye, and proud of it. If it weren't for the pistol you bear, I'd have scarce recognized you without your wig and fancy robe."

"Ye'll see me soon enough on the bench, once I determine yer part in all o' this."

"Forgive my ignorance. Part of all what?"

"Thievery of a horse, as well ye ken."

"And where might I be hiding the animal?"

"Yer Cameron clan, then." Gunn waved the pistol in the direction of the woods. "A pair of them stole a fine Irish mare no' ten minutes ago."

Standing close beside Robert, Meagan felt him tense.

"Irish, you say."

"Aye, like yer bride." Gunn glanced at her, then did a double-take, giving her a more thorough study. "This be the unfortunate lady?"

He said the last with a sneer.

"Unfortunate fer sure," echoed the bailie.

The sheriff crept closer, his steps marked by a slight limp. Robert put an arm around her while she tried to hide within the plaid.

"Gi'e us a peek at her," one of the men said. "She must be ugly as me own wife for ye to bring her out the eve ye were wed."

More than ever she sensed the tension in Robert, but a quick glance at his face showed no change in his expression. If he could be so brave, she must be the same, and she let his courage flow into her.

"In truth, men, after an afternoon together, she's robbed me of my strength. We've come for a stroll before finishing out the night."

Gunn's dark button eyes turned to slits. "A stroll, is it? Ye're a mile from Thistledown."

"She's a hardy one," Robert said, "this new lady of Cameron land."

They might have been discussing the merits of a hunting dog. Meagan fought back a retort.

"Och, mon, gi'e us a look at her," another put in.

Robert pulled her so close her face was buried against the rough, earthy fabric of his coat, his one-arm embrace as strong as a vise as he held her tight to his broad chest.

"She's hardy, but she's shy." He patted her reassuringly. Just the way he would a dog.

"About the mare. Who's the owner?"

"He dinna say," Gunn replied. "But I suspect he's kin to ye now, what with so few of his kind in these parts. Strange, I trow, he wasna at the ceremony."

"Strange, indeed," the bailie growled.

"And where might this Irishman be?" Robert asked, still calm as you please. "I'll put the question to him about his neglect."

"Took off into the gloaming after the thieves."

"There was more than one?"

"A pair of them, lads from the look of them," said the man with the homely wife. "Or so the Irishman claimed afore he ran after them inta the woods. He'd need be swift as a roe deer to catch them, I'll be bound."

Meagan felt more than heard someone draw near. A hand reached out to grab her shawl.

"Away, Gunn. Dinna be touching my wife."

Robert's voice was low, menacing. Only a fool would have ignored him.

Gunn must have been such a fool, because he did not let go.

"I've a need to look at her. 'Tis my duty to ken all in the county by sight."

"'Tis your duty to catch thieves. Except that you'd be after yourself then, would you no'? And the tacksman I sent scurrying off Cameron land."

"Cameron land," Gunn said in mockery, and the bailie echoed, "Cameron land."

"Aye. Does the sound of it make you bilious? Your quandary, Edgar, is that I returned from my wanderings too soon to suit your greedy purposes."

Meagan understood about half of what they were saying, but she had no trouble picking up on the tension in the air. It fairly prickled over her skin. Outnumbered as they were, and unarmed, she had a hard time holding on to her faith in Robert.

And yet she did.

Why that was, she would think about later. Hoping maybe she could help, she pushed away and opened her mouth to speak. If any questioned her accent, he could tell them she'd been deaf.

"Ah, lass, I'm neglecting my duties. You'll have to forgive me," Robert said with a shake of his head, and promptly kissed her. Long and hard. She started to fight him, but common sense told her to remain calm, especially with enemy witnesses nearby. When he touched her tongue with his, instinct told her to touch him right back.

He pulled her within the warmth of his coat; slipping her arms inside, she pressed her body to his. She knew this was wrong, elicit, foolish, but it was also enticing, thrilling, and strangely right. He was too much, too strong, too overpowering, and at the same time his kiss wasn't nearly enough.

He was the one to break away; reality hit her in a rush. What was she thinking of? Could they really be in danger if he could take such advantage? Clearly he was an unconscionable cad, and she was just as clearly a fool. She eased from him and stood with her back to the others, staring blankly into the woods, slowing her breath, stilling her wildly beating heart. And wondering what came over her whenever this determined Scot came near.

It wasn't wimpdom, she feared, but a weakness far more serious.

The men talked, but she shut out what they said. Something crude about her, no doubt, something ugly passing between Robert and Edgar Gunn, subjects she could not be part of, problems that were not hers.

She had enough problems of her own without taking on more. Sighing, she thrust her hand in the pocket of her skirt, and started when her fingers touched an object thrust deep inside. Shifting to hide her actions, she pulled out her mother's handkerchief, the one she'd brought with her as

85

something old for her wedding.

She clutched the soft fabric and the hard object it was wrapped around. Her engagement ring. She'd forgotten all about it. Worth thousands of dollars in 1997, what would it be worth now?

The calculations almost made her forget Robert's kiss. Remembering the men behind her—including an armed sheriff of questionable honesty and his cretin bailie, including, too, a strapped-for-cash, sort-of husband she barely knew—she hastily shoved the treasure in her pocket just as the latter stepped to her side.

"Let's go home, lass," he said, then more softly, where only she could hear, "We're losing too much time."

Go home? If only she could.

This time they walked side by side, letting the rising moon light their way. She kept an air about her that appeared amazingly at ease, considering the way memories of his lips on hers thrummed through her veins. The memories, together with the effort from the walk, kept her warm against the night chill.

Too, she kept worrying about the blasted ring. What if she accidentally lost it on this dark trail? William would never understand, provided, of course, she ever saw him again.

Without warning, Robert grabbed her wrist and dragged her off the path. For just a moment she wondered if he planned to have his way with her somewhere in the bushes. To her relief—her great relief, she told herself—he kept on dragging her through the brush and high grass, her feet painfully striking stones as she ran.

A particularly sharp rock caused her to yelp.

He halted, motioning her to silence as he listened to the wind and the cry of unseen birds in the night. Dim moonlight played on his face, casting shadows across his features, sharpening the lines of his cheeks and his mouth, making her forget the ring. She tried to picture this man walking the streets of Manhattan, entering boardrooms, ordering lunch at Tavern on the Green.

She couldn't do it. He fit no place but here in the Highlands, at ease in the wild countryside, a chill Scottish breeze ruffling his hair.

"We've put distance between us. They'll no' be hearing your howl, not with Gunn too lazy to follow."

"I did not howl," she hissed, and then, speaking in a hard whisper, added, "What are we doing, anyway?"

"Chasing down my bride."

"But you said we were going home."

"I dinna always tell the truth."

"I'll remember that."

His harsh expression softened. "Are you injured?"

She thought of her throbbing foot. "No," she lied.

"Could it be, Meagan the Elder, you're no' being honest with me?"

He moved close. What was he going to do? Her heart quickened. If he tried anything she'd fight him this time. She had her pride.

Instead he growled. "You shouldna be here. But I've little time to get you back to safety. No' if I'm to keep on her trail. I hadna planned, you ken, on the lassie finding herself a horse."

"I've not held you up yet, Robert Cameron. And you seemed to enjoy my presence all right when you kissed me."

"We shared the enjoyment, did we no'?"

"We did not."

"Strange it is that I gathered otherwise."

"I went along to avoid arousing suspicion."

"And unlike me, you dinna lie. You're a noble woman, and I'm a cad to think you drew pleasure from it. Should there be another time when such a demonstration proves necessary, I'll remember 'tis your honor and nobility that puts your tongue against mine."

If she could have thought of a smart retort, she would have thrown it at him. But he had her, and he knew it. She chose silence instead, which was just as well because he seemed to forget her presence, concentrating instead on the night.

"Do you think it was the brother whose horse was stolen?"

"Aye."

"And the thieves? Two lads, they said."

"Or a lad and a lass."

"Meagan-Anne?"

"She's supposed to be a fine rider. It was a point of pride in MacSorley's description of her. And a lass who would break her word would no' refrain from theft."

"So who's the second thief?"

"There the possibilities grow complicated. Gunn has a nephew visiting from the north. The lad was supposed to meet him at the change-house, but he's no' yet been seen this night."

"You think he ran off with the girl?"

"I see it as a possibility."

"Ah," Meagan said. "Complicated indeed."

She had no chance to contemplate the situation, for Robert chose that moment to take off away from the trail, warning her with only a quick "Hie close" before renewing the chase.

They soon broke through the brambles, and he quickened his stride. Most of the way wound across hills of low grass at the edge of a thick woods. Never a Girl Scout, she had no idea the direction they took, but Robert seemed in little doubt they were headed in the right direction. She followed close in his path, and luck was with her, for she didn't stumble once and only rarely came down upon a bothersome rock.

She estimated they'd gone a quarter mile when he turned toward the trees. He halted shortly, and this time she was out of breath from the chase. He seemed not the least affected, however.

"Are we lost?" she asked.

"Dinna speak foolishness. I'm considering what t' do. 'Tis clear she's given up her plans for the post, if she ever had them. She'll be heading south and west, toward the ocean, toward Ireland, believing she can get away."

"Which she can't," Meagan said, thinking the poor girl seemed more and more like a hunted animal.

But one who's gone against her family's honor, she reminded herself. *Like Shakespeare's Juliet, and look what happened to her.*

"She'll have streams and lochs to hinder her way, and most difficult of all, the Great Glen."

"Assuming she's the thief."

"Aye. For the while, I've little choice but to believe she's taken the horse."

"What about the nephew? Assuming he's the one with her. Won't he bring her back?"

"Any kin of Edgar Gunn's will no' behave honorably. Nor will he have much sense about the lay of the land, being a stranger to these parts."

Meagan had a dozen questions bothering her, but she set them aside for a time when she was more likely to get her answers. It occurred to her she should be frightened of the night and of the

trees, the way she would have been at this hour in
Central Park. But in this impossible earlier time
her only worry at the moment was that in some
way she might fail.

How strange it was that she kept slipping in and
out of panic, of fright, and, she admitted, of lust.
She, Meagan Butler, who kept her feelings tightly
bound except when lost in a book. In whispering
that blasted incantation, she'd not only lost her
century, she'd lost her sense of self.

"So what do we do?" she asked.

"We've been circling the forest without a sign
they've broken through to the pasture. I've little
doubt they're wandering somewhere not far away.
She's a lass; she'll need to bed down for the night."

"Being weak, you mean."

"And not a jogger, whatever that be. The lad's
the puzzle. Maybe she promised him favors if he
helped her escape."

"You're talking about your future wife."

"Aye, that I am."

Meagan the reader understood something
about past customs and the importance placed on
virginity for a young bride's wedding night.

"What will you do if they . . . well, if the favors
are given?"

"Make an honorable Cameron woman out of
her. If I have to lock her in her room."

Meagan had no doubt he meant it. Suddenly the
night chill got to her, and despite her resolve she
shivered.

"So what do we do in the meantime?"

His answer was to motion her deeper into the
woods. They came upon a small cottage almost
before she knew it. A thin ribbon of smoke curled
from the roof, but there were no windows to offer
a welcoming light.

Still, she felt relieved by the sight. Until, that is, Robert spoke.

"We'll remain here for the night, then leave before first light to track down our errant pair. I'd planned something grander for our wedding night, but at least"—here his eyes glinted darkly—"we'll have a roof over our heads and beneath us a bed to ease the passing of the time."

Chapter Seven

"The fire'll warm you soon enough, unless you've a mind for a heated body next to yours."

Robert purposefully said the words with innocence, but there was little innocent in how he planted himself sideways in the doorway, gesturing for her to precede him inside.

"Humph!" his bride said as she squeezed past him. Praise be to the crofter whose home this was for making the portal so narrow; her choice was to rub him with her front or her rear. She chose the latter. Robert gave her no room to spare.

Sweet torture it was to feel her bottom graze his thighs. He caught her intake of breath as she passed; sweet torture, too, for her. He knew when a woman wanted him. Despite her spinsterish *humph*, here was such a lass.

Curse the promise to leave her alone.

In compensation, he took his pleasure teasing her. She seemed to ask for it, always having a rejoinder for whatever he said, her fine violet eyes unknowingly revealing hidden hungers, her chin tilted in defiance even as her lips invited a kiss.

A little looby, without doubt, fighting what was clearly between them, a great deal touched in the head as she clung to her wild story about traveling through time. And yet so must he be, the way he sometimes almost believed her.

No one inside the cottage waited to greet them, a fact not entirely unexpected. The low peat fire at the center of the room sent out uneven heat, its smoke drifting upward through a hole in the roof. On the iron tripod built over the fire, there hung a cauldron of simmering broth.

The room was lit by a blue haze from the hollowed-out hearth, its earthy smells that of peat and potatoes and venison.

When Meagan looked around her, surprise and interest lit her eyes. Wherever she came from, she'd clearly never seen a crofter's cottage before.

Putting himself in her place, he lit a taper and studied the walls made of alternating layers of turf and stone; the rafters supporting a sod roof, whose center hole took the place of a proper chimney; the earth floor; the rough table, which was already laid with wooden goblets and bowls, and two chairs; a pair of box beds against one wall, in front of which hung a plaid tossed over a rope for privacy, and at the end of one bed a small wooden chest.

The place was poor but neat and welcoming, and while he cursed the dampness that might give its people coughs or crippling rheumatism, he knew there was nothing different here from dozens of other such places on his land. Highlanders had lived thusly for hundreds of years; he was determined the Cameron clan would not do so for many more.

With that thought in mind, he'd provided each

cottage with something few homes elsewhere could boast: a spinning wheel. This one sat in a dimly lit corner quietly, patiently, waiting for the woman of the house to make it sing.

When Meagan looked past the spinning wheel as if it had no particular significance, he felt a stab of disappointment.

"Sit, Meagan. We've the place to ourselves."

She nodded toward the cauldron. "Surely whoever lives here will be returning soon."

"Nay. Angus and his wife will sleep in a cottage nearby. Good folk that they are, they've prepared the food for us."

Her thick lashes lifted and she stared at him with troubled eyes. He realized with a start that not once had he seen her smile.

"How did they know we'd be here?" she asked.

"Afore we left Thistledown, I sent word to the crofters in the area I might be needing a bed for the night. We Scots are a hospitable lot, no matter how poor."

"But not necessarily friendly."

"Because they dinna choose to greet us? They know 'tis our wedding night. They've learned to expect the unexpected from their laird, and from the appearance you made today, running from the keep, then fleeing back inside, they've gathered I've met my match. Though they're none too sure about the swooning in the chapel." He couldn't resist sidling close. "They doubt you'll prove a lustful wife."

Her retort came as fast as he'd expected.

"William has no complaints."

Discomfort akin to jealousy bit him, apt punishment for teasing her. "Perhaps the fish is no' so lusty himself."

She looked away quickly, too quickly. So the

lass was sensitive about her man's coldness, was she? Should he take advantage? Aye, he should.

Easing out of his jacket, he dropped it on a chair, then turned to pull the plaid from her shoulders and toss it beside the coat. She shivered, but he knew it was not from a chill.

"Whoever he be, you're wasted on him."

He stroked her cheek. She pushed him back.

"You promised," she said, eyes flashing angrily. "Aren't Scots honorable as well as hospitable?"

He shrugged, refusing to take offense, noticing how her gaze dropped to his chest and his legs before returning quickly to his face.

"The trouble is we're also beset with a powerful lust."

"Is that all you think about?"

"'Tis a madness that takes hold, turning us to savage beasts of unsurpassable strength. Worst of all, the madness continues 'til we've had our release."

He braced himself for another *humph*, yet hoped for something more encouraging. She laughed. None too steadily, but still it was a laugh. Not what he would have chosen as a reaction, but it had its charm, like a silver bell tinkling in the night.

Too bad it did not include the warmth of a smile in her eyes.

"What a crock," she said with none-too-silvery certitude.

"You doubt my lust?"

"I'm sure you'd like to get me in that bed. But struck with madness to do it? Hardly. You're too calculating for that." Walking around the fire, she gestured to the cauldron. "How convenient to have everything waiting for us on this night of unexpected events. If we hadn't been successful in

Evelyn Rogers

finding news of your bride, would you have found
another excuse for getting me here?"

Robert watched her in fascination. She had a
tongue on her that should be put to better tasks
than lacerating him with words. She'd also managed to put the fire between them for safety's sake,
mayhap needing it for protection. Did she not ken
how the light played on her face and over her
body, reminding him of its valleys and peaks, of
the strange garment she wore beneath her skirt?

With great patience, he held to his place. "I'm a
cautious man, and one who must consider all con-
tingencies."

"I know," she said, tucking her thick hair behind
her ears. "Be prepared. I've heard the motto before."

"You're a cynical lass, are ye no'?"

"It comes with my time."

"You still insist on your preposterous tale."

"Preposterous or not, it's the truth."

He wanted to believe her; he had detected signs
that it could be—her unseen apparel, her genuine
surprise at everything she came upon, the pain in
her eyes when she'd gazed down on the ruins of
Thistledown.

Too, she had an air about her that equaled that
of no lass he'd met in any of his worldly travels, a
manner of confidence that misted over the confusion and trepidation she did not want him to
see.

And then there was her scent. When it caught
in his nostrils, he did in truth come close to being
a savage beast.

He tried to remember her family name. She
wasn't a Cameron, despite the vows they'd shared.
Butler, that was it. Meagan Butler, or so she'd
said. A bold miss, with her skillful kisses, bold yet

96

tremulous at the same time. Which was the real woman? Someone in between, more than like.

Enemy to his resolution, that was certain. Keeper of secrets. Traveler through time? He'd never heard of such. What sort of a fool did she take him for?

A fool who wanted beneath her skirts, and honor be damned.

Life was proving, year after year, to be more challenging than he'd dreamed when he was but a lad.

Without another word he took refuge in activity, ladling each of them a bowl of stewed venison, potatoes, and broth. A loaf of coarse barley bread sat on one of the stones banking the fire. Tossing the coat and plaid to one end of the table, he settled in one of the chairs and gestured for her to join him. She did just that, watching as he scooped up the rich food with a portion of the bread, copying him awkwardly, as if she did not ken so much as the way she was supposed to eat.

Like him, she managed to clean her bowl, then downed another until the food was gone. He filled the goblets with whiskey from a small cask he found by the table.

She took a cautious sip. "Scotch. I should have known."

"Whiskey. And what else should it be but Scottish?"

"Now—that is, in the future, it's distilled in many parts of the world. But the best comes from Scotland and it's called Scotch."

More nonsense, but within it lay a compliment he took without argument.

She took another sip. "This is different from what I'm used to, almost a smoky taste, but good."

"Aye. *Iusge-beatha*, 'tis called in the old language. The water of life."

In fascination he watched her drink, watched the play of muscles in her throat as she swallowed, spied a hint of liquid on her lips. How would the whiskey taste if he licked her lips dry? Smoky indeed, and rich as cream.

Ah, what a torment she was. He must be paying penance for past sins.

With a little laugh she set the goblet aside. "I'd better stop. It's going to my head."

For his part, Robert downed the drink, then finished hers, taking care to place his mouth on the goblet where hers had been. She watched him, and she understood.

Pushing away from the table, she picked up the bowls. "Where do I clean these?"

"Put them by the door. They'll be got."

Were her hands none too steady? Aye, he thought with satisfaction. They were.

She looked less than pleased at the suggestion, but she did as he said.

Brushing her hands together, she walked past him to one of the beds. "We'd better get some sleep. We'll want an early start tomorrow."

"That we will," he said, keeping to his chair, watching the lithe way she moved, the way her smooth black hair bounced against her shoulders, the twitch at the corner of her mouth that proved she was not so calm as she might wish.

If she could see the fit of his breeches, she'd ken that neither was he.

She hugged herself. "What I wouldn't give for a bath."

"What would you give, lass? Be specific, and we might come to an agreement."

Her hands stilled on her arms. He stared for a

moment at the curious—nay, the intriguing—pink nails.

"You'd ask too high a price," she said.

"Nothing I wouldna give you back in kind. I'll toss in a good back-scrubbing for free."

"And a front scrub, too, I'll bet."

He let out a long, slow breath, imagining how her damp breasts would feel, silken like her underdrawers, only warm instead of cool. "We Camerons," he said huskily, "are a thorough lot."

"Aye," she said, then scowled. "You've got me talking in your brogue."

"'Tis a start."

They stared at one another through the blue haze. Everything about her tore at his system. He wanted to rip the clothes from her body, entwine his fingers in the slip of silk that covered her treasure, stroke the dark hair at the juncture of her thighs, discover the sweet secrets of her intimate parts.

And put his parts against hers, rubbing, stroking, teasing until she cried out his name, then thrusting deep inside her, a thousand times until passion erupted and he could start to discover her once again.

His breath came in short gasps, so vivid were the images in his mind, and for an instant he did not know himself. He stood with such violence the chair fell to the floor behind him. In the firelight she saw his breeches, saw what she did to him. Her eyes darkened to rich amethyst. Did she not know she'd started a hotter fire inside him than any hearth could contain?

He walked slowly around the table, more stalking beast than man. She watched each movement, each step. The wind whistled wildly around the cottage; his heart thundered with the roar.

"You frighten me," she said as he halted scant inches away from her.

"You frighten me. I've never wanted a woman more than I want you. And 'tis our wedding night."

She closed her eyes. Her lashes curled thick and long against her tawny skin. "I mean it. You frighten me. I've never felt like this before."

The tremor in her voice gave proof she spoke the truth. He stroked her hair lightly, marveling at the texture of the smooth, straight strands.

He lifted her chin. "I'll take your maidenhead with gentleness, if that's what you fear. And I'll give you a pleasure that matches my own."

"My . . . oh. I don't have . . . that is I'm not—"

"—a virgin," he said, finishing for her, hearing the regret in her voice. Or was it simply surprise he could be so blunt? She ought to ken by now he knew no other way.

She nodded but held her silence. Jealousy twisted inside him. What man had taken her prize? Had she been hurt? He'd thrash the bastard, head and shoulders, then sever his manhood, making certain he would never hurt a lass again.

He tried to tell her something of what he would do. Her regret turned quickly to anger.

"I'm thirty years old, Robert. And I come from a different time. What I've done may not have been wise, but it was my choice and mine alone."

There it came again, the strange tale to which she clung. It put between them a barrier that he knew not how to scale.

He was not so much a savage that he couldn't see the lost light glimmering behind the anger in her eyes. He cupped her face and brushed his lips against hers, then stepped away.

"The taste of you burns into my soul, Meagan Butler Cameron. You make me forget my task, but

I've no' the power to make you forget your plight, whatever it be. Take your rest. I've a need to feel the chill of the wind if I'm to lie chastely close to you throughout the night."

Meagan barely made it to the bed before her knees buckled. She listened as he pulled the length of plaid along the rope that stretched high in front of the beds, forming a wool wall as protection against—against what? Iron bars wouldn't keep Robert Cameron from her bed if he chose to sleep there. And neither would her resolve, which was about as substantial as warm ice cream whenever he came near.

Cursing the two of them, she huddled beneath the covers as he went out the door and closed it firmly behind him. Cursed him for being so una-bashedly physical, and herself for letting it matter so much. The moment he found out she'd slept with a man before, he decided he didn't want her after all. She didn't care; at least, she shouldn't care.

So why did she feel more lost and alone than ever?

This whole situation was getting out of hand. She didn't know why she was here, or if she could ever leave, but she'd convinced herself to be strong until she tried out the incantation again.

She was making every effort. Back in the future she could have held off any of her three fiancés— the pseudointellectual college student, the preening actor, even William, who was the love of her heart.

But Robert Cameron was something else. Rob-ert, with his broad shoulders and tapered hips and his great calves and knees. The three men she'd planned to marry all had cool eyes in shades of blue. Not Robert. He looked at her with brown eyes so heated and hungry they reminded her of hot fudge.

Most of all she thought about the lips he used with such devastating skill each time he kissed her. It seemed shallow to think she could be undone by something so inconsequential as a touch of one mouth to another. But she was.

She'd told him he frightened her. She could have told him why—how he was so much more than she could handle, so virile, so manly. She felt foolish using such terms—she would never use them in her ads—but she'd not met this overwhelming Highlander back in New York.

How clearly she remembered reading *The Forever Bride* and wondering what the husband did to the wife to keep her satisfied between visits.

Robert would know.

When she thought about how he would make love, she soared beyond simple fright. She was terrified.

Not that she had a thing to worry about, she thought as she tossed about in the bed. Because of her past associations, he didn't want her so much anymore.

Chapter Eight

Robert strode the perimeter of the clearing outside the crofter's cottage, staring up at the moon, at the smoke whirling in the wind above the roof, at the woods, at the stones over which he trod. Everywhere he looked he saw a pair of violet eyes staring back.

The frenzy of his wanting her still pounded through him, and the trace of a violence he did not recognize as being part of himself. He'd seen a similar violence in his wanderings as a youth, after the slaughter at Culloden when both British and Scot, under the guise of seeking traitors to the Crown, raped and pillaged and burned.

During those sad days he'd learned to hate the depths to which a man could fall; he cared naught for it now, these twenty years hence.

Thistledown Castle had fallen during this time, though ill health had kept his father from taking a place beside his fellow Jacobites. The so-called justice-seekers had not cared. They'd wanted vengeance; they'd wanted blood.

Evelyn Rogers

As for himself, he'd been too young to join in the battle to bring Bonnie Prince Charlie to the throne, too powerless to halt the ugliness that followed, though he'd tried. His body still bore the scars of more than one fight, and his soul the memories. When he was no more than a lad he'd sworn that he would never fall prey to such degradations as he had witnessed, either in the giving or in the taking.

But he could have taken Meagan on the cottage floor. He thought she might have succumbed with hungry willingness once he'd kissed her as he had before, but he was not sure. Worse, he knew not whether her submission made a difference in what he did.

A half hour of walking and breathing in the cold air eased the fever his almost-bride had given him, at least to a tolerable degree. And he saw the necessity of keeping his hands to himself. To do otherwise would be a sin against all that he believed, all for which he fought, and all he hoped yet to do.

He'd provided his people with spinning wheels and tools and the practical knowledge he had picked up in his travels, details about farming and a hundred other tasks. Yet too many still lived in hovels like this one. Too many bairns died too young.

They were the ones who needed his dowry, not he.

'Twas a burden indeed his father had put on his shoulders, dying and leaving his wishes behind. When Robert returned from Quebec, seeking peace above all else, it was to find a wife and infant son buried on a Cameron hill, and his father close to joining them.

His gravestone had already been carved:

The Forever Bride

To the honored memory of
DONALD CAMERON
who loved in the serene
evening of his life
to look around him here
May his children's children gather here
and think of him

But the only child of Donald's only child had died before him, along with Iona, the beloved daughter-in-law who might have borne others to fulfill the old man's final wish. Robert, gone too long with little news of home, had not known of his son's birth until he saw the evidence of his death.

It was a cruel blow to a man seeking comfort, seeking love, seeking peace. He must marry again, must bring more grandchildren into the world. And he must keep Cameron land—his father's *land*—intact.

His orders came from the grave.

Most of the time he buried the memories of his lost wife and child, though his sense of obligation burned hotly in his soul. In stirring his passions, this rare, fascinating woman who called herself Meagan had also stirred up remembrances of what drove him on.

Hellfire and damnation. The more he wanted her, the more he knew he should keep his hands to himself.

So she wasn't a virgin. It was of little import. Neither was he.

'Twas a pity he knew so little else of her. She said she'd seen Thistledown Castle restored, and his name sung in praise for being the cause. She was either a visionary or a dissembler who knew how to flatter him. He would give a portion of his land to know which she might be.

A stirring in the trees at his back drove all other considerations from his mind. He whirled and dropped into a crouch, watching as a dark figure came stealthily into the clearing.

"Halt," he said, pulling out the dirk he wore in his boot. "Halt and identify yourself."

Hands flew into the air. "'Tis only a poor wreck known as Tully MacSorley. I mean no harm to any man."

Ah, Robert thought, just the lad he wanted to meet. For once something was going right.

"Step close, Tully MacSorley, and reveal yourself."

The man he saw, if he could be called a man, looked no older than twenty, short and slight, his youthful features screwed into a frown of worry.

"I'm in search of my lost sister. Ye've not seen her, by any chance? Red hair, sharp tongue, no more sense than a salmon, but mettle enough to make St. Patrick himself wince."

"What makes you search these woods?"

"She's stolen Gertie from me."

"Gertie being your horse?"

"Aye, taken from the tavern where I'd stopped for a wee dram to ward off the night chill."

"You saw the theft?"

"I could not name her as my kin, not at the time, but later I spied her in these woods, riding like the hobgoblins were at her tail, lost as Mac-Killiguddy's sheep. She had a lad wi' her, which should come as no surprise. She always has one lying about."

"Did she know she was seen?"

"Not likely, what with all the noise she was making, scaring off the goblins. She's got a real fear of 'em, ye see. She's gone to ground somewhere with

106

my horse and her lad, clever kitten that she is, and won't come out until the light o' day."

"Is she clever or senseless? You've described her as both."

"So she is. Clever in getting her way, but without the sense God gave a flea in knowin' what that way ought to be."

Tully dropped to the ground as if he were too weary to go on. "Drat it all. Da will flail the skin from me bones when he hears what's happened. If only that rascal Robert Cameron had kept her under his roof, none of this would have happened."

"You've the right of it there. Cameron's known far and wide for the rascal and fool that he is."

"Ye know him?"

"Aye. Happen you're looking at the rascal himself."

Tully made the sign of the cross and turned his eyes to heaven, his whispered prayers coming fast and unintelligible.

"I want to find her, too," Robert said, helping Tully to his feet. "The lass and I have not had the chance to meet."

"But I left her at Thistledown yesterday eve. Saw her inside meself."

"And then departed."

Tully stared guiltily at his boots. "She had no funds. I'd little reason to suspect she would run."

"She chose to spend her time in the room I'd prepared," Robert added. "When the hour came for her to appear, she was gone."

"Told you she was clever and senseless, did I not?" Tully sighed. "There was talk at the tavern that ye'd wed. I thought all was well."

"It was talk I encouraged," Robert said, seeing no point in telling the lad that a wedding had taken place, although with unexpected results. "I intend to find your sister and make her my wife."

Robert found no pleasure in the declaration, just an unfortunate and inevitable truth.

"Ye have a sheriff that'll be a wee upset at the news," Tully said. "Though he believes like the rest of 'em the vows have already been said. Seein' his temper, I kept my kinship with Annie to meself."

"I was told her name was Meagan-Anne."

"Annie is what she prefers. Da calls her Brat."

That particular news concerning his betrothed brought Robert little cheer. He put it alongside her brother's admission that she always had a lad "lying about."

Tully moaned in agony. "'Tis a dilemma I'm facing, and that's the truth. I'll no' be finding the lass without letting out she's stolen me Gertie, but if I do go braying about wi' the news, like the veriest jackass, word will get back to Da—it always does—and I'll never leave home again."

"Then let's keep it to ourselves that his daughter is temporarily misplaced. Once she's found and we're married, 'twill all be the same."

"Ye'd really have her after what she's done?"

"I'm a man of my word. I said I'd relieve your father of the burden of a daughter"—*and of her dowry*—"and I will."

"Ye'd do that? Ye'd keep my secret?"

"I would, and so I swear."

Tully's brow furrowed as he thought through the offer. "I'd have to know she fares all right."

The consideration came a wee bit late, Robert thought. "That's my responsibility now."

"Ye let her get away."

"I didn't understand her then. Now I do. Trust me, Tully. I know these woods. If she's heading for Ireland she's got rivers and lochs to cross.

She'll no' be away from me for more than a day."

He could see the lad weakening.

"Let us reach a compromise. I'll not tell your father of the change in wedding days and you don't mention your missing sister to anyone. Let the sheriff believe the thieves escaped unidentified."

"But—"

He sweetened his argument. "There's another crofter's cottage just beyond these woods. Bed down there for the night, and I'll provide you with funds to set you on as fine a hunting trip as you've ever known. You are a hunter, are you no'?"

"Aye," Tully said, his doubt clearly edging into interest.

"Take your time. Try some trout fishing, if you wish. I'll even send along a guide and companion. And a flask of the finest whiskey in all of the Highlands."

The whiskey proved the prime inducement. Tully tried to make his agreement sound reluctant, but it was clear he would set out tonight if he could.

"I'll even get you another horse to speed you on your way. Not so fine as Gertie, but one that will carry you where you want to go."

With the lad in complete agreement, he took him to the nearby crofter, and after a short consultation returned alone to his waiting bed.

His cold waiting bed, he thought as he entered the cottage. Throwing peat onto the smoldering fire, he knew whatever heat the flames provided would not warm him on this night.

Too restless to seek sleep, too weary to go out for another walk, he threw himself on one of the chairs, poured a goblet of whiskey, and stared at the plaid that stretched in front of the occupied

bed. The taper had long burned down, but he
could see all too well each fold of wool behind
which Meagan lay. Fate did indeed play cruelly
with him, to place him in the path of such a de-
sirable woman, yet put her out of his reach.

Tomorrow he would find his true bride; tonight
he would think of the bride he had wed.

Sometime in the night he fell into a troubled
slumber, his head resting on the table. As was his
habit, he awoke shortly before dawn, stiff and little soothed by the few hours of sleep. Again the
fire was low; he fed it more peat, welcoming the
warmth and light it spread across the room.

His eye was caught by a scrap of white on the
floor by the plaid. He retrieved it and sat back in
the chair. A fine handkerchief it was, of the softest
linen, with a delicate border of pink embroidery
around the edges, and in one corner an elaborate
letter *B*.

The quality of the linen paled beside the hard,
cold object around which it was wrapped, a ring
the like of which he'd never seen before, a diamond with a hundred facets set in gold sufficient
in weight to ransom his land.

He rested it in his palm; it lay heavily, sparkling
in the firelight like the purest star fallen to earth.

The jewel must belong to Meagan; certainly no
crofter could possess such a thing.

Holding it close to the light, he inspected it further, taking special note of the date inside the
wide band. *May 12, 1997.* He read it twice, and
then again.

The day was two hundred and thirty-two years
in the future. Could her wild tale have been true?

Impossible; he could barely comprehend such
an occurrence.

Still, here was the ring, whose size and cut

would rival a crown jewel. He weighed it carefully, then weighed all that she had said. Legs stretched toward the fire, he studied the date again. It had not changed since the last time he looked.

He remembered the lost look about her when she'd stared down at the ruins of Thistledown, the frantic search of the bedchamber, the dash down the stairs, and the sadly determined return.

He remembered, too, her underdrawers.

A woman from a future century, whisked from her wedding to his. Impossible, he told himself again, yet he held the proof in his hands. No wonder she'd fainted when he kissed her, sealing, he thought, their union, but to her mind opening a door to hell. He was lucky she hadn't given way to hysterics and run screaming from his arms.

In a land whose people believed stones could talk and spirits walked the heathered glens, where monsters lurked in lakes and bogs and invisible creatures dwelt in trees, why should there not appear a woman from another time?

The university man in him wanted to deny the possibility; with great reluctance, the Scot accepted in his heart that it was so.

Was she an alien ghost, come back through the centuries to haunt his troubled keep? In a thousand tales told 'round a thousand fires, he'd ne'er heard of any apparition so soft and warm of skin or so saucy of tongue.

Spirited she might be, but 'twas certain she was no spirit. A woman of flesh and blood and hungers she could scarcely deny, a woman lost, in her own strange way as troubled as he.

Possessed of a jewel worthy of any Oriental potentate, she gave no sign she feared hard work, not with the manner of her racing through the woods. The ring must have been the gift of her betrothed.

How wealthy was this fish of hers? She'd said he toiled because he wanted more. A man bent on acquisitions, that was William.

Robert shrugged. So was he. 'Twas another point they had in common, along with wanting the same lass.

"How do you make love?" he whispered to the plaid that separated them. "You kiss with heat to warm every Highland hearth, yet you carry in your heart a great fear, not only of time and place, but of me."

At that moment he admitted his talk of keeping his distance from her was just that—talk. She was his wife, whether she ought to be or no. 'Twas time she realized all that the title entailed. Wrestling with his tarnished honor would come after she was gone.

He allowed himself a small smile. "I'll not hurt ye, that I vow. But I'll know your ways of making love, or else I'm no' of the Cameron clan. As to the how and the when of the learning, I canna yet ken."

He would have speculated more about the fate that brought her here and whether, outside of bed, this woman from the future would be a hindrance to him or a help. But too many other demands tore at him, too many obligations, to submit to indecision. He would have his impossible bride. And then he would let her go.

In the meanwhile, he would keep the discovery of the ring to himself. He slipped the jewel inside his jacket, then, on a whim, hurried outside to find a small round stone of equal size and weight. As he wrapped the stone in the handkerchief, he noticed dim hints of light in the eastern sky. Day would soon be here. Two horses neighed at the edge of the trees, but they brought him no alarm.

The crofter had done his work well.

He returned to the hut and pulled back the plaid curtain by the bed. Meagan lay on her back, tangled in the thin blanket that served for warmth, her black hair spread against the mattress, light bruises beneath her eyes. She must have tossed and turned throughout the night. She'd got no more rest than he.

Was he the cause? Nay. She was lost in time, and frightened. She'd said it herself. The lass needed comfort. It was something Robert was prepared to give.

A bittersweet thought struck. Here was a woman he could fancy above others, found when he was obliged to take another, and in and of herself, strange beyond his understanding.

Jaded man that he was, he'd thought to have seen all the world could offer, all the ways the world could offend. Then Meagan Butler had come from another time to let him know how little he understood of the world after all.

With great delicacy he slid handkerchief and stone beneath the covers. He could not resist stroking her cheek.

Her eyes flew open. She came close to smiling, and then wakefulness hit her and she sat up in bed.

He leaned close, both hands resting beside her. "'Tis time to get on with our adventure, lass. We canna ken just what this day will bring."

Chapter Nine

Meagan had a wild urge to put her arms around Robert's neck and start the day with a kiss. It seemed fitting, it seemed right, and she knew it would be very, very good.

The trouble was that whatever she did wouldn't stop with a kiss. She knew it, and so did he. Last night she'd decided he didn't want her; this morning she saw that he did.

She hugged herself, holding the hot urges inside, calling herself a few choice names for being such a dunce. Had she no sense of what was safe in this crazy adventure? Did she really want to endanger her self-control?

Clearly control must remain the uppermost factor here, control and toughness, no matter how much she had to fight for them. And fight she would. During her restless night she'd dreamed in fits and starts that she might wake up returned to her twentieth-century world, but her dreams had been wrong. Here was her Highland husband, in the flickering light looking as manly and enticing

114

as ever, with his burnished face darkened by morning whiskers and his chocolate brown eyes darkened further by desire.

She sighed despite herself. Try as she might to deny it, she still longed for that kiss, and more. Why wouldn't he go away? Why couldn't she?

Heart pounding, she could draw no more than shallow breaths, and she actually felt her body lifting from the bed . . . toward him, toward disaster. The ferocity of her reactions sent a shiver through her. Self-control, she reminded herself. And toughness. She forced herself to press away from him, knowing he watched everything she did, fearing he could read all the wanton thoughts skittering through her mind.

What was wrong with her? She'd never lost herself to passion. Such a thing was found only in her books.

But she was out of her place and out of her time. She needed to return. Agreeing to remain had been the most foolish thing she'd ever done. The decision she should have made yesterday at the keep came to her now. The key to sticking with it was not to let Robert have his way.

He straightened, but he did not step so much as an inch away. Drat him, he was reading her the way she'd read *The Forever Bride*. Though she'd slept in her skirt and blouse, she pulled the thin cover to her chin.

"I can't get up with you standing so close," she said, proud her voice was stronger than her will.

"'Tis the standing close that has the opposite effect on me," he said, sounding sadly forlorn.

But there was little sadness and much devilment in his eyes. He should have been the actor instead of her second fiancé.

115

"Then back away, and we'll both get relief," she said.

"You've a saucy tongue on you, wife, e'en so early in the morn."

"I'll get worse as the hours go by." She meant it. He thought she'd been blunt-spoken before, did he? Wait until he heard her today.

She twisted in the bed and felt something sharp against her hip.

"Ouch," she said, and felt beneath the covers. Her fingers grasped what was unmistakably her mother's handkerchief and, more important, the ring around which it was wrapped. They must have slipped from her pocket during the restless night.

"Have you an ailment?" he asked.

Something in his voice made her suspicious that he knew what she was hiding, yet that could not be. As surreptitiously as possible, she thrust the handkerchief and ring back into their hiding place.

"It's just a cramp. I need to stretch."

Stretching was indeed how she started each day, but that was in her apartment in front of no one but the commentators on the morning television shows.

Robert would be very interested in her routine. Especially when she was wearing her latex shorts.

He stepped aside. "Please, stretch 'til you're satisfied."

She scrambled from the bed, away from him, and her knees buckled. The tramp through the woods had been harder on her than she'd supposed.

She caught herself, but not before he saw her weakness. She waited for a comment on her thighs, but all she got was a knowing smile.

"How else do you start the day in this time of yours?" he asked. "Surely you still have need of a chamber pot."

"I'd rather visit the woods," she said, remembering the unpleasant container she'd found beneath his bed.

"As you choose," he said, backing away.

He seemed surprisingly accommodating and not nearly so harsh. More than ever she was aware of their isolation. Accommodating Robert Cameron might be, but he was also intensely watchful. And he considered himself still in charge.

He stared at her wrinkled clothes for a moment longer, then without another word he went out the door, leaving her to draw her first deep breath since waking.

What was he up to, she wondered, asking about her time? Did he finally believe her? Why had he changed his mind?

Most important of all, should she tell him now of her decision to leave? *To try to leave,* a warning inner voice whispered. She refused to pay the voice much mind. The incantation would work; she could believe nothing less.

Still, she decided the declaration of her decision could come later. At least after she'd had her morning Power Bar and cup of herbal tea.

She caught herself. The only available food she knew about was half a loaf of bread and a jug of whiskey. Her stomach turned at the thought.

She pulled on the stockings that she had tossed on the foot of the bed sometime during the night, stared ruefully at the woebegone slippers, then put them on, too. Grabbing the plaid, she went out into the misty morning. The chilled air got to her right away; she pulled the wool shawl tighter and set out to find a place both open and private. In the grayness, the search took longer than she'd counted on.

For a moment, as she wandered through the brush, a fear of getting lost panicked her. She fought it down, took care of business as quickly as she could, then returned to the warmth of the indoor fire, in the process losing her way for no more than a minute but for what seemed like a year. It was clear she couldn't just take off on her own back to Thistledown. To find the way she would need help. And there was only one person she knew to ask.

Robert was not to be seen, though she felt his presence everywhere. Waiting on the table was a bucket of water, a worn rag, and a pile of clothes. They looked as beautiful to her as her tiled shower and crowded closet had ever appeared.

She did miss her special soap, however, her shampoo and her Water Pik, the small luxuries that seemed like necessities now. Oh well, she'd have them back before long.

She made the best of what she had, feeling relatively clean when she had bathed. She recalled a magazine article she'd once read about people who flossed with their own hair. Should she try it? No, she wasn't that hard up. And the inconveniences besetting her were only temporary.

The clothes presented a challenge—brown trousers and saffron-colored shirt, thick wool socks, and a pair of sturdy buckled boots.

Was she supposed to wear all of this? Everything looked far too small for Robert, and too large for her.

But they looked very, very warm. They felt warm, too, as she put them on. The pants were tight in the rear, hung loose in the waist, and dragged on the ground. The shirt, a better fit, smelled of strong soap—lye, she guessed—and of the smoke from a peat fire. She rolled up the pants and shirtsleeves, tying the shirttail at her waist to serve in place of a belt, then put on the socks and boots.

The latter fit far better than she would have expected. She was wriggling her toes inside them when Robert returned, walked around her slowly, then lowered himself in one of the chairs as he placed a plate of cheese in front of him, along with an extra coat.

Beneath his jacket he was wearing a different shirt, and she saw that he had shaved. His hair lay damp and thick around his rugged face. He looked at her so long and so thoroughly, she decided she'd done something wrong.

Before she could ask what it was, he broke his silence.

"You'd best put the skirt over the breeches. We've less chance of a riot that way."

The woman in her warmed to the compliment. In fact, everything about her warmed to everything about him. Warmed and hummed and hungered, and all he'd done was walk into the room. She felt like a woman who'd never had sex, or one who wanted it all the time. Neither description suited her in the least. Good grief, what was she turning into? She'd best leave as soon as she could.

"Women's breeches are very common in my day," she said, her fingers working nervously at the collar of her shirt, then tucking her hair behind her ears. "Only we call them pants. Or jeans. Sometimes dress slacks. They're practically all I wear."

Amusement glinted in his eyes, but she knew he wasn't laughing at her. If only he were.

"And do the men no' fight in the streets o'er you?"

"Not very often." Now was the time to tell him. Now while she had the nerve. She cleared her throat. "Robert—"

"I've changed my mind about your thighs."

"What?"

"They're no' so thin after all," he added.

Meagan sighed. Talking with him was like playing mental hopscotch, except that he kept changing the rules, kept drawing new squares in the dirt. She saw right then that pulling the skirt over her pants was a good idea. Under his watchful gaze she did just that, making sure the ring was still hidden away in the pocket.

He offered her bread and cheese for breakfast, and a goblet of whiskey, explaining it was the way when tea was not available. The repast, he said, had come from the crofter Fergus, along with the clothes.

Declining the whiskey, she settled in the chair opposite him. She'd never been a particularly willful woman, but she'd better be one now.

"Robert, I need to tell you something. I've decided to go home."

"Aye," he said, downing a swallow of whiskey, "and so you shall, as soon as the wrong you wrought has been righted."

She didn't bother with a defense; he wouldn't accept it and she had more important matters on her mind.

"No, now," she said.

He pulled off a thick piece of bread and with careful deliberation selected a slice of cheese to go with it. "Are you no' a woman of your word?"

"I've been seen. Everyone believes you have your Irish bride. Isn't that all you wanted?"

He set the food aside without taking a bite. "You know better. I made no secret of what I wanted. I wanted my wife." His eyes bored into her. "I wanted you."

The simple act of gazing at her pinned her back in her chair. How could her heart sink and pound at the same time?

It was easy. Any feminine heart would, with a man like Robert Cameron sitting so close, staring so intently, looking rugged and handsome and bronzed and broad, and as intractable as the Scottish hills.

I wanted you.

His soft words thundered in her mind. The Robert Cameron who spoke with such frankness was not the man who'd wheedled yesterday to bend her will. In his bedroom he'd been willing to compromise. Here he demanded his way, simply by refusing to agree with anything she said.

And by looking so cursedly sexy it was all she could do to keep from jumping him where he sat.

He would accommodate her, all right, over and over again. Lost forever was yesterday's man of reason, the man who'd requested her help. She knew beyond doubt she was seeing the real Robert Cameron now.

The terrible thing was he wasn't all bad. As a matter of fact—

Meagan told her heart and libido to behave themselves. He might want her—what did he have to lose?—but she couldn't afford to want him.

She tried again to make him understand.

"Be honest with yourself, Robert. You'd gotten worked up because you expected to have a real wife. You didn't want me. Any woman would have done."

"Another woman I could have had wi'out looking far."

"Ermengarde?"

She cursed herself for bringing up the name. He'd believe she was jealous, which she most certainly was not.

"You've learned much in a short while. But I plan to teach you more."

Meagan had little doubt about what he meant.

"And aren't you a man of honor? You promised to leave me alone."

"'Twas your request I do so. During the night, while I listened to your restless turnings, I kept to myself, though I needed to do otherwise. Do you no' think I can make you change your mind?"

"Never," Meagan said with more fervor than veracity.

As a sickly child she'd fought to gain her health, exercising, resting, eating food no other child her age would even taste, like spinach and the dreaded green beans. She'd been a stubborn little thing, lonely, turning to books as her companions, somehow growing stronger all the while.

Through the years she'd lost some of that stubbornness. She needed it now. Leaving was her spinach, something good for her; it was a healthy, hard-to-swallow serving of green beans. Shoving the chair away from the table, she clinched her fists in her lap and squeezed her eyes closed.

"*A ghràidh mo chridhe. A ghràidh mo chridhe. A ghràidh mo chridhe.*"

Holding her breath, she waited for the dizziness she'd experienced on her first journey through time, for the change in the atmosphere she'd noticed right away, for a change in the air. Much to her regret she felt sadly clearheaded, if somewhat panicked, and she still smelled the earthy peat fire.

She opened her eyes to see Robert regarding her, a shuttered expression in his eyes.

"You'll need the kirk for your escape. I've nay the time to get you there."

Meagan felt as though someone had hollowed out her insides. It was all she could do to remain in the chair without crying, without begging, without losing all her pride.

"I'll get myself back."

"Nay. You'll stay with me." His dismissal was curt and cold. It was the wrong approach. It brought out the fight in her, the grit she'd been searching for.

"You can't watch me all the time." She threw the words out as a challenge. He took it up right away, standing and coming around the table, pulling her to her feet.

Meagan stood tall, stood proud, stood trembling inside as his nearness shot her temperature up a dozen degrees. Another phrase from her books came to mind. Around this Highlander, she was nothing but a shameless wench.

And a foolish one, too. She wouldn't have had the vaguest idea how to return to the kirk on her own.

He brushed a thumb across her lips, then dropped his hand. Without thinking, she licked where he had stroked. She tasted sweetness. He smiled, but there was little of humor in his expression and much of heat.

"I'll not touch you, wife, until you touch me first. I'm thinking that you'll not be letting me out the door."

She didn't know whether to hit him or slap herself; instead she stamped her foot.

His smile broadened, and this time he truly looked amused.

"Do you ride?" he asked.

She wondered if maybe he were being crude, asking about her lovemaking techniques; then she caught herself. Around him all she could think of was sex.

"I suppose you mean a horse."

"What else? The deer are much too swift to catch and saddle."

"Of course I ride," she said, not entirely lying. She had been on a pony once, when she was a child and her father had believed riding would help build her strength. All she remembered was bouncing around a great deal as she sat very high, very far from the ground.

But if she told the truth, he'd probably have her sitting on his lap atop some beast, or else bouncing around behind him, holding on to his waist for dear life.

"I was just a little girl when I got on a horse for the first time," she added.

"Good," he said.

Silently she disagreed.

Donning the coat he'd brought her, she thrust a portion of bread and cheese into her pocket. The day might well offer no opportunity for a better meal, and she needed to keep up her strength if she were at all successful in defying him.

With the plaid draped over her head, its long ends wrapped around her throat, she followed him out to the gray day. The mist still lay heavy against the ground, obscuring the trees and the rising sun. It was not thick enough, however, to hide the waiting horses. All she noticed about them was that they were brown and huge, and they watched her as suspiciously as she was watching them.

Hunched in the overlarge coat, she closed her

eyes and tried to recall the hundred Western movies she had seen. Hiking her skirt to her waist, she made what she hoped was a passable bluff as Robert helped her into the saddle on the smaller horse.

His hand on her rear gave her a momentary respite from fear, but then he abandoned her as she settled into the small strip of leather that passed for a saddle. Where was the saddle horn, for crying out loud? What was she supposed to hold on to?

She gripped the reins so hard she snapped off an acrylic nail. At home it would have been a catastrophe. Here it meant nothing at all.

Especially when she inadvertently pulled back and her horse reared a startled head. She stifled a scream, but she could not hide the terror in her eyes.

Without saying a word Robert adjusted her stirrups, then took the horse by the bridle and walked her around the clearing, giving her time to adjust, being maddeningly considerate just when she'd gotten used to his arrogance.

If he thought a little walk would help her adjust, he didn't understand the situation. At the least she'd need a year or two of lessons, but she thought it best not to tell him.

Amazingly she gradually grew more at ease, and when he described for her his meeting with Tully MacSorley the evening before, she forgot for a moment she was supposed to be terrified.

What she decided was that this riding business wasn't as bad as she'd thought. All she needed to do was watch carefully everywhere they went, figure out how to get back to Thistledown and to the kirk, then whisper the incantation in the setting where it just might work.

He let go of the bridle; she immediately lost all confidence. Calling on the stubborn child in herself, she sat very, very still. Much to her surprise the horse didn't buck her off, or head out on its own through the trees. Instead it stood as quiet as she.

Robert mounted his own horse and took off in the lead, picking out a trail in the woods she hadn't noticed before. Her own mount needed no encouragement to follow. He rode slowly, or at least what must be slowly for him. Bouncing around in the saddle, Meagan thought she could have won the Preakness at that pace. Her knees pressed with deathlike fervor against the horse as she followed, grateful she had nothing to do but concentrate on staying in place.

And watching the way Robert sat in the saddle, graceful as he was on the ground. Oh, she definitely needed to get away. He thought she would come on to him, did he? Never. Not if they both lived to 1997.

Her fingers worked through the folds of skirt at her waist until they found the reassuring hardness of her engagement ring. On the strength of that ring, she vowed to get back to her home, to her work, to her true love's arms, if it was the last thing she ever did.

The trouble was that, with Robert's rear view burned in her mind, for the life of her she couldn't remember her real fiancé's name.

Chapter Ten

"Keep your rear low to the ground, slip in slow and get out fast, soon as the deed is done. 'Tis the only way."

Annie rasped out the words, clearly caught in the intensity of what they were about.

"You're daft," Fitz said, on the off chance the lassie would listen to what he said.

"And you're a virgin, are you not?" she threw back. "Never done the likes o' this before."

"I've never had the need, no' in such a manner," Fitz returned, stung. "And I am not a virgin."

"Then why act so shy? You've a hunger inside you that won't let go 'til it's satisfied. 'Tis little use denying it. I feel the same meself."

Fitz's stomach growled. He was hungry, right enough. And daft as the lass, to be where he was, about to do whatever his companion said. If his father ever found out, or his uncle . . .

He'd never see his twenty-first birthday, that was sure.

Why he'd ever jumped on that horse, he couldn't

ken, even though Gertie was as fine an example of horseflesh as he'd seen in a long while.

Annie MacSorley was the one he'd been watching outside the tavern. And she wasn't a beauty, not like the mare. A slip of a thing, with wild red hair tumbling about a high forehead, eyes too deep, nose tilted, and chin most definitely too strong.

But when she smiled, ah, she was a sight to behold. 'Twas like lighting a lamp inside her. She glowed. Basking in her warmth, so did he.

Trouble was, she wasn't smiling now. Dead serious in fact, as the two of them huddled on the downside of the slope leading to a small fenced poultry yard, planning their strategy on just how to become thieves.

At least Annie was planning. Fitz was wondering how he'd gotten himself into such a plight. A sober lad, he was caught between a feuding father and uncle, sent by the former to spy on the latter and in the process to grow to manhood.

At least his father's version of manhood, which included more than a hint of cruelty.

His uncle the sheriff, brother to his gentle, oppressed mother, was even worse.

When he'd jumped onto the mare, he'd acted without thinking, but the thoughts had come fast enough as they twisted and turned through the trees, the thrashing sounds of Annie's furious brother never far behind.

At last they'd lost him. Stumbling upon an abandoned hut, the lass had insisted on bringing the mare inside.

"Tully will find her for sure if we leave her outside."

The night had passed without event—if one considered huddling inside a roofless hut with a bonnie, crazed lass and a flatulent horse being without event.

Fitz had judged the passing of time by the regular plop of manure on the hut's hard dirt floor. Inspired by the noise, in the hour before dawn he'd gone out to relieve himself. He'd returned to find Annie saddling the mare—and announcing the intended crime.

Riding toward town they'd come upon a crofter's place, and the poultry yard.

"I stole a litter of piglets once," she'd told him as they surveyed the scene. "And they were squealing for their sow's teats the whole while."

Tully had found little encouragement in the tale.

In the hour since, as they waited for dawn's first light to grow strong, she'd come up with several suggestions as to the exact procedure. The decision was to lie low, slip in slowly, and move out fast with one of the fat geese from the yard wrapped in the horse blanket under her arm.

Steal the goose, kill it, cook it, and eat the evidence of their crime.

Eating was the only part Fitz knew for sure he could manage. Hungry as he was, he could have eaten Gertie if he weren't fearful of catching her flatulence. Too, he felt a kinship for the mare, both of them being captives of a green-eyed, looby Irish lass.

Curse her though he did, somehow she brought out protective feelings inside him. At least she had until she mentioned stealing breakfast.

Fitz sighed and burrowed against the hill. He had no notion where they were; nothing seemed familiar, but why should it? He was from a country far to the north.

At least they weren't near the town where his

uncle kept office. It was the lone bit of good fortune in his predicament.

"Wait here," she whispered, then was off before he could respond.

Trying to decide just what to do, he heard the squawking of a dozen geese, and a man's hoarse shout. Panicked, he stood, prepared to charge forward to the rescue. Before he could move, Annie hurtled over the hill, a quacking, twisting bundle under her arms. She flew past him, and he could do naught but follow.

She scrambled down the hill, managing to hold on to the horse blanket and let out a shrill whistle at the same time. Gertie galloped out of the woods, heading straight for them, and behind he could hear the loud curses of someone in hot pursuit.

'Twas a familiar sound when he was with the lass.

Fitz wasn't sure how they both managed to mount the horse and escape to the protection of the forest; all he was able to ken was that they did. Gertie rode swift and sure, twisting through the trees, forcing Fitz to hold on to Annie else he would tumble to the ground.

When his heart settled from his throat to its proper resting place, he took pleasure in the gallop. Indeed, it was exhilarating to charge through the woods with such wild abandon. The exhilaration scarcely ceased when Gertie slowed, trotting at a more sedate pace under her mistress's sure hands on the reins.

As they moved along, little could he help it if his hands slipped at times to the curve of Annie's small, firm breasts. Wayward hands they were; he kept returning them to her slender waist, but before he was aware, there they went again, seeking out the comfort of her curves.

He'd never felt a lass's breasts. Not that he was a virgin, to use Annie's regrettable word—he'd spoken the truth before—but his lone experience had been with a milkmaid who ordered he keep his hands to himself while she put the necessary body parts where they should be.

Nay, the life of a thief was not such a bad one after all, he decided when they found a place in the woods for their feast.

Soft as her body was, and the touch of her hair against his face during the wild ride, there was little of softness in the way she wrung the goose's neck and plucked the feathers from its plump carcass.

His tasks were to build a fire and erect a spit for the bird, both of which he managed with passable efficiency. He and Annie collapsed onto the soft grass of their woodland lair to rest and contemplate the savory scents coming from the fire.

Using her mantle as a blanket, she lay back in the grass, arms folded beneath her head, and stared upward. He rested on his side and stared at her. In repose, she looked gentler than when she was mischief-bound. She looked younger, too, fragile, almost vulnerable. He liked her this way, but he knew the image of a guileless Annie MacSorley would not long endure.

Little more than a bairn she seemed at the moment, but with hints of the woman she would be.

"You coulda been killed, you ken," he said. "We shouldna take such risks again. And don't be giving me that look about you facing the dangers alone. I was coming up the hill to your rescue, that I was, when I saw you running the other way wi' an angry man in pursuit."

She smiled at him, and her inner lamp burned

bright. Far too soon the smile died, and she returned to looking at the sky.

"Better to suffer a cudgel against me head than the fate awaiting in Robert Cameron's bed."

"'Tis a difficult choice to make."

"Not so. I heard me brothers talking about him, back in Ireland, without them knowing I was about. Oh, such tales they spun, of how he'd abandoned his poor ailing father, choosing to roam the world and take his pleasure in far-off battles. Leaving his wife heavy with child, not returning until the two of them were buried in the cold, cold ground."

"At the tavern, you claimed to have heard Cameron describing plans t' beat you."

Her eyes widened. "Oh, I did, I did. His words served to prove everything I'd learned in me own land."

Fitz wasn't sure which story was the truth, but the fear in her voice and in the depths of her green eyes seemed genuine enough. Never having met this Robert Cameron, he took a strong dislike to him. He must protect Annie from him however he could.

"I was running from a fate worse than the goblins, that's for sure," she said, a shudder running through her slender body. When Fitz spied tears running down her cheeks, he scooted awkwardly closer and took her in his arms. She nestled against him. He held her tighter. With a strange new warmth trickling through him, he decided he could take easily to this life of crime.

Too, he felt very much a man.

She rested her head against his chest. 'Twas almost his undoing, the way his body tightened and grew. He liked the way she smelled, like flowers and new grass and the wind. More, he liked the way she felt, soft as a pillow in places, warm as a kitten curled next to the hearth. Hungry as he'd been a moment before, he wished the goose would never get done.

"I must return to Liam," she said.

Liam! She'd mentioned him before. 'Twas a name Fitz could readily hate.

But whoever he was, Liam was far away in Ireland. And Annie was here in his arms, needing his protection and his company. 'Twas likely, too, the Irishman had never helped her purloin a meal.

Settling back down, Fitz dared to stroke her hair, all in the way of soothing, he told himself, wondering what else she would allow him to stroke.

"Liam O'Toole's my one true love. He's the man I plan to wed."

For sure, she was a stubborn lass.

Fitz swallowed hard and lifted his hand from her hair. "You were promised to two men at once?"

"Liam and I had an understanding. Papa wouldna pay us any mind, claiming if I married an O'Toole I'd be living in the same county and could torment him the rest of his days. Papa, that is, not Liam, although he might have meant the two of 'em. Me father never passes a chance to chide his Brat."

A sigh shook her body.

"Whether Papa wishes it or no', I must return to Ireland."

"You'll find few boats passing this way."

"I'm no' a fool. I must needs get to the coast. And don't be saying it's a hundred miles away. A thousand would no' be too far to go for a lass's true love."

Enough torture, he told himself, more than any

man should endure. He let her go and stood, taking his place by the fire.

"Is something amiss?" she asked his back.

"Looking to see if the goose is cooked through." He couldn't refrain from adding, "'Tis not honorable to hold another man's betrothed. While I'm no' sure about two men, I'd say 'tis even worse."

"Blather. Don't be a prudish lad. Besides, you weren't holding me *that* way."

Fitz grimaced in the direction of the spit. A prudish lad, was he? Mayhap he should have fondled her breasts in the manner he was wanting, taking his pleasure while he could. She'd have known right soon which way she was held.

He turned to face her. She was sitting upright, arms wrapped around her knees, looking for all the world as innocent as a new bairn.

Beneath that shower of red curls, though, lurked a mind of devious intent.

He would not fall beneath her spell again; alas, neither could he abandon her.

"Tell me true, Meagan-Anne MacSorley. When you filched those piglets, did you kill and roast them the way you're doing the goose?"

Chapter Eleven

Robert rode beside Meagan through the unpaved street of the hamlet known as Buscar-Ban, moving south, farther away from Thistledown, searching for a wife he did not want.

The lass he preferred sat the saddle far better than when they'd begun their journey two hours past, but she still held to the reins as if fearful relaxing would pitch her to the ground.

He liked looking at her, liked remembering the temptations that lay beneath her bulky clothes, liked, too, the brave way she stood up to him and faced whatever challenge he threw at her. Trouble though she was, and a distraction he could ill afford, he liked having her at his side. But then when had he ever acted smartly in his own behalf?

After the splendor of the countryside through which they had ridden, he hadn't wanted to bring her to this poor place, to its half-clothed bairns lying in the street before miserable huts and yapping collies torturing the horses's heels. But given the direction his betrothed had taken before going to ground last night—if her foolhardy brother could be believed—Buscar-Ban lay directly in her path.

Though Annie wouldn't like exposing herself to people, hampered by the shortcomings of her companion and of herself, she would be needing civilization if she planned to survive.

Not that Buscar-Ban was an example of a civilized Scottish society, being little more than a row of huts housing impoverished peasants under the power of the high sheriff and under a genuine fear of the bailie who served him. But it offered food, and a place to ask directions.

Most of its people were remnants of scattered clans from across the Highlands and up the Great Glen past Loch Ness and to the seacoast town of Inverness. While Robert fought on foreign soil and his father was falling into the decline that would eventually kill him, they had fared passably, working Cameron land for the tacksman who'd been in alliance with Gunn. When Robert returned to Scotland to reclaim his heritage and that of his clan, they'd lost what little they had.

Having little choice but to bring his own people the property they'd lost during his absence, he tried to help the weak of Buscar-Ban, but Scots were a stubborn lot, even the poorest, and they wanted nothing to do with any Cameron.

And so they suffered an existence harder than most. A glance at Meagan showed her deep violet eyes widening in dismay as she looked at the passing scene, her attention so caught she'd apparently forgotten she still sat the horse. When her gaze fell to him, he saw questions in her expression that she could not bring herself to ask.

They were questions he'd be hard put to answer so she would understand.

As was his wont when he took her to new places, he tried to see the village as she must be seeing it. Knowing she came from a different world, one far richer than his if the ring hidden in his pocket was any sign, he viewed the poverty more sharply, more painfully than ever before.

The huts were separated by gardens of potatoes and kale and hemlock, all growing wildly amidst stalks of nettle on the unleveled ground; flanking most of the front doors were black stacks of turf and a malodorous family dunghill.

Behind a few of the cottages he spied a tumble of stones that might be taken for a barn, where a horse or a milch cow could be kept. Most of the peasants were too poor for such luxuries.

The children, with their skin burned black by the sun and their hair bleached white, appeared far too indolent to move out of the street, making it necessary for the riders to rein around them as they made their slow forward progress.

Except for one lad who drew to his feet and stood directly in his path, hands on hips, ragged clothes hanging limply on a scrawny frame.

"Oh," Meagan said in alarm, jerking on the reins. Long used to her erratic manner, her mount did not respond.

"Be careful," she whispered, but Robert could not tell whether she spoke to him or the horse or the lad.

No need to warn the lad, who understood what he was about. He looked no more than twelve, but there was the shrewdness and the insolence of the ages in his hard brown eyes, so much so that Robert felt a stab of pain as he reined around him to ride on down the street. Until the year he was fifteen he'd enjoyed a happy childhood. This lad had no such memories.

Occasionally he heard the shrill command of a matron for the bairns to come inside, but few stirred and the dogs kept up their incessant barking. Once or twice he caught a glimpse of an old man peering out from a doorway, his eyes rheumy, skin furrowed, body bent. None of them stirred farther than the door to satisfy their curiosity.

He looked not for the younger men, who would be out in the fields hunting or tending cattle, or by a stream casting for fish to put on the family table, or perhaps getting into mischief at some change-house drinking away their hard-earned coin. A small number had gone to the coast, where they gathered kelp to be used as fertilizer, but Robert knew the industry offered meager pay.

The maidens remained at Buscar-Ban. Bolder than the matrons and the old men, they came out to watch as he and Meagan rode by. They wore simple blouses and skirts, their head and feet bare, hair bound neatly in long, thick braids. More than one would be called a beauty if she bathed and powdered herself in the way of a city lass.

None of them—not the bairns nor maids nor the old men—looked stupid. On the contrary, like the lad, they all had a wary intelligence in their eyes, darkened by hints of defiance and despair. None had his spirit, though, nor his audacity.

At the far end of the street, a quarter mile away, he spied a common field, where the villagers cultivated rows of rye, oats, barley, and peas, the bare necessities to keep them alive. All in all, it was a poor place indeed, as different as could be from the model village he'd built for his clan. Intensely proud of it, he would take Meagan there before she left.

Before she left. They were words he did not consider often. Not once since they'd departed the crofter's hut this morning had she mentioned returning home right away, but he doubted that leaving had strayed from her mind.

Again he watched her from the corner of his eye as she looked around, the drape of plaid shielding her face from most who would look upon her. She stared thoughtfully at each detail, as though she would memorize it. For what purpose? He must ask her to describe this New York town where she lived, later when they were alone.

For now she needed distraction.

"You've ridden well," he said over the noise of the dogs. "I'll no' be tying you to the horse when we pick up the pace."

"You think I'm getting back on this beast once I get off?" She lifted her chin in defiance, but she had a pinched look around her mouth. She had not, after all, forgotten where she sat.

Her lips needed kissing to softness. He added it to the things he planned to do.

His gaze dropped to the grip she had on the reins.

"Have patience. We won't be lingering here for long. I fear we have a ways to travel before we can rest."

"Maybe not. Maybe we'll find Annie right away."

"Is that what you truly want?"

"Of course," she said quickly—too quickly, to his way of thinking. "And you do, too."

Her face, framed by the plaid, looked too lovely, too intense for him to gaze on her for long. Without answering, without knowing exactly what to say, he pulled his eyes from her and back to the uneven row of huts. Find Annie they must. He knew it all too well. He had responsibilities.

When he'd made his way toward the village, it

was with little hope of discovering her crouched by one of the dunghills. But he did have hope someone might have seen her and her companion.

Who to ask? Among these unfriendly folk, who would tell? They had no leader, other than the despotic Sheriff Edgar Gunn and his sycophant bailie Fergus Munro, and they lived in a fancier town. The chieftain who'd ruled these hills had long ago died, his once proud mansion now in ruins beyond the common field, hidden in the double rows of horse chestnuts and sycamores that lined the avenue leading to what had been a grand front stair.

No one had come forth to promise a restoration, the way Robert had done at Thistledown. A pity it was, and inevitable, that times must change.

Concerned with the future, Robert intended to hold on to the past.

It was the present that concerned him now.

Glancing down the street, he saw the squat, square figure of the bailie Munro standing like a post to block their way. A cur snapped at his heels; Munro kicked him aside. No one else seemed to be paying him any mind. It was as if they'd grown used to the mean little man, the way they had the hunger gnawing at their bellies and the anger dulling their hearts.

Robert reined to a halt in front of him and dropped to the ground. Before he could instruct her otherwise, Meagan tried the same. He caught her just before she fell.

Her skirt dropped in place over her breeches. Smoothing it, he felt the kerchief-wrapped rock hidden in the folds. She shook him off and tried to stand on her own, then grabbed his arm for support.

"Everything's harder than I think it's going to

be," she said. Something about her words and the desperate, determined edge to her voice stirred a response inside him. It wasn't solely the urge to protect her; it was a feeling more urgent, a sensation more intense.

Something very basic that existed between a woman and a man.

He placed himself between her and Munro, holding her close until she found her strength.

"Not everything, wife. I'll show you what I mean when we're alone."

He pulled the plaid tight around her face, anchoring it in place with the collar of the oversize coat. But not before kissing the corners of her lips. Her gasp came quick and sharp, but she did not pull away. What a cad he was to take advantage of her this way.

An unrepentant cad. He kissed her again, and then, with his arm around her, he turned back to Munro.

"What brings you here?" he said. "Some thought of charity? A bit of food to help these poor folk?"

"I meant to ask ye the same," the bailie growled.

Bareheaded, his black hair snarled and limp, Munro came no higher than Robert's chest. With his short arms hanging at his sides, hands curled into fists, and his flat face twisted into a frown, he looked like a bulldog set upon by bigger hounds, ready to defend his territory without knowing exactly how.

"I'm showing my wife the sights of the county, did you no' ken? And are you by chance looking for people to torment, to put under the whip?"

"Just one. When she's found," Munro said, "she'll get more than the sting of a lead tip. Stealing one mon's horse and another's goose could put her at the end of a rope."

"I've heard no word of the goose," Robert said with measured indifference. "Nor that the thief of the Irish mare was a lass. That's what happens when a man takes on a new wife. He's apt to forget all else."

Meagan squirmed in his embrace, but he did not ease his hold.

Munro stared at the pair of them and spat at the ground, narrowly missing the cur who roamed just out of kicking distance of his pointed boot.

"She was seen clearly enough. A lass, all right, with hair the color of fire, the crofter said, and feet that flew across the ground, so fast he claimed the wind could no' have o'ertaken her."

"This crofter, is he the unfortunate man who lost the goose?"

"She snatched it from his pen while he saw to the feed. No' a quarter mile t' the north o' here, just off the road, fleeing on her stolen horse into the woods."

"I suppose she had her companion by her side, the lad who rode with her away from the change-house."

"Aye, she—"

The bailie stopped, and a crafty look stole onto his face. "Ye seem uncommonly interested, fer a mon newly wed." He turned his attention to Meagan. "Is the bride not gi'en ye enough to ponder? Why bring her to Buscar-Ban?"

"I asked him to," said Meagan.

Her strange, strong voice hit the air like an explosion. Robert wanted to throttle her.

The bailie's eyes widened in surprise.

"'Tis true," she said, and it was all Robert could do not to roll his eyes at her attempt at a brogue. "If I'm to ken all about this new country of mine, I must see the bad along with the good."

142

A poorer excuse for a Scottish or an Irish lass or any nationality in Robert's ken he could not imagine.

With his free hand he pulled the plaid ever tighter around her face, coming close to muffling her, though not nearly so close as he wanted.

"You'll catch cold, my love," he said, though now that the sun had burned through the mist, the day was turning fair and warm.

Munro stepped close. "Let's have a better look at ye."

"Do you have in mind losing a hand?" Robert asked. "If so, you need do no more than touch her sleeve."

"Ye wouldna dare. I'm an officer of the law."

"Named by a sheriff who's named by the Crown, and there's few in these parts have love for the latest German George."

"I'll have ye before the sheriff for treason," the bailie puffed, his flat face growing red.

"I'm trembling in my boots."

Stepping back, the bailie pulled a pistol from inside his coat and waved it about. Meagan jumped; Robert loosened his hold and stepped in front of her as a shield. Taunting Munro proved pleasurable, but only when he alone risked danger from his foolish wrath.

"Ye'd best tremble," Munro snarled. "I've reason enough to arrest ye without adding the charge of treason. 'Tis said you wore the kilt at the swearing of the vows."

"Do not be saying one of my people spread such a tale."

Munro puffed with pride. "I have my agents." He sneered at Meagan, who was peering around Robert's shoulder. "'Tis also said yer bride could no' stand yer kiss." He licked his fat lips, the only

143

feature in his face that wasn't flat. "Mayhap she needs the taste o' another mon to compare."

He waved the gun to gesture her closer. Robert looked at his bride's tight face, at the gun, at the leer in Munro's eager eyes. Rage flashed like lightning through him, and he struck the bailie with his fist, feeling the give of the fat lips against his knuckles.

Munro went down and the gun went off. Meagan screamed, the cur barked, and behind him came the yelps of a dozen scattering hounds as the echo of the blast filled the air.

Wiping his mouth, the bailie stared at the blood on his hand. "Ye're under arrest, Cameron," he said over the din.

Robert reached down to remove the pistol from his grasp and toss it aside. "And who's to carry me to jail?"

"Ye'll hang for yer resistance." Munro talked bravely, his fist waving in the air, but he made no attempt to stand, instead choosing to remain sprawled on his back in the dirt.

Robert doubted the incident would lead to such extremes as the gallows, but he was rational enough to realize some sort of trouble would ensue. He should have held his temper, but he was not a man who always did what he ought.

A discretionary retreat seemed wise. The presence of his almost-bride made it essential.

He looked at her, then at her mount.

"You'll have to ride," he said.

She nodded dumbly, giving him no argument, for which he sent heavenward a prayer of thanks.

Hiking her skirt to her waist, she accepted his assistance, but she could not disguise the wince that came when she settled her rear onto the saddle once again.

The lass needed a thorough massage. He was not so plagued by the bailie he failed to see his husbandly duty in that particular regard.

He would make her feel better, that he swore, and in the process give a more thorough inspection to her underdrawers. What a rascal he was to consider such matters with a lawman sprawled at his feet and calling for his head. Or mayhap not such a bad 'un. Every man had to set his priorities.

Mounting, he reined north, in the direction from which they had come, cursing the ill luck that had made him miss Annie, at least making the attempt, thinking that the delay in their meeting had one fine result. Meagan the Elder would not be leaving so soon.

He smiled to himself and forgot Munro. In a world of strife, a man had to look to his luck and take the good times wherever he could.

Riding beside him, Meagan could scarcely believe the smile on his face. Was he crazy? He'd just been threatened with hanging by a mean little man who'd do everything in his power to see that was just what he got.

She was not a stranger to the cruel use of authority. She'd seen it at more than one business meeting of Bernard and Roberson, her advertising firm. None of the men went so far as to pull a gun, but they fought over accounts and they calculated how to steal clients from one another, while she sat quietly to the side, the lone, lowly woman looking tough, grateful her cosmetics company was doing so well that she didn't have to join the fray.

At Bernard and Roberson she understood the rules, though she didn't like them. Here in the Highlands, two centuries from her time, she had no idea what was real and what was bluff.

They rode slowly down the street, but the dogs had fallen silent and the children stayed close to their yards. All but one, the same boy who had defied Robert by standing in his path. Watching their approach, this one was edging back onto the street.

How thin he was. Her heart went out to him. Remembering the bread in her pocket, unmindful for the moment of the rocking of the horse, she tossed it to him before grabbing the reins again. He caught it, but she couldn't stop to see if he threw it to the dogs or ate it himself. Whatever happened, it wouldn't go to waste.

She caught Robert watching her, but she couldn't read his mind to know if she'd done something wrong.

Feeding a starving child could never be wrong, she told herself, especially one who lived in this poor place. Thoughts of Buscar-Ban reminded her of the bailie, and she forgot the boy as her terror returned. She could still hear the gunshot, still hear that mean little man's snarled threats.

"You shouldn't have hit him."

"Do I hear rightly? Are you defending the fool?"

"Of course not. But didn't you make matters worse?"

"I cared not for the way he spoke to you."

Meagan looked at him in astonishment. "You hit him because of me?"

He grinned at her, and Meagan's pulse went into triple time.

"A mon can have poorer reason for what he does," he said.

She looked away, fast, before she launched herself from her horse to his, or at least made the attempt. He'd struck the bailie because of her. He'd been defending her honor, and he'd been held up in the pursuit of his true bride because she was along.

Fighting the thrill of satisfaction, she told herself again and again she had to leave. She had no choice.

Another cause for panic struck, the doubt that the incantation would work even in the kirk. There was only one way to find out for sure.

Stealing a glance at her almost-husband, she admitted she didn't really want to go. To deny her feelings was not only foolish, it was wrong. But she had to get away, for the safety of them both. Back to—she thought with all her might—back to William Stuyvesant Sturgeon IV. What a relief it was to remember his name.

That didn't mean he supplanted Robert in her thoughts. She'd have to be back in New York for that to take place.

Riding the past two hours beside him, listening to his description of his land, eating the wild berries and flaxseed he gathered for her, along with a handful of barley, drinking the clear, cold water from a Highland stream, she'd forgotten her panic at being on a horse. Well, almost forgotten it. It would take more than a little eighteenth-century trail mix and an occasional glance at Robert to make her completely forget her sore rear.

Her confidence in her riding skill growing, she loosened the plaid from her head and shook her hair free. She knew he watched, and she knew he both approved and disapproved. With his eyes on her, she felt warm. No, make that hot. Like Maggie in the Tennessee Williams play. Like a cat on a hot tin roof, skittery because she wanted sex. Not just any sex. She wanted Robert Cameron, a man practically married to someone else. As was she.

Evelyn Rogers

A shameless wench, that was what she was, going as far from her sense of right and wrong as she was from her right and natural time.

Oh, yes, she'd better get the heck home as soon as she could. ASAP. Pronto. Right away.

"I have to go to the ladies' room," she announced when they were well out of town, back out on the road, returning north the way they had come. She believed they were headed in the direction of Thistledown; she'd better be right.

They both reined to a halt.

"Is your meaning that you need relief?"

"Oh, yes," she said with more fervor than she'd intended.

"Would you be needing assistance to gain it?"

He spoke innocently, but she caught the glint in his eye.

"Definitely not."

He slid from his horse with the same masculine grace that marked everything he did. With his hands at her waist inside her coat, he eased her to the ground, but he did not let her go. And she could not bring herself to pull away.

"Later," he said, "mayhap I can help."

Her breath caught, and her heart pounded in her throat. What was this wild urge to kiss him every time he came near? Why in her own time had she never felt such urgency?

It must be something in the air, or in the water.

Be honest, she told herself. It probably was the idea of this eighteenth-century man, this savage Scot, this rugged bronzed brute with the intelligent and all-too-lustful light in his chocolate eyes. She'd decided early on he was a cross between Conan and Sean Connery. Nothing he'd said or done had changed her mind. Except now she added a soupçon of Mel Gibson in his movie role

148

as an early Scottish hero.

Maybe more than a soupçon. Robert and Mel had similar legs.

"Aye, lass, you need relief. As do I."

What a rich, deep, entrancing voice he had, not to mention wonderful hands. She swayed closer, then caught herself.

Meagan the Cat, hotter than the bailie's pistol. She definitely had to leave.

He slipped his hands upward from her waist, coming dangerously close to her breasts, swollen to attention at his approach. And then he was no longer touching her, but from the look in his eye she knew he'd found out what he wanted to know.

The next time they ended up in the same room at night—if there was a next time—she couldn't, and she wouldn't, keep him out of her bed. The shared, unspoken knowledge bounced between them like heat from a furnace. She felt the beads of sweat on her brow.

He stepped back, gesturing gallantly toward the woods that lined the road. "Be quick. I dinna like it when you're out of my sight."

Meagan didn't hesitate taking leave of him, fairly running into the woods, calling herself every synonym for stupid she could think of, and that was quite a few. If she kept on running, generally heading north, as best her feeble scouting skills could tell, she would come upon Thistledown kirk. At least she ought to see the keep rising from the top of the hill overlooking Loch Lochy, and perhaps the castle ruins. Meagan was a fast learner. She knew how to survive in the wilderness, at least enough to pick out the same berries and seeds Robert had chosen, and there was always a fast-moving stream nearby to provide water.

The trouble was he would follow, and he would find her. No telling what he would do.

She corrected herself. She could figure out how he would get back at her . . . get to her . . . get in her. . . .

She shook off the image that burned into her mind, a picture of Robert lying naked on top of her, their legs entwined. How could prim, serious-minded, honorable—all right, somewhat prig-gish—Meagan Butler even think such things?

Because she was inspired, that was how.

With a sense of defeat and, yes, a bite of antic-ipation, she relieved herself, then began the fate-ful walk back to the road. A rustle in the bushes stopped her. A bear? A wolf? Robert said neither had been spied hereabouts for years.

A wild boar, maybe, or—if there were such a thing—a feral sheep. With her luck, a whole herd of them lurked within the stand of trees.

She tried to hum, to whistle, but she couldn't make a sound. So she held still, wondering if she could survive attack from a wild beast long enough for Robert to come to her rescue.

Searching about the ground, she found a sturdy fallen limb. It felt good in her hands. She turned toward the bush, which parted. She lifted the limb and was about to bring it down on whatever at-tacked her. She caught the downward progress just in time to keep from hitting a child.

The boy looked up at her with defiance in his eyes, and little sign of fear. She remembered him as the one who had stood in Robert's way in the middle of town, the one who had caught her gift of bread.

She lowered her weapon with trembling hands.

"What are you doing here?" she asked. "I could have killed you."

He stood. He came almost to her shoulder, but he must have weighed no more than eighty pounds.

"I've come t' pay ye back for the food. Jamie MacRae always pays his debts."

She started to tell him not to be silly; the bread had little worth. The pride in his expression and in his bearing stopped her.

"And how do you plan to do that?" she said as her trembling subsided. "I doubt you have any money."

He cocked his head. "Ye've a strange way of talking."

"But you understand the question."

"Aye. I'm offering my services t' ye. Not t' yer man, ye ken, just t' ye. I move quickly through the woods, as ye see. I fetch and carry, and I can dance a lively jig if I've a mind."

Meagan could have grinned when she pictured those gangly arms and legs keeping time to music. But she had no use for entertainment. What other services could he possibly provide?

I move quickly through the woods. A crazy thought struck. She tried to thrust it aside, but it just wouldn't disappear.

"Will you be wanted back at home soon?" she asked.

"I'm the last of the MacRaes," he said as if it were a point of pride. "I take care o' meself."

"Of course you do," she said, trying to sound as though his words hadn't affected her, as though she didn't want to take him in her arms and promise all would be well. She knew he would have run if she tried.

And it was a promise she couldn't possibly keep.

"What I'm about to ask is a great deal for just a bite of food."

151

"'Twas the kindness I'm repaying. No' the crust o' bread."

More than ever she wanted to hug him. It was the frustrated mother in her, she knew for sure.

She put the matter to him as bluntly as she could, feeling strong, feeling tough.

Smiling broadly, he promised to do what she asked.

Chapter Twelve

With Meagan's skirt bound out of the way about her waist, Jamie led her through the woods away from the road, away from Robert, away from where her heart lay.

She shook her head, even as she scurried to keep up with the boy. What a stupid thing to think, romantic, out of a book. A line of copy from one of her ads. No one could leave her heart away from her body. And she'd known the man less than twenty-four hours. The journey through time had definitely addled her brains.

In contrast, her legs seemed in surprisingly good condition, especially her thighs. Though they carried the painful reminders of her horseback ride, it took only a short distance of trying them out before they took her quickly over the ground, keeping her close to the boy. His bare feet seemed not to notice the rocks, but she felt them through her boots.

After a few minutes they broke through the trees onto a broad rolling glen where a dozen head of shaggy cattle grazed. Without consultation, Jamie led her right into their midst. She told herself cows were no more dangerous than horses, but they moved about too erratically for her to believe it.

City girl that she was, dodging taxis was more her skill than milling with beasts of the field, no matter how domestic they were supposed to be. Besides, like the feral sheep she'd wondered about, might there not be feral cows?

She saw what the boy was up to. Robert was probably very good at detecting footprints, but even he would lose all trace of them in the cattle tracks. If, that is, the hairy monsters didn't trample her into the dirt and leave her body for him to find.

Robert was definitely good at finding her body. He'd proven it time and time again.

Cattle must have been grazing in the meadow since winter, for everywhere she looked she saw evidence of their presence. More than once she had to jump carefully over a clump of that evidence, some of it still soft. She determined that in no place would he find her bootprints, or the marks of Jamie's bare feet. She allowed her confidence to grow.

A clap of thunder ended her complacency *tout de suite*. The cattle jumped and stirred. She shifted quickly to avoid being caught by one of their hooves. Good grief, she could be caught in a stampede if she didn't hurry. She dared a glance at the sky; she hadn't seen the dark clouds moving in, so intent had she been on Robert, on the horse, on the dangers they had faced.

And on her own plans.

Fat splats of rain hit the ground around her. Jamie grinned, took her hand, and, as the drops quickened, ran with her across the glen to the far woods, outpacing the restless cattle and the coming storm.

"We've lost him," he crowed as they reached the shelter of the trees.

"I doubt it. We escaped too easily."

"He'll not be knowing ye've got Jamie MacRae as yer guide," he said, "though he'll ken ye've met up with someone."

Thunder rolled in the distance while the boy danced a quick jig, all arms and legs as she had pictured. Watching his youthful exuberance, admitting a growing affection for him, she saw the vulnerability of them both. Depression dark as the clouds settled on her. Somehow, she felt sure, Robert would figure out the truth.

And would that be so bad?

Of course it would.

"Aren't we headed toward Thistledown?"

"No' just yet. That's what he'll be thinking, is it no', since it's where ye asked to go? I figured to lead him astray by going away from the keep."

Meagan wasn't sure his plan was wise. She was the adult here and he was the child and she ought to be the one to make decisions. Unfortunately there was nothing she could tell him he didn't already know, certainly about the present time, and there was everything he could tell her.

She kept quiet. Robert would have been proud.

The thought of her Highlander cast her deeper into a depression. With the cold rain making its way through the thick oaks, she pulled the plaid over her head and followed Jamie, all the while thinking of the man she left behind.

This was the right thing to do. For him and for her. She didn't belong here. Why the journey had ever taken place would always be a mystery; how she learned to care about someone she'd known for only a day a greater mystery still.

She tried to concentrate on her escape. They seemed to be following no path or particular trail, but Jamie never hesitated in his choice of direction. With the lessening of the rain, they seemed to be shifting their course.

"Are we headed toward Thistledown now?" she called out over the noise of the spring shower.

"Aye," he called out, but he did not slow down.

She glanced behind her. The rain still fell with enough force to cover their tracks. If it stopped altogether, however, every step they took would be clearly visible.

She would take the stopping of the rain as a sign she wasn't meant to get away. It didn't let up in the least. Instead, after the brief lull, the storm again grew in intensity, growing more fierce the farther they walked. The length of plaid, her coat, her skirt, her boots caught every drop, and she felt a chill down to her bones.

But she kept on walking. She tried not to look at Jamie too much. He looked so cold in his scant clothes, but when she offered to share some of her clothing with him, he'd scoffed. Especially at the skirt. What did she take him for, a weakling lass?

When they paused, she asked if they could make it to the kirk before dark.

"Not wi' the circling around we did," he said with a shake of his head. His fair hair had darkened in the rain, and water clung to his dark lashes. Despite his thinness he was a handsome child, his features fine, his carriage proud. And he seemed old beyond his years, which he'd told her numbered twelve. Or so he believed. He wasn't certain of the year when he'd been born.

"So when will we get there?"

"No later than t'morrow's eve."

Meagan's heart sank. Could they really evade Robert for so long? Could they each keep up their strength? She admitted to being hungrier than she'd ever been in her life, even when she was on one of her many diets. But she couldn't say so, not with Jamie obviously in far more need of nourishment than she.

They took off again, and in her mind she built the biggest cheeseburger of all time, with a thick grilled patty of beef, a slather of melted cheddar and another of Monterey Jack, mustard, lettuce, tomato, two slices of crisp bacon for good measure, all heaped on a toasted poppy-seed bun. She left off the pickles and onions. Somehow they seemed too much.

She made up for their absence in a side serving of curly fries. She hadn't eaten a French-fried potato since she was fifteen. Nor a hamburger, for that matter, certainly not the one of her dreams. She'd make up for the loss as soon as she returned home.

If there was anyone who knew what good food tasted like, and how bad it could be, it was a chronic dieter. What copy she could write for a restaurant ad. Trouble was, her musings served only to make her hungrier. She must think of something else.

Robert shot to mind. Another kind of hunger struck her, one that was just as acute. With a sigh, she plodded on.

The rain ceased, and after another hour of walking Jamie said they must stop and rest.

"If I stop, I don't know that I can start again."

"If ye dinna stop, ye'll collapse afore long. Strong as I am, I'll no' be able to bear ye on my back."

Reluctantly she admitted he had a point.

Besides, Robert was far, far away. She was safe, if lying in a strange forest with a chill wind blowing over her, clothes and shoes soaked, unsure of herself and lost, questioning whether she was doing the right thing—if all of that could be called being safe.

Leading her to one of the thousand small streams that must lace the Highlands, Jamie left her for a short while. He returned with seeds and berries and, miraculously, a couple of small, hard apples, more tart than the ones she knew but delicious nevertheless. She tried to eat slowly, but that had never been her way. She gobbled her portion down before the boy had barely begun.

With the heavy cloud cover holding low, daylight was fast departing. Jamie was right; she needed to rest. Taking off the damp skirt, she removed the handkerchief and ring, considered giving them a quick look, then thrust them into the pocket of her pants. They were with her. That was all she needed to know.

Draping both skirt and plaid over the branch of a tree, she shook out her coat and found the dampness hadn't penetrated completely through the thick wool. Grateful for small favors, she put it back on. She even found her socks dry within the muddy boots.

She performed each act, each inspection, with great care and total concentration, struggling to keep from acknowledging how miserable she was. She came close to success.

Trying to get comfortable, she gathered a pile of dry leaves from beneath a fallen log and spread them on a patch of grass on the bank by the water's edge. Here the rain had not fallen so hard, and the bank had been protected by the branch of an ancient oak. With a sigh she settled down, the leaves crinkling and crackling as she curled into a tight ball. At first she thought the comfort would never come, but after what seemed an hour of worrying and thinking and shivering, she closed her eyes.

With a start, she opened them to the beginnings of dawn, and a feeling she was not alone. Shifting about on her bed of leaves, she sat up and blinked to orient herself. It didn't take long, not with a thousand sore muscles crying out in reminder of yesterday.

She shook her head to clear the cobwebs. Had she really slept through the night? She would not have believed it possible. Yet she saw the hint of yellow streaks breaking through the deep gray sky.

And she knew she was not alone.

"Jamie?" she whispered into the still air. She got no reply.

"Jamie, where are you?" she said louder, peering up and down the stream, looking past the huge oak tree behind her and on deeper into the woods. Again she was met by nothing but silence. Not even the birds had chosen to sing.

The skin crawled at the back of her neck. The far side of the stream seemed equally deserted. She shoved herself away from the bank, sliding over the ground until her back came to the hard, rough surface of the oak's trunk.

Startled, she cried out, then clamped a hand over her mouth. Why didn't she just stand up and dance one of Jamie's lively jigs? She wouldn't be calling attention to herself any more than she already had.

She held herself very still, trying to hear whatever had awakened her, trying to figure out what was different about her surroundings, trying to understand what was wrong. She glanced at the limb where she'd hung both skirt and plaid. The garments were gone.

Over the pounding of her heart, she heard a rustling somewhere behind her. She forced herself to stand, to turn, to watch a dark figure moving toward her. She thought of the hobgoblins that Meagan the Younger feared so much. She imagined them rather small and fleeting. This figure, this dark shadow lumbering in her direction, was definitely a man.

Unfortunately, large as it was, it was definitely not Jamie. Somehow she knew it was definitely not Robert, either. Robert didn't lumber. Robert glided, stalked, strode.

She stifled a cry. It was trouble, that was what it was.

Too late, she turned to run. A strong hand caught her by the wrist and jerked her back.

"George, bring the lantern," a deep voice growled.

Her panic grew. There were at least two of them. She struggled to get away, but he kept his grip. Taking a deep breath, she turned to face him.

This time she did cry out. She'd never seen the man before, but he was the essence of every villain she'd ever read about. Hulking body, shaggy black hair, Cro-Magnon forehead, dull sunken eyes, blunt nose, bearded cheeks, thick lips grinning over mottled teeth. The only feature he lacked was a chin.

Everything about him was magnified to grotesqueness by the surroundings, and by their isolation. He looked so bad, he was almost a caricature, almost a joke. But she saw no humor in him, nor in the companion who walked up behind him holding a lantern.

"Look what we got here," her captor said.

She looked with hope to George. The light cast ugly shadows across his face, revealing features much like the first man's. They resembled each other so much she decided they must be brothers, maybe even twins.

She found no consolation in the thought.

Still, she cleared her throat and tried to speak. No sound came out. Terror had left her mute; she'd thought Robert had struck terror in her heart, but her feelings around him and for him had been sweetness and light compared to this.

She tried again. "You're hurting me." As if that would matter.

"Listen t' her, Ned," the man called George said as he waved the lantern about his head. "Yer hurting her."

"Mayhap I am."

She heard no regret in either voice.

Her mind raced. She'd lived thirty years in New Jersey and New York—she realized with a start this was her birthday—and not once had she seen any bloodletting violence except in a movie or on TV. But she'd imagined it, thinking it was only a matter of time until she ran into trouble. For that reason, she had taken lessons in self-defense.

Somehow she was supposed to relax. Lull the attacker into complacency. Talk to him. Distract him. Then become the attacker herself before getting the hell away.

It had seemed so easy in the gym.

"Are you brothers?" she asked.

"Huh?" George said.

"Brothers," she repeated. "You look so much alike."

"Aye, that we be."

"The lassie's got a queer way o' talkin'," said Ned. He stared at her trousers. "And a queer way o' dressin', as well."

His grip tightened. It took all her strength of will not to fall on the ground blubbering. Robert would expect more of her, and so would Jamie. Why they should make a difference now, she didn't know, but they did.

"Is it lassie or laddie?" Ned asked. He wiped his thick lips across a filthy sleeve. "I've a notion in me head t' find out."

"The notion's in yer breeches, ye mean," George put in.

Ned's laugh came out half growl. "Aye, 'at's a good 'un, George. A notion in me breeches." He laughed again.

"I'll have 'er when yer done."

"The wee bit that's left."

George set the lantern on the ground, then clamped a broad, hairy hand on his brother's shoulder.

"Then I'll go first."

Ned shook him off. "Ye went first last time. I found 'er. She's mine."

They commenced to argue over who should take precedence in the rape. In the jawing, Ned eased his hold on her. She slipped her wrist from his grasp, then took a small step backward. Very small. But it was enough to catch George's eye.

"Ye fool, ye'll let 'er get away."

She raised her hands in innocence. "Oh, no. I'm not running. It's clear you two big strong men would catch me right away."

They stared at her in puzzlement, not knowing what to think of her or her words.

Ned was the first to recover.

"Ye'll no' be running, lassie. No' 'til I've had me fill."

This was too much. She couldn't handle them alone.

Jamie, she thought with all her energies, calling out for him with her mind before guiltily realizing she could not endanger the boy.

Robert, she cried in silence. *Robert.* He was someone to defend both her and himself.

But she'd done too good a job in eluding him. She was on her own. So be it. A chilled calm settled on her. It seemed she was hovering outside herself, a being apart from the ugly scene, someone who could think clearly and do whatever must be done to bring about her escape. What she needed was a distraction, maybe something from the twentieth century. But what?

She rubbed her hands on her pants and felt the ring. She breathed a sigh of relief.

"I have something better than what you're thinking of," she said, practically in a singsong voice.

"There's nothin' better," Ned said.

"How about being rich?"

"Rich is better," said George, and she found herself almost liking him.

She nodded in his direction.

"You're right. When you're poor, rich is always better."

"Ye look no better off than George or me," the first brother said.

"But I have something you don't have." She saw right away it was a poor choice of words.

"Aye, an' so ye do," he said and lunged for her.

She stepped aside, but she did not run. He righted himself, and she could practically see the drool coming from his lips. Standing tall and sure before the pair of cretins was the hardest thing she'd ever had to do.

"Do you know anything about jewelry? About gold?" She smiled encouragingly. "About diamonds?"

It was the *gold* that lit their eyes.

"I have a ring I'll give you. If you'll let me go. It will bring you wealth beyond belief. You can buy the biggest mansion, a ship, a town—" She stopped herself from getting carried away.

"Can it buy a horse?" George asked.

"A dozen, at least," she said, smiling encouragingly. "And all the whiskey you can drink for the rest of your lives."

"Let's see it," said Ned.

"If I show it to you, and you like it, you have to promise to let me go."

"Ye're looby!" Ned snarled. George elbowed him in the ribs, and both men nodded.

"We gi'e ye our word," Ned said, a sickly grin turning his features into a grotesque parody of sincerity. "Once we hold the ring, ye're free."

Liars, she thought as she eased the handkerchief from her pocket. Centering it on her palm, she slowly unfolded the corners, then held out her prize where all could see. She stared in astonishment at what she revealed.

She looked up at Ned.

"Ye canna fool us," he snarled. "That's naught but a stone."

"You have to look closer," she said in desperation. "It needs a bit of polishing, that's all."

Ned bent his head. She tossed the rock onto her makeshift bed. As he went for it, she kicked him hard in the groin with the tip of her pointed boot.

That particular maneuver was one she understood. She'd learned it in class.

He went down with an anguished moan, holding himself with both hands. George lunged for her, but he tripped over the lantern, spilling its fuel, and fire spread to the leaves, then onto Ned's dirty shirt, which went up like a torch.

She didn't wait around to make sure he was all right. Sprinting through the shallow stream, she took off on the opposite bank and lost herself in the woods. She ran for what seemed a month, twisting and turning on a path she made up as she went along, pausing to listen for pursuers but hearing nothing over her pounding heart.

Crossing glens and slogging through a bog, trying to keep to the protection of the woods whenever possible, she had no idea where she was headed, only that she was separating herself from the brothers. Sharp drop-offs and ragged rocks slowed her, challenged her, sharpened her fear. Just when her energy seemed to flag, her endorphins kicked in. She might as well be running in Central Park, she thought with a strange exhilaration as she quickened her pace.

Another quarter hour and reality settled in. She wasn't in Central Park; she was in a Scottish Highland forest without the vaguest idea where to go or what to do. Her step slowed, and at last she came to a halt, holding the throbbing pain in her side. She looked around her. Until she could calm herself and make some plans, she'd best find a hiding place.

Where that might be, she couldn't imagine. One tree looked about the same as all the others, and trees were all that she saw. As she looked up, she saw the return of dark clouds. The wind quickened, colder than she'd yet felt it.

Oh well, she thought, resorting to an old adage, any port in a storm. She headed for the nearest oak.

Chapter Thirteen

"I'll kill her."

Astride his winded horse, moving slowly through the forest, Robert took pleasure from the thought. Though he'd slept little the past two nights—one spent in the crofter's cottage, the second under the shelter of an oak—he admitted to no weariness other than a fatigued exasperation with his futile search.

He had the energy to go on. Find Meagan Butler he would, and she would pay for all she had put him through.

First he had to find her alive; urgency drove him wild.

His hands shook on the reins; he tightened his hold and rode onward, eyes darting to right and left, and to the ground, searching for signs she'd turned from the path, stiffening himself against what he might see.

He imagined her graceful figure dashing through the trees—jogging, as she put it in her strange way. For a moment he pictured her injured, lying at the side of the trail, mayhap in a forgotten bog, unable to cry for help. Images crowded his mind, of a once graceful leg twisted and broken, a gash on her brow that rendered her unconscious, or worse.

Such injury could not be. For Meagan with the intense stare and the quick wit, and the passionate heart she did not want him to see, death was too final, too complete.

"I'll throttle her," he amended, having more use for a warm body than a corpse.

His hands would be gentle on her, but nay too gentle. She needed to ken he was not a man she could cross.

He remembered her throat and the slender neck and the slope of her shoulders. Within his gloves his fingers itched to stroke her.

He settled on a milder, "I'll turn her over my knee and teach her to do as she's told."

And what exactly might that be?

The question brought a dozen answers to mind, each more satisfying than the last.

First he had to find her . . . alive.

That he would; nothing else was thinkable.

He stared at the soiled skirt and the length of damp plaid draped across his thighs. He'd spied them separately, one in the middle of a glen, another in the woods, a half mile apart, each time at a moment when he thought he'd lost her trail.

It was as if she were marking her path for him.

An unlikely occurrence, given the circumstance of her attempted escape from his company. From the signs he'd found, the attempt had been voluntary. But escape from what? He'd treated her kindly. He'd not forced himself on her, though the chances had been often enough, and the need for force doubtful at best. His conduct had been more than gentlemanly, given the temptations she'd presented. Given the fact she was his wife.

Nay, the lass had run as soon as she could for no reason other than the presence of opportunity and an inclination to defy him. She'd been with someone for a while—a lad, from the look of his tracks. A woman and a lad, helpless creatures, the pair of 'em, scampering through the wilderness like a pair of undisciplined pups, as though the world presented little danger.

Far too well, Robert knew otherwise. The strange leavings on the bank of the stream, the evidence of a scuffle and the tracings of burned leaves, hinted that Meagan might now know otherwise, too.

What was there about him lately that made his women run? He did not know; 'twas new to his experience. He would ask them, one by one, when they'd returned, Meagan the Elder most decidedly first.

He tucked the garments into the packet behind the saddle. Guiding the horse through the trees, he listened, he watched, he grew impatient. In the absence of a high noon sun, the wind was cold, and the rain that had been threatening most of the day appeared ready to fall, worse than yestereve.

If Meagan was not injured, then what? Gone back to her time? It could not be, and yet he knew it could. A lost, wild sense took hold of him. How cruel it would be if she had returned so soon, cruel because in too many ways she was still a stranger to him. He wouldn't allow it. Not yet. Not yet.

But where could she be?

"Robert!"

The hoarse, fervent whisper seemed to come from nowhere and everywhere at the same time. His senses quickened, and his heart began to pound. Reining to a halt, he looked about him.

"It's me, Meagan. I'm up here."

He spied her boot on a high branch of the tree by which he'd stopped. Peering higher, he could see little else except thick leaves that blocked his view. The boot jiggled, as if in greeting. Knowing she was here, knowing she was alive, he admitted to unbridled joy and a sensation of triumph that had little to do with reason.

Then rage took control, and with it came a return of the need for revenge. How dare she sound all right?

"Who else would it be, pray tell, but Meagan the Elder?" Calm. Very calm. "No sensible Scottish lass, 'tis sure."

"I'm so glad to see you."

"Are ye now?" He held tight to the reins and to his temper, wondering how long it would be before she changed her mind.

Something in his voice must have given her warning.

"I'm—I'm coming down."

She seemed none too happy about it, but down she came, tossing her coat first. It landed on the ground by the base of the tree and spooked his horse. He settled the animal and waited, watching as she placed her boots with great care on the branches strong enough to hold her slender body, one step at a time, gradually edging closer. He watched the trousers work across her buttocks, taking what pleasure he could in the descent.

When she drew close, he reached up to take her in his arms and bring her down to sit in front of him, her legs dangling to one side of the horse, her bottom warm against his thighs. She felt no lighter than a breeze as she rested her weight on him; her hands stole around his neck, and she

169

buried her face against his chest.

He wanted no tenderness between them, not with fury and the desire for retribution burning through him, but he could not long resist putting his arms around her and holding her close.

Despite himself, despite the anger, he felt a rush of relief because she was well, and a momentary return of joy. He held her longer than sense or circumstances dictated. The horse shifted; she tightened her grasp. He was tempted to put the animal to the gallop to see what else she might do.

At last she pulled back and stared at him, her lips scant inches from his. Should he begin his lesson now? What a temptation the lass was, with her raven hair and violet eyes and spirit of a brave, high-flying lark.

Aye, a temptation to be sure, but he'd not take her astride a horse in the cold in the wood.

Not unless he had no choice.

A light mist began to fall.

"Robert—"

"Hauld your whisht, lass. I'm taking you on to Thistledown, where we'll have a friendly gab."

She shivered. He doubted it was from a chill. "Thank God you're here," she said, sounding as though she meant it. "I knew you'd come."

"You've been expecting me?"

She nodded, smiling at him—her first real smile since coming to the kirk. The smile and knowledge filled him with more pleasure than they should.

"I'm sorry, oh, goodness, I'm sorry, but I acted without thinking, hoping to save you trouble, and then Jamie, Jamie'd been helping me but he disappeared and Ned and George were there, and the fire, and I ran so hard—"

Her voice broke over the tumble of her words.

Out of all the nattering, Robert heard only the names. Jamie he knew not, but the other two sent hot fury knifing through him. The Dundas twins he knew far too well.

"Tell me of Ned and George."

If she heard the tightness in his voice, she gave no sign.

"They found me asleep but I kicked one, I forget who, and he caught on fire, and—"

"They dinna harm you."

"No, they did not, though they tried."

She sounded proud. Well she ought if she escaped the wretched Dundas pair. But then she never should have been where they could hurt her. She nay was blameless in the matter, though she must have been extraordinarily brave. Later he would hear the scene in more detail.

"You spend your energy in talk. No more havering about until we're home."

"Have we far to ride?"

"No more'n a quarter mile."

Astonishment lit her face. "A quarter mile?"

"You almost made it to the kirk, dinna you know?"

"Good grief," she murmured, then slumped against him and did not move again during the short, slow journey through the dampness, to the edge of the forest and across an open green, through the stone gate of the ancestral Cameron home, stirring only when he reined to a halt by the entrance to the keep.

The anger at all she'd put him through returned, a fury at the delay in his search, he told himself with great righteousness, at the discomfort, at the sleepless nights of torment away from his bed. Had she never appeared to him as she had done two days ago in the kirk, he would have found his rightful bride and taken her in the tranquillity of his bedchamber, assuring himself in the way between husband and wife of her loyalty and devotion and his right to use her gold.

But appear she had, and his frustration was the result.

Meagan sat up to gaze around her; her attention lingered on the castle ruins rising gray and jagged in the afternoon mist. Always a challenge they were, mysterious and incomplete, taunting in their want, in ways not too dissimilar from his almost-bride.

Janet Forbes came out to greet him, and he saw from the corner of his eye a dozen of his people milling about the grounds: Ermengarde, his cousin Colin, and others well known to him, all of them with a claim on his soul. Close as he was to his people, it was this stranger/wife who claimed him now.

He spoke only to Janet, asking her assistance in getting his lady to their bedchamber. She put no question to him, but held the lass upright beside her while he dismounted. He reached to take her in his arms.

"I can walk."

"Aye. And run."

She eyed him with the spirit he was wont to see in her. "I suppose you're going to be difficult."

"'Tis possible."

"Well, I've got a little matter to take up with you—"

He grew impatient. "Whisht."

Sweeping her against him, he barked orders to Janet, then carried Meagan up the stairs, unmindful of the many watchful eyes that saw them go. His wife gave no more than token resistance until he'd closed the bedchamber door.

"Look," she said, squirming in his arms, "I really am all right. Tired and hungry and filthy, but otherwise fine."

He set her on the feather mattress. "Good. I've no joy in beating an afflicted lass."

"Beating!"

She jumped to her feet, then grabbed her head and dropped back to the bed. "What happened to the friendly gab?"

"I lied."

"Oh yes, I forgot you do that sometimes."

"I'm no' the only one."

He could take his revenge now, but he saw the sweetness in making her wait, allowing her to worry, to speculate over what he had in mind.

Clever lass that she was, she must ken what he planned to do. He went to the wardrobe and rummaged until he came up with a gown and petticoat. He tossed them beside her.

"You'll have a hot bath and hot food afore long. Do you have a preference which should come first?"

She answered readily. "The food."

Well chosen, he thought; the lass looked lost inside her trousers and shirt.

He strode toward the door, hands curled into tight fists to keep from touching her.

"Thanks for the clothes. These are a bit ripe, I'm afraid."

He looked back, not taking her meaning. Their eyes locked. She seemed not in the least subdued, but her cheek was streaked with dirt and her hair hung limp against her shoulders, and there were dark circles under her eyes. Lost indeed, and needful of his care.

He felt a moment's pity; he thrust it ruthlessly

aside. She read his mind. He saw it in the panic on her face.

Well she might give in to fear. For the past few years he'd forced his step down an unselfish path, his heart and his will bent to the needs of others. He'd thought that path would extend through the last of his days. But not today. Not for a while.

Slamming the door behind him, he visited the turret where the MacSorley gold was hidden, then went below and helped himself to the mutton and roasted potatoes Janet had prepared. Feeling soiled himself— What was it Meagan had said? Ripe. He'd thought of another meaning at the time.

Feeling ripe, he went out to bathe by the cistern, stripping to his bare skin as was his habit, applying the keen edge of his dirk to the stubble on his face. A tub would be carried up to his wife while she ate, along with buckets of heated water. He preferred the out-of-doors. The rain had ceased and the sun had broken through the clouds. He felt a grim glory in the beauty of the day and, more, in the hours that lay ahead.

Colin approached when he was almost done. The Cameron most like him in appearance, he was two years his junior and still unwed, not from lack of choices for a bride but from too many. Like Robert, he was a man who liked women. Unlike him, he'd not been given the chance for travel or education or for battle; the lack had left him more settled than his cousin, and far more content.

It was to Colin that Robert turned for help and advice. He turned to him now.

"There was trouble in Buscar-Ban," he said as he wiped the soap and stubble from his dirk.

"Ye took yer bride to such a place?"

Robert hesitated before answering. Because of

the newlyweds' hasty departure the evening they were wed, Colin knew they faced difficulty in the marriage, but not what or why. He knew, too, his laird searched the countryside for a lass and a lad, but not who. How much to tell him was a particular Robert had yet to decide.

At his request Colin had spread the word that he might need help in the search; it was why the crofter Angus had been ready to share his home and belongings, why the horses had been available so fast.

A good man, he deserved to know more. But not yet. And not everything.

"Fergus Munro gave offense," he said.

"Our bailie bastard gives offense wi' each breath. Ye stopped him."

"With my fist."

"He threatened jail, did he no'? I can hear him now."

"He'd received word of the wearing of the kilt, and the scene in the kirk. There's an informant in our midst, Coz. Learn his name."

"Or hers."

"Aye, or hers."

"'Tis done."

"There's more. I've got it on good authority Ned and George Dundas ride on Cameron land."

"Did ye no' frighten them half the way t' Inverness these two years past?"

"They're none too bright. It seems that they've forgot. And they're dangerous."

Colin regarded him with great care. "They will be found. I swear it on forfeiture of my life."

"For which I thank you, Coz, but I prefer you alive and well. Besides, 'tis a search I prefer to make myself. Alert the people they should no' be traveling about except in pairs. And with the usual precautions."

These precautions being the dirks and cudgels and, for some foolhardy souls, the pistols denied them by a vengeful Crown.

Colin's gaze drifted up the keep to the window of the bedchamber. "Ye've had a strange start t' yer marriage, Rob. The Irish were e'er a peculiar lot."

Robert hated the deception that was forced upon him. He could only hope Colin understood when he learned the truth, as much as could be told without the teller counted out as hopelessly daft if not outright insane.

"She waits for me," he said.

"From the look o' ye, she'll no' be waiting long."

Colin smiled in lascivious suggestion, though his puzzlement was still much upon him. The two clasped hands, more friends than cousins, and Robert returned to the keep, where he donned the shirt and trousers the housekeeper had set out for him, along with a clean pair of boots. A good woman, she knew his needs. And was that not how all good women served their men?

He took the stairs two at a time, meeting Janet outside the bedchamber, a tray of empty bowls in her hand.

"The lass ate like a starved kitten," she said, shaking her head as though he were the culprit who had deprived her of food.

He shoved at the closed door.

"She's at her bath," Janet warned.

"'Tis as I wished. Do you no' remember we're wed?"

Not waiting for a reply, he entered the bedchamber to give his almost-wife all that she deserved.

Chapter Fourteen

Meagan sat in the cramped wooden tub, her knees bent well out of the now tepid water. Small waves splashed against the tips of her breasts as she rubbed a small wedge of soap along her arm.

She'd washed her hair first and toweled it almost dry with a linen cloth Janet had brought. Her concentration turned now to the forearm where the cretinous Ned had held her. No matter how she scrubbed, the feel of his hand would not go away.

The slam of the door did the trick. She looked up to see Robert enter the room. The posset Janet had brought with the food, a strange mixture of warm sweet milk and wine, had served to leave her light-headed and heated, but not so much as Robert with his half-buttoned white shirt and tight black trousers and polished boots, his thick, as always looking mussed, his harsh, rugged features the color of aged oak, and last, the most captivating feature of all, a provocative twist to his lips.

Coward that she was, she could not bring herself to look into his eyes. She'd been worried about feral sheep and cows, had she? How foolish when she had a feral husband on her hands.

When she'd dropped from that tree to his waiting arms, she'd thought him the most gorgeous, marvelous man she'd ever seen. Furious for him and furious at him, it was true, but she'd wanted to crawl inside his jacket and hug him for a week.

He looked even better now, except that she dropped *marvelous* and put in *menacing*.

A thrill not quite akin to fear shot through her, and she almost rose out of the tub.

Discretion kept her in her place.

"I'm still bathing," she said, as though he couldn't see.

He could see, all right, far too well. His eyes raked her, and she saw the evidence in the fit of his trousers that he did not remain unaffected.

He was aroused, was he? Her heart began to thunder. So was she, suddenly, wildly, as if a blast furnace had been turned on inside her. Thinking of Robert standing there naked, his body slick and hard and contoured with marvelous muscles, she gripped the soap until it came apart in her hand. With steady sureness and implacable desire, he would pull her from the water, clasp her wet body to his, rub her against him, rub his sex against hers. . . .

Meagan licked her lips. Unlike him, she planned to fight her desire.

She tried to sit with dignity in the cold water. "Could I have a few minutes of privacy?"

Her words came out dangerously close to a squeak.

"Nay."

He strode deeper into the room, glancing at the

gown and petticoat on the bed where he had placed them, then at her soiled garments resting on the floor by the tub. He seemed puzzled, as though he didn't see what he wanted. Except when he looked at her.

"The skirt you wore, as well as the plaid, are below with Janet," he said. "I found them as I tracked you down."

"Where?"

"Along the path you left as you ran."

"But I didn't—"

Meagan stopped herself. She'd last seen the skirt and plaid where she'd tossed them over a tree branch to dry. When she'd awakened to Ned and George, the clothing had been gone. What Robert told her didn't make sense. But what else lately did?

He glanced at the windowsill, where she'd draped her laundered panties and bra to dry in the afternoon sun. He went to inspect, holding up the panties first, stretching them a time or two, then returning them to the sill.

"I preferred them on you," he said.

And when had he seen them? Oh yes, she knew. When she'd been unconscious after her collapse in the kirk.

Next came the bra. His puzzlement was clear. At least he hadn't completely undressed her when she was unconscious. She got the distinct impression he meant to make up for his neglect.

He waved the bra in the air. "'Tis a strange kind of sling your people use."

"It's a brassiere. Put it down."

He held it by the ends and gave it a thorough inspection.

At last he smiled. "A wee corset, is it no'?"

"Put it down. Please."

He returned it to the window's edge. "Are you asking favors?"

"I'm asking you to keep your hands off my underwear."

"Here's the Meagan I've grown accustomed to." He walked slowly to the tub, picking up the linen cloth Janet had brought. "Dry yourself."

She grabbed for the cloth, but he held it just out of her reach. Water splashed onto the floor.

"Robert, quit teasing."

"I'm no' teasing you, wife. Threatening would be a better word."

"At least you're honest. Remember we had an agreement."

"Aye," he said, all innocence. "If you make no attempt to abandon your place beside me as my wife, I make every effort to leave you untouched. One promise, you should remember, was dependent on the other."

Wrong approach. He was trying to confuse her with selected facts. The trouble was that he succeeded far more than she liked.

Closing her eyes, she tried to remember the motivation for her run, the fight in Buscar-Ban, the gun, a threatening officer of the law lying on the ground.

And Robert, proud, stubborn Robert, seemingly oblivious to all danger as he protected her against the silly insults of a nasty little man.

She understood now why he'd done it, understood because of her own skirmish with Ned and George, understood because of the exhilaration that had overtaken terror when she made good her escape. When Robert hit the bailie, defying the pistol he waved about the air, he must have felt a little the same way.

She shook off the momentary pleasure. It

wasn't like her at all. Men fought, and foolishly so. She'd hurt her attackers and got away, but only because she'd had no choice.

One rude detail of that escape came to mind, the part where she'd tried to offer a bribe. She had something to battle Robert with, something to keep her tough.

Something to make her mad.

"Where is it?"

Once again, he was all innocence. He had the look down very well.

"Don't lie to me, Robert. Tell me where it is, and you know exactly what I'm talking about."

He shrugged in resignation. There was nothing slow about Robert Cameron.

"You found the kerchief and the stone."

"Obviously you expected me to. So where is my engagement ring?"

"In a place of safety."

"It was safe enough with me."

"I found it on the floor of the crofter's hut. 'Twas the date inside that told me you spoke the truth."

Meagan's thoughts went back to that first night she'd spent in the eighteenth century. She saw how it must have been. The handkerchief had fallen from her pocket during the restless hours of tossing about and trying to sleep. Of course Robert had found it. He wasn't a man to let details get past him. Consider the way he was looking at her now.

"So you picked it up and kept it."

"In fear you might lose it again. 'Tis obviously valuable. In all my travels I've never seen the like."

She summoned all the dignity she could while sitting naked in a cold tub. "I want it back."

"I'll not use it to buy my way out of debt, if that's what you're thinking."

"It's not," she said, and knew she spoke the truth. "If you'd wanted to steal it, you wouldn't have put that rock in its place."

"A rare word of confidence in your laird? I'd have you confident in more than just this issue."

"Don't change the subject. I want it back."

"You'll have it before you leave."

"Is this another way to keep me here?"

"Think what you will. I promise the ring is yours."

She could have argued further, told him how his little joke had almost gotten her raped, or worse. But it would do little good. And she needed to save her energies for other issues that would rise between them. Like the matter of having sex.

It was clear from the look in his eye that he hadn't been distracted from his purpose. At least not yet.

Meagan sighed. Except for handling a pair of inept rapists, she'd done little lately that worked out. She hadn't even had a thoroughly comforting bath.

"I'm cold," she said, somewhat needlessly, since her skin was turning blue.

"I've a plan to warm you."

Here she must dig in her figurative heels. "Forget it. I'm not only cold, I'm exhausted. I just want to go to bed."

"'Tis a sentiment I share."

He spread the towel wide, just out of her reach. Conan the Stubborn. Meagan the Stubborn didn't have the same natural rhythm to it. Unfortunately, Meagan the Hapless did.

She gave up. Unless she intended spending the next few hours sitting in a dirty tub, she had no recourse but to stand and step into the barely adequate cloth.

He looked away, after a not-so-quick glance at her nakedness. A gentleman laird, was he? Ha!

Wrapping herself as best she could, she edged around him toward the bed.

He grabbed an arm and spun her around. "Forget the gown."

"Robert, please."

"I plan to please the both of us."

"Please don't." She snapped the words at him.

"A challenge? Nay, wife, I'd call it more a mistake."

She tried to back away. He pulled her near, his warm, rough hands splayed against her bare shoulders. She clutched the thin cloth as if it were armor, but nothing could keep her from feeling the hard contours of his body as he held her close, his palms rubbing in small circles as they moved slowly down her back. She pressed her hands against his chest and sensed the heat, the coursing blood, the heart of the man.

She closed her eyes against his intensity. How frightening he was, and, worse, completely compelling. For all her resolve, for all her reasoning, she could not fight, she could not pull away.

"Are you punishing me for running?" she asked.

He cupped her buttocks and held her against his erection.

"Aye. The both of us need punishing for waiting so long. Can you no' feel the pain, lass? Can you no' tell how I hurt?"

The sharpness of desire hit her in private places and spread like wildfire through every nerve, every vein, engulfing all thought and sense that what they did was wrong.

The cad, the brute, the rat, she called him to herself, sadly with little effect. No name she came up with diminished him in her mind, nor lowered her body temperature by so much as a single degree.

"The punishment's not working," she said, her breath mingling with his as she forced herself to look at him. "It feels like a reward."

There was nothing wimpy about such honesty, she thought. She knew exactly how she felt. No need to keep it a secret; he knew it, too.

He held her even tighter, thrusting his hardness between her legs. It was as if they were having sex, standing here clothed beside the bed. At least one of them was clothed. She felt a sense of shame. He was too much, too hot, too hungry. She'd never known a man like him before.

She could not let herself acquiesce to what he offered, not honorable Meagan, not practical Meagan, Meagan who was engaged to another man.

Robert Cameron did indeed frighten her, but not because she thought he would inflict pain. The fright came because around him she did not know herself.

"This is a bad idea." Inadequate. Ad copy she would toss in the trash. "You must stop." Still inadequate, but it expressed how she felt.

"In time."

He eased his hold, gentling his approach, putting her off guard. Then he slanted a kiss across her lips. "You're as changeable as the weather, lass. Do you no' think we've had enough of storms?"

"Not nearly enough," she said in a whispered rush. "Don't make me fight you."

"I won't." He kissed her again, putting more force into it. "You won't."

And then he just looked at her, not touching her except where his hands loosely held her waist. She

184

thought of the inadequate foreplay of her three fiancés, how they never seemed to get it quite right.

Robert got it right with just his eyes.

She'd known from the start he would, like the hero from *The Forever Bride*.

But this was real life, not a fantasy. And she was no heroine who'd fallen madly in love.

Or was she?

The idea struck hard. It would not go away. Was she in love with Robert? The thought stunned her more than she would have believed possible. It had taken her two years to learn to care for William. She'd known Robert barely two days.

She did indeed fight him, shoving away so unexpectedly he let her go. Defying him, defying the unwanted questions crowding her mind, she stood with the towel clutched to her front.

"I'm not ready for this."

"You taste ready."

He dropped his gaze from her eyes to her bared shoulders, to the damp towel that clung to all the wrong places, down her legs to her bare feet and up again to her kiss-dampened lips.

"You look ready. What's yet to be done?"

Not much. If only he knew how her body had prepared itself for him. In the most basic of ways, she was more ready than she had ever been.

But she couldn't go through with it. She was a wordsmith. She had to make him understand.

And he wasn't quite the barbarian he was trying to be; otherwise he would already have her on the bed. Her heart went out to him all the more.

"You have to understand me. That's what is left to be done. I ran away because I was afraid. You could have gotten killed in that poor little town, and I blamed myself. It's clear I don't belong here.

It's equally clear I'm not helping you out any. You're engaged to someone else. So am I. When I return to my time, and we both know I have to try, it can't be with memories of how I made a fool of myself and did things that brought me shame."

"There's no shame between us. You're my wife."

"Only by chance. And not for long."

She was proud of herself. She'd expressed herself in ways that he must accept. She was wrong.

"Aye," he said, "my wife but no' for long. 'Tis why we canna let opportunity escape. And I'll no' be the first. You said it yourself."

The bluntness of his words stunned her.

"That's a terrible thing to say. You know nothing about me. Nothing about my past."

His eyes hardened. "I remember what you've told me. Have you lied?"

"Perhaps I should have. In this world of yours do only virgins deserve respect?"

His expression softened, and the half smile that tugged at his lips melted the sharp hurt of what he had said.

"Ah, is that what this is about? I respect you, lass. Let me show you the many ways."

With such a voice the serpent must have tempted Eve, and countless women since must have been seduced by such a smile.

Unwilling to be so weak, she tightened her hold on the towel. "What is it you call women like me? Fallen angels? Soiled doves? Round-heeled harlots? You'd be wrong every time. I made a few mistakes, damned few, and I made them out of a need to belong to someone. In my time, there's nothing wrong with that."

"Nor is it wrong in mine," he answered, his voice turned sharp once again. "You've lain with others. As have I. In truth, I want you to belong to me, for as long as you can."

"But don't you see—"

She broke off. He didn't see at all. He hadn't meant to be cruel. He'd spoken the truth as he saw it: in taking her to bed, he wouldn't rob her of her innocence. Rather he was offering her a respite from the difficulties they both were going through; in words a twentieth-century lover might use, he was offering her a good time.

In a very basic way, he wanted her, and Lord help her, despite all her high-flown sentiments, she wanted him.

Chapter Fifteen

Meagan knew her hunger was in her eyes; she saw it reflected in his. He eased the towel from her hands. Making one last effort to flee, she turned to run. He caught her by the wrist and pulled her backward against him, his sex hard against her bottom.

When his arm came like a steel band around her waist, she tried to pull it free. He did not move, except to hold one of her small breasts within his grasp. Broad and callused and brown, his hand easily covered her. She swelled as she had never done before, and when his thumb stroked the hard tip, she felt her betraying body nestle against him and her betraying lips whisper his name.

Hot lips kissed the side of her neck. "You've a silver tongue, lassie. It must be put to better use than simple talk."

She caught the hand on her breast, meaning to pull it away; instead she felt herself increasing the pressure. She moaned, or was it Robert? She didn't know.

He relaxed the arm around her middle. "Tell me to leave."

She tried. She failed. No sound came from her lips except another moan. A crazy time this was, a crazy situation, and she must be a little crazy, too. She gave in to frenzy, a feral wife turning in his arms, rubbing her breasts against his shirt, her heavily lidded eyes unable to look above his parted mouth.

"What use would you put to my tongue? This?" She licked his lips. "Or this?" She dipped inside his mouth for just a moment.

"Aye, and more. I want ye, wife. I've ne'er wanted a woman more."

His brogue was thicker than she'd ever heard it. It flowed like hot honey across her skin.

Lost in time, she was more powerfully lost in his arms. He kissed her hard and with a thoroughness she would remember all her life. He tasted of mutton and wine and wildness, but then so must she.

Her fingers stroked his hair, his muscled neck, his throat; her palms pressed hard against his chest. "Undress."

He eased her onto the bed and did as she ordered. Making Robert obey her was not so difficult after all. She simply had to order what he already planned to do.

Sunlight streamed into the room. In its brightness she watched the quick, efficient movements of his hands, the baring of his chest, the play of fair body hairs down to his waist. And then the removing of his boots and pants, each movement, each view, etched like acid into her sizzling mind.

She was not used to so much light in such a moment. But then, neither was she used to such a moment, not like this.

Everything around her was of a piece—the hand-carved oaken bed, the earthy peat fire licking against the stone hearth, the wool rug on the floor, the coverlet, the man, who looked hand-carved himself, sculpted from copper, his skin slick and tight against sinewed muscle, his stomach tight, his thighs and calves powerful enough to crush her, to hold her to him against all her protests, if protest was what she had in mind.

Her gaze fell to the hard, thick shaft he brought to her, taunting in its size and promised pleasure, making her hunger to learn what this part of him would taste like. Desire knifed through her, stunning in its ferocity, and for an instant she saw herself in ways she did not like. Uncontrolled. Lustful. Wanton. She tried to rise from the bed, but he was upon her and she could not think or judge herself at all except in what she needed for him to do.

And what she needed to do to him.

"Ye come from an untamed time," he whispered as she dropped her head back to give him access to whatever part of her he chose.

"I never knew it before."

"I excite ye?"

"Aye," she said hoarsely, "ye do."

He ran his tongue across her throat and around her ear. She shivered from the pleasure.

"Ye've a terrible brogue, lassie, but ye do everything else in a pleasing way."

"Everything?"

He licked the tip of one nipple, then the other. "'Tis a point well taken. We've scarce tried everything yet."

She ran her hand down the contours of his arms and across his chest. "Your tongue is golden, Robert. Everything about you is golden."

190

"I've something harder than gold between my legs."

She licked his nipples as thoroughly as he had licked hers. "We've got a saying in my time. Talk is cheap."

He took her measure; the talking ceased. He stroked, he rubbed, he massaged until she felt thoroughly kneaded and needed all at once. She laughed at her foolish use of words, but kept the laughter to herself lest he misunderstand and think she laughed at him.

There was nothing laughable about Robert Cameron, and all that was glorious. Even as she knew she was doing terribly wrong things, she did them, stroking and rubbing and massaging, taking his harder-than-gold erection in her hands, running her fingers up and down the thick, slick column as his fingers sought the folds of flesh between her legs.

He found her wet and waiting; he hesitated no more, settling himself on top of her, his powerful thighs between her slender legs, thrusting deep while his tongue thrust in her mouth, again and again and again. This might not be her first time, but it felt as though it were, with her body reacting as it had never done before. They fit together, his sex against hers just as it ought to be, and she exploded against him as he exploded inside of her.

She'd never had a climax during intercourse, but always afterward or before, when she'd needed special attention. She liked it Robert's way. She loved it. She loved him.

For all his bluntness, his stubbornness, his inclination to see things his way, she truly loved him.

With fearful intensity, she held tightly to him, unwilling to let the sensations get away from her.

She'd traveled through time to find the love of her heart. No other truth would do, for if she had not, if she had betrayed her sense of loyalty for no reason other than lust, she didn't know how she would live with herself.

And so she held him tight, as he held her, eyes closed against the light, welcoming the dark where things could be as she imagined them, as she desperately wanted them to exist. In her perfect, shadowy world each of them owed allegiance only to the other, a solitary couple high in a medieval Scottish keep away from the cares of the world.

In that darkness she wanted to tell him that in all the important ways, this was the first time for her. If she opened her eyes to him he could surely read the truth: that in her other life she'd been innocent of what lovemaking was meant to be. He'd taught her in such a sweetly thrilling manner that she would never forget, even when the time came—

She broke off the thought. This moment was too precious to destroy with predictions of what must be.

It was as though he sensed the urgency of her embrace, for he did not ease away, or say anything, or do anything but kiss her hair and stroke her arm and rest his powerful hand against her naked back.

She should have dozed; she couldn't, fearful she would wake and he would be gone. As it was, he was the first to shift away. A blast of cold air hit her from the window. Blinking against the harshness of day, she looked over to see her underwear fluttering to the floor.

Like dying birds. What a strange, inappropriate thought, coming just when she'd felt the rapture

of love. He'd said the weather was changeable.
And so it was.

A chill went through her that had nothing to do
with springtime or love or too-long-delayed ful-
fillment, and everything to do with inevitability.

"You've traveled from a fine time, lass, if all the
women are such as you."

His voice was deep and gentle, not in the least
harsh. Still, she swallowed an anguished cry. The
room darkened. A cloud had passed over the sun.
She closed her eyes against the sudden shadows,
but she couldn't close her heart to what he'd said.

This time the darkness brought only wounding
thoughts. He'd meant to compliment her; she felt
it in her heart. But oh, it would not do, it would
not do. The glory of the moment shattered like
broken crystal. In an instant love turned to hate,
sudden, sharp, breathtakingly painful. It was a
hate for him, for her, for all her circumstances.

Scant seconds ago she'd wanted him to see the
love in her eyes; now she kept her eyelids lowered
so that he could not see the hurt.

"I'm not so special."

*In New York alone there are lots of love-starved
women no smarter than me.*

Than I, she corrected, ever the grammarian.

Ever the fool. Looking for love in all the wrong
places; looking for love in Robert Cameron's arms.
Reality struck like the tolling of a bell. He wasn't
being purposefully cruel to her. He was simply an
eighteenth-century laird with an eighteenth-
century view of sex. She didn't belong here. A fish
out of water. A woman out of her own time.

She tried to be practical, a fraction of the self-
sufficient woman she used to be. With William
she'd found love, or at least a reasonable substi-
tute. If she ever felt worthy of him again, she'd

confess all and beg him to forgive and forget.

Except that with her luck, she was probably carrying her temporary husband's child. The man she hated. No, she thought, calmness returning clarity to her mind. She must be honest. He made her hate herself.

So many thoughts rushed through her mind, she could hold on to only one: the possibility of pregnancy; it robbed her of all energy. In that sliver of time, she discovered another of her oft-read expressions was true: a heart really could break and at the same time turn to stone.

Robert stirred, his muscles rippling beneath her hands, burning her fingers as if he were on fire. He planned more, wanted more.

"Please," she said, using the last of her strength, "no more pillow talk."

"A curious phrase, but one I ken."

He tried to kiss her lips. She turned her head.

"I'm tired. And I'm not good for more than once at a time."

With Robert it was a lie, but he would not know.

"You're tempting, of course," she said, unable to keep the truth from him entirely. She pulled away from his embrace, the covers carefully held in place between them, and a little more of the truth slipped out. "I told you my experiences were few. I've never made love like this." She stared beyond him. "Never."

"Then why—"

"Because if we go on I'll feel loose, promiscuous, sinful, if you want to put an old-fashioned name to it. I've never thought of myself as any of those things."

She forced herself to look at him. "At least not until now."

His expression hardened, and his eyes turned to brown glass.

"You think little of yourself for what we've done? Wife?" He put great emphasis on the final word.

"What difference does it make? You wanted me, and for a short while you made me want you. That ridiculous ceremony in the kirk had nothing to do with it. In your time and mine, we wouldn't call it a marital consummation. We'd call it lust."

She ought to shut up and let him go. But she was not through. She had one more thing to say, one last remark to make certain he didn't tempt her again.

"You wanted to punish me for running, and I called it a reward. I want you to know it was a great deal of both."

As though she'd slapped him, he stood and dressed. She could not watch with any of the attention she'd given to the undressing, but as she sank into the soft depths of the feather bed, she saw him in her mind, the trousers slipping over powerful calves and thighs, covering the damp shaft that would be immense even in its laxness, and the wiry dark hair she had stroked with such care.

He would shrug into his shirt, covering so many places she had kissed, had tasted with her tongue.

And wanted to taste again.

This was all insane. Why did she still feel his hands upon her? Why must she endure the wetness between her legs? When he was gone she'd get into the tub again, no matter how cold and dirty the water, and she'd try to wash all feeling away.

He stared down at her, looking for all the world like a conquering male. "I said you had a silver tongue, but it can be a harsh one as well."

Pride gave her the strength to sit up and lean against the headboard, unmindful of its cutting hardness against her naked back. Courage forced her eyes to his. Belated modesty kept her holding the cover at her throat.

"Words are how I make a living."

"You earn your keep?"

She nodded. "By writing."

He stared at her for a long while, as if by staring he would grasp the mysteries of her life and of her soul.

Little he knew how simple she really was. If he understood the language of a woman's heart, he could read her like a book.

"I would know more about this strange occupation," he said, just as her pride and courage faded. "Rest, then dress and come below where you can tell me all. I've doubts the clothes will fit, belonging as they do to the youthful Meagan, but they're the best my poor household can provide."

He spoke formally, all familiarity between them gone. Maybe now he'd let her get to that kirk and get home.

And maybe taxicabs had wings.

He strode toward the door, then paused before making his exit, dragging out the moment, dragging out her despair.

"I'll hear more, too, of the lad who led you through the woods, and of Ned and George. The matter of this adventure is not yet done, lass. Not done by half."

He left, and it seemed he took the sweetness of the air with him. Always the laird, she thought, the dominating figure in this Scottish fantasyland. He wanted her with him in the great hall, entertaining him with talk as she had entertained him in bed. This time he would be disappointed. She would eventually tell him all, but not this afternoon, and not even tonight.

It was a small rebellion, this choosing to stay in her room, far less decisive than her effort to leave him in the woods. After her shameless behavior today, it was the best she could do, remaining in seclusion to figure out all the ways she'd done things wrong and how she could make them right.

Meagan woke from her third night in fantasyland with an unexpected consideration pounding in her mind.

One man, one night.

Would such a marriage work?

An eternity had passed since that moment in her other life when she'd sat in the kirk and asked herself the very same thing. This morning, after hours of restless tossing and juggling more questions than she could possibly answer, and then more hours of a deep-as-death sleep, it struck her slowly awakening psyche with far more urgency than it had done before.

Had she really made such wild, abandoned love to Robert?

A few details burned their way into her mind. The answer was a resounding *yes*.

With all her sense of right and wrong and honor and fidelity, how could she have let him do anything he wanted to her and have done the same to him in return?

Remnants of common sense told her she was asking the wrong questions. The one issue to deal with was this: did she have any choice? All consideration of emotions aside, there wasn't a woman alive with a normal supply of functioning hormones who could have resisted him. He was magnificent—she'd be a liar if she thought otherwise—and he knew all the right buttons to punch. Most appealing of all, he'd wanted her, private, predictable Meagan who had never, in all her life, attracted much attention from virile men.

Her appeal had always been to the intellect.

But Robert had wanted her. And not for her mind. Good grief, he didn't understand half the things she said. It was a hard point to ponder when her tattered emotions remained divided between equal parts enchantment and regret.

Calling this time and place a fantasyland was a lie, especially with the sex and violence she was encountering. She and Robert were not and never could be truly married. Besides, her practical side reminded her, she hadn't been with her man for an entire night, just one erotic afternoon. And their parting had been scarcely amicable, much less amorous.

She didn't love him. She couldn't. She saw that now. They had nothing in common, and they must part very soon. She admired him, and she feared for his well-being, and she seemed more alive than she had ever been because he had come into her life.

But that wasn't love. She couldn't put a name to it, but it wasn't love. That she knew for sure.

Since he'd left her the previous afternoon, she'd not been visited again in his bedchamber except by the housekeeper Janet, who brought her broth. Later she'd returned with an additional posset, strong enough to knock her mistress out for the night. Meagan hadn't heard whoever it was who removed the tub and her dirty clothes and laid the fire against the nighttime chill.

It was bright daylight now. Tub and clothes were gone, the sun was streaming in the window, lighting her laundered panties and bra on the rug, and she was lying naked in Robert's bed with the feel of his hands still on her and more memories than she could handle before her first cup of tea.

Across the room from the bed, burning coals in the fireplace needed only a peat log and some stirring to erupt into flame.

The way she needed only a kiss from Robert to—

Meagan shuddered. Such thoughts could serve her little good, not if she were to deal with all that had happened, and more, what was yet to come. She could imagine his striding in and thinking she was waiting for another session. She was honest enough to ask herself the all-important question: was she doing exactly that?

Most definitely not.

To prove it, she slipped from the bed, grabbed up the underwear, rekindled the fire, and hopped back under the covers in less time than it would take to say *Robert Cameron* three times.

Easing into her panties was easy enough, the bra harder, but she managed.

"You'd like to see me right now, wouldn't you?" she said to her absent husband. "You'd like to know just how they fit."

And how they were removed.

Her husband was a thorough man.

Her husband. Her Highlander husband.

No. She had to quit thinking that way.

She wondered where he could be lurking. Wherever it was, he would be thinking, remembering, planning what to do. According to what he'd said before leaving, he wanted to talk. Curling into a ball, she pulled the covers over her head. Maybe if she hid he wouldn't find her.

That seemed as unlikely as—

She tried to think of the most preposterous thing she could, but that turned out to be traveling from 1997 to 1765.

Her head throbbed. Wine and milk would never be her favorite drink. She needed to be clear-headed this morning, enough to figure out what to do now that she and Robert had consummated their accidental vows.

She thought about the kirk, so close, so taunting. Head pounding and heart lying heavy in her breast, she saw her leave-taking as long overdue.

What if she did go, right now, before she had to face him, breaking her word for the good of them both? A new and terrible consideration struck. What if she returned to the twentieth century and found the castle still in ruins?

It was possible. Unlikely, but possible. Because of her interference, Robert might have to forgo the dowry, might lose his land, might forsake his dream of restoring Thistledown.

Whatever else happened, Meagan knew she could do nothing that would change the past. Right now that meant hanging around.

What a mess. That was how she would have to look at the situation. A mess, not heartbreak or devastation, no matter how depressed she felt at the moment. Once she left, once she was back in New York at work, once she was back with her true fiancé, she would probably have a difficult time remembering Robert's name.

The way she kept struggling to remember . . . William, that was it. William Stuyvesant Sturgeon IV. It all came back in a rush, and if wasn't exactly a rush of joy, she wouldn't worry about it just yet.

All the thinking warmed her, and she pulled back the covers, glancing at her hands in the process. Glancing at her fingers. Not an acrylic nail was left. She must have lost them in the scuffle with the would-be rapists and in the scramble up the tree. She hadn't felt them snap off, a fact that gave fair testimony to the emotional straits she'd been under.

Her own nails had grown long beneath them, but, fragile as they were, they would sliver and peel before long. The lost nails seemed symbolic. Was she shedding all the traits she'd brought with her from the twentieth century? All her outer toughness? All her pride?

Not all. She got out of the bed, shivered at the briskness of the air, and scurried in panties and bra to close the window before warming her backside by the fire.

Definitely not all.

She was struggling into the small petticoat and gown Robert had laid out for her when a brisk knock sounded at the door and Janet Forbes entered.

The housekeeper's cool dark eyes gave a quick assessment. "Ye'll need clothes," she said, turning Meagan around, working at the fastenings that ran down the back of the gown.

Meagan took a cautious breath, relieved to discover that the fastenings held, and faced the woman. "Not many," she said.

Janet's grunt told her little about whether she agreed.

"He's gone," the housekeeper added.

Alarmed, Meagan squeaked, "Where?"

"T' find the lass we're no' supposed t' mention."

"He left without me?"

"Aye."

"Alone?"

"Colin."

It was clear Janet thought the new companion was wise.

"What am I supposed to do?"

"Wait."

"Where?"

"Here."

Monosyllabic conversations had their drawbacks, Meagan decided; she could not keep up with Janet, no matter how hard she tried.

"Am I to remain in this room?"

"Laird Cameron did no' say. But he wants ye here—those were his words—when he returns."

Of course he did. In the room, in the bed, or perhaps naked in her bath.

He had to learn he couldn't always get his way, but when—and how—she had no idea.

There was no telling how long he would be gone, hours, maybe a day . . . or more. Meagan's inventive mind suggested how she would fill the time.

Requesting breakfast, she rummaged through the wardrobe until she found a comb, then spent a few painful minutes tugging it through a thousand tangles. Satisfied as best she could be while wearing a pale blue dress that was too tight across the bosom and came two inches above her ankles, she went down the winding rock-walled stairway to begin her day.

She started with a self-guided tour of the keep. Three floors, the bottom used for storage, the second the great hall, kitchen, a small library filled with leather-bound tomes, and a pair of alcoves for overnight guests. On the top floor were the laird's private quarters, his bedchamber and a smaller room that apparently was used as an office.

At the end of the hall lay the locked door to the

tower. From the outside she recalled the arched roof of stone slabs and the encircling parapet which must have once been used for defense. It was inside the tower that Robert must have stored the as-yet-untouchable dowry and her engagement ring.

Janet caught her trying to jimmy the lock.

Meagan started as though she were in the wrong, though she met with no accusations.

In answer to her questions, the housekeeper said the keep had been built in the late fourteenth century, then added onto through the centuries until it became the quadrangle that was Thistledown Castle.

"'Twas a fine place," she said, her eyes turning inward as she stared out the corridor's lone window onto the ruins. "I was but a lass during the last of the building, but I remember what seemed t' me a hundred rooms, for meeting and greeting folk, for visitors to stay the night, a grand ballroom, and crowning it all a finely paneled oaken roof."

"Yes," said Meagan, picturing the castle she had toured more than two hundred years hence.

"The old laird, Donald Cameron, saw it burned after Culloden, as did our Robert. But fifteen, he was, staying with his father when his heart yearned t' be in the thick o' the battle. He saw his share o' the ugliness, though, the raping and the pillaging that went on, English and Scots preying upon other Scots. He took t' wandering, in places high and low, even down t' London, as low a place in my mind as ye're likely to see."

"He mentioned once he'd been a scholar," Meagan said, afraid to ask too much and end the discourse, wanting to know everything about her Highlander.

But Janet, her thoughts stirred by remembrances, showed no inclination to stop.

"An uncle, brother to the old laird's late wife, saw him in Edinburgh, slaving t' pull a sedan chair for one of the wealthy Lowlanders bloated wi' fat from too many meals. Our laird says 'twas naught but an adventure, the manner in which he earned his way, but the uncle, a pompous sort, saw otherwise and paid for his schooling in Holland. The thing t' do, ye ken, then as now, was t' send the sons of lairds t' study law at the university in Leiden. Our Robert admits t' a poor performance in his studies, having more interest in the foreign ways of cultivation and drainage, learning how they could be used on Cameron land."

That sounded like him, always thinking of the future, of what must be done to better his clan. Proud of him, respecting him all the more, Meagan felt an ignoble bite of jealousy, not of any one person, but of a countryside full of them.

"You say his mother died."

"When he was a wee bairn. The last of twelve babes he was, and the only one t' survive beyond birth."

Meagan looked through the window beyond the ruins to the rocks and hills and forest that made up the Highland wilderness, trying to picture the powerful man she knew as the motherless little boy he once had been. She felt such tenderness for him that her eyes blurred with tears.

"He grew up wild, which led to his wandering days. After leaving the university, he settled down, but no' for long. Hard times threatened the loss of all the Camerons owned. He joined wi' other Highlanders, serving beside Simon Fraser himself under promise his home would be saved from taxes. Brave lads, all, who went t' Ireland, then on t' a strange land across the sea."

"Quebec," Meagan said. "He mentioned it to me once."

"He'll no' reveal the details, I'll be bound. 'Twas a bloody time for our laird. He returned to find the horrors he'd been through were all for naught."

"The taxes—"

"We've a sheriff here who dinna ken right from wrong. With the old laird sick in his bed and his son across the sea, he threw people off the land they'd worked all their lives, brought in a bastard tacksman who collected rents that left those who remained wi' little t' eat and a poor roof over their heads."

"Edgar Gunn," Meagan said, remembering the gaunt, weasel-faced lawman she'd seen outside the change-house.

She saw, too, a clearer, harsher picture of this time into which she had tumbled, the sacrifice, the heartbreak, the loss. Strength and goodness were here, and evil, too, just as they were in the late twentieth century.

She must do something for Robert, something tangible to leave behind when she was gone. Her heart grew heavy at the thought, but she saw no other way.

"Do you have any drawing materials?"

"Aye," Janet said. "The first bride of our laird was taken with sketching."

"The first bride?"

"Did our laird no' tell ye he'd been married afore?"

Meagan shook her head, unaccountably hurt. So many things about him remained a mystery, despite all that she had learned today.

"Iona Cameron was a frail lass, but bonnie.

After Leiden, our laird came home t' fall in love, though he was promised to a MacSorley. A stubborn mon, he married against his father's will. She and the bairn died while he fought in the battle of Quebec."

"He had a child, too." Meagan's voice was scarcely above a whisper.

"The news of his birth and death came hard when our laird returned."

"So he didn't know he had fathered a child until it was too late," Meagan said, comprehending a little of the loss he must have felt. She felt ashamed for being hurt, however briefly. Robert was not one to speak of sad times; he was not one to confide. But, made of flesh and blood and heart, he would feel the devastation, and the frustration of never having held his infant son.

"His father taken to his bed, the land gone for taxes . . . It was a sad time at Thistledown. Seeing the pride in the people, the crops in the fields, the cattle grazing on the hills, ye'd no' ken how it was but a few years afore."

"I've been to Buscar-Ban."

"Then ye've seen our worst."

Meagan saw, too, the way things must turn out. It was a way in which she had no part.

She took a deep breath. "The drawing materials," she reminded Janet, and went with her to assemble them, doing all that she could for Robert before she told him good-bye.

Chapter Sixteen

Having spent the second night of their escapade
in the open woods, on the third Annie and Fitz
sought refuge in a deserted shed at Buscar-Ban.
She woke scratching and feared she'd taken on
some fleas.

Fitz did the same. As he stood to inspect his
arms and legs, barely pulling back his clothing to
expose his skin, he was not so sanguine about
their fellow travelers.

"If I were a foulmouthed man," he said, scratching at his rear, "you'd hear some cursing now."

Given the innocent look about him and the ex-
cessive modesty, Annie suspected he knew few
words to utter. She told him several she'd heard
her brothers use. He scowled at her and slapped
the side of his neck.

Served him right, she thought, though she was
tempted to slap herself in a dozen places. Despite
the fact she and Fitz had spent three nights together, he had not tried for so much as a peck on
the cheek. She most certainly would have refused

such forward favors. But it wouldn't have been remiss for him to *try*.

Peering out the half-hinged door, she saw that dawn had edged onto the eastern horizon. They slunk out of the shed, glad to leave the damp, fetid enclosure behind. Keeping low, they headed for the stand of trees a hundred yards away, each of them scratching as the urge arose. Southwest they ran, in the general direction of Ireland, in the specific direction of water where they could bathe.

They'd hidden Gertie in the forest, far off any noticeable trail, and taken refuge from the rain in the town. Annie would have given much for a change of clothes. Though she'd complained about her father often enough, he did supply her with a wardrobe the envy of every lass she knew.

She'd brought a half dozen dresses with her; unlike her, they remained at Thistledown.

Running was the right thing to do, even with Fitzroy Sutherland alongside, Annie told herself as she scurried through the woods. Through too-quiet woods, she thought as they neared their destination. Through the deserted woods, she realized when they arrived. In hiding the mare, they'd obviously made a mistake. Gertie was not where she had been the night before.

Annie ran frantic circles in the clearing, thinking maybe she'd remembered the hiding place wrong, saying over and over, "She must be close. She must be close."

Fitz said nary a word, just walked after her in his own calm way, searching the woods with his eyes, irritating her until she wanted to scream. Last night he'd argued against leaving the mare behind, but she'd seen no choice but to do so, else they would have attracted a crowd in that pitiful town. This morning she saw he might well have been right.

She saw little purpose in telling him so. The most she could concede was that the search had best come to an end.

Fitz took the pronouncement with typical male superiority.

"'Tis a good thing," he said, slapping at his arm. "You've come close to obliterating the few clues we have."

She looked down to where he'd gestured, to the hoofprints still visible in the mud. Gertie's hoofprints, along with the marks of heavy boots. They led from the clearing in a southwesterly direction.

Annie fought back tears. She never cried. Whined maybe, on rare occasions, and loudly protested all injustice, most definitely at the injustice directed at her. But she never cried.

A tiny voice reminded her she'd done just that while the goose cooked two days past, when she'd wondered about ever seeing home again, then again through that dreadful night in the woods.

All right, she amended, she seldom cried.

The tears came again today. She brushed them aside before Fitz could see. Between the two of them, she was the stronger. Still, she didn't want to disgust him into abandoning her. She didn't want to run away alone.

As delicately as possible, she scratched her rear, then concentrated on the tracks. Once she'd followed Tully in just such a way, when he'd taken off on an adventure with one of his mates. It was a good thing she'd led such an exciting life. It gave her experience.

For all his innocence, Fitz seemed equally adept at following Gertie. Heads bent to the ground,

Evelyn Rogers

they walked in silence for what seemed half the morn. The sound of voices brought them to a halt.

They tiptoed toward the sound, keeping low, inching forward to thick brush that could serve as a hiding place. Crouching in the mud, they parted the shrubbery and saw Gertie pawing the ground next to two of the ugliest men she'd ever seen. They looked so much alike, they might as well have been looking into a mirror as they stood practically nose to nose.

Blunt nose to blunt nose, belly to belly, beard to beard. They were big, hairy, and dirty. And they looked very, very mean.

"I ride her first, Ned. Ye had yer chance wi' the lass."

"Ye saw I was in trouble." The man he'd called Ned spat in the mud. "Ye let her get away. I've the burns on me back t' prove it."

They commenced to toss accusations back and forth, using language even Annie's rascal brothers had never dared. Through all the curses and threats, she learned that Ned's cohort was called George, that they had taken a lass and tried to do her harm and in the process been injured themselves.

Annie thought she might like to meet the lass who managed such a feat.

In their roaming, the pair of louts had come across Gertie, but with the ongoing argument between them, had been unable to decide which of them would mount her. Poor mare. Annie had to get her away.

The men began to shove one another; the shoving separated them farther from the mare. Gesturing for Fitz to follow, Annie crept through the brush toward Gertie, away from the men. She

210

reached through the leaves, inches short of grabbing the dangling reins.

The horse bobbed her head and snorted. Annie stilled.

"By God, George," Ned snarled, "ye're letting this one get away." He came at a run to the horse while Annie and Fitz slunk low as possible against the ground.

Patience was never one of Annie's virtues, but she saw the need of it now. Such rascals as these would be at each other's throats again afore long. Her purpose must be to shun timidity, to take Gertie and run.

Maybe she could use Fitz as a diversion. He could set up a clatter, turning the men's minds and eyes away from Gertie. Annie smiled at the thought. She'd stolen the goose, giving them food the past two days. It was time for him to do something, too.

The sound of an approaching horse kept her from outlining the plan. A flat-faced man half the size of George and Ned rode into view. Fitz gasped, but the sound was lost in the trample of the two horses, who neighed at each other in greeting.

Annie stared at her companion.

"The bailie," he mouthed. "Fergus Munro."

Annie tried not to be discouraged. An officer of the law must surely be after these two thieves, little thinking she might be put in the same category. He probably had a pistol somewhere on his person. Her spirit lightened. Maybe he would have to shoot the pair of them. Escaping with Gertie would be easy then.

Much to her dismay, George greeted Munro with a wave of his hand.

"Just the men I hoped to find," said the bailie,

who sounded not at all as though he planned to put them under arrest.

"Ye've got work for us?" Ned asked.

Munro dismounted. "Aye. Would ye care to be representatives of Her Majesty's government?"

"Like yerself?"

"No' so grand," he said with a strut. "But I need yer help w' a bit of trouble and the government is willing to pay."

George scratched his head. "The last time ye had us throw people off their land. They dinna want t' go."

"That was because of that devil Robert Cameron. He stirred them t' rebellion. 'Tis time we made him suffer fer it."

Annie sighed. Robert Cameron, always Robert Cameron. Would she never escape the brute? Still, it was a mark in his favor that he had enemies such as these.

Both Ned and George grinned. Annie saw they liked the idea of his suffering. She also saw they had bad teeth.

A flea bit a very private place. She jumped, ignoring Fitz's warning glance. The others took no note.

"Wot do we do?" Ned asked.

"How much do ye pay?" George asked.

"Take Cameron into custody," he said; then when the two men blinked, he translated, "Put him under arrest. He needs to feel the kiss of the whip."

"Ye'll beat him?"

"Aye." For which act, he added, he named a sum so low Annie would have laughed in his face, even given her current state of poverty.

"He'll no' be easy," said George.

"Between the two o' ye, he'll have little choice."

Ned puffed. "We've a horse now t' help in the work."

The bailie glanced at Gertie, then with a start gave her a closer look. "Whered ye get her?"

"Found 'er wandering in the woods."

Munro came closer to the mare. "'Tis the Irishman's horse, fer sure. Stolen these three days past."

"She's ours," both George and Ned growled.

Munro's flat face took on a crafty look. "Aye, bring Robert Cameron t' me, and she's yours." He reached for the reins. "In the meanwhile I'll keep 'er. One horse fer the two o' ye will only cause trouble. Ye need to concentrate on yer task."

The two set up a howling protest, stamping and arguing, and the bailie turned to bring some calm to them. Annie saw her chance. Standing, she whistled sharply. Gertie's head jerked, and, brave mare that she was, she came through the brush toward the summons.

Just as she'd done at the change-house, Annie leaped upon the mare's back, helped a surprised but willing Fitz scramble up behind her, and with a yell, circled, then galloped toward the three men, spooking the bailie's horse and riding on, letting out another yell to show her exhilaration. She kept to the trail for a while, then reined through the trees, twisting, turning, always heading away from the morning sun, so filled with excitement she forgot the fleas.

They rode for miles, how many Annie couldn't count, breaking into grassy meadows, galloping up and down glens. They rode until they came to the crest of a rise that overlooked Loch Lochy. A beautiful sight it was, glistening in the morning sunlight, on the near bank a blanket of grass so green it could have come from Ireland. On the far side a hundred yards away huge tumbled rocks lay close to the water's edge, and behind them were rising hills dotted with dark stands of pine.

Giving Gertie a rest, the two of them dismounted. Annie hugged herself in sheer joy, twirling round and round until she grew dizzy. She felt Fitz's eyes on her. She paused and saw the admiration she was used to seeing on the faces of lads she graced with her attention. It was about time.

Suddenly aware of how she must look, hair tangled, everything about her person soiled, she welcomed the admiration all the more.

He was a handsome lad, she admitted. A bit on the young side, certainly, and stocky, but pleasant enough. If he kept up with her, he'd lose the stockiness soon enough. The youthful part, too. Annie knew she could be hard on a lad.

Least, that's what Liam said.

"I'd kiss you," she said, "if I thought you knew how."

He took the insult poorly. The admiration died.

"I could kiss you well enough so that your toes would curl," he said. "If I had the urge."

She planted her hands on her hips. "And why wouldn't you? Am I so painful t' look at?"

"Nay. No' so long as I stay upwind of you. And don't be forgetting you've got fleas."

Annie had never been so insulted in her life. "If Liam O'Toole could hear you, you'd be sitting on your backside rubbing at a broken jaw."

"I'd like to see him try."

"Well, he would, and there're more lads who'd—"

She sputtered, so angry she couldn't tell him just how many they numbered or exactly what they would do.

She turned on her heel and tromped down the

incline toward the loch. Without looking back, she knew the lad and the horse followed, as they ought. Stumbling over a stone, she righted herself, along with her dignity, and kept to the march, not stopping until she came to the water's edge. Tugging off her boots, tossing her mantle aside, she continued walking, letting the low frigid waves strike like tiny picks against her stockings and the hem of her skirt, still walking until the water came to her waist, moving slowly now, the rocky bottom feeling none too comforting against her tender feet, the weight of the loch holding her back toward the land.

She stopped before the water got deeper, being not so angry she wanted to drown herself. The waves were icy cold against her; without considering the consequences, she dropped below the surface and came up shaking her wet hair.

The water around her turned brown, and when she saw dark flecks on the surface, she bade goodbye to the fleas.

At last the cold got to her. Her teeth chattered. Fitz came up beside her, looking just as shivery as she felt, despite the sun that was beginning to spread its warmth across the land. Having little mind to hear more affronts, she splashed him with water.

"Wha—" he said as she caught him right in the face.

"It's what you deserve for being so rude."

He splashed her right back.

"And you for being so cocky," he said.

The two of them commenced a hearty water fight, getting into the fray so completely they forgot to be angry or chilled, and in the process losing from their separate persons a pound or so of dirt and a few dozen fleas.

Quickening the pace of the fight, Annie lunged forward to shove him under the water, but she lost her footing and sank like a rock. She swallowed more water than she ought. Panic set in. She couldn't seem to find which way was up and which was down. Strong hands lifted her to the blessed air. She choked, unable to draw a breath. A strong fist hit her between the shoulder blades. She coughed and coughed before settling into a ragged kind of breathing.

Fitz took her in his arms. "You frightened the life out of me, lass."

She nodded against him, trying to say she'd been frightened, too. She rested her hands against his wet shirt. It was easy to feel his body, and personal, too. He was harder than he looked, more man than lad, and she took comfort from it, leaning against him longer than the situation required.

Then she didn't know quite how to back away. He must know she was enjoying the moment, which was the last thing she wanted. And why her heart was fluttering, she couldn't say. He lifted her chin and touched his mouth to hers. There wasn't much to the kiss, but it set up little tingles of pleasure inside her that were new to her experience.

She backed away. They looked at one another for a moment, then looked toward other points of interest, her to the distant hills, him to the sky.

"Race you to the shore," she yelled and took off as fast as the waist-high water would let her. She barely beat him; she suspected he let her.

As well he should, for stealing the kiss.

Squeezing the water from her hair and gown, she dropped to the dry grassy ground and stared up at the sky. Dark clouds formed in the distance, but overhead all was blue. Fitz lay on his back beside her and after a while he took her hand.

Neither spoke for a while. He didn't try to do more, nor did she wish him to. The moment seemed perfect just the way it was. They'd outsmarted three grown men with mischief on their minds, taken one horse and spooked another, and had a fine swim and fight. And there was, of course, the kiss. She couldn't forget the kiss.

That was probably because of the connection with his hand. It was like they were linked together. Not for long, she reminded herself. She had Ireland waiting, and Liam O'Toole.

The thought of the man she loved didn't thrill her as it ought, so she did what she always did when something troubled her. She put it from her mind.

She fell asleep. A cool breeze awakened her. The sun was high overhead, but the clouds were moving in fast, robbing the day of its warmth. She jiggled Fitz's shoulder. He sat up with a start.

"We're like to being dry," she said, running her fingers through her hair to separate the tangles. She must look a fright. The glint in his eyes said maybe she didn't. Annie smiled to herself. The admiration had returned.

She stood and shook out her skirt. "I've an idea."

Fitz rose beside her. "And when have you not?"

She liked him teasing her. She knew better what to say.

"I'm so hungry my ribs are rubbing against my backbone. Are you of a mind to find another goose?"

She waited for the lecture that was sure to come.

"Let's make it a chicken this time," he said. "They take less time to cook."

"Aye. 'Tis a bonnie idea."

217

She took a few steps down the hill, toward her boots and mantle lying by the water's edge, alongside Fitz's shoes and coat. She glanced at him over her shoulder. If there was one thing she knew, it was how to flirt.

"If you do the plucking, I'll show you how to kiss."

Chapter Seventeen

Edgar Gunn, High Sheriff of Darienshire, had need of a hanging.

Little else would call proper attention to the importance of his post.

He straightened his wig, smoothed his robe over his gaunt frame, and stroked the handle of the newly carved gavel that was his pride and joy. The symbols of office were his in appropriate splendor, if he overlooked a rent in the hem of the robe; the high bench behind which he was sitting was itself adequate, so far as high benches went. It was the quarters, two small rooms in front of a one-room lockup, that lacked the grandeur he deserved.

Little in the way of pronouncements or verdicts or sentencings awaited him late on this fine May day. In the past months few such acts of power had come his way, few smugglers apprehended, fewer thieves.

A hanging was definitely overdue.

He would let his haughty brother-in-law

Humphrey Sutherland hear of the accomplishment soon enough. Edgar knew himself to be far superior to Sutherland. His downtrodden sister Sophia, whom Humphrey had taken to wife twenty-five years past, must feel the same.

Edgar had Humphrey to thank for his limp, slight though it was and disguised by the robe. Too much wine at the wedding, too much forced celebration. He'd been thrown by his horse.

Damn the man. He'd sent his son to spy on him. "Make him a man," he'd written by way of instruction, "take him under your official wing." But Edgar couldn't be fooled.

Where his nephew was now, he didn't know for sure.

To find him, these two days past he'd ordered the bailie out on a search. It wouldn't do to let Humphrey learn he'd been misplaced, although, as far as Edgar was concerned, it was a relief to have the lad out from underfoot for a while.

With any luck Fitzroy was sequestered somewhere, becoming a man.

Thrusting Fitz from consideration and having little to do in the way of official business, he went back to his favorite subject, the hanging. And he knew just which victim would provide the greatest spectacle.

Robert Cameron.

No more than the thought of the hated name sent fury racing through him, the name and the fact that he was married now. At least word had it that the wedding had taken place, to a woman of riches. He'd seen her himself at the changehouse, though not up close, as she'd chosen to huddle against her husband, acting like the touch of another man would poison her fair skin. Edgar had been immediately suspicious. Something

220

about the pair suggested the marriage was not what it seemed.

He'd heard talk the bride was comely enough, but she'd acted more like a whore than a lady, accepting her husband's kiss readily enough for one and all to watch. Cameron received good fortune that he ill deserved.

Cameron! In mindless outrage, Gunn threw his gavel across the room. It broke against the wall and fell in pieces to the floor. It was another reason to hate the man.

The bastard would take a strong rope and a long drop to break his solid neck. But it could be done. The contemplation of the event soothed his rage. He was working on the particulars when Fergus Munro slammed into his office to present himself in front of the bench.

The bailie was a proud little man who more often than not o'erstepped his abilities, but he had one unfailing trait: his enthusiasm for seeing justice done without putting too fine a strain on the legality of method.

"Did ye find him?" Edgar asked.

Munro slapped at the dust on his coat and trousers, then wiped a sleeve across his sweaty brow. "Find who?"

Edgar sniffed in disgust. "My nephew, you dolt. Ye've been searching for him two days and nights, ha' ye no'?"

For once the bailie did not take offense at one of Edgar's insults.

"Aye, I traced him to the woods west of Buscar-Ban. 'Tis from there I've come riding hard t' bring ye the news."

"So where is he now?" asked Edgar, losing patience.

"When last seen, he was riding the stolen Irish

mare with a redheaded lass I've no' seen in these parts afore."

Becoming a *man*, thought Edgar, who doubted redheaded lassies had been in his brother-in-law's mind when he wrote the words.

"Ye let him go?"

"I had bigger game t' pursue." A sly smile stole onto Munro's flat face. "Who else would ye like t' find under yer power? Someone better than the lad."

"Cameron." Edgar's spirits lifted. "Ye've got the bastard?"

"Good as."

"What does that mean?"

"I've set two men on him."

Edgar's pleasure was short-lived. "Dinna be telling me it's Ned and George. I'd heard they were once again in the county."

"They're no' so bad."

Edgar snorted in disgust. "Have ye no' forgot two years past? They couldn't evict women and children when they had the chance."

"Only because Cameron returned when we thought he'd been killed in battle."

Edgar remembered those days with bitterness. With Cameron gone as part of Fraser's regiment and his father ill, the Crown had confiscated vast territorial riches in lieu of taxes. It had been the sheriff's task to get what money he could, by taking on a tacksman to supervise the taking of rents, best done from nonrebellious people, like the poor fools of Buscar-Ban.

And not like those of the Cameron clan. The laird had a cousin in particular who'd given them trouble. He'd needed subduing more than once when the tacksman had been at collecting rents.

If some of the hard-gathered coin failed to make

it to the Crown, such was the way of things in these turbulent times.

If some of that same coin remained with the sheriff, such was the way when a clever man like him was in power.

"And what is the charge against him?" the sheriff asked.

"The wearing of the kilt at his wedding."

"Bah! 'Tis no' a hanging offense."

"And assault on an officer of the law."

Edgar's impatience abated, and his already narrow eyes narrowed further. "Tell me more, Fergus."

The bailie preened under the sound of his name.

"He struck me down when I wasna looking. Before witnesses in Buscar-Ban. His wife was a witness, too, though she'd no' be willing t' testify, I suppose."

Edgar sat back in his chair and drummed his fingers on the bare surface of the high bench. "Describe her."

"He wouldna let me get much of a look, though she spoke up in as false a brogue as I've ever heard."

"Did she sound Irish?"

"She sounded like no one I've e'er heard afore."

"Surely ye got a glimpse of her. Was she young?"

"No' a child. A woman more'n a lassie."

Something was definitely wrong. Edgar felt it as strongly as he had that night at the change-house. The marriage was not right. For one thing, 'twas said far and wide the new lady of the land would be little more'n a child, yet Fergus claimed otherwise.

And there was the fact that Cameron had been gone from the keep these two days past, taking with him his bride. For what purpose? Certainly not for the stroll of Cameron lands, as he'd claimed outside the change-house. Nor for the chance to slake his lusts while others watched. If Edgar owned such a woman, she would be locked in his chamber and visited whenever he chose.

As to what he would do on those visits . . .

Edgar smiled. He preferred using women in unusual ways.

"I thought ye'd be pleased wi' the news."

The bailie's words brought him to the present. "I've little confidence in that pair of idiots you've hired."

"They've orders t' do what's necessary to bring Cameron in."

"What's necessary, eh?"

"Aye. An' if they fail, it can be only because Cameron has taken to violence against them. Being representatives of the Crown, they must be avenged, do ye no' agree?"

Again Edgar smiled. Twice in one hour was rare indeed. As rare as his bailie doing something right.

It was highly possible that the quick-tempered laird would continue to break the law, in a manner that would force the sheriff to call for assistance far more efficient and brutal than the bailie's George and Ned.

And if he did not? There were other ways to bring him to ruin. He'd already dispatched a letter to Glasgow, a letter that hinted of troubles Cameron could ill afford.

With a wave of his hand, Edgar dismissed Munro. As evening drew into night, he settled back to contemplate the sweetness of Robert Cameron's destruction, the return of the tacksman, the return of good times.

And the scowl on the face of his brother-in-law when he heard the news.

Chapter Eighteen

Meagan had little trouble passing the time while Robert was on his search. Swallowing the lump in her throat, she'd taken the drawing material Janet had promised and gone out to the grounds where members of the Cameron clan worked, past the stable built into the twelve-foot-thick wall, past a cobbler's shop, a blacksmith, and others she could not name.

No one approached, but they were curious enough—men and women both—to stare at her in silence. She'd smiled, but in their taciturn Scottish way, obviously—and rightly—sensing something was amiss in their laird's new marriage, they had not smiled in return.

How different was their reception from the raucous greetings she'd met with on that fateful wedding day.

Never comfortable with strangers, she'd found herself a shady spot on the grass close to the keep, one that offered a good view of the castle ruins, the wall, and the stone gate, and, wrapped in the plaid she'd brought with her across the centuries, she'd thrown herself into her work.

Occasionally she heard the sound of voices, Robert's people speaking among themselves, but their thick brogue and low tones kept her from understanding a word they said. More than ever she felt like the interloper that she was.

Once she could have sworn she saw the boy Jamie peer around one of the castle walls, but he disappeared so quickly she wasn't sure. She wanted to call to him, to say she understood his running from Ned and George. For all his street-smart ways, he was still just a boy. But she had no chance and, in his absence, feeling lonelier still, she threw herself into her task.

She spent the next day in much the same pursuit, driven indoors by an afternoon rain. By candlelight, with the scroll of paper spread out on the long table in the great hall, she put the finishing touches to her work. She'd always been good at drawing; no artist except with words, she nevertheless had a good eye for a straight line and a sense of perspective.

Perspective in other ways would do her good, she told herself when she thought of Robert's circumstances. He must find Annie MacSorley. He must.

Just as she must never make love with him again. Honor, morals, her sense of decency told her so.

She slept late the next morning, troubled by a restless night. Janet woke her with the announcement that her husband had returned.

"He awaits ye below."

"Alone?"

Janet nodded. "The lass eludes him yet."

Shamelessly, silently, Meagan rejoiced, then

lectured herself for being so selfish. In all things she must be circumspect, especially physical concerns. She could not leave carrying the burden of memories she would forever regret.

Tucking her work at the back of the wardrobe, she struggled to put on another of the true bride's dresses, combed her tangled hair without giving more than a second's thought to her blow-dryer and brush, and with a pounding heart descended the stairs, slowly, to see what disasters awaited her.

She had no doubt there would be a minimum of one or two. The only point in question concerned their magnitude.

Big, she thought, when she found Robert waiting for her at the table in the large hall one floor below, skin the color of polished bronze against his open-throated saffron shirt, his brown eyes gleaming like those fireplace embers in the bedchamber hearth.

Enormous, she amended when he stood in all his masculine magnificence to greet her, looking as if he planned to throw her over his shoulder and carry her back upstairs.

Gigantic, she decided when he strode to her side and took her in his arms, rendering her speechless and stunned.

When he kissed her, she quit coming up with adjectives or arguments about leaving with honor and thought only of him.

Having waited days for this moment, Robert put all he could into kissing his bride. Tall though she was, she felt slender and slight as she leaned her body into his. The feel of her breasts against his chest, the touch of her tongue against his ignited a raging fire in his loins.

227

What fine, long legs she had, and magnificently strong thighs, for all their lack of girth. Remembering how they'd wrapped around him in his bed, he considered taking her on the table. In truth, there would be none to say nay.

He cupped her buttocks and held her hard against him to let her know of his arousal. It seemed she clung to him with desperate need, and when she moaned, the flames within him raged higher.

And then he let her go, surprising the pair of them, he was sure. This lass from another time deserved better than a mounting such as he envisioned. He cursed his conscience, and the hard, sharp pain of denial, but still he let her go.

No longer could he call Meagan his almost-bride; temporary bride, sad to say, but bedded bride beyond doubt, which made her both official and more precious to him. With a wife a man had responsibilities. He'd forgotten it as they rode through the woods, when he'd failed to guard her properly; he wouldn't forget it again.

As he stood back, his hands trembling like a woman's against her narrow waist, his body holding on to the pain and not the pleasure, he managed a smile, expecting a similar expression of welcome on her face.

Instead he saw darkness in the depths of her violet eyes, and while he wanted to credit lust for the reaction, he feared another cause. She hungered for him, yet she could not rejoice to see him return.

At least, she could not rejoice to see him return alone.

"You rode without me," she said.

"You had a need for rest."

"After the night in the wild, you mean."

And an afternoon with him in bed. The blush that darkened her cheeks gave proof she shared his thoughts.

Her rest was not all that motivated his leaving without her, since her participation in finding the MacSorley lass had come to an end with the Dundas twins.

"Annie has the luck of the Irish," he said.

"She got away."

"Though she seems to ride in circles, the occasional rain obliterated her tracks."

No need to say he might have pursued her further, but a dark-haired vixen lured him back to the keep. Revealing such a weakness would be wrong for them both. She would think he cared for her in improper ways; caring for Meagan Butler was something he could scarce afford.

"She's in the county?" Meagan asked.

"Aye. I've men in pursuit. She'll no' escape for long."

"Good."

He heard scant enthusiasm in her reply. He allowed himself to hope that lust drove her as it was driving him, that the pain of denial burned equally hot in her loins. In this strange bond that they shared, lust was all that they could share. It would have to be enough.

He would have her tell him so when he embraced her another time.

For now, sensing her distress came not because she'd missed him nor even because he'd ridden without her, he sought other, more plausible causes. The subtleties of women were ofttimes too much for him; he sought the reason in the obvious, by considering how she had come to him on this beautiful morn, striding into the hall with a confident step, easing back when she caught sight of him, watching his approach with a mixture of pleasure and apprehension she could ill disguise.

He stepped back for a more thorough perusal. Dull witted he could be about the complexity of womanhood, but he recognized a wrong-sized gown when he saw it. 'Twas something his first bride would not have tolerated. He doubted such displeasure would change in two centuries.

"You're in need of clothes," he said, proud he'd settled so quickly on the problem, yet irritated because it had nothing to do with sex.

Her frown said he'd done something wrong.

He tried to make amends. "Mayhap you'd rather have none on a'tall. If so, the disrobing can be quickly done."

Meagan shook her head.

"Robert, Robert, Robert," she said with what sounded far too much like disgust. "You look good enough and you kiss adequately. All right, the kiss was more than adequate, and you look more than just good, but you don't know the first thing about what to say to a woman."

"I'll not take offense, lass, since two of your three observations are compliments."

She started to speak. He held up a silencing hand.

"As to the third, since my return to the Highlands these two years past, I've become dedicated to the improvement of self as well as property. Teach me what I should say."

"That's ridiculous."

"You've an understanding of words, have you no'? So you led me to believe when last we were together."

"Not a complete understanding. I know enough to get by."

She brushed her hair behind her ears. He noticed the fingernails were no longer pink, no longer smooth. The encounters in the woods, mayhap the encounter in her bed, had faded the color and smoothness away.

Or had she been engaged in physical pursuits during his absence? Janet had said she'd whiled her time between the grounds and her room, but sometimes, unless specifically instructed otherwise, his housekeeper did not choose to tell him the truth.

He led Meagan by the hand to the table. Gesturing to a chair, he sat across from her but he did not release her hand, not until Janet had set porridge, barley bread, and a cup of tea in front of her.

"Tell me about this work you do, this use of words by which you earn your keep."

"You're not going to understand."

He shrugged in confidence, but she proved herself prophetic, eating a while, talking a while, describing tasks that were beyond his ken in a field of endeavor called advertising. Trying to concentrate, attempting to forget the way her hair glistened like black silk caught beneath a full moon, he took in what she said, tried to make sense of it, but could hold his silence only so long.

"You draw pretty pictures and create fancy words to make lads and lassies long for what they do no' have."

He'd meant the assessment to be critical, but she gave no sign she took it in such a way.

"That's about it. I don't do the actual drawing, of course. We have artists and draftsmen and computers for that."

"Computers?"

"That's a lesson for another time."

"And these pretty pictures and teasing words

are printed and sent across the land in hopes that those who see them will spend money on fine objects they dinna need nor want."

"They want them if the advertising is good enough. You should know that not all the objects are fine. It's up to the words and pictures to make them seem so."

Worse and worse, he thought. "This advertising does no' always present the truth?"

"Not always."

"False claims are made."

"Not exactly. We've laws against outright lies, so we get our message across by association. We show the products used by beautiful women and virile men, all very happy, very contented, very proud. The implication is that the product itself makes them beautiful and virile, even if what we're selling is a brand of soap."

Robert slapped the table in disgust. "Building cloud-castles for the poor souls, that's what you do. 'Tis no more honorable than a tacksman collecting unconscionable rents."

"Not true," she answered with equal force. "The people understand the lies. They want to believe them. Belief gives them hope."

"Bah! What if the wanting exceeds a man's ability to pay? What then does he do?"

"Sometimes he borrows, that is if he wants something bad enough."

"He goes into debt?" Robert said, thinking the manner of this advertising worsened with each added detail.

"Everybody's in debt in the twentieth century. We've something called credit cards that let you keep borrowing as long as you pay a little bit each month on what you owe."

Robert shook his head in disgust. He'd borrowed money from the Glasgow bank based on his good name and the reputation of Camerons before him and, most of all, the expectation of an advantageous marriage. This credit card allowing more and more borrowing seemed like a dangerous thing indeed.

Better to stake one's future on the turn of a playing card, as men had done since long before Robert's birth.

"I dinna believe I'd care for this twentieth century. Unless there are fulsome dowries sufficient for the demand."

"There are no dowries. Besides, women borrow as much as men."

The thought left Robert speechless.

But not for long. He was about to explain why women should have little borrowing power when his cousin strode into the hall. Cleaned up like himself from their two-day ride, Colin ignored his scowl, turning his smile onto his laird's new lady, his long, strong legs, encased in tight-fitting trews, taking him to her side, where he might give her a thorough study.

His grin spread from ear to ear.

"'Tis little wonder ye called short our search. Unlike the lass we seek, she's no' a child, Robert, but a woman full grown. One to make any man proud. And ye took her on yer few days together frolicking about the countryside. The pair o' ye shoulda remained at the keep in bed."

Meagan looked from one man to the other and back again. "He must be related. Not only do you resemble one another, he knows equally little about tact."

"The difference between Colin and myself is that I can be taught. My cousin's dense as day-old porridge."

233

Ignoring the insult, Colin introduced himself and kissed the back of Meagan's offered hand.

"Where would you be learning such as that?" asked Robert, none too pleased that his bride did not pull her hand away.

"I've been to Edinburgh, well as ye. Though I've little use for Lowlanders as a rule, their ways are no' entirely bad." Again he turned his attention on Meagan. "I've little reason to give offense, nor wish t' do so. I'd heard ye were a comely lass, and 'tis so. Such is the only message I bring t' ye on this fine morn."

Meagan smiled. Smiled! At Colin, when she'd scarce given him civil words this morning after their very torrid afternoon, then two days of separation.

"I have no wish for anything other than compliments, Colin. May I call you that?"

"Aye, ye may," the cousin said, but his expression of pleasant surprise was tempered with bemusement. "Robert tells a strange tale of yer arrival. I've scarce given it credence, but 'tis clear ye're no' from the northern shore of Ireland. Ye sound like no Irish lass I've ever met."

"Sit, mon," said Robert, "and tell her what I've said. You'll hear from her very own lips I've no' told a lie."

Which didn't mean he'd told the entire truth. He'd spoken little during the hard-riding days, saying what he had to say, concentrating on the task before him, which was finding a runaway lass. Colin had sensed the urgency of the situation and put few questions to him, though Robert knew his cousin doubted much of what he had said.

If Meagan was of a mind to reveal all, she'd find Colin a difficult man to convince.

234

"Did you tell him about my deafness?" Meagan asked, her fine eyes wide with pretended innocence.

The lass wanted kissing, that she did.

And more.

He glanced at Colin. "'Tis but a jest between us."

Janet entered to serve tea while Robert waited impatiently for what was to follow.

"He told me ye were no' the bride I believed ye to be," Colin began. "I in turn said few o' them are. But ye"—he gave her another perusal—"should arouse other than complaints."

Meagan gave no reaction, other than to sit back in her chair, hands folded in her lap, and settle a watchful gaze on her husband.

Robert smiled. "I'm no' complaining. What I said, if you'll but recall, was that she's no' the Irish bride I was promised."

Colin shook his head. "I'll scarce be finished by the lamplighting hour if you continue to interrupt."

"Continue then. I'll keep to silence."

Colin went on to relate with close to accuracy all that he'd been told, that Meagan had come from Glasgow, and before that the colonies far across the ocean, but difficulties in travel had sent her to the kirk at the wrong time on the wrong day. Separated from her fellow travelers, she'd been seeking help, but with her name being Meagan, in the confusion of her arrival she'd somehow ended up as his bride.

"Since the right Meagan-Anne MacSorley had chosen to flee her responsibilities," Robert put in, "and this lass, covered from head to toe with a Cameron plaid, seemed no' to ken where she was."

"So ye said. But how could—" Colin stopped, then started over. "Dinna ye—"

Evelyn Rogers

Again he paused and scratched his head. "Do ye
take me for a looby lad, Coz? Yer story sounded
daft enough as we rode along, but in the woods
with the goblins and spirits hovering about, it
seemed possible. Now I'm no' so sure."

"I've told you nary a lie." He looked to Meagan
for affirmation. "Tell him. He's more like to believe you than me."

She shook her head. "You'd make a good ad
writer, Robert." And then to Colin. "He has not
lied. In the kirk I truly did become confused.
Crazy as it sounds, I heard the name Meagan and
said 'I do' without knowing quite what it meant.
It's the true bride you've been following, the one
who ought to be here now."

"So I was told," Colin said, frowning in disbelief,
but he refrained from calling the new lady of the
land a liar, as he clearly wished to do. Instead he
drummed his fingers on the table. "He claims t'
have learned of the mistake when he carried ye t'
the keep."

"And so I did," Robert said. "She had scant inclination to participate in the consummation."

"She's changed her mind about the matter, has
she no'? She has the look about her of a woman
who's been loved."

As answer Robert chose a discretionary silence,
in preference to the enthusiastic *aye* he wished to
give.

Meagan rolled her eyes. "Would you two like me
to leave so that you can get down to the details?"

Robert grinned. "I'm developing a fondness for
your sarcasm, wife, though it's taken a while."

"I guess I'll have to resort to temper tantrums."

"You can try it once. I'll allow ye that."

"Allow!"

"Dinna be using up the one time too soon."

A fine-spirited creature she was, Robert decided as he watched her fight to control her irritation. 'Twas clear from the expression on his face Colin enjoyed the watching as well.

If they were alone he would explore this matter of anger further, as well as the other powerful emotions it could arouse. He'd missed her more than he expected. For the first time in memory, with his blood pulsing hotly in his veins, he found his closest cousin and best friend decidedly in the way.

Reluctantly he drew his eyes away from his wife and turned them to Colin.

"You see the difficulties this causes. 'Twas why we had to ride so hard, and why our failure came bitterly."

"Aye. The dowry."

"For an uneducated man, you've a quick mind."

"For an educated man, ye've got the same."

It was an old form of teasing that showed the affection existing between them, neither taking offense.

"I believe ye, hard though it be," Colin said. "'Tis truly the MacSorley lass we've been searching for, riding a stolen horse, her companion the nephew to Edgar Gunn." He whistled. "I've seen matted sheep wi' fewer tangles."

"Well said. As you can see, I've a need to keep the matter private until the problem can be resolved."

"As to the how of it, I canna guess what ye've got in mind."

"I've asked for the trust of those who dwell on Cameron land, and their help and discretion as much as they can give. They're bound to question my actions of late, and the woman who is little like the new mistress they had long heard described. To that end I put a question to you before we parted at the cistern these two days past. Have ye received word of the answer?"

"The matter of the informant's identity, ye mean. I came to report the mystery is solved. While in the alehouse at Darien, our very own Sandy MacLean, cobbler to all Camerons, was heard to boast about yer bravery in wearing the kilt. Little wonder Fergus Munro learned of the crime. I've talked with Sandy this hour past. He'll no' be making the same mistake again."

"Still, the damage is done. And now Munro has against me the added charge of assault. He'll no' try to arrest me here at Thistledown; his way is to catch me when I'm unarmed."

"Which ye ne'er are."

"Never have been, more t' say."

All the while they spoke, he felt his wife's eyes on him and sensed her growing distress. It was the brief scuffle with the bailie that had sent her running from him, blaming herself for his troubles. Wrong though she was in the matter, he liked her attitude.

He liked, too, the hint of tenderness he saw in her eyes when she thought he was not looking. Brief it was, but it was new to her. He liked it far too much.

"I'd learn more of the Dundas twins," said Colin, speaking once again to Meagan. "If ye've a mind t' tell me."

"Ned and George?" Meagan asked. "Is that their name?"

"Aye," said Robert. "Like Colin, I'd hear more of your encounter. Afore we parted you mentioned setting one of them afire."

Colin grinned, and even Meagan managed a small smile. Briefly she told of being accosted by the pair "while on a stroll." While Robert appreciated her attempt to hide the trouble between them, he knew Colin would see the truth.

In an attempt to bribe the brothers, she said, she'd offered them a prize she thought she carried with her.

"It turned out to be a worthless rock," she said, all trace of a smile replaced by a frown of remembered trouble.

Robert avoided her censorious eye.

"I kicked one of them," she continued. "Their lamp spilled into the leaves, and he got caught in the fire. That was when I took off across the stream and hid in the tree where you found me."

Colin stifled a cough. "These two days past, Coz, I've heard no mention of this tree."

Robert ignored him. "And the lad who guided you through the woods. You made mention of him, too."

"He'd disappeared by that time."

"You called him Jamie. Are you claiming he appeared like a benevolent goblin to do your bidding?"

She cleared her throat. "I'd rather not say any more."

"No need. He's the lad you fed in Buscar-Ban, returning what he supposed to be a favor."

"Maybe. Maybe not. But should he turn up again I would like your promise not to hurt him in any way."

Robert felt Colin's eyes darting back and forth as though he watched the tossing of a ball, but he was little inclined to explain all of what his wife said.

He nodded solemnly to her. "You have my word." He turned to Colin. "Before the problems with Munro can be resolved, we must find our pair of runaways."

"Aye, that we must."

"Annie's a slippery one, for all her youth. If we learned little these past two days, we saw the truth of that. Had us running in circles, that she did."

"And the lad who rides with her. If he's aught like his rascally uncle, she may already have come to harm."

Robert shook his head in disgust. "I owe her my protection, though she cares not to share my name."

"A tangle," said Colin with a shrug of his broad shoulders. "They've not gone far, circling as they have. Heading west they were, when we lost their trail. I'll return t' the search this very day."

"What about the Great Glen and the lochs?" Meagan put in. "Won't that stop them?"

Both men looked at her.

"It was just a thought," she said, twisting a curl of hair behind one ear.

"The MacSorley lass little knows the extent of the barrier," Robert explained, "and I doubt Fitzroy Sutherland understands any more."

"I was thinking—" Meagan began.

Before she could continue, a woman entered the great hall bearing an armload of woolen cloth in shades of purple and lavender.

"Ermengarde," Robert said, none too pleased to see his former mistress.

A buxom widow close to his age, she boasted a mass of fiery, untamed hair and a lustful nature to match. To keep her skillful hands occupied, he'd asked her to supervise the use of the spinning wheels he distributed among the crofters' wives.

"Janet said I shouldna hesitate t' join ye," she said.

Robert remembered distinctly asking the housekeeper to tell all that the bridal couple could not be disturbed, even during his absence. The trouble with Scots was they had minds of their own.

Ermengarde glided to the table in the hip-swinging manner he'd been wont to admire, dropped the wool in front of him, and with hands on hips, bosom thrust close to his face, said, "I've come to display me wares, laird, since I've not seen ye these few days past."

She leaned close, and the top of her blouse fell loose. Robert had only to lower his gaze to see the dark tips he remembered from days and nights past.

He kept his attention on her face. He had no interest in her ample figure; of late, he preferred more subtle shapes.

"I'll look at them later," he said, meaning the cloth.

Colin sputtered in poorly suppressed laughter, while his bride just sat and watched, her eyes the color of the darkest wool.

It would seem he was in need of more instruction from the silver tongue of his wife.

Before he could make amends, Janet entered, followed by a nattily dressed man he knew all too well, the last person in the world he cared to see. The housekeeper must have decided to bring him to ruin; he saw no other explanation for her disobedience.

He stood and extended a reluctant hand. "Mr. Balfour," he said. "Welcome to Thistledown." He turned to Meagan. "Love," he said, a warning glint in his eye, "this is Thomas Balfour, family friend to be sure, and representative of my Glasgow bank."

Chapter Nineteen

Meagan opened her mouth to say hello.

"Dear heart," Robert said, his voice thick with brogue, "dinna be putting a strain on yer voice."

He smiled indulgently at her, then turned to the banker. "Caught in the rain, she was, when we were on a ride to observe Cameron land. I fear she has a bad throat. I've been telling her she ought to remain in bed, but—"

He shrugged as if there were no explaining women.

Banker . . . mortgage . . . dowry. Putting them together, Meagan saw the need for subterfuge. Feeling more than ever like the fraud she was, she tried to smile sweetly back at him and look ill at the same time. Both Colin and Ermengarde gave her a sympathetic nod.

"Ye know me cousin Colin Cameron, do ye no'? And this fair lass be the weaver of the fine cloth you see before you, Ermengarde Drummond. We were inspecting her work as ye arrived."

"What a pleasant gathering," Thomas Balfour observed wryly.

What a bunch of liars, Meagan thought.

In appearance the banker was unlike the men she'd seen thus far, from the short, curly red hair brushed back from his clean-shaven face to the high-heeled shoes and white stockings. He wore a blue wool frock coat trimmed with gold frogs and braid, an ecru waistcoat and white ruffled shirt, and dark breeches that fastened well below the knees. His gloved hand gripped a cord-trimmed brown felt hat.

He seemed very much the town gentleman, more English than Scottish, though she'd picked up the hint of a brogue in his few words. He was also rather handsome, by Meagan's standards, with even features, deep-set green eyes, and a firm chin. His complexion was far paler than that of Robert or his cousin, or even Ermengarde. Obviously he spent much of his time indoors.

He was, in short, the sort of man who might have appealed to her—before Robert, of course. The Highlander had changed her in this and in a thousand other ways.

With a nod to the others, Balfour bowed from the waist in her direction. "Please accept my disappointment at your affliction. I'd hoped to talk with you of your homeland, to which I have oft traveled. The north of Ireland is, most especially, a favorite place of mine."

Something about his tone alerted her suspicion that he wasn't entirely sincere. For a change, she appreciated one of her husband's lies.

Gesturing to her throat, she fluttered her hands helplessly, as if she would chatter away about the dear old Emerald Isle if she only could.

Colin and Ermengarde continued to smile

Evelyn Rogers

benignly, though there was a hint of real humor in Colin's dark eyes and a trace of grudging respect in Ermengarde's.

Robert offered tea. "Or perhaps whiskey," he said, sounding as if he would like a cup of the latter.

"Neither. I've come about business. Is there someplace we can talk?"

For all his natty appearance, Thomas Balfour sounded like every banker Meagan had ever met. There was a harshness, too, in his voice that boded little good.

Asking to be excused, Robert escorted him to the side room opening off the great hall. It was, as she recalled, the well-stocked library. The door closed. The three in the hall stared in silence at one another. Nervously Meagan glanced at the wool Ermengarde had brought for her laird to inspect. At least, it was the excuse she'd used to get inside the keep.

"Trouble," Colin said, his eyes on the closed door.

"Aye," Ermengarde said.

The two words managed to make Meagan feel on the outside, a stranger, someone who didn't belong. Beyond reason or common sense, the realization hurt more than usual. Of course Robert had trouble, she wanted to say. When did he have anything else?

She stared down the length of the hall, past the closed-off room where Robert met with his banker, past other doors, past the alcoves, along the wooden floor, up the stone walls to the lanterns hanging on iron standards, to a lone chandelier whose hundred empty candleholders spoke of grander days long ago.

In modern times the keep was closed to the pub-

244

lic, used for storage and apartments for the Thistledown Castle staff. When she returned, she would ask for a private tour.

When she returned. The words made her shiver. *If* perhaps more than *when,* but only because the incantation might not work. She rubbed at her arms. Despite the long sleeves, her borrowed gown was made of too light a wool to keep her really warm.

"Where do ye come from?" Ermengarde asked.

The question caused her to start, and she saw that both the Scots were regarding her with uncommon care.

"If it's Ireland," the woman continued, "I'll eat me cloth."

Meagan looked to Colin for help.

"Tell her what ye told me. It's what Robert would have ye do."

"I don't know—"

"Ermengarde," Colin said, "swear on yer late husband's grave ye'll not repeat what ye hear."

The woman gave Meagan a thorough inspection, taking in most especially the ill fit of her gown. "I swear. I'll no' go havering about it no matter what she says. Unless our laird tells me t' do otherwise." Her green eyes glinted. "I allus behave as he wants."

Meagan matched her stare for stare. "I'm sure that you do." She looked at Colin. "I'll wait."

"Has he got ye so flummoxed ye canna speak wi'out he be near?" Colin's expression was friendly enough, as was the sound of his voice, and Meagan knew he meant no harm.

"The matter is complicated, that's all. You know it. You've heard the story yourself."

She could read the sharp curiosity in Ermengarde's expression, and the admiring amusement in Colin's. Suddenly she could abide their scrutiny no longer. Pushing from the table, she mumbled something about needing fresh air, hurried down the last flight of stairs that led past the storage rooms, and walked into a glorious day.

The glory contrasted with the sense of dread that lay within her heart. In any century, bankers had a way of spreading gloom.

Despite the sun, she still felt a chill. As if she could read her mind, the housekeeper appeared with a full-length cloak in her arms.

She thrust it into Meagan's hands. "No need t' catch a true illness. 'Tis heavy enough t' keep ye warm."

"Thank you," Meagan said. "How did you know I wanted exactly this?"

The tall, formidable woman looked past her to the ruins of the castle. "I know many things. I have the gift."

"The gift?"

"Of sight. I see into a person's heart. Into his past, his present, and what lies ahead. 'Tis why I told ye all that I did."

Meagan's heart quickened. "You saw something for me? Something concerning Robert?" Foolishly, she let her spirits rise.

Janet's dark eyes took on a still darker cast. "'Tis no' for me t' say."

Meagan let out a long breath. "In other words, nothing good."

"If ye're strong enough, all will be well."

It was obvious the woman's loquaciousness of two days before had disappeared. Before another question could be put to her, she turned and disappeared inside the keep, leaving Meagan to the blue sky and the brisk wind, and the curious stares of a half dozen Cameron men and women at work on the castle grounds.

Nothing had changed for her over the past days except that she knew a little of what they'd suffered. Not that they would care for her sympathy.

More than ever she felt like a freak. How could she have entertained for one fleeting second the question about whether her marriage to Robert might work? She was here because of some fluke in the universe, the butt of a cosmic prankster's joke.

She threw the dark green cloak over her shoulders; its warmth enfolded her like central heat, but it brought no comfort. Like her borrowed dress it was part of the costume she wore for her role as Robert Cameron's stand-in wife. So, too, were the wedding clothes she had allowed the modern-day housekeeper to provide her, the skirt and blouse and length of plaid wool. Costumes all, and she was playing a part.

Even the part of loving fiancée, she saw all too clearly. What she felt for William was nothing compared to what Robert aroused, and she meant far more than just incredible sex.

She looked to the right, to the kirk with its promise of a return to home; she looked to the left, to the castle ruins that promised hope for Robert's future; she looked to the keep, where he met with the man who could bring him to bankruptcy.

Last, she looked inside her heart. Janet warned her to be strong. Strong enough to leave? Strong enough to stay? Her heart gave her the answer. Stay, it had to be. She made her way to the ruins.

Sometime later, she had no idea how long, Robert found her scrambling over the interior stones on the second floor, moving in and out of the shadows cast by the high, jagged walls, staring to where another floor and the roof should have been, going over her secret drawings, deciding where she needed to make a change.

"Most of the inside is still intact," she said, brightly, crisply, from her perch atop the tumbled rocks. She hoped he didn't catch in her voice the breathy nervousness that the sight of him evoked.

"You have an optimistic way of looking at the matter."

She heard no sign of tension in his words, but only the ever-present deep strength and shrewdness and masculinity.

"I'm not discounting any of the loss." She looked away, fearful that if she kept staring down at him she would make a swan dive into his arms. "Everything's been rebuilt by my time." Her voice trailed off at the end of her declaration. *My time* was a time that didn't exist.

"So you said."

Hearing herself blather, unable to stop, she went on to describe the restored castle as she had seen it, the great hall, the sweeping stairway, the upper rooms, the landscaped grounds as she had drawn them. He stood quietly, and she couldn't tell if he listened or not.

"It makes a grand bed-and-breakfast," she said, then saw she had to explain the concept to him. All the while he simply watched her, as if waiting for her to say something he wanted to hear.

What that could be, she didn't know, and she fell silent.

"You didn't leave."

She caught her breath. "The kirk, you mean."

"I feared after my return you would do so."

"It seemed wrong to run out while you were with Thomas Balfour. What did he want?"

"Money."

"That's what I was afraid of."

"He hinted of rumors in Glasgow that our marriage is not what it should be."

"How would he know?"

"I fear our high sheriff has a part in the tale. Suspicious though he might be, Balfour's given me more time."

Time to find her replacement. The words were almost visible in the air that separated them.

"Can't you just give him the dowry? Isn't it enough to clear the debt?"

"'Tis more than ample, but it's no' yet mine to give."

Something in his voice gave her pause, and a foolish, impossible sense of joy. He spoke as if he did not want the money, as if to use it would seal a fate he did not choose.

How glorious he looked at the moment, standing with legs slightly apart, the sun falling golden upon his rugged face. Glorious and powerful and able to take on all the troubles that he faced.

If only it were so.

"Has Balfour gone?" she asked.

"Colin is riding with him as guide to the improvements we're making."

"And Ermengarde?"

She hadn't meant the question to sound so sharp.

"Returned to her cottage."

"Where—"

"I want you, Meagan."

Her breath stopped. She had no trouble understanding him; her problem came in not telling him the same thing.

"You'd take me to your bed?"

"Nay. I want you here and now."

"Outside? With no roof over our head?"

"We'll no' be disturbed." He took a step onto the stones.

She held up a hand, but he took another step.

"We can't." Dismay and hunger and eagerness roiled inside her, so much she could put little force behind her words. It was mostly the hunger that she felt.

"'Tis no' the words to say to a Cameron."

"But it's not honorable," she said, the protest sounding feeble even to her ears. "You belong to someone else, and so do I."

"Why did you no' make the attempt to leave while I've been gone? What's changed from the day in the woods?"

"I'm . . . interested in how things turn out for you."

"And nothing more?"

"Leaving now would be like putting down a book before I finished reading it."

Meagan thought the last an inspired response. The glint in Robert's eye told her he was not so impressed.

"I'm like a book to you." He was close to her now, his steps steady on the bank of fallen stones. When he took her by the hand, she did not, could not, pull away. "Strange books you have in this twentieth century of yours."

Splaying her free hand against his chest, she felt his heartbeat beneath the saffron shirt. She felt, too, her body grow warm and pulsing and damp for the same thing that she read in his eyes.

Being close to Robert like this, touching him in less than intimate ways, was more erotic than anything she had ever experienced in her life. He couldn't possibly want her more than she wanted him.

What had happened to her wishes? her ethics?

her honor? Empty words without heat or meaning. Robert was her all. He had suffered beyond all belief, he was pushed, he was threatened by forces and circumstances beyond his control. She could not make too much of the session with Thomas Balfour, nor its effect on him. And what did he do? He dispatched those closest to him, people of his own time and land, and he came for her.

He made her feel powerful, important, desired. That must suffice for feeling loved.

With a cool breeze ruffling her hair and the sun shining bright in the sky, she bent her head to kiss him. Lightly, and then not so lightly.

He slipped his arms inside her cloak and held her close, returning the kiss. He broke away long enough to whisper, "Open your mouth," and when she did she felt his tongue dance against hers and his hands stroke lower until he cupped her buttocks and held her hard against him. Eyes closed against the harshness of the day, she slipped into the velvet darkness of a make-believe night.

All of this was make-believe. But his kiss and his hands and his tongue were all too real. As was her love. Less than a week with him and she was altered beyond return, no matter the century in which she lived.

Meagan was pragmatic enough to take what she could while she could, and too much in love to care about the consequences. Right and wrong had no meaning for her; joining herself to Robert had become her everything.

She threw herself into the kiss with all her strength and all her heart. He groaned when her tongue invaded his mouth, and his hands eased up the skirt and petticoat until he pressed his palms against the flesh of her thighs. Clever fingers found the elastic of her panties; she heard him groan again. While she clung to him, he fondled her buttocks, her thighs, fingers stroking between her legs until she went a little mad.

He tugged at the panties; they fell to the ground. Lifting her into his arms, he managed to scoop them up and thrust them inside his open-throated shirt, then nimbly stride down the pile of rocks and stone, carrying her to the shadows that fell across one of the castle walls.

With the little bit of mind left to her, she thought he'd lay her on the hard floor. Instead he stood with his back close to the wall, bunched her clothing around her waist, and, as if she weighed no more than a leaf of heather, lifted her until her legs could wrap around his waist, then lowered her so that her wet, pulsing sex pressed against his erection. He rubbed her up and down; the feel of his wool trousers against her throbbing body drove her wild.

"Now, Robert, now," she ordered, hugging him with arms and legs, running her tongue against the salty warmth of his neck, tasting him and wanting him and wishing she could put her lips and tongue everywhere on his body all at once.

With dexterous speed he unfastened his trousers, freeing himself, giving her what she needed as he lowered her onto his shaft.

The effect was electric. She came at once, and with no more than a thrust or two so did he. She used her inner muscles to hold him inside her as long as she could, kissing his neck, his ear, his eyes, his cheek, his lips. This was what mating was all about, this joining and sharing and loving and wanting, even as the tingles of satisfaction faded and gave rise to the bite of hunger once again.

This was the way sex was meant to be. No book could describe it. Only Robert could make it real.

And Robert belonged to someone else.

Meagan tried to feel shame, but she failed.

Failed until Robert eased his sex from hers, let her skirts fall between them, set her away from him so that she stood with only her hands touching his shoulders and his hands holding her lightly at the waist.

Letting go of her long enough to refasten his trousers, he took her by the waist once again, murmured something in Gaelic, and kissed her gently, sweetly, almost forlornly, as if he were telling her good-bye.

Then he said the words she would remember the rest of her life.

"I have to find her. God help me, I dinna want to, but I must."

She saw herself as he must see her, a trollop from another time, sent to soothe him while he found his true forever bride.

Was she too harsh on the both of them? Perhaps, and then again, perhaps not. She lifted her hands from him and curled her hair behind her ears, her fingers shaking, her insides hollow except for her pounding heart. Despite her best intentions, she gazed at his hair and skin that in the shadows seemed the same coppery color, at the chocolate brown eyes, at the lean line of his jaw, the tempting lips, the strong neck, the cluster of dark hairs at his throat.

The odor of sex hung in the air between them. She tasted him on her tongue.

She felt, too, the dampness he'd left between her legs, and she thought again of bearing his child. Why did she never think of the danger before they made love? It seemed as if she wanted his baby, as if she could leave more easily if she had a part of him to take with her.

Wrong thinking, she told herself, and unfair to him, to her, and most of all to the child.

But pregnancy was only a possibility. Reacting to his need for Annie was all too real. She managed a smile. Oh, how tough she was, how strong, and so brittle that if he embraced her again she would surely break.

"I know you have to find her."

A bird cawed overhead; did Scotland have crows? She knew so little about this land.

She rubbed her palms against the sides of her cloak. "I also know we can't do this again."

He started to speak. She held up a hand.

"I agreed to stay until all was made right here. I will honor that agreement. All I ask is that we be friends."

He laughed sharply. "You ask much."

"Have you never had a woman as a friend?"

"Never."

"Not even your wife?"

"You heard about her."

"Yes." *And about your child.*

He searched her face as if he would read her thoughts; she hid them behind a gentle smile.

"We were lovers," he said, "and then I was gone."

He said the words quickly, but she sensed a world of hurt behind them. Oh, to take him in her arms again and tell him that she understood. But she kept herself apart, and kept all loving sympathy to herself.

"Two hundred years from now men and women are still arguing whether friendship between them is possible."

"I've little trouble knowing on which side of the argument you put yourself."

There seemed nothing more to say between

them. She needed very much to be alone.

"I'd like to freshen up." His look of bemusement drove her on. "That's a euphemism. In my time it means cleaning oneself."

"In another time, I'd do it for you. I've a need to touch you, Meagan. Everywhere."

"Oh," she said, her fingers pressed against her lips to check her startled cry.

He made no attempt to stop her as she turned to leave the castle ruins. She was halfway up the stairs of the keep before she remembered he still had her underwear.

Friendship with a woman?

Impossible, Robert told himself as he returned to the keep. Friendship by his definition meant sharing a whiskey, a bawdy tale, a song, offering conversation when needed and silence when desired, providing advice when asked and aid when want was seen.

Friendship was what he shared with Colin; it was not what he experienced with Ermengarde.

His conscience struck him. In no way could he compare his feelings for Meagan with the mutual convenience he'd known with the widow, a convenience she shared with others. He couldn't put those feelings into words, except that this woman from another time lingered in his mind when other thoughts ought to prevail, and that around her he felt more alive and closer to happiness than he had felt in years.

He knew, too, that more than he wanted anything else, he wanted her to stay.

More than saving Thistledown? It was a question he could not ask himself.

Most definitely, he admitted, remembering the underdrawers still tucked inside his shirt, he did not care to have her as his friend. He could have spent eternity inside her body. He wanted her now; he throbbed with the need.

And she asked for a platonic relationship. Impossible. They did not have forever, a bitter fact he could little ignore. They must use their little while for what they both desired.

Still, he waited in the great hall for her descent so that he could give the relationship she asked for a try. Until he could convince her otherwise.

In the meantime he had a friendly gab with Janet Forbes.

"I must be remembering wrong. Did I no' ask you to keep all visitors away?"

"Thomas Balfour has a crafty way about him. He woulda been suspicious had I sent him back on the long road wi'out so much as a drink of water."

"Would a warning of his presence ha' been much to ask?"

"I had faith ye could manage the problem. As ye did."

Robert always got suspicious when Janet resorted to compliments, such rarely being her way.

"If I dinna ken otherwise, I'd think you wanted him to discover the wrong wife."

"'Twas no' my intent."

Before he could push her further, Meagan arrived, still wearing Annie's gown and the cloak. What did she have on underneath? What protected her finely rounded bottom; what covered her silken flesh? He'd have to ask, all in the cause of friendship, not wishing her to catch a draft and fall ill.

What a crude, lascivious brute he was to consider such a detail. But then his wife had a need for hands to warm her, did she not? He must do what he could.

"I'd like to show you about the grounds and the fine view we have of the loch. That is, if you've no' had a look already. I've little knowledge of how you spent your days while I was gone."

"I stayed close to the keep. What about Annie?"

"You get right to the point, do you no'?"

"I'm not the only one."

He knew she spoke of the scene in the ruins when he'd spoken his intent. His fingers burned to lift her skirts, to stroke her skin, to cup her buttocks, to fondle her private parts. She'd be quick to wetness, just as he was quick to grow hard.

"Please don't," she said.

"I'm doing something wrong?" His voice was thick; the words came out slowly.

"You're looking at me as if I were naked."

"'Tis my most fervent wish."

A blunt-spoken woman, in truth, was Meagan the Elder. He liked it, then wondered if such a liking was the start of friendship.

Such a relationship would not be all bad, though if he were as blunt-spoken as she, he'd tell her he would rather be carrying her up to bed.

"You've heard me say I've got men searching for her and the lad. When Colin joins them, she'll be here soon enough."

Men and dogs were both on the hunt, but he wasn't sure she would appreciate his thoroughness. He looked around to find Janet gone, and on the table a knapsack filled with food. Sometimes the woman seemed to read his mind.

With Meagan at his side, he strolled the grounds around the keep, pointing out the cobbler Sandy MacLean, the blacksmith, the stable boy, and on beyond the walls the few people who lived close

Evelyn Rogers

by, tilling the land, caring for the grounds.

Atop a grassy knoll overlooking Loch Lochy, they shared the bread and cold meat and the flask of whiskey Janet had prepared.

"Tell me about your first wife," she said when they were done.

"Janet told you about her."

"We had to pass the time somehow." He heard no censure in her voice.

A private man in matters of the heart, he found himself willing—nay eager—to share the details of his past. Wise woman that she was, Meagan would ken all that he said, and all he didn't say.

"I was long promised to the MacSorley lass," he said, "though she was but a child. I was to wait. Iona was an orphan, a lovely thing to gaze upon, fragile as the petals on a rose. I'd traveled far, wanderlust driving me most of the time. I'd seen all that was interesting in the world, or I so believed, and when I returned to take my place beside my ailing father, I saw her."

"You fell in love."

"Aye, and wanted her above all else. I was young and foolish and thought love conquered all."

"But it doesn't." She spoke unsurely, or so he thought.

She was looking out at the loch, her eyes clear, her features without expression. He must have been mistaken about the quaver in her voice.

"It did not hold off the tacks man," he said.

"Janet told me. About Gunn, about the loss of your wife and son. You hadn't known about him, had you?"

"When I served with Fraser's Highlanders, letters were a sometime thing."

She touched his hand. He felt her heat, and her sympathy. Never had he wanted such a weakling

258

feeling directed at him, but he saw no harm in it now. Indeed, it gave him the strength to talk of matters he had long kept to himself, of the horror of the battle, of the stench of newly spilled blood, of the crushing agony that came with seeing his companions fall beside him while he was spared.

One after the other, the words spilled out in rapid progression, like water pouring through a broken dam. In the spilling, he felt an unexpected relief.

"We were victorious on the plains of Abraham, or so they were called. But at a very great cost. Our leader General Wolfe was lost riding into the French fire. I heard the last words of a brave man: 'Now God be praised, I die happy.' But I saw little of happiness in his eyes as he stared sightless at the smoky sky."

He sat in silence for a moment until the terrible memories faded and the sharper images of a closer time returned.

"I came home a man of peace to find my own land in a different kind of war."

"Oh, Robert."

When he stood to help her to her feet, her warm gaze stirred something inside him, a new kind of hunger he could scarce afford to slake. He wanted to take her hand, to walk with her in quiet communion, to bask in the warmth aroused by sympathetic hearts.

Instead he looked away, and the moment of reflection that they'd shared was gone.

"Enough of my troubles. Mayhap word awaits."

He did not have to tell her what kind of word.

She stood beside him, her gaze on all around her except him, and they returned to the keep. Two days passed before a clear sign of the pair turned up. Days spent in showing Meagan the model town he'd build close to the loch, the land drainage that Colin oversaw, the crops newly sown. Brave man that he was, he even took her to Sunday service in the kirk. No matter where they were, she took everything in, asking questions always to the point, keeping her distance, avoiding his eye.

Mostly she took pleasure in the shaggy cattle and the black-faced sheep, claiming she never saw animals so close in New York.

"Unless you count a cockroach or two."

Once, after the evening meal, as they sat beside the great hall's warm fire, she told him the curious tale of *The Forever Bride*, describing the illustrations of her personal copy, declaring it was the romantic aspects of the almost-lost lovers that kept the book close to her heart.

"Are you thinking of returning to Thistledown each year on the date we were wed and lying in my arms?" he asked.

"Of course not," she said. "It's only a story."

"Aye. And I canna scoff at the foolishness of such an arrangement. It was the tale that brought you here."

They looked at one another, and Robert admitted to a great warmth stirring his heart. He heard her small cry, but when he reached for her she backed away and hurried from the hall and up the stairs to the lonely bedchamber where she spent her nights.

Leaving him to stare into the fire and curse the fates that forever brought him pain.

They were at breakfast the next morning when Colin entered with the news. Seeking the teasing banter of the past, Robert had just returned the taunting underwear to her with the admonition that he would see her in them again, and she had said that under no conditions would that take place.

"They've been seen on the road to Glasgow," Colin said as she thrust the garment into the pocket of her gown. "'Tis believed they've been hiding in one of the glens."

"At last," said Meagan, standing. "Here's the good report we've all been waiting for."

"So it would seem," Robert said, unwilling to commit himself to more.

They shared a glance, and he saw new depths in her fine violet eyes. Try as he might, he could not read the meaning that they hid.

"I'll get out of your way," she said, "and let you bring them in."

With a nod to Colin and a brief, sharp sideways glance at Robert, she strode toward the stairway and disappeared.

Chapter Twenty

At high noon Meagan decided she had played the dutiful wife for about as long as she could stand.

Restlessness set her to pacing in the great hall. Cabin fever, that was what it was. No, keep fever. Ever aware of words, she wanted to be precise.

More likely, she decided with a sigh, it was the realization that this strange drama—this stolen time of happiness—was approaching its end.

Whichever the case, a thousand needles pricked at her insides every time she tried to settle down. And each time she thought of Robert's finding—and embracing—his true bride, a weight the size of an anvil settled on her heart.

"Have you got those trousers I wore the other day?" she asked Janet, approaching her in the large, dark room that served as the Thistledown kitchen.

Around her, iron pots hung from iron hooks on the smoke-smudged stone wall, heat pulsed from an adjacent oven, utensils rested on oak shelves, and all of it was organized and utilitarian, just as she would have pictured any work area used by Janet Forbes.

The woman eyed her carefully. Ever since she'd mentioned having "the gift," Meagan was afraid to so much as think around her, in case she could read her mind.

"Aye," Janet said.

"Could I please have them?"

"Aye."

Another one-syllable day, Meagan thought, but she refused to get impatient.

Janet exited the kitchen through a back door, returning in a moment with both the shirt and trousers, and also with the skirt she'd worn over them on her ride with Robert.

"Thanks," she said, grateful for no questions and no lecture. Robert could take a lesson or two in communication skills from his housekeeper.

Meagan hurried to the bedchamber, changed clothes, then with the cloak and hood thrown over her against the almost constant Scottish chill, she went down for her first solo confrontation with one of the Cameron clansmen, specifically the stablehand.

He proved to be no more than a lad, and when she asked about the mare she'd ridden, he proved also to speak in a brogue so thick she could understand nothing of what he said.

Gestures worked little better; maybe she wasn't pantomiming a saddle and bridle very well, nor the riding itself. Or maybe he didn't want to understand, feeling safer taking orders from his laird.

"Ye need help."

Meagan whirled to see Jamie standing in the stable door.

A rush of pleasure overtook her, and relief that

he was all right. She wanted to run over and hug him, but he was looking so sure of himself, so adult for his twelve years, that she figured it was the last thing he would want, especially when in full view of another youth.

She glanced at the stablehand, who had a decidedly unwelcoming expression on his face. Stepping closer to Jamie, she assumed a confident air, the lady of the keep who could welcome onto Cameron land anyone she chose. A fake, that was what she really was, but the stablehand didn't know it. With a shake of his head he backed away.

"What happened to you in the woods?" she asked.

Jamie hiked his trousers, the same shabby pair he'd worn before. "I dinna desert ye, if that's wha' ye're thinking."

"Maybe I did a little bit, at least at first," Meagan confessed, "but mostly I worried that something bad had happened to you."

Remembering Ned and George, she shivered within the warmth of her cloak.

"I knew there was nothing you could do to help me with those two men," she added with a sympathetic smile.

The boy shrugged, his lanky body looking thinner than she remembered it. "I did wha' I could."

He sounded modest and proud. She figured he wanted further prodding. "And what was that?" she asked.

"I took yer skirt and plaid. Did ye no' wonder why Cameron had them when he found ye? 'Twas me that led 'im t' ye, dropping the skirt here, the plaid there t' serve as guides as he wandered about."

"I should have known," Meagan said, wanting more than ever to hug him. "You saved me after all. It's I who owe you now."

He flipped his long hair out of his eyes. Standing tall for his twelve years, looking cool, he had a prouder-than-ever air about him, and she saw he was not unmoved by her praise.

"Ha' ye a mind to run again?" The boy's dark eyes glinted with delight at the prospect, and his teeth showed white against his sun-darkened skin as he smiled. "He beats ye, does he no'?"

"No, he doesn't beat me." It would be better, she thought, if he did. If such were the case, she would have left long ago.

"I simply wanted a ride," she added.

It was clear he didn't believe her, but he made no protest. "I'll get the horse for ye."

"Why can I understand you and not this other boy?"

"He's no' been about so much. I wasna born here, ye ken, but to the south where there's more o' the English. 'Tis where I learned me fine speech."

"Oh, I see."

"But I can talk wi' a brogue when I've the need."

He strode around her to the stable door and proceeded to demonstrate, launching into an intense, unintelligible conversation that bordered on argument, and she had to hold herself back to keep from interfering. For a moment the tempo and volume increased, so much so she feared someone might come to see what was going on and pitch the young visitor out on his ear.

Watching, she thought that during his wild young days Robert might have been a little bit like Jamie, not so gangly perhaps, but just as independent and resourceful, just as willing to throw himself into situations in which he took an interest, and the danger be hanged.

At last the stablehand led the mare from one of the back stalls, saddled and bridled her, and with a sullen look at Jamie and a worried look at her, stepped back as if he would dissociate himself from the proceedings as much as he could.

Now it was up to Meagan to mount. The horse wasn't big, certainly not so big as the beast Robert had ridden, but it looked more than adequately challenging as she walked close, threw back her hood and cloak, and hiked her skirt.

The stablehand gasped and averted his eyes; Jamie grinned and watched.

"I need your help again," she said.

"Ye've got it, if I can ride ahint."

"Oh, yes," Meagan said, glad of the company.

Mounting proved difficult and certainly undignified, if not downright ludicrous, with Jamie's hands splayed against her bottom and then her foot and again back to her bottom, shoving her with surprising strength until she lay stomach-down across the saddle while she valiantly struggled to swing her right leg into place.

At last, mount she did and the boy sprang onto the horse behind her, his long thin legs gripping the mare's flanks.

The mare took a step, then another while Meagan concentrated on straightening her tangled garments. She forced her muscles to relax and move with the shifting saddle, remembering Robert's instructions, gradually accepting the rhythm of the slow ride.

A hundred eyes must be watching the scene. As if she would block them out, she adjusted the hood over her head, the skirt at her waist, and the cloak over her trousered legs, looking in her mind like a lady likely to be wed to a laird.

She quickened the pace, but only slightly, hold-

ing the reins as she had been taught, guiding the
mare away from the stable and toward the gate.
Except for one small snicker, Jamie kept his silence, for which she was grateful. They rode past
the cobbler's shop and on to the blacksmith's open
doorway. Ermengarde strolled out to watch her
go by. Hands on hips, red hair spread like wildfire
about her head, the woman wore a wanton, satisfied air, as well as a glint of curiosity.

Meagan looked beyond her to the burly, dark-
haired smitty standing at the edge of the darkened
interior, chest bare except for the bib of a leather
apron, the glow from the coals licking at his muscled, sweat-slicked arms.

She could practically smell the aura of sex rising
from the pair of them.

"No' much doubt wha' they've been about," Jamie said, none too softly.

"What would you know—" Meagan began, then
caught a sideways glance at the boy's knowing
smirk.

"I can tell you know more than you should," she
said, feeling a little prissy, then grinning at him.
"Sorry. At your age I was very ignorant."

"Ye're a lass," he said, his smirk turning to a
superior grin. "'Tis t' be expected."

She nodded at Ermengarde as they rode by and
was surprised at the elation she felt because the
woman had found satisfaction with someone
other than Robert. How easy it was to like her
when she was with another man.

Oh, Robert. The thought of him brought on a
rush of memories, drawn sharper as the mare
walked past the ruins and Meagan remembered
what they had done in the high shadows close to
the half-formed walls.

There was nothing half-formed about Robert.

267

Her pulse pounded. Nothing half-formed at all.
Once again, the anvil lay in place against her
heart.

With a click of her tongue she urged the mare
to a faster trot and they passed through the open
gate and onto the hard-packed dirt road that
wound across the rolling hills in front of Thistledown.

On the route to the north lay the change-house
and the county seat of Darien, where Sheriff Edgar Gunn and his bailie Fergus Munro held sway.
Loch Ness nestled in the Great Glen beyond, and
farther on the northern coastal town of Inverness.
The road curved to the south in the other direction, toward the poor town of Buscar-Ban and,
two days' ride away, Glasgow.

It was upon this segment of the road that Annie
and the sheriff's nephew had been spotted. Somewhere to the south her husband rode, searching
or, very possibly, riding back with his true bride
in tow.

The thought was depressing.

No, it was devastating.

Robert belonged to her, not a child who had
abandoned him.

But of course that was a lie. If Robert could be
said to belong to anyone, it was to whoever had
the money to help him out. And that definitely
wasn't penniless Meagan, whose savings account
would prove meager indeed to help his needs,
even if she could get to it.

There was always the engagement ring. But it
wasn't really hers, and besides, converting it to
cash might prove complicated in this land that
still bordered on being a wilderness.

Thoughts of the ring reminded her of William,
the man to whom she owed allegiance, and she

found herself devastated more than ever.

Being honorable and noble and honest was not all it was cracked up to be.

She reined the mare toward the south, thinking that at least she wasn't a wimp anymore. She hadn't so much as considered the possibility for days.

They rode in silence for close to a mile. The road proved surprisingly smooth except for the ruts from carriage wheels, but these were none too deep, carriages apparently being in short supply in the Highlands. Once a post chaise thundered by, all creaking leather and pounding hooves and snapping whips. She and Jamie watched unseen from the shelter of a stand of oak. Back on the road, they journeyed through Buscar-Ban, stirring only the dogs, then another mile without passing a vehicle or lone rider. How privileged they were to ride on such a glorious day.

Dropping the hood, she welcomed the cool breeze in her hair. Tilting her head, she basked in the warmth of the sun on her face. The mare stumbled, reminding her of her precarious position, and with Jamie chuckling behind her she straightened and held the reins with all good seriousness.

"Why do you dislike Robert so much?" she asked.

"He's a Cameron."

"That doesn't explain anything."

"Where'er ye belong, 'tis no' here. 'Tis our way t' dislike those who would hold power o'er us wi- 'out seeing t' our needs."

"That sounds like something you've heard and not something you believe."

"My father used t' say it, afore he took off."

"How long ago was that?"

"When Robert Cameron came home to throw good workers off his land."

"But the land had been taken illegally. He was only returning it to families that had labored on it for generations, and who had themselves been thrown off."

Jamie had no response, and she left the argument to his own good sense. For the past few years he must have heard nothing good about Robert, and he would not admit he was wrong from anything she might do or say, certainly not in the time left to her.

Which might be only hours.

"What about your mother?"

"She died soon after my father disappeared."

"Leaving you alone."

"I've no complaints."

"I'm sure you don't."

This time the silence that fell between them was uneasy. She floundered around for a topic that would bring neither of them distress. The weather was all she could come up with, but before she could ask about Scottish springtime storms, he spoke.

"Ha' ye e'er tasted trout caught fresh from a clear stream?"

"No," she said, realizing that she was starving. Porridge and barley bread had been a long time ago.

"Would ye care t' try it?"

She didn't need to think twice to agree. Directing her off the road, he proceeded to give her directions in a general southwesterly direction. They rode cross-country, away from the winding road, across a series of glens and bogs, through stands of pine and fir. At last they topped a pine-edged hill that looked out upon a grass-swept valley dotted with bracken and boulders, and with the purple flowers of wild heather rising on the distant side to rolling hills and more dark woods.

At the base of the shallow valley a meandering stream sparkled in the bright afternoon sun. Meagan caught her breath at the beauty of the scene. City girl she might be, but she felt very much at home here in this open, clean-aired land. It was as though her soul were enriched and her spirit set to soar.

Only the ever-present anvil kept her heart from celebrating the glory of the land. This wasn't home, no matter how much she had grown to love it. Hers was a place of subways and taxis, of crowded restaurants and theaters and guarded walks in the park.

She was about to guide the mare down the hill and to the stream when she felt a nudge at her waist.

Glancing back at Jamie, she saw him staring past her to another hill on the same side of the valley, to a wall of trees, to another horse standing at the edge of the pines. She could make out two people riding double, a woman and a man.

Little else about them was visible, except that the woman had long red hair, the man sat behind her, and they appeared to be young.

Her breath caught as she realized who they must be.

"Annie MacSorley," she whispered, then floundering around for her companion's name, came up with it. "And Fitzroy Sutherland."

Robert hadn't found them after all.

Her first instinct was to warn them away, to send them fleeing, to keep Robert for herself. Her breath caught, and then gave way to a sigh. She couldn't do it, no matter how much she wanted to. But neither could she call to them in joyous welcome. Annie and her young man needed a quieter approach, and a talk to settle the girl's troubled mind.

She feared riding toward them might frighten them away.

"Get down," she whispered to Jamie. Surprisingly he did as she asked, and she eased herself to the ground, stretching her muscles, then straightening her back as she adjusted to holding up her own weight.

She turned in their direction, estimating the distance between them to be a hundred yards. From this distance Annie looked young and slight, her companion not so much, but neither did he give any sign of being as villainous as his uncle. In truth, as they stared out at the valley, the two looked like nothing but a young, carefree couple out on a lark, and as little like fugitives as they could be.

"Hello," she called out as she strode toward them, waving a friendly greeting.

Annie shouted out, and in a flash the horse and its two riders disappeared into the woods.

So much for strategy. Muttering a few curses, Meagan ran back to throw herself at the mare, who skittered in a circle at the sudden attack. Jamie helped her to mount, a floundering exercise much like the one at the Thistledown stable, then climbed onto the horse behind her and they were off in pursuit.

Ignoring the fact that she didn't know anything about riding a galloping horse, she leaned forward and slapped the reins sharply against the mare's neck. The horse took off like a shot, Jamie gripped her waist, and she felt the thrill and the terror of her first fast ride.

It seemed to her they were flying, yet the steady bounce of her bottom against the saddle told her they were still crossing the hard, cruel ground. She reined the horse into the woods at the spot she'd last seen Annie, but there was no sign of her in the trees.

"Which way?" she asked.

Jamie gestured straight ahead. She glanced back at him. The imp was grinning. This was nothing but a romp for him. For Meagan it was her everything.

Realization of her precarious position atop the horse struck her, and in a delayed reaction she became more afraid of the slower, cautious walk through the woods than she had been of the gallop along the ridge of the hill. Reining to a halt, she listened for a sound that would indicate Annie's whereabouts, but she heard only the wind in the trees and her own unsteady breath.

Tears burned at the back of her eyes, a sign of her frustration and of how important finding Annie had come to be. For the past two days she'd dragged out her time with Robert, the two of them being polite as they could manage, keeping their hands to themselves while she learned about him and his troubles, learned even more the depth of her love, but always keeping the knowledge and the pain to herself.

What would he have done if she had jumped him as she had wanted to do so many times?

He would have taken her on the spot, no matter where it was, and then the parting would have begun all over again, and the return of honor and of being sensible.

That Annie and Fitz had made love seemed obvious, certainly to her twentieth-century sensibilities, both of the runaways being at an age of raging hormones. Too, they'd been together in a situation parallel to hers, strangers in an alien land, and despite her best intentions she'd not been celibate.

But Robert had already indicated he would forgive his rightful intended and make her his wife. Ah, yes, honor and duty must rule the day.

She spied a scrap of cloth caught on the sharp twig of a shrub.

"Look," she said.

Jamie scrambled to the ground and brought it back to her. A triangle of blue wool; it must have come from Annie's gown. They were heading in the right direction after all. The boy chose to walk ahead, looking for other signs; after a while they took separate paths, never straying so far the other one couldn't hear a shout.

She stumbled upon the fugitives without warning. They had stopped at the edge of a small, rock-strewn glen, both still astride the horse, their backs to her. They did not turn around when she called Annie's name, nor did they attempt to escape.

Riding closer, she saw the cause of their altered behavior. Ned Dundas, broad and brutish as ever, stood close to the horse, reins in hand, while look-alike George watched a couple of feet away, a long-barreled gun in his hand. She might have the names reversed, but she little cared, her attention occupied by the gun. It was pointed at Annie's head.

Icy terror took hold of Meagan. She'd been far too noisy. George looked beyond the current captives, blinked his beady eyes, and stared right at her face. The light of possibility gave a hint of rare intelligence to his Cro-Magnon eyes. He shifted the gun to her.

"Luck be wi' us, Ned," he said in a growly voice. "Behold. 'Tis a real treasure we've got here."

Ned looked. The smirk that cut across his swarthy face was not a pretty sight to behold.

Heart thundering in her throat, she reined away from them, and all hell broke loose, the twins shouting, Annie screaming, horses neighing, a bullet whizzing past Meagan's head as the air around her exploded with the sound of the shot.

In the midst of the din she felt herself falling and looked down to see a hairy fist tugging at the tail of her cloak. She slapped at the fist with the reins, tried to slip free of the garment, but she kept on falling, falling, it seemed forever, yet in an instant she came in contact with the ground, wincing in agony as her shoulder hit first, then, when her head bounced back against a boulder, experiencing a shooting pain that obliterated all thought. With a low cry she slipped into the blessed, dark vacuum of unconsciousness.

"I'm thinking, Rob, that ye've no desire to find the lass."

Robert stared at his cousin, but could come up with no answer that would satisfy either of them.

They rode side by side down the winding road to Glasgow. A dozen Cameron men rode into the woods and fields that flanked the road, coming back from time to time to report no sign of the fleeing pair.

"What makes you think such a thing?" he asked.

"Ye've a talent for tracking that would put us all to shame, yet ye keep t' the road, sending others t' do the looking."

"Annie was seen on the road."

"Aye, hours ago. If the Irish mare was up to a

hard ride, she could be halfway to the coast by now."

"She's nowhere near the ocean. Dinna ask how I know, but I do. She's somewhere close by."

They were on a rolling stretch of road that wound across open glens, no trees or shrubs or even boulders to provide a hiding place for a lass, a lad, and a horse.

And certainly no towns or isolated houses. They'd passed a roadside inn a mile or so behind them, but no one reported seeing anything that would give them any help. Neither did the driver of the post, who had gone by several hours past.

Still, Robert sensed the presence of their quarry.

Or maybe it was that he feared it. Not ordinarily a man given to trepidation, he felt it now.

He looked down the road and saw Meagan striding toward him, her long skirt catching against her fine legs with each step. Knowing the sight was an apparition, he enjoyed it nonetheless. Meagan with her raven hair that curled gently on her shoulders; Meagan with her splendid woman's body that was both soft and strong; Meagan with her dark-heather eyes that told more than she knew and less than he wanted. In the depths of those eyes he could see her hunger for him, but she shut off all else. How she truly felt, whether she regretted leaving, how she judged him were all beyond his ken.

She approved what he did to help his people. She had told him so in open honesty, but such was not enough. If he could but manage the feat, he would see into her heart.

And, too, he thought with truthful insight, he would see her lying naked beneath him, her lips swollen from his kiss, her nipples wet from the laving of his tongue, and a cry of pleasure whispering from deep in her throat.

What a rogue he was to want her when he sought another lass.

"Rider's a-coming."

Deep in gloomy thought, he scarcely heard Colin's words, but he caught the urgency of them as his cousin repeated the news.

"Two riders," he amended. "A woman and a man astride a single horse."

A curious hollowness took hold in the pit of his stomach. He knew who they must be. It seemed a strangely unsatisfying ending to all that had occurred since that afternoon more than a week ago when Meagan-Anne MacSorley had run from Thistledown.

Unsatisfying, aye, without triumph or elation. Unsatisfying and unwelcome. He reined to a halt, as did Colin, and they awaited the approaching pair.

Annie rode toward him with an anguished cry, her long red hair flying loose, the sheriff's nephew Fitz holding on to her waist as the horse covered the distance in a frenzied gallop.

"Help!" she shouted as she rode.

It was not the call he would have expected.

"They've got the woman."

The words came out raggedly, but Robert heard every one. A knife pierced his heart. It could not be Meagan, he told himself. She was safe at Thistledown.

Annie reined to a halt beside him, the slathering mare jerking in protest at the bite of the bit against her jaw.

Colin grabbed the reins to keep her from riding on. The horse pranced in place. "Describe her," he said.

"Dark haired," Fitz said, "with violet eyes. I noticed 'em 'cause I've no' seen such a color before."

The knife twisted. "Who has her?" Robert barked. "Where?"

"Two men—a pair of hairy devils we'd seen earlier in the woods—came upon us with a gun."

"We were riding, thinking how pretty everything was, and then this woman came walking toward us," Annie put in, her words pouring out in a rush. "She was waving, calling something I couldn't understand and we ran but the bad 'uns caught us and she showed up riding a horse, and, oh, I understand not what happened except we got away."

She stared at Robert, tears streaming down her pale cheeks.

"Once the bastards got a look at her," the lad put in, "they forgot about us."

Robert could well imagine who the men might be. He quickly described the Dundas twins.

"Aye, they're the ones," Fitz said.

"And the woman?" Robert asked with a cold calm that surprised him. "You say they've got her."

"I dinna believe she got away."

"You left her."

"We had no choice," Annie put in. "They had a pistol. One of them fired at her, and she fell. That's all we know."

A splash of red across a slender shoulder flashed through Robert's mind. Wild rage threatened; he fought to bring it under control. Wildness would help no one now.

"You're Robert Cameron," the lad said.

Robert nodded, though who he was meant little to him now.

"Take me to where you saw them last." He spoke coldly, brusquely.

Annie gestured behind her. "The next bend in the road, to the west, through the trees and on to the edge of a field. That's where we left them, everything smoky and loud and confused."

Her eyes, a wide, wild green, studied Robert for a moment. And then, without warning, she brought a stick down sharply on Colin's hand with such unexpected force, he dropped the reins. The mare bounded forward, away from the scene, Annie grabbing for the reins, Fitz Sutherland hanging on to her for his life, and all of it done as quick as a flash, horse and riders hurrying down the road in a cloud of dust.

Colin gave a sign he would go after them.

"Nay," said Robert. He took off in the opposite direction, toward the bend of the road, his thoughts not on Annie but on Meagan. She needed him more than he needed his true bride. He blocked out all worry or consideration that he would find her too late.

She would be saved, and she would be all right. A man who yearned for peace, he would snap the necks of those who brought her harm.

Chapter Twenty-one

"Fine bait ye be, lass."

Ned kneeled low, his weight on his heels, to stroke Meagan's cheek.

She shivered as his long, dirty nail trailed across her skin. Sitting cross-legged in the midst of purple heather, cloak tossed aside, hands tied behind her, mouth bound with a filthy rag, there was little else she could do but shiver. And put all the hate she could into her stare.

Oh, for another trick like the one she'd come up with the last time these cretins had caught her. But she was out of tricks, out of luck, and just about out of spirit.

When they'd pulled her from the horse, she'd thought herself shot, but the bullet had passed harmlessly through her cloak. Terror had sent her into oblivion, that and the hard rock she'd had the misfortune to crack her head on. Too soon she'd awakened to her second captivity by the Dundas boys. Fool. She almost deserved what she got.

Ned grinned and shifted his massive bottom, his

bent knees crackling from the weight. His finger trailed down her neck. She closed her eyes. He cupped her breast, then squeezed the nipple hard. Her muffled cry brought on a chuckle, and he did the same to the other breast. This time she swallowed a moan of pain, but she could not still the tears that spilled onto her cheeks.

If only Robert didn't find out her predicament. If only he kept riding on. Pain was not the main part of her worry. Bait she was, an enticement to draw her husband to his death, though why the Dundas twins wished to kill him she didn't know.

Yet here she was, brought back to the field where she and Jamie had planned to picnic, the boy gone, her inevitable rape postponed by the Dundas twins until the celebration of their success. She hadn't known they could be so restrained.

Bait for Robert, a reward for his killers. She sat in the middle of the cruelly beautiful glen with Ned all too visible, his armed brother lying in wait in the shadows of a nearby woods, and Robert possibly on the way.

The plan couldn't go right, not with these fools executing it. But sometimes luck was on the side of such villains. Look at the crime statistics in New York.

By all that was logical, Robert wouldn't find out she'd been captured. He should be riding toward Glasgow, intent on finding another wife. She prayed that was the way things were. But she couldn't be happy about it, no matter how hard she tried.

What a confused mess. She didn't know how she wanted to feel, what she wanted to believe, except that she yearned for the happy ending she loved in her books. Deep in her heart, despite her

281

practical nature, she'd always believed in miracles. But not now, not now.

Was the cosmic prankster who had brought her here chuckling as evilly as Ned? Or was he ruing the day he ever let her read *The Forever Bride?*

She sighed. Pranksters didn't hang around to see the results of their deviltry. And the only part of all this she truly regretted had taken place in the past hour, when she'd blundered into the sight of an unfriendly gun. It was, sadly, bad enough to make up for all the rest.

Ned pulled himself to his feet and spat into a clump of bracken. His narrow, dark eyes scanned the trees at the top of the hill. He grinned down at her. "Wha' say we gi'e the laird a bit o' somethin' t' bring 'im down."

Meagan shrank away from him. Her shoulder pained her where she'd fallen, as did her head, but they seemed inconsequential injuries now. There must be worse things than being raped by one of the Dundas twins, but she couldn't think what it could be.

She tried to talk through the gag, and then she truly did gag, choking on vile tastes she hoped never to identify, pleading with her eyes for him to loosen the dirty kerchief.

Miraculously he did just that, and she sputtered to clear her mouth.

"He's not coming," she declared when she could speak. "You're wasting your time."

"He'll be here soon enough. When he hears we got ye."

"Who'll tell him?"

He looked at her as if she were as stupid as he. "The lass."

"She's running from him." Meagan's head reeled from exasperation and the lingering effects of her fall, but she hurried on. "I tried to tell you that before, but you wouldn't listen. Robert is the last person in the world she wants to talk to."

Ned screwed his mouth and narrowed his eyes, signs he was thinking.

"He'll find ye. Ye're his wife."

She could have explained how she wasn't, not really, but she'd need a week to make him understand the rudiments. And a week she didn't have.

She reduced her story to the basics.

"He wants another woman."

Ned snorted his disbelief.

"I know what I'm talking about. As soon as he finds her I'll be on my way. Tossed out. Thrown away."

Something in her voice must have gotten to him, for he eyed her with all the care he could manage, concentrating primarily on her breasts.

"Cameron's a fool, but I dinna believe he's looby."

He stood just as the wind shifted, and she caught a stench of body odor that turned her stomach. He belched and took a step away.

Somehow, in the midst of sickening revulsion, she found inspiration. "Oh, he's looby all right," she said, "and more. He wants . . . unnatural things from a woman."

Ned slowly turned, and she caught the glint of curiosity in his pinpoint eyes. Encouraged, she hurried on.

"He wants me to do things I—" Staring toward the distant hills, she had no trouble coming up with a very visible shudder. "Things that disgust me. Things with my mouth while he—"

Her voice drifted off and she let Ned's imagination take over. Even he should be able to come up with something specific, something he might want her to do, too.

She was acting on instinct, coming up with details as she spoke, using as her guides all that she knew and everything that Ned did in reaction. With supreme effort, she made the ultimate sacrifice and regarded her captor with open admiration.

"He's not man enough to make me want to do them."

But you are. She said it with her eyes.

She shifted to her knees, rising until her mouth was level with his crotch. She concentrated on the growing bulge in his trousers. Swallowing bile, she licked her lips. Even one of the Dundas fools should get the picture.

Ned did.

He rubbed himself.

"You need a woman to do that," she said, figuring she'd been about as subtle as she could be.

He rubbed harder.

"Free my hands and I'll do it for you. And you can touch me. Have you ever had a woman who was wet? I mean really wet? You know, down there."

She disgusted herself, the words as nasty as his stench, but she saw she was getting to him.

"I'll bet you haven't," she whispered, speaking lower, huskier, drawing him closer to catch every word. "That's what a woman's body does when she wants a man very much. It makes him slip inside her very easily. In and out, you know how it goes."

He grunted to show that he did. He glanced toward the trees where George was hiding. She used her voice to draw him back.

"Danger excites me, Ned. I'm afraid of you, oh

284

yes, I'm trembling, but that makes me want you all the more."

She was going too far, much too far. Even Ned could not be such a fool. He'd see the trap; he'd pull away. The sound of his ragged breath and the sight of his hairy hand cupping himself told her otherwise.

"Untie my hands and we'll undress each other."

He growled something she took to be a no.

"Then we won't undress," she amended quickly, "not all the way. Just the parts that matter."

She rubbed her breast against his knee, back and forth as long as she could stand it, then eased away. His legs buckled beneath him, and he came down hard on the ground beside her.

She smiled, trying to be sweetly calm while every nerve within her tightened to the breaking point. She felt crazy and wild and desperate, but more than anything else, she felt strong.

"I'll be good bait, all right. Just think how crazy Robert will be when he sees us having a good time." She added an extra twist. "And so will George. You'll get to me first."

"Aye," he said, grinning broadly, teeth mottled black between his thick lips. "I'll be the first."

With a prayer for continued strength, she twisted her wrists toward him. His fingers fumbled, but at last she was free.

Now came the difficult part. She had to put her hands on him . . . and more.

Resisting the temptation to rub the bruised skin where the rope had been, she raised her hands. "I'd like to touch you first. To kiss you. Have you ever had a woman really kiss you, Ned? I mean really, where she used her tongue?"

He shook his head with such vehemence, she knew for sure he had never had a woman except

by force. Raped women didn't offer kisses freely.
Kisses or anything else.

She cupped his face, and the bristles felt like
razors against her palms. She leaned close, and
the smell of his breath almost caused her to retch.

Blanking out all senses, she put her mouth to
his cheek. And like an animal she bit down hard,
feeling his flesh give way, tasting blood, jerking
her head violently.

He screamed and pushed her away. She jumped
to her feet. He moaned, gripping his face, and
then, with a howl, he launched himself toward
her. The veins in his temples pulsed with uncon-
trollable rage. She kicked out, catching his jaw
with the toe of her boot. It was a lucky kick. His
chin jerked up and he fell backward striking his
head on a jagged boulder, landing hard against a
thorny shrub.

He lay still, eyes open and glassy, his neck bent
at an unnatural angle, purple flowers haloed
around his head. She didn't pause to find out if he
was alive or dead. Hiking her skirts, she ran like
hell away from the woods where George lurked,
down the valley, toward the stream where Jamie
had planned to catch her a trout, the taste of death
and blood defiling her mouth.

Her feet flew over the stones along the bank of
the stream; she knelt at the water's edge, plunged
her hands into its iciness, and washed her mouth
out time and time again, scrubbing at her teeth,
wondering if she would ever rid the nastiness
from her tongue. Crying, trembling, gasping for
breath, she concentrated on what she did and not
on what she had done.

Drops of blood marred the front of her blouse.
Splashing cold water on them, she rubbed and
rubbed and rubbed. A shout from the direction of

the hill stopped her. She stood to see George, gun in hand, lumbering from the direction of the trees and down the uneven slope. For all his awkwardness, he closed the distance between them fast, a hundred yards, fifty, forty, thirty. She seemed frozen to the ground. Another shout, this time to the right. As if she had summoned him, Jamie popped up from the bracken and heather, waving his arms wildly, not toward her but toward George, drawing his attention, drawing his fire.

The barrel of the pistol shifted toward the boy.

"No," she screamed, running toward the gun, running and screaming, "Me, me, me." Her words echoed across the waving green.

She felt the beat of thundering hooves vibrating beneath her feet, even as she saw a horse and rider emerge from the woods behind George, pounding down the hill, wind caught in dark copper hair, a savage snarl on a coppery face, the wild-eyed mount snorting and lathering in a headlong gallop.

"Robert!" she screamed.

George whirled. Robert raised his arm; a knife hurtled through the air. George stumbled, fired, then stumbled again, swaying, then fell backward to lie not ten yards from his brother, the bone-colored handle of the knife protruding from his chest.

He twitched once, twice, then lay still as the stones that dotted the ground around him.

Robert reined to a halt between the two brothers, his gaze sweeping the scene before settling on her. He didn't smile, he didn't speak, and neither did she. He dismounted, checked the bodies, then walked toward her, his strong legs carrying him solidly, steadily forward. Her heart thundered with pride and love and the remaining tremors of fear, for him more than her.

"Robert," she whispered when he drew near.

"Both dead," he answered. And then he added, "One for you and one for me."

There was as much question in his voice as statement of fact. She looked beyond him to see his cousin Colin and a half dozen Cameron men emerge from the trees.

"Yes," she said. "I did it. And I'm not sorry."

"Nor should you be."

She looked around for Jamie, but again he'd disappeared, and then her thoughts were all for Robert and for nothing else.

He looked her over with such thoroughness she felt unclothed, untamed, and very much in need of his loving hands.

Just when she thought her heart would die if he didn't touch her, he swept her into his arms and kissed her, and all seemed right once again in her crazy world.

Sending Colin back to Thistledown with a report of what had passed, Robert took her to the roadside inn they'd passed on their search for Annie. Cradling her in his arms, gently, terrified he might hurt her, he took her by horseback, just as he had done when he rescued her once before.

This time he had no anger in his heart, but a relief and a gladness she had not come to harm, and the somber realization that he had come upon the ugly scene almost too late.

Dishonorable man that he was, he also wanted to explore every part of her, making certain she had come to no harm.

He told her exactly that, once he'd ordered a room vacated for the two of them, clean linens put on the bed, and a cask of whiskey with two tankards placed before a crackling fire.

288

She needed warming. And so did he.

Once all was done as he'd ordered, once the door to the small, dank room was closed and the first dram of whiskey downed, they set their tankards aside and stood before the fire to stare at one another.

Now was the time for revelations, for clearing the ugly memories of what had passed on this once beautiful afternoon. They'd both killed, but out of necessity, and though he'd once sworn never to kill again, he would fling that knife at a thousand Dundas bastards to save her precious life.

From the trembling of her hands, he suspected she did not feel so sanguine. She'd need of talk, of what she would consider confession, of letting out all she had done. She needed, too, to hear how brave and bonnie she truly was.

"Meagan—"

She pressed her fingers against his lips. The smile she gave him was not quite happy, but it was determined and served to silence him. She threw off her cloak, stepped out of the skirt she wore over her trousers, and proceeded to unbutton her blouse.

Though she had a dark, unthinking look in her eye, he made no move to stop her.

Nor did he wonder about declarations of honor and belonging to someone else.

The only thing he pondered was whether or not he could hold himself back while she disrobed. He found his nobility in the waiting and the watching and the half-smile of encouragement he could not keep from his face.

She opened the shirt slowly to reveal the strangely cupped band that she'd given a fancy French name. Brassiere, she'd said. It looked like

289

something the French would come up with, a cradle for each breast, lifting and separating, holding its treasures out for a man's hands and a man's lips.

She shrugged out of the shirt, tossing it aside. Her raven hair lay soft against soft shoulders, her skin a satiny gold against the whiteness of the undergarment. Her nipples, dark and large, beckoned through the thin lace cloth.

He was ready to answer the call.

Still, he restrained himself.

Next came the trousers. Loosening the waist, she eased them over her naked hips. Good God, she tormented a man, but it was torment he could easily endure. For a while.

He knew what to expect: the resilient scrap of silk that had so fascinated him the day they were wed, the silk he had stolen in the castle ruins, the silk he had returned with more reluctance than she could ever know.

He liked it better on her than thrust inside his shirt.

The trousers fell to the floor. With her usual grace she stepped out of them and stood before him in her twentieth-century undergarments, apparel that showed little practicality while it demonstrated all that was possible in allure.

Did these people ne'er think of anything but sex?

Much to his regret he knew it was not so, if he could go by Meagan's example. She thought of honor. But not today.

What glorious long legs she had; he cursed himself to think he'd ever questioned them. Gentle hips, a narrow waist, firm breasts high and tempting, a lifted chin, parted lips, heathery eyes that glistened with desire.

He looked back at the underdrawers. A man could be only so strong.

She lifted her arms and slowly turned around, a gentle bird ruffled from stillness as if she would take flight.

"My shoulder's a little sore, but no bruises," she said when she faced him once again. "I told you I was all right."

The bruises were inside, he knew; they came with memories of killing a man. 'Twas clear she saved them for another time. He saw the wisdom of her way.

Lord help him, his swelling strained his trousers and made him ache. He stepped close and snapped the underwear.

She caught her breath, but she did not catch his hand.

"When first I came upon these, I believed them the invention of a crazy Irishman. Then I thought, nay, a clever one."

"You said you'd see me in them again. And I said no. Looks like you were right."

He placed a palm against the flatness of her abdomen and eased his fingers inside the top edge of the lace. He felt the soft, black hair curling against his fingers. "I'd see you out of them, too."

"You will."

No contradictions, no arguments, no nays. He liked that in her. He'd like himself in her as well.

He put his other hand against her lower back, letting his fingers explore as carefully as he had the front of her. He traced the separation of her buttocks, spread his palm across the tight, full swells, and all the while his fingers eased lower in the front, parting the sweet folds of skin between her thighs, finding the small hard nub of her desire.

Her hands gripped his sleeves, eyes closed, teeth caught at the edge of her full lower lip.

"You should have stayed at the castle," he said, showing no mercy, rubbing in tiny circles between her legs while he gripped her buttocks with his other hand.

Within his grasp he held a treasure beyond all else. He felt her muscles contract with each of his strokes, felt the pulsings as she rubbed herself against his hand and fingers.

Her eyes fluttered open, their centers deep and full and rich with raw hunger.

"If I had stayed," she whispered huskily, "we would not be doing this."

"Aye," he said, and dipped a finger inside her, brought out the wetness and rubbed it across her nub, then returned the finger to the channel that would bring him ecstasy, his own great glen and the only one in all the world that mattered.

"The bed, Robert. I want you in the bed."

"'Twould be cruel for me t' deny you, lass."

"And you're not a cruel man."

He eased his hands from her and lifted her in his arms. She clung to him, and he felt a shudder rush through her. She was remembering particulars of the day. It was his fault for moving too slowly. She must think of only one thing: the glory of life that pulsed between them, and not the deaths they both had seen.

He laid her on the sheets, then stood back to disrobe. No shy lass, his Meagan watched every move, and he saw the terror in her eyes give way to other considerations.

Was that a smile tugging at her lips?

"Do I amuse you?"

Her gaze was pinned on his powerful erection.

"I've a need to be vulgar and dirty, Robert. I've

a need to make wild love."

"I'll rise to the cause."

"You already have."

She kneeled at the edge of the bed and licked the skin at the end of his shaft, nipped the tip ever so gently with her teeth, enfolded him with her lips, taking him deep in her throat, using the pressure of both mouth and tongue to drive him to the wildness that she craved.

Pleasures such as he had never known lanced through him. He craved the wildness, too.

But he could take only so much. She was stronger than he. It took a good, brave man to ease his manhood from her mouth, but he proved himself to be just that, much to his surprise and, he suspected, to hers as well. And then he was upon her, stretching his body against hers, feeling far too big and far too hairy and far too brutish to lie against such delicate warm satin, but if she had complaints, she said nary a word.

She showed him the curious hooks that held her brassiere, but he was too hot to notice the workings, and she had to ease it from her breasts while he observed.

The bottom garment he handled for himself.

She cupped him, fondled him, kissed her way down to lick him, but he could not let her take his sex in her mouth, else he would climax too soon.

He returned her favors, kissed his way down her soft curves, lingering at her breasts, suckling at the full dark tips, licking at her navel, kissing the private hair, sucking at her womanhood. She writhed beneath him, and when she tugged at his arms he did her the same courtesy she had done him, and he kissed his way back to her lips, lingering where impulse led him. Her moans, her cries, the scratches of her nails against his back told him he chose well the places where he stopped.

"Rough wool," she said as she laved a hairy patch on his chest. "I need rough wool."

He would ask her later what she meant.

She was the one who spread her legs and pulled him down atop her, the one who guided his pulsing shaft to her wet great glen, the one who began the thrusts. Between the two of them they quickened the rhythm, rocked the bed, shook the rafters of the ancient inn, and found the wild sweet love that they both craved.

They did it again and again and again, throughout the evening and the night, and when the old springs finally gave way and fell in a cloud of dust to the floor, they laughed and held tight to each other, and they did it another time.

When the first light of dawn crept through the cracked panes of the window, with the pair of them entwined on the fallen bed, she woke from a troubled sleep and confessed all that she had done in that damnable field where she had been held captive.

"I was like an animal, Robert. Not like myself at all. I bit him like . . . like some wild beast—"

"Whisht, lass. Think on it no more. We both were not ourselves. Or maybe we were, doing what we had to do. When I rode over that hill and saw the gun on you and you begging to be shot, I was lost to a white-hot rage. It had never happened to me afore, even at Quebec. I dinna know rage could come in colors." He held her close. "I know it now."

"Oh, Robert, we've both got so much to remember. I thought I'd never get the taste of him from my mouth. And the splashes on my blouse. I felt like Lady Macbeth scrubbing at her bloodstained hands."

"Nay, in that you're wrong. She was a villain. There's none such in this room, save those in our misbegotten thoughts."

But she was not so easily appeased. "I don't know where I got the idea. I must have read it somewhere." Her eyes took on a faraway cast. "Maybe I read too much."

"Nay, 'twas cleverness and strength that came to your rescue."

"And my laird."

"Almost too late." He shuddered at the thought of what might have been. "They had the devil's own luck to have passed a dozen Camerons wi'out being seen." He stroked her hair. "But the luck ran out when they tried to bring harm to you."

She didn't answer for a while, and then she wept. He held her close, assuring her what a brave and bonnie lass she truly was.

"Why did they want you?" she asked when the weeping was done.

"They've served as hirelings of Fergus Munro afore. 'Twould seem likely this be his handiwork."

"The nephew, Fitz. I got only a glance at him, but he didn't seem a bad sort of young man. I know you can't always tell from looking, but still, sometimes I get feelings about people that prove to be right."

"And what, lass, is your feeling about your laird?"

"That you're brave and good and honorable," she said, her voice soft and low.

Honor was a subject he cared not to explore.

"I was thinking of my shaft. What be your view of it?"

"Let me sleep awhile, and then I'll demonstrate how I feel. You must be a very slow learner, Robert Cameron, if you don't already know."

Chapter Twenty-two

Fitzroy Sutherland jumped as though the devil had walked across his soul.

"Are you pinching me?" he asked.

Annie MacSorley glared at her companion, or at least she gave him an angry stare he would have seen if they weren't buried beneath a load of wool in the bed of the oldest wagon she'd ever seen, a heavy canvas cloth serving as a tent between them and the loosely packed bales to allow for room to breathe.

"I've not laid a hand on you," she answered, rocking uncomfortably on the hard wagon bed. "Where would I have an interest in pinching?"

"'Tis my backside that smarts."

"Sure and that proves it. I've no interest in that part of your anatomy. A surprise it is that a bug would be so entertained."

She meant what she said.

At least she wanted to mean it.

The springless wagon hit a rut in the road; she bounced awkwardly, painfully, falling against

296

Fitz, pushing away as if he'd burned her.

Why was she so skittish around him? She hadn't been so at the beginning of their adventure. The past three days confined in the cottage they'd found close to Loch Lochy had done it. Three days of looking at him and watching him fish and clean the plump trout he'd caught, days of sharing stories about their lives—at least about hers, for he'd been selfish with any information concerning his kin.

Three days of sharing silliness, too, and laughs. Then had come the disaster.

He'd kissed her. Last night before they went to sleep. And it wasn't just a peck on the cheek or a brushing of his mouth against hers. He'd really kissed her, long and hard, managing to get his tongue between her lips for a moment or two. They'd done with their meal, were lying in front of a small fire, the only kind they could risk, all comfortable and cozy, and he'd taken upon himself to steal a kiss. She'd forgotten about Liam and about running and about everything but kissing him right back.

She'd used her tongue, too, but the taste of him had frightened her. A terrible mistake it had been, too personal, too intimate. He'd made her feel undressed, or at least put the idea of getting that way into her mind.

She'd slapped him right soon enough, when his hands took to wandering, but she knew there was little force behind the blow. He'd known it, too. He'd grinned.

Men!

He hadn't bothered to kiss her again, for which she was grateful, but matters hadn't been the same between them since. All the past night and then in the early hours of the day the both of them had grown quiet and irritable and not the least bit content as they used to be.

At midmorning, both so tense they jumped when the other came near, they'd risked leaving, having heard no Camerons stalking about the woods, the loch, the glen. And what had happened? They'd ridden into a trap set by those two villainous, no-good—

Only her brothers would know the language to call them rightly what they were.

When the woman had appeared they'd run, but they'd had to tell someone that she'd been caught.

And who did they choose?

Robert Cameron himself.

"Cameron looked little like you described him," Fitz said into the gloomy darkness of the wagon.

"Are you reading me thoughts? If so, your ears must be a-burning."

"I'm saying you were wrong about him. He's no' the man you've talked about. Are you sure you saw him at Thistledown?"

She refused to answer. He'd only accuse her of lying.

He'd be right, but that was beside the point.

It was true her betrothed was nay so old as she'd imagined him to be, and best as she could see, he had all his teeth. Perhaps he was nay so ugly, either. Perhaps a lass or two might find him favorable to look upon. Perhaps her father had not been so wrong.

She stopped herself from going too far. Men thought they knew everything. Her father, Liam, every one of her brothers. And now Fitzroy Sutherland. So smart, catching the fish, trapping the rabbit, patching the roof when the rain came on unexpectedly.

It was his fault Gertie had pulled up lame. If he

hadn't dared her to ride away when he'd gone for
a drink at the stream, she wouldn't have taken off
across that rocky glen. And the mare would not
have turned her leg and dumped her rider onto
the hard, cruel ground.

It was her idea to leave the poor, dear horse at
the farm of the crofter whose goose they had
taken. They'd walked Gertie along the road, moving slowly and carefully lest the mare hurt herself
further, little caring whether they were seen. Good
fortune had been with them. No Cameron had
come near. With a few hundred tears and reas-
surances, she'd tied the horse to a post by the
poultry yard and bidden her good-bye.

It was Fitz's idea to hide beneath the wool when
they'd heard the sheepman talking to the crofter
about taking his goods down the road to Glasgow.

He'd family there, the sheepman said. 'Twas
time he paid them a call.

In Glasgow she could find a ship that would take
her to Ireland. Fitz said he would pay the fare,
though where he would get the funds she had no
idea. When she'd tried to question him, he'd told
her with all his masculine pride that he was a man
of his word.

Men. They liked to be in control. It was clear he
wanted to be rid of her. For certain she felt the
same about him.

His arm rubbed against hers. She wiped the per-
spiration from her brow. Though she'd removed
her cloak to use as cushioning beneath them, in a
woolen gown and petticoat and a binding chemise, she still wore too many clothes.

And wouldn't Fitz like her stripped naked?

Or would he care?

"'Tis warm in here," she said.

Without a word he shifted the canvas, tugging

at the edge until a sliver of daylight slipped through to their woolen cave. With it came a wee current of cool, fresh air, sweet as the breezes of Ireland itself.

Scottish air was nay so bad, she had to admit.

And neither were Scottish nights, not when she had a friend to share them. She'd scarce thought of hobgoblins throughout the past week.

Feeling charitable, she edged closer to Fitz.

"I'm no' sorry I kissed you," he said.

Was she charitable enough to be honest?

Aye, that she was.

"If the truth were told, Fitz, I'm of the same mind."

"You've a poor way of showing it, slapping me as you did."

"And you've had little experience with women. You should have kissed me again."

"Is that what Liam would have done?"

She waited a long while to answer, listening to the creak of the wagon, feeling each rut, each bend in the road, deciding whether to tell the truth.

Thinking things through.

"He's never kissed me," she said in a small voice.

He laughed sharply, as if he didn't believe her.

"Never," she said.

"Is that the Irish way? No' to kiss when a man and woman are promised one to the other?"

"We're not promised."

"But you said—"

"I bespoke more than I should. We were going to get promised, I know we were, but me father sent me away."

Fitz did not answer for a while. And then he took her hand, finding it smoothly in the dark, the way a lover might if he were used to seeking out his lass's hand. She liked his firm grip. For the first time she thought of him as a man full grown, and not a lad.

"Liam O'Toole has no sense about him," he said.

"Not so."

"Aye, 'tis the truth. You're a fine lass. Daft at times, but fine. And bonnie. Has he no use for hair the color of a cloudless morn when the sun burns night into day? Has he no use for eyes that flash like emeralds? Or for a lass with courage to defy unwanted fate?"

Annie's cheeks burned and her eyes misted.

"I'm not so bonnie."

He squeezed her hand.

"I dinna think so at first meself, but I've changed my mind. When you smile, you light up the world."

Somewhere in what he said lay an insult or two, but she was not of a mind to remember what they were. If he said her smile lit up the world, who was she to carp?

She snuggled close.

"We might have starved if not for you, these past few days," she said, surprising herself that she was so quick to give him his due.

"'Twas need that drove me, there being few geese lying about to steal."

"Will you ne'er forget the theft? We paid back the man far more than we took."

"I'll see that Gertie's cared for," said Fitz, then added solemnly, "after you're gone."

"Aye, that would be a kindness."

She could barely get out the words.

After you're gone. How could he be so uncaring? How could he be so cruel?

All charity fled her heart.

"Will your uncle beat you?" she asked, almost wishing it would be so.

Almost, but not quite.

"He's afeared o' my father. He'll keep his hands to himself."

"Your father is a brute, is he?"

"Some believe 'tis so."

"Is he poor, t' send you to an uncle he's no liking for? It's little concern of mine, you know, whether you're rich or poor, but I was wondering. You've said so little about yourself."

"T' my mind, he's poor indeed."

"Me father's rich. I could send you money. To pay back the sailing fare, though where you'll get it—"

"'Tis no' your money I want, Annie MacSorley."

His hand moved up her arm, effectively silencing her.

In the little bit of daylight straying inside beneath the canvas, she could make out his profile. Strong and straight it was, and she realized for the first time he was a handsome lad, leaner than he'd been when first they met, and he was decidedly growing a beard.

She stroked the bristles of his cheek. He jumped. She pulled her hand away. But he kept on moving up her arm, past her elbow, until he reached high enough to feel the curve of her breast.

"You can touch me if you like."

"Touch you?" His voice was barely a whisper.

"Aye, you know." She rubbed herself against his knuckles, brazen the way everyone thought she was. But everyone was wrong. Except for a few dry kisses stolen from one of the neighbor farmer's sons and that when she was but fifteen, she was as innocent as the day she was born.

Innocent in body, that was. Possessed of a vivid imagination, she had a very experienced mind. Hadn't she peeked when her oldest brother had taken to the barn the fair young lass who tended the goats? And did her father not know she understood the nights he spent with the widow Killeen?

"There," she said, rubbing against Fitz once more. "No other touching, you understand, nor kissing."

"I understand."

His voice seemed to have dropped two octaves. He shifted to his side so that he might face her and brought his hand against her with great slowness, caressing her waist, the heat from his palm like a mangle iron hot from the hearth. He moved so slowly upward she wanted to scream, but, too, she wanted to squirm and draw out the taunting moment. With everything inside her in a turmoil, her stomach clenching, her heart pounding, her breath turning ragged and shallow, she decided that touching was better than a kiss.

Nay, she revised, but it was just as good.

Alas, she couldn't take them both, the kissing and the touching, not at the same time. And so, when he cupped her breast, she put her hand atop his lest he move away or try to do more, smiled into his shadowed eyes, then stared into the dark, no longer mindful of the crude wagon bed or of the ruts over which they rode. Too, she made herself forget where they were going and what she had to do when they arrived.

Now was not a time for thinking things through.

Chapter Twenty-three

Sheriff Edgar Gunn brought his newest gavel down hard on the top of Bailie Fergus Munro's head.

"Ow!" Munro howled. He held his head against another blow.

Gunn raised the gavel, then lowered it. The bailie was unworthy of the energy it would take to hit him again.

"Ye're a dolt and a fool," he rasped instead, then with a whirl of his robe sought his rightful place on the perch behind his high sheriff's bench.

High bench, high sheriff. He liked the coupling.

He hated Fergus Munro. Sniveling, weak, stupid, that was what he was.

He was an ally, true, one of the few men he could trust to follow his will. Trouble was, the fool made too many mistakes. Taking a gun to Cameron, for one, and not using it. He could have killed the bastard right there on the street in Buscar-Ban and sworn 'twas in self-defense, with no one to say nay. Once again Cameron land would

304

have gone for taxes and Edgar Gunn, high sheriff of Darien, would have again been in control.

Wealth beckoned under such a circumstance, and a chance to spit in the face of his brother-in-law.

Inside him, rage warred with fierce anticipation, but as he looked down on the poor squat figure of his bailie, he spoke with a deadly calm.

"Ye say no word has come from the Dundas pair."

Munro rubbed his nose with the back of his hand. "Nay, but Cameron's left Thistledown, this time wi'out the wife."

"Ye're sure the information is correct?"

"He was seen by one o' the poor souls from Buscar-Ban, passing the inn on the road to Glasgow. The man rode hard t' bring word. I promised him coin."

"Then ye'll be the one t' pay 'im."

Munro spluttered and his face grew flushed. Ignoring him, Gunn tapped the gavel against the desk. Something was going on with Cameron. Why did his men roam the countryside? It seemed unlikely they searched for his nephew Fitz. And now the laird himself had joined them, leaving his amorous wife at the keep.

What was there about her that drove him away? Edgar had heard tell of women who could exhaust a man with their bedtime demands. Mayhap Lady Cameron was such a one.

Damn Cameron and his good luck.

Gunn's temple throbbed. Too much thought, too much speculation based on damned few clues.

He took his rage out on the only victim at hand.

"If the deed is no' done soon, indeed if no' done a'tall, I've a plan ye will little care for."

Munro shuffled his feet and blinked up at him. "A plan?"

"Aye."

He started to tell him more when the door behind the bailie flew open and Colin Cameron strode into the room. For a second Gunn took him for his cousin, so much alike did they appear. One was about as hated as the other, but it was Robert who held the power and the title and the land. For such, he would be destroyed.

The cousin's death would come in due time.

"We've business, Gunn," Cameron barked without so much as a greeting to the high office before which he stood. Rebellious fool. He'd pay for every insolent word that passed his lips.

Gunn leaned back in his chair, hands resting on his stomach. He regarded the intruder with contempt. "Ha' ye come to turn yerself in for some heinous deed? If so, I'll provide ye wi' the punishment ye deserve."

"So should we all get what we deserve. There are those who've done so already. I've come t' tell ye they're dead."

Gunn sat up. Excitement tingled within him. "Who?"

Too much to hope it was Robert Cameron and his bride. But still he hoped.

"The toadies ye set upon my cousin. Did ye think such a pair could do 'im in?"

Gunn's excitement died as fast as it was born. "I dinna ken wha' ye mean."

Cameron looked from him to Munro and back to the high bench. "Ye're a liar as well as a coward."

Gunn fumbled for the gavel and brought it down hard on the desk. "I'll fine ye for contempt!"

"'Tis no' enough money in all of Scotland to

306

cover the contempt held for ye, Edgar. I'm here to say the scoundrels met their fate when they tried to kill my laird and his bride. The fight was unfair, right enough. The fools attacked a pair o' their betters. That is t' say Robert and his woman have sense about them, and honor as well. Poor Ned and George dinna have a chance."

Munro spoke up. "Did they say anything afore they died?"

Cameron's grin was hard and lacking in goodwill. "The pair o' 'em pissed in their trousers, tha' was all. But they declared right loud enough they were after Robert."

His cold stare shifted to Gunn. "We ken the reason, do we no'? Paid assassins, if we were t' give such a fancy name to the wretched pair. Unpaid, more 'n like. Ye're no' the sort to pay afore a task is done."

"There's naught o' what ye say that ye can prove."

"And if I did, who's t' hear? 'Tis a pitiful thing when the Crown seeks violence upon the heads of its citizens. The ones who pay the taxes wi'out so much as a farthing slipped into a pocket or two."

Gunn's blood boiled. "I say—"

"I'm wondering wha' our German George would say if he learned all that was done in his name."

" 'Tis treason t' speak ill of the king."

" 'Tis treason as well t' steal from 'im."

Sweat beaded Gunn's brow. He glanced at Munro. "Toss the fool into the street."

The bailie's eyes bugged. "And how am I t' do such a thing?"

Cameron shook his head, disgust as strong as ever in his eyes. "I've done wha' I've come t' do. And that be to warn ye off, Edgar Gunn. Robert Cameron is a friend t' the people of Scotland and an enemy t' all that would do his country harm. He's a good man and true, but more, he's strong enough t' bring about yer ruin. This time ye brought harm t' his wife."

He came around the bench and grasped Gunn by the front of his robe, pulling him halfway to his feet. "This time, fool, ye went too far."

Gunn fell back in the chair, scarcely daring to breathe until Cameron had slammed his way from the room. He looked at the wrinkled folds of his gown, the primary proof of his high office.

And then he looked at Fergus Munro. He threw the gavel at him; it broke against the wall over his head.

"I warned ye I had a plan if ye failed. Be gone from this room, from the office. No longer are ye bailie of Darienshire. No longer are ye a Scot. There be ships leaving Glasgow for the colonies. Be on one o' 'em or ye'll meet the fate o' those Dundas fools."

"Ye can't!" Munro cried.

Gunn rose to his feet, blood pulsing at his temples. "Be gone!" he yelled.

Munro scurried from his sight, and Gunn collapsed into the chair. The walls closed in on him. He could see Sutherland's mocking face hanging in the air above his desk. Worse, he could hear the cackle of mocking laughter echoing across the room.

Another fear struck. Where was that cursed nephew? He'd scarce given him a thought over the past few days. Sutherland would have his liver on a plate if harm had come to the brat.

He rubbed at his aching bad leg but found no relief. Damn Fergus Munro for being so inept, leaving Fitz unfound.

Fitz was definitely a complication, but not the

main one, of course. That was bringing about his fondest wish. Before the week was out, without the encumbrance of his former bailie, he would see that Robert Cameron was destroyed.

Chapter Twenty-four

William Stuyvesant Sturgeon IV stared at his mother across the nineteenth-century Karastan Bigelow rug, one of the many American treasures in his parents' Upper East Side apartment.

Hortencia, by birth a Back Bay Bostonian, took pride in all things American, most especially those objects whose high-quality lineage could be traced back generations.

She felt the same way about people.

"I never cared for the girl," Hortencia said with a sniff, settling herself onto the walnut-and-velvet Hunzinger sofa, origin circa 1870, that was her special pride. Behind her a wall of windows provided a spectacular view of Central Park.

She seldom enjoyed the panorama, preferring instead the "exquisite loveliness" of her three-thousand-square-foot "modest" home.

"Meagan was well aware of your feelings," William said. He was trying to be patient with his mother, truly trying. But her welcome on his arrival from abroad moments ago left much to be desired.

"It's time you came to your senses and returned home," was the sum of her greeting as she'd offered him her rouged cheek.

"She's been missing less than two weeks," he had offered in protest, but his mother had already turned to take her place on the Hunzinger sofa, and he wasn't sure she was aware of what he'd said. His mother had what his father called a "convenient ear." She heard what was convenient to hear.

It was the closest William Stuyvesant Sturgeon III ever came to criticizing his wife. William Number Four believed Number Three found the characteristic admirable. Unlike his father, at most he found it amusing. But not today.

Dutiful son that he was, he had followed her into the living room, then watched as she sat, smoothing the skirt of her pink wool suit over her thin thighs, crossed her legs at the ankles, and, with her hands on her lap, went on the attack.

"Vulgar, I call it, running off that way. It's in the blood, I suppose, and should have been expected."

Hortencia barely topped five feet in height, weighed no more than ninety pounds, and would soon reach the sixty-fifth year of her birth. Without raising her voice, she controlled her husband, the six civic and cultural committees on which she sat, and most definitely her only son.

Or so she thought. Marrying Meagan had been William's lone way of rebelling, and now even that had been taken from him. His frustration knew no bounds.

He settled into a matching Hunzinger side chair, wondering if this might be the day the museum piece splintered under him. With the way his luck was running, it very well might.

"I do not believe she 'ran away,' as you put it," he said.

"Naturally not. Men can be such fools about women. I've Sybil's report, do not forget. She was there. She knows."

There was something particularly bitter in his mother's voice that he was unused to hearing, especially the part about women fooling men. Could his father have engaged in a dalliance of which he knew not? It was an intriguing thought.

He brushed it aside.

"I believe something dreadful has happened to her."

"Don't be dramatic, William. It's unseemly."

"When the love of one's heart disappears at the altar, drama seems called for."

Hortencia's gray eyes snapped in a succession of quick blinks, a sure sign she was roused. "For heaven's sake, 'love of one's heart'?"

He tapped the book on his lap, the volume she had been dutifully ignoring since admitting him into the foyer.

"A phrase I read in here. *A ghràidh mo chridhe.* It's Gaelic for 'love of my heart.'"

"It's one of that woman's trashy romances, no doubt. I might have known."

William let the comment go.

"I've spent a week trying to find her. And so have the authorities."

Hortencia shuddered. "I suppose it was made public in that barbaric land where she insisted on dragging you. Thank goodness the media have not picked up the story here. We would never live it down."

It would have been futile to point out that business had taken him to Glasgow, not his fiancée's fanciful plans.

Therefore he plodded on, but the going was getting difficult with all the interruptions. As always, his mother was like a difficult jury, one that had the power to speak.

"There was no sign of her after she left the kirk."

"Kirk?"

"The chapel where we were to be wed. People were there, tourists, groundskeepers. It's not at all private."

Hortencia's eyes grew hooded. "I know."

But more private, he could have said, than the Fifth Avenue church where she'd planned a wedding spectacle. The difference lay in the fact that Hortencia wanted the church. Meagan preferred the kirk.

He stood, unable to remain still a moment longer, and began to pace back and forth the length of the rug. His mother hated his pacing on the irreplaceable Bigelow, but at the moment he little cared. Meagan was irreplaceable, too.

He slapped the book against his leg as he walked.

"I tell you something has happened to her." Turn. "She needs help." Turn. "Honor would keep her from doing anything that might bring discomfort or pain to anyone." Turn and halt, with a lifting of hands. "My God, Mother, she was to bear my children. Your grandchildren. And don't get that look in your eye and say 'I know' as if it were a fate close to contracting leprosy."

"Sit down, William," she said through pinched lips. "You're straining my neck with all that movement."

I'd like to wring your neck.

William stopped. Had he actually thought such

313

a thing? Thank God he hadn't put it into words. He'd never hear the end of it and, possibly, neither would his father.

He held out the book. "This was with her when she disappeared. Except for the belongings in the room she had reserved, it was all she left behind. Somehow the secret of all this lies within its pages."

"You're becoming dramatic again, William."

"But that doesn't make me wrong. I feel the book's importance. No, I know it. I have but the particulars to figure out."

"You speak almost mystically," she said, her voice taking on an uncharacteristic wheedling tone. "Is this my Harvard attorney I hear? Your ancestors must be turning over in their graves."

"If they're as stubborn as the current generation, they need a good stirring."

"William!"

Hand at her throat, his mother looked truly shocked. He'd never managed that before, not when he'd told her of his engagement, or even his revised marriage plans. It was a reaction he rather enjoyed. And in that enjoyment he came to a decision that must have been lurking unbidden in the recesses of his thoughts ever since he'd boarded the Concorde hours ago.

He grew bold, seeing little recourse but to shock his mother again.

"Thank you, Mother, for helping me make up my mind. I came home because your call convinced me my efforts in Scotland were futile. But I'll find no peace here, not with Meagan's disappearance still a mystery. I must return. Immediately."

The result of his announcement was all he could have wanted, and more. Hortencia bounded to her feet and commenced to pace.

"You can't. Already I have made excuses to our friends, but they grow curious and less satisfied."

"Screw 'em."

That stopped her.

"William!" She clutched her chest and sank down on the Hunzinger in a most uncharacteristic slump.

He started to go to her, but caught her quick sideways glance in his direction and held up.

"Don't be so dramatic, Mother. It's vulgar."

She fanned herself with her hand. But she did not speak, and for that he was grateful.

He also felt a twinge of conscience. He knelt before her, *The Forever Bride* clutched in his hand.

"I tell you the secret is in here," he said, ruffling the pages, letting the gilt-and-crimson illustrations flutter before her eyes. The obvious quality of the book brought her upright.

"Nonsense."

He kissed her cheek. Her eyes widened. He couldn't remember the last time they had shown affection for one another. Emboldened, he kissed her again. Had he not known better, he would have sworn she blushed.

And then he stood. "I must make arrangements to return immediately."

"But two transatlantic flights back-to-back. Is that wise?"

"A man in love cannot afford wisdom, Mother. Even if I have to forgo the Concorde and take an overnight flight, I must go. Somewhere between this book and Thistledown kirk lies the answer to the mystery. Ask Father to explain my absence at the firm. I do not know when I shall return."

Hortencia gripped the sleeve of his coat.

Gently he removed her hand. "Don't ask me how

315

I know it, but wherever she is right now, something terrible is happening to Meagan. And it's up to me to see that she escapes her terrible situation with no permanent harm."

Chapter Twenty-five

Meagan ran a trembling hand down Robert's spine. Though he lay on his side, back to her, he was as always a beautiful creature. From any angle, she thought. She especially liked the sight of him lying on top of her, powerful and proud as a lion, yet gentle as a cub, using both power and gentleness to create a devastating effect on her body and her senses. And her heart.

Forget the heart. That line of thinking led to disaster.

She snuggled against him in the broken bed, more comfortable than she had any right to be.

"Are you awake?" she asked.

"Aye. But dinna let that sway you from your task."

She managed a laugh and kissed the indentation below his nape, trailing her lips down to his waist, using the light filtering in through the inn's curtained window to guide her way. Using her tongue, too, to feel her way down. She would have gone lower, but, just when she was getting truly involved, he turned, pulled her up to face him, and caught her mouth with his.

A most satisfying kiss it was, and one that was welcome far more than common sense told her it should be. With eyes closed, she curled her nakedness against him, fighting the urge to cling to him, to bare her explosive needs.

All night and into the morning they'd made such incredible love, like two people out of the *Kama Sutra*. He'd exhausted her, or rather she had exhausted herself, but she doubted she'd slept for long, each moment with Robert being far too precious to waste. And here she was, awake again, all sorts of lascivious desires pulsing through her. The longer she lay beside him, the more desperate they became.

She could not let him know, at least the desperate part. Lascivious he probably expected, given her conduct through the night.

She kissed one corner of his mouth. "Is it much past dawn?" she asked, then kissed the other corner.

"Closer to the hour of noon, I would judge."

Her eyes flew open. "Noon! But I was only going to sleep for a little while."

"You had a busy day and night, lass. Dispatching a bastard without so much as a weapon, and wearing me down with insatiable lust. You're hard on a man, Meagan Butler Cameron, and that's the truth."

He covered a lot of territory with just a few well-chosen words, so much he made her shudder. Stretched out as she was on her side, facing him, she felt terribly vulnerable. Somehow she must keep up the badinage.

"You know what they say about a hard man."

"Pray tell me."

"He's good to find." She laughed self-consciously. "It's a corny joke."

"Corny?"

"Well, no, that's not right." She sighed. "Forget it. I'm sorry I brought it up."

"It's up, for sure, and you're the cause."

"You've got a twentieth-century way about you, Robert Cameron. For sure."

She tried to say more, but suddenly she could no longer feign an easiness between them. Despair threatened with an intensity she could not bear. Instead of laughing or sighing or coming up with a quip, she wanted to cry. But she couldn't. If she did it wouldn't be a trickle of tears, something delicate she might be able to hide, or if not, attribute to fatigue.

Great, heaving sobs would take hold of her. And she wouldn't know why.

"Meagan—"

She pressed her fingers against his lips.

"I've never told you much about me, have I?" She kept her voice casual, and if each word came out close to brittle, he gave no sign he noticed.

It was his turn to kiss the corner of her mouth.

"I was born in a town about as far from New York as Thistledown is from Glasgow," she said, trying to ignore him, which was about like ignoring a tornado that threatened her with its winds.

He kissed the other corner. "Thirty years past, in your time, that is. Thirty years one week and—"

She groaned. "Would you forget about my age? And if you can't, at least give me the respect it demands."

He fingered her hair. "I respect you, Meagan the Elder. You're as well preserved—"

"I know. As smoked ham." Why did she have to

319

remember everything he'd said to her? Why did she have to wonder about the things he'd never said?

Summoning her courage, she hurried on. "My father worked for the post office, delivering mail until he became a supervisor. I was a sickly child, and Mother stayed home to care for me. Many women had jobs, you see, so it was good she was able to do so. We didn't have much in the way of possessions, but we had each other and that was enough."

He stroked her arm and shifted his hand to her hip, paying close attention to her outer thigh.

" 'Tis hard to believe the sickly part."

Her stomach knotted. She could almost hate him for his effect on her, if she didn't love him so much. Taking a deep breath, she determined to blunder on. Maybe he wanted to know about her and maybe he didn't. But her past was a far safer topic than their present circumstance, and as for the future—

She came close to breaking down.

Ah, but she was tough now. She was growing tougher every day.

"I caught every disease that came along, stayed in bed a lot, took to reading. But I ate right and I exercised and gradually I became the healthiest kid on the block."

He cupped her buttocks. Tough, she told herself. Tough.

"That reminds me," she managed, unable to keep the quaver from her voice or, worse, to stop the shift of her hips closer to him. "Did I ever tell you that your diet is terrible?" She gave him no chance to answer, but kept rambling on, holding back the sobs, concentrating on what she said. "Too much fat. You need more grains and vege-

320

tables and less meat. Some of MacFerron's figs wouldn't serve you ill, come to think of it."

He shifted his hand to her breast. "Aye, in that we agree."

She arched herself into his wonderfully callused palm. A knock at the door sounded with the explosive effect of George Dundas's gun.

She shrank into the mattress. Cursing, Robert eased from the bed and strode toward the door. God help her, she couldn't keep from watching the movement of his buttocks and his strong legs as he moved away from her to speak through the door. Everything about him rippled in a wondrously erotic rhythm. He mesmerized her as much as he'd captured her heart.

Hearing the voice of a man she didn't recognize, she pulled the covers over her head to block out the world. Whoever he was, he brought no good news. In truth, the only good news she could imagine was that Robert had won the Scottish lottery and the castle could be restored without the MacSorley funds.

But there was no Scottish lottery, at least not in 1765, and miracles didn't happen twice in one lifetime. Meeting Robert Cameron had been miracle enough.

The door closed and Robert fed the fire before returning to her. She listened to everything he did, listened to the pad of his feet against the bare wood floor, the crackle of logs that fed the flames, the creak of the bed as he lay beside her and took her in his arms. His skin had chilled in the brief moments he'd been out of the bed. She rubbed his arms, his chest, his stomach.

He caught her hand.

"I wanted to warm you," she said.

"Can you no' feel the heat within me? Does it no' burn your hand?"

"It burns me." She kissed his throat. "I share the heat."

"Meagan—"

She kissed his lips, sensing a stillness in him, terrified of what that stillness meant.

"Hush," she said. "Don't talk. Please."

She licked his teeth, the inside of his mouth, his tongue, and all the while her hands worked against his chest, palms rubbing against his nipples, feeling them grow tight, hearing the deep groan of pleasure in his throat, a rumble like distant thunder promising a storm.

"Touch me," she said.

He stroked the wetness between her thighs. A bolt of pleasure shot through her, so sharply provocative it was almost pain.

"Now," she ordered. "Do it now."

"Hush, lass. Dinna talk," he said huskily, mocking her orders to him, and she loved him all the more for it.

When he suckled her breast, she lost all train of thought except of where Robert touched her, where he stroked, where he kissed.

He paused long enough to curl her fingers around the oak spindles of the headboard.

"Hold tight," he said.

"But—"

"You'll no' regret it."

She tightened her grip. "Promise?"

But he was already back at work on her breasts, unable to answer because his lips and tongue were otherwise engaged.

She closed her eyes. In the velvet darkness that enfolded her, she knew nothing but the feel of

Robert, the scent of him, the sound of his ragged breath.

His hands teased, his lips taunted, the sound of his voice whispering erotic-sounding phrases in the ancient language of his people eased over her like a rare warm Scottish breeze. He kissed her breasts, her stomach, brushed his mouth against her private triangle of hair, then used his tongue to send her beyond the limits of words, into a world of pure sensation. He loved her with such expert intimacy that though he had not yet penetrated her body, she felt the heat and power of him all the way to her womb.

Her heart sang for him, her body wept its intimate tears so that he might take possession of her as she hungered for him to do. So frenzied was her passion, she almost snapped the spindles of the headboard into splintered pieces, much as he was splintering all that she had been, all that she ever could become.

Suddenly she could not wait for him to lower himself on top of her. This was the last time for them; she knew it, and, worse, she knew that he realized it, too. The last time. She wanted to drag it out two hundred years, but, too, she wanted it done, wanted to halt the torture of anticipated ecstasy, to take what he offered, and begin the agony of telling him good-bye.

The sooner begun, the sooner finished. With a spurt of strength that surprised both of them, she took his hands from her body and she pushed him back onto the mattress, straddled him, and, as she ran her tongue around his lips, ordered him to grip the spindles of the headboard where she had been holding.

"They're hot for you."

"Have your way with me, wife. I feel the heat."

How cruel it was for him to call her the one thing she could never be; yet in the truest sense of the word, she would be his wife forever, no matter which century served as the setting for her life.

Only a wife had the right to do this, she thought as she rubbed her dampness along his shaft, seeking refuge from the torturous throbs, wanting them sharper, faster, in the rubbing receiving everything she sought. Her gaze fell to his face, to the parted mouth, the flaring nostrils, the skin pulled tight against his magnificent cheekbones, his eyes a burning brown, like molten lava from the cauldron of desire.

She felt omnipotent to hold such a magnificent creature within her power, if only for this fragment of time.

Watching him, she lowered herself onto his shaft. She rotated her hips, a true and total wanton, her muscles tightening around him in welcome. She eased forward so that he might lick the tip of one of her breasts. Fire shot through her from every place they touched until her whole body, her entire being, was in flames.

Let her cosmic prankster laugh at the cruel joke he'd played; she was the one triumphant because she'd found the love of her heart.

"*A ghràidh mo chridhe,*" she whispered, but she knew he could not hear above the ragged breaths that tore from them both.

With a low groan he released his hands from the headboard and he stroked her back and cupped her buttocks while he laved one nipple and then the other. When the final convulsions came, she kissed him, swallowing his cry, letting him swallow hers, cries and breathing and separate climaxes melding, holding him tight, holding in the pleasure and the torment, knowing she should let him go but unable to do so.

Never, her heart cried out, and her soul answered, *Not yet.*

A sharp rap at the door told her the time that she most dreaded had come.

"Carriage approaching," someone called out. As if such an event could matter in the least, though it brought King George himself to the inn.

Impossible. She still felt the last waves of completion easing through her. When she lay in his embrace, it was in some ways the sweetest time of making love, when the two of them were the closest to being one.

But he let her go. Having little choice, she did the same to him. How shameful it would be to end this glorious moment with cloying embraces and with tears. Shameful and inappropriate, too, for a woman as strong as she.

If she didn't hurt so much, she would have laughed. Strong? She lay back on the fallen mattress and stared at the low rafters that striped the inn's dark ceiling, wondering if she had the energy to get out of the bed.

Robert stretched out on his side, the length of him touching the length of her, and he brushed the sweat-dampened curls from her face. She wanted to catch his hand and kiss his fingers. But she did not.

" 'Tis believed they're on the way to Glasgow, hidden in a shepherd's wagon."

No need to ask of whom he spoke.

"The horse they stole was found abandoned and lame near Buscar-Ban, and the cart departed soon after."

"When?"

"Yestereve. They've been traveling through the night. Cameron men watch."

"To make sure they don't escape again."

"Aye. There was much anger and embarrassment that they'd got away afore."

"We'd best hurry, then. You'll want to be there when they're found."

"The cart moves slowly."

"And the approaching carriage?"

"From Thistledown. I'd guess 'tis Janet come to see how matters lie, and to help as best she can."

His hand moved from her hair to her cheeks, her lips, her throat in gentle touches, but he made no move for a more intimate caress. Strange how she felt all empty inside, yet heavy-hearted enough to find sitting up impossible.

He was the one to rise and dress. She did not watch, instead finding the rafters of uncommon interest.

"I'll wait for you below," he said, and then was gone.

The luxury of a moment's solitude was denied her when Janet Forbes entered almost immediately.

"I've ordered ye a bath," she said after a brief look at the condition of the mattress, "and brought ye new clothes. The laird is none too attentive to a lass's needs."

Meagan came as close to smiling as she could. Not see to a lass's needs? That was one thing the laird could handle with incredible skill.

Surely Janet knew it. She'd noticed the broken bed.

Meagan stayed beneath the covers as a tub and buckets of water were brought to her. Laying out the garments she'd brought, Janet left her to the privacy she had wanted only a few minutes ago. But it was no longer what she craved. She had a lifetime to be alone.

The Forever Bride

She bathed quickly, then put on the chemise and petticoat and the gown, the latter made of a violet-colored wool the exact shade of her eyes. She supposed Janet had made it from Ermengarde's cloth; if so, she'd done a good job. High necked, long sleeved, fitted at the waist, it swept over her hips in gentle folds, ending at her ankles. Stockings and hand-sewn leather shoes had been brought, too. Everything fit. Everything felt right and good.

Combing her hair, bundling up her few possessions, she steeled herself to stoicism and went down for a small repast before setting out on the ride. A single glance from her husband told her what she wanted to hear: she looked pretty in her new clothes, so pretty he'd get her out of them if he could get her alone.

Janet stayed behind to wait for the post that would take her back to the keep. Meagan sat in solitude in the closed, rocking carriage; Robert chose to ride alongside a half dozen Cameron men, as well as Colin, who joined them after a hard ride from Darien.

Robert checked on her from time to time, but always she waved him away. With a smile, of course, and a nod of encouragement.

They spent the night in the home of a laird who had long been Robert's friend. She asked for a private room, claiming a headache from all that happened the past few days. Their host readily agreed to her request, and Robert made no protest.

If he seemed particularly brooding and silent, she attributed it to his sense of duty taking over when he would have rather indulged himself in the pleasures he knew with her.

Robert was a good man. He had been hard to find.

Another night was spent on the road, this time in an inn at Dumbarton. Early the next day they crossed the river Clyde and entered Glasgow. She remembered the way it was in the 1990s, a hundred times larger, with squalid tenements, true enough, like any modern town, but with enough Victorian-era homes remaining to give it a charm that other British cities lacked.

In 1765 Glasgow was smaller than she had expected and yet more civilized, with little more than ten thousand residents, but the streets seemed so busy with pedestrians and carriages alike, she would have guessed the population far higher.

Robert, riding alongside the carriage, served as guide. On their short journey to the docks they passed the town's fifteenth-century cathedral, and then Glasgow University.

"Three hundred years old, it is, and more," Robert said.

He pointed out Tollbooth Steeple and a road he called Gallowgate, at the end of which, he said, "the hangman awaits." Of all the sites he pointed out, only the hangman was not still around in 1997.

Crowded streets branched off of High Street, little more than teeming alleyways whose residents looked poorer than the people of Buscar-Ban.

Too, they passed brick mansions built close to the street, some so new they were not yet complete.

Over it all, over the stench of poverty and horse dung, she smelled hints of the waterfront and, stronger, another familiar odor. It took a while to figure out what it was: tobacco.

When she asked Robert about it, he answered that the importation of the product from the colonies financed many of the fine houses she had seen.

The high masts of sailing vessels guided them to the dock. Leaving the carriage, Meagan walked alongside Robert, with Colin and the other Camerons close behind, her feet moving without her will, the smile on her face plastic and insincere. Curious eyes turned to them—to her, she felt self-consciously, longing for her cloak and hood. Once again she felt out of place, a freak, an alien.

Robert seemed not to notice, his attention directed toward searching the crowds.

When he halted, she knew they had found their prey. Forever she would count that moment as the end of all her joy. She followed his gaze to the woebegone couple standing at one of the piers, the young man talking in earnest to a man she guessed to be the captain of the schooner anchored close by. The creak of the wooden hull, the sway of the masts, the shouts, the bustle—all served to make her dizzy.

Or so she told herself.

Annie MacSorley looked so very young, she thought, even younger than when she'd seen her astride a horse across the purple field. On foot she looked smaller, her red hair wildly tangled about her slender shoulders, her cloak bedraggled, dark circles looking like bruises beneath her eyes. They stared at one another. Meagan knew the moment she was recognized as the woman in the field. Robert had told her of Annie's warning concerning her danger, risking capture to save a woman she'd never met.

Meagan had thought only of how wonderful it was that he'd ridden to save her from harm and let his quarry get away. Though Annie could not have known exactly who she was, nor her situation, on this bright morning she seemed to understand the significance of her presence, and the bond that they shared.

All of it seemed so anticlimactic, with Meagan staying back and Robert walking forward, and no one shouting or running or crying as he spoke to the runaway pair. Over the caw of seabirds and the din of daily work that echoed along the docks, she could hear nothing of what was being said among the three of them, but she could imagine it. Robert would be quick and to the point. The powerful lion and not the gentle cub.

Colin remained by her side, her friend, she thought, providing the support she needed. The effect was to make her realize all the more how much she had gained from her journey through time, and how much she would lose when she was gone.

For she knew that no longer could she keep her engagement to William. To marry him would be unfair to them both. That part did not make her sad, except when she considered the family they had planned.

Unless she carried Robert's child—and somehow she doubted it, even after all that had passed three nights ago—she would never be a part of a complete family, never hold her own infant in her arms.

But she could not, must not think of herself right now. With the finding of Annie, Robert's intended destiny was now assured. That would have to be enough for her.

Chapter Twenty-six

They arrived home three days later, Meagan and the errant pair in the carriage, Colin and the other Camerons riding as escort. Robert remained in Glasgow to confer with the bankers who held the mortgage on his land.

"I'll follow as soon as I can," he said, speaking to no one in particular as they prepared to leave the docks.

Only Colin answered, promising to deliver all safely back to Thistledown.

Annie slept most of the way, as did Fitz, although sometimes he held her hand and watched each breath she took. There was an infinite sadness about him that she recognized in her own heart. The inevitable, that which they'd fought against, would soon take place.

When they arrived at the keep, Meagan and Annie went upstairs to freshen themselves. Bathwater awaited them in two separate tubs, as well as clothes laid out in preparation for their return. Janet had outdone herself.

For Meagan there was another hand-sewn gown, this one the color of amethyst, so lovely in its detail and fit that she almost broke down.

Annie wore one of the dresses she'd left behind when she ran away with Fitz. It suited her better than it ever had her temporary replacement. And so must her role as lady of Thistledown.

Neither spoke during the time they were alone, one being as lost in thought as the other. Annie descended first. Meagan lingered to lay out the Thistledown drawings for Robert, a going-away present she knew he would like.

Her plan was to slip away to the kirk and leave before she was forced to face him again. But Sheriff Gunn was waiting below in the great hall, and the boy Jamie MacRae, and even Ermengarde, with Janet looking on. The crowd of them cut off all chance of an easy escape.

"I found the little bastard lurking about outside the gate," Gunn said, waving at the boy, proud as if he'd brought in a culprit on a par with Jesse James.

Jamie sniffed in disdain, then winked at Meagan. "He couldna' catch his arse wi' both his hands and a chart. I came of me own will, wantin' to learn if ye be safe and well."

"I am," she said and then, with Colin seeing to the horses and to all that had occurred at Thistledown while he was gone, and Annie keeping quiet as a stone, she took on the role of lady of the keep, for the first time really, just at the time she must vacate the post.

"And why else are you here, Sheriff?"

Ignoring his nephew, who like the women had bathed and donned fresh clothes, he kept his attention on Meagan.

"Ye're no' from Ireland, though yer accent is one I dinna ken."

"I was deaf as a child," she said. "Why are you here?"

"And ye're no' a young lass."

"My people age early. Why are you here?"

His gray eyes darted about the room. "Where be the laird?"

"Why are you here?"

Each time she uttered the words, she snapped them out more harshly, while the others stood back and watched. From the corner of her eye she caught an encouraging nod from Janet, a smirk on Ermengarde's lovely face, and an open, toothy grin lightening Jamie's dark skin.

Gunn twisted a hat in his hand. He was dressed in finery to rival that of the banker Thomas Balfour: black frock coat, ruffled shirt, tight black breeches on skinny legs, high-heeled boots to give him height. His face was pale, his features sharp, his eyes darting and cold.

As a sheriff, he was certainly no Matt Dillon or Wyatt Earp. He wouldn't even make a credible Barney Fife.

An uncomfortable silence settled over the hall.

"I'd received word my nephew had been found," Gunn said at last. "I've come for him." He smiled at Fitz, who seemed none too glad to hear the news. "Ye were naughty t' put such a fright on me, lad."

Annie took Fitz's hand. She looked as though she would speak, but the young man silenced her with a shake of his head.

"I was sent here to become a man, do you no' remember, Uncle?"

"And have ye?" Gunn asked, his gaze shifting to

the girl by his nephew's side. She looked back wide-eyed but unafraid.

For all her stubborn pride and bravery, she had an air of innocence about her, and Meagan knew that in the area of sex the girl was still untouched. She knew, too, from the way Annie was gripping her young man's hand, that the two cared much for one another.

The contrast between them and her situation with Robert hurt all the more.

"I'm man enough to need little looking after," Fitz said.

"Hauld yer whisht, lad!" Gunn took a halting step forward, but there was nothing halting or lame in his voice. "I'll have none of it. Ye're coming wi' me."

"If Fitz says he's not coming, then he's not coming."

It was Annie who made the declaration, the most she'd said since leaving Glasgow. She spoke more softly than the sheriff, but her words had an equally steely edge.

Gunn's eyes turned hard. "Is this the whore ye took wi' ye on yer adventure, lad? Yer father will be none too pleased."

Fitz drew back a fist.

"Making friends as usual, I see, Edgar, and keeping the peace."

Meagan's heart stopped. She turned to watch Robert entering the hall. She had not heard him until he spoke, but, oh, how glad she was to see him. He was backed by Colin and two of the clansmen who had ridden with them on the Glasgow journey.

She told her heart to start its beating. She had no right even to be glad that he was near.

He kept his eyes on Gunn.

"I've had an interesting time in Glasgow. On the docks I met Fergus Munro, who told a curious tale."

"Fergus is nay my concern," Gunn said with a sniff. "I relieved him of his bailie's duties days ago."

"Aye. And bitter he is to be heading for the colonies."

Robert walked closer, his step solid against the wooden floor, his eye steady, a hint of a smile upon his face. But there was nothing pleasant about the smile, or welcoming. Meagan thought he had looked much this way when he tossed the knife at George Dundas's heart.

White-hot rage beneath a cool veneer.

"Do you have no interest in Fergus's tale? It very much involves yourself."

Gunn shifted nervously, his calm demeanor cracking under Robert's stare. "I've come for my nephew. We'll be gone. As for the charge against ye of assaulting Fergus, I've decided t' overlook it. And the wearing of the plaid as well."

"What a generous man you are. As generous with your forgiveness as you were with the taxes off my land."

"We've been o'er this subject when ye first returned, Cameron. No need to go through it again."

"There's need. I've Munro's testimony about the collections and where they ended up. And information, too, about the location of the tacksman who did your greedy work. Greedy and very much illegal. He's come upon hard times and hopes to sell what little he knows to whoever wants to hear it."

"And who's t' believe the likes of ye? Representatives of the Crown dinna turn on one another. I

335

take me orders from the king's men and no' from
ye."

"These representatives are newly appointed. I
found them more responsive to a Scotsman's
plaints than those who went afore. But then, of
course, I dinna then have the testimony of one of
your thieves."

Gunn glanced nervously about the room. "Ye
lie."

"You have only to return to Darien to find that
I tell the truth."

Gunn's gray face flushed red. He looked at Fitz.
"Yer father is behind this somehow."

"Nay," said Robert. "I am solely to blame. When
I go to my grave, in hopes as a very old man, I'll
consider this one of my life's finest accomplish-
ments. A blow for Scotland it is, and against the
oppression of a misrepresented Crown."

With a roar of rage, Gunn went for his pistol.
Robert moved swiftly and flattened him with his
fist. The weapon clattered harmlessly to the floor.

Standing over the sheriff's sprawled body, Robert seemed little the worse for the one-sided scuffle. "I've not mentioned the plan to set a pair of
idiot twins on me, nor the danger they presented
to my wife."

"But I'm not—" Annie began.

"Quiet," Fitz ordered, and she obeyed.

Robert paid neither of them any mind.

"You'll find I'm a generous soul, Edgar. You
have a carriage below, do you no'? I'll provide
fresh horses to get you to Glasgow. I suggest you
leave immediately. Alone."

Propping himself on his elbows, Gunn rubbed
his jaw. "And why would I be fool enough t' go
there?"

"Why, to join Fergus on the long sea journey.

I've taken the liberty of booking you passage on the same ship."

Meagan could not keep her silence. "You're sending them to America?"

Robert shrugged.

"We've enough criminals already without adding more."

Gunn sat up. Robert scooped up the pistol and tucked it inside the waistband of his trousers. "One as inept as this should prove of little trouble."

Meagan had her doubts, but she saw Robert had made up his mind.

He hauled the sheriff to his feet. "Colin will see to your leaving. Your passage is paid, and there are funds awaiting you at the bank to provide the necessities for your journey. The bare necessities, but then the sooner you get used to the lack of luxury, the easier you will survive in the wilderness to which you're headed."

Gunn started to speak, but Robert was not done.

"The rest of the stolen coins will, unfortunately, revert to the Crown. I tried to claim them for the people who were your victims, but a man can do only so much."

It was the first note of regret she'd heard in his voice since he entered.

Colin took over Robert's hold on Gunn's collar and, with his captive howling in protest, dragged him from the room.

And that left the central players in Meagan's drama standing beside the great hall's long table, each given to separate thoughts, none of which would be in agreement with anyone else.

Each second that ticked by was like a pin pricking at her nerves.

"Excuse me, please," she said, daring to look

Robert in the eye. "I need to rest before any more decisions are made."

The lie was delivered with a certainty that made her proud; it was a skill she'd picked up from her laird.

Without waiting for an answer, she hurried from the hall, but instead of going up the stairs to the bedchamber that was no longer hers, she hurried down past the lower floor and out into an overcast day.

The sheriff had already departed; she was proud of Colin's fast work. Just as she turned toward her true destination, a rider came through the stone gate and onto Thistledown grounds. He dismounted beside her.

"Pardon, miss, but I'm looking for me sister Annie. Has the Brat been seen hereabouts?"

"You're Tully MacSorley, aren't you?" she said. "Annie's in the great hall with her betrothed."

Her voice almost broke on the words.

"Praise be the Lord," he said, making the sign of the cross.

"And the laird, as well," she said as she turned from him. Lifting her skirts, she ran down the path that led to the kirk. She didn't stop until she was standing beside the pew where her adventure had begun.

She'd grown so used to calling it her adventure, but today the word seemed inadequate. Here was where her life had begun, and where the soul of it would end.

Her gaze drifted to the high vaulted ceiling and to the paintings from the Bible, the seasons of the year, the depiction of the myths. A strange collection it was, showing the love of the Scots for learning and for beauty, no matter their source. Brilliant men had come from this time, among them the economist Adam Smith, the diarist James Boswell, the poet Robert Burns.

Brave men, too, like Robert Cameron, men who strove to preserve the past as well as provide a decent present and prosperous future for people long oppressed. Living in the midst of a vast and beautiful wilderness, he was also part of a brilliant civilization. For all its hardships, it was an incredibly exciting time to live.

But she must go.

She prayed the incantation would work. Taking a deep breath, she sat and prepared to utter the ancient words.

"I love you." The declaration came from a voice that was heartbreakingly familiar and dear.

She looked up to see Robert standing beside the pew. She brushed a tear from her eye, then looked down to her lap.

"You shouldn't be telling me now."

"I feared you dinna know."

"It doesn't make any difference."

"Lowering words, wife." He sat on the pew beside her and took one of her hands. "I thought you'd be pleased."

She tried to pull away. "I'm not."

"I've turned you into a liar."

"I'll find it useful when I get back home."

"Your home is here at Thistledown."

She sighed in exasperation. Why did he have to make this so hard?

"Did the bank give you the money? Did Thomas Balfour say that since you're such a good and honest man, with goals that make Scotland proud, you do not have to worry about repaying the loan?"

"Since my return from the war, I've been a realist, Meagan. Looking at matters without coloring them as I would want, taking the death of my wife and infant son as a sign I never should have gone. The lingering illness of my father and the wish upon his grave guided me in all that I did. But it was always a dream, Meagan, and I'm no' a man for dreams."

"What of your people?"

"They will survive. I will make sure of it. The land is here; it will no' be taken from them again, though the bank in Glasgow holds title. I've the word of good men that such will be."

"And what of the castle restoration? I've told you it must be done. You cannot change history."

"I can but try. Stay as my bride, my wife, though I can promise you little of luxury. Together we will see how matters go."

Opening her fisted hand, he placed a gold-and-pearl brooch on her palm. She stared down at its intricate loveliness, and her heart broke a little more.

"I've no ring to give you, but this belonged to my mother. Now 'tis yours."

And then he placed beside it the engagement ring she'd received from William. Beside the delicate brooch it looked gaudy and out of place.

"I told you I would return it, lass. Though I bend the truth from time to time, I'm a man of my word."

Meagan thrust the ring in her pocket, but she could not let go of the brooch. Not yet. She wanted to hold its beauty and all that it represented for as long as she could.

She clutched it tight and saw that her nails were stronger than they'd ever been in her life. Before long, once she was in her rightful time, they'd probably start splitting and peeling again, and she would have to resort to acrylic fakes.

The Forever Bride

Pulling away from Robert, she stood. He was all that was temptation, so much so that her lungs constricted and she could hardly breathe. She didn't need luxury. She needed him.

And as the years passed, what then? If she stayed would they wander about the countryside? About the world? Or would he remain close by and view the ruins of Thistledown with a growing regret? She'd read a thousand romances where true love lasted forever, but she'd read other books as well, stories of the dying of love, crushed by the realities of daily living, by hard times, by the happenstance of fate.

She'd preferred the happy endings; she'd believed them as possible as their alternate.

But she could see no happy ending for herself. And so she toughened herself for the final lie.

Placing the brooch on the pew, she took a step backward, but she did not flee as she would have liked.

"Listen carefully, Robert, to everything I have to say. And do not interrupt, please. It's true I feel a strong affection for you. What's not to like? You're handsome and brave and witty and educated and, most of all, you have a sympathetic heart for your people and your land."

"I can see where you'd find it hard t' love me."

"Don't be so smug," she said through a throat so tight she barely got out the words. "You're not perfect. You're sarcastic and untruthful when the need arises and you very much prefer to have your way."

He stood and took a step toward her. She managed to hold her ground.

"What of my lovemaking?" he asked. "Dinna you care for me in bed?"

Standing in the middle of the kirk, feeling

341

terribly sinful, she could imagine his hands on her, stroking, caressing, arousing. She could feel his penetration of her body, the hot convulsions, the whirling madness of the passion that they shared.

And only through the suggestion of his words.

But it wasn't really sinful, was it? They had been wed in this very church.

"I care for you in bed. I'm not so skilled a liar to deny it."

"Can you abandon all that we've shared?"

She saw he was about to touch her, to kiss her, and she knew that if he did she would be lost.

And so she told the ultimate lie.

"After we're married, I'll pass on to William all you taught me. He'll be very appreciative."

He blinked once, and then he was still, so much he could have been carved from ice. She waited for his fury, his scorn. But she got only silence extending into eternity.

When he spoke, it was hard and brusque and so low she could barely hear him.

"You're no' the woman you were when you first fell into my arms."

If he could summon up anger, she could, too. "And who's fault was that? I wanted to leave here right away."

"And so you should have. I was wrong to ask you to stay."

If she told the ultimate lie, he offered the ultimate rejection. She thought she took it rather well, considering he might as well have cut out her heart.

But his coldness was what she wanted. No, it was what she had to have.

She stepped past him, prepared to sit and utter the incantation, wondering what in heaven's name she would do if the words did not work. It was a consideration she would handle only if her worst fears proved true.

Before she could sit, before she could say a word, a dizziness overcame her, something akin to what she had felt the day of her wedding, the moment when she had tried to pledge herself to William, the moment she had passed through time. Robert must have sensed something was wrong, for he was suddenly beside her, taking her hand.

And then the second miracle happened. A haze formed across the pew, and then was gone, in its place her fiancé William Sturgeon, dressed as always in his Brooks Brothers suit and Italian shoes, the Rolex watch still strapped to his wrist.

Strange it was to notice such details, but they were easier to comprehend than the presence of the man.

"Eureka!" he shouted out. "I broke the code." He saw her as the haze evaporated, and he grinned like a schoolboy, a sign of unalloyed pleasure she had never seen in him before.

"Meagan, I don't know where we are or what's going on, but I've found you at last. You're rescued. I've come to take you home."

Chapter Twenty-seven

Meagan welcomed William's embrace, simply because there was nothing of arousal or desire in it. He was like a friend; he *was* a friend, the only one she could accept. And he was so glad to see her. Unlike the man who stared at them close to the doorway of the kirk.

When William stepped back, he took his first good look at her, at her strange floor-length gown and the windblown way she was wearing her hair, and he stared at her face for so long she began to shift nervously.

"You're different," he said.

"I've been gone more than two weeks."

"There's more than two weeks of change in you."

He looked around her at the kirk, at the air so much cleaner than he was used to, at the brighter color on the ceiling, at the open pews that were closed to the public in 1997.

And then he saw Robert standing behind her. Robert, with his thick, dark-copper hair and his saffron shirt and his trousers tight against his muscular frame. Robert, with his strong features and piercing brown eyes and skin the color of bronze.

Robert, who looked as one with the magnificent land on which he was raised, and at the same time comfortable in the confines of the medieval church.

"What the hell is going on?" William asked.

She'd never heard him use any form of profanity before. She wondered what he would say when he got the full report.

"It's 1765, William, that's what is going on. We're still at Thistledown. Only the century has changed."

He shook his head in disbelief.

"What was the date when you broke this code?"

"I don't know. Somewhere toward the end of May."

He *had* changed. He always knew the exact day and time, no matter the circumstance. Even when they'd shared a bed, she'd known his inner clock was always ticking.

"You said *The Forever Bride*'s incantation three times, didn't you? While you were sitting in the kirk."

"Yes."

"That's exactly the same thing I did."

"But you said it in the middle of our wedding ceremony." He sounded accusing. He had the right.

"I felt faint." What a wimpy thing to say. Not at all in keeping with her newfound strength. She would have to improve. "I said it because I needed bolstering to get through the vows, and the next thing I knew I was back in time."

He started to comment, a declaration of

disbelief more than likely, but he took another look around him and said, "I'll be damned. You're telling the truth."

"I am."

He believed it far faster than she had, but then he had her to tell him the truth, that and her mysterious absence over the past weeks.

"What's more, when I went back in time I landed here in the middle of another wedding ceremony." She wanted to laugh, to show how casually she treated the whole crazy happening, but nothing came out except a pitiful squeak. "Funny thing about that ceremony. Guess who was the bride."

For the first time since his arrival, William's visage took on its usual lawyerly cast.

"Considering the look on your face, I'd say it was you."

She nodded, and William's attention returned to Robert. "And the groom?"

Robert bowed.

William's face reddened. He was actually flushed. She hadn't known he had enough blood. And then she felt ashamed for putting him down. He was as good a man as he had ever been, and he'd offered a Hoboken postman's daughter his highly prized name.

"You didn't—" he began. "He didn't—"

She spoke up fast, before Robert could do so. "What has happened here is beside the point. You've come for me, and I'm returning with you."

She shot Robert a look that was supposed to warn him against speaking up. She wasn't in the least surprised that the look didn't work.

"Meagan Butler Cameron is my wife," he said. "'Tis here she should stay."

She shook her head in exasperation. "I already

told you I can't. You seemed to believe me. I didn't think you even liked me anymore."

"I've altered my thinking. I like you, lass. And you've no' convinced me you need to go."

"That's because you're a stubborn Scot."

"It's been my charm, dinna you ken?"

"It's not in the least charming, and I—"

William cleared his throat, and his gray-blue eyes darted from one to the other. "Is there something going on between you two?"

"No," said Meagan.

"Aye," Robert snapped.

The opposite answers came out simultaneously.

"I believe him," William said.

"A wise man," Robert said.

The two men eyed each other with a mixture of admiration and hostility. She knew them both to be abominably stubborn; she saw it as a Y-chromosome trait.

"Maybe there was something going on," Meagan said, "but no longer."

William took her left hand. "You're not wearing a ring."

From her pocket she pulled the huge diamond he'd given her to signify their engagement. "That's because I don't belong to either of you." She placed it in his hand. "Here. Thank you for the honor of wanting me, and thank you very, very much for coming after me. But the truth is, we'd make a terrible couple."

Robert spoke up. "You'd make a poor Sturgeon, indeed."

"She's told you of me," William said. "You knew she was engaged."

"When she vowed to be my lady, I assumed the betrothal was o'er. Tell me, pray, where my thinking went astray."

Meagan saw William's fist clenching and unclenching, and she was struck with dismay. All she needed was for him to challenge Robert to fisticuffs. He'd boxed a little in Harvard, but that had been years ago, and she didn't think he had been very good.

In contrast to Robert, who had flattened the sheriff with one blow.

She'd had enough. "Look, guys, this is the way things are. William, I'm returning with you but not as your wife. Robert, accept it. Once I'm gone our marriage will surely be null and void, by reason of abandonment if nothing else. You'll marry Annie the way you should have—"

"Nay, I'll not have him as my husband."

The three of them turned to Annie, who'd slipped unnoticed into the kirk, followed by Fitz, Colin, Janet, and Ermengarde. Meagan didn't remember the place being so crowded even on Sunday.

William regarded the newcomers with open curiosity, especially Ermengarde.

"Annie, you must marry him," Meagan said, having put up with all the argument she could take for one day.

Tully MacSorley joined the others. "Brat's a stubborn one, she is. Da claims he's never seen the like."

"She's honor-bound to do so," Meagan said. That brought a look of skepticism to every face in the kirk.

"All right, honor hasn't figured into much of what's gone on, but it should have."

"And love?" asked Robert. "Does the heart have nary a say in what we do?"

Everyone present seemed to draw a collective breath.

She looked at him, and it was as though they were alone in the chapel. He looked so wonderful, so strong, so manly, so . . . Robert. Every part of her cried out for him, yearned for his comforting embrace. How easy it would be to give in, to say, *Okay, everybody wants me here—well, almost everybody—and that ought to be good enough for me.*

But it wasn't.

"I know you care for me," she said. "But your heart belongs to Thistledown. And your honor. We've thrown the word around a lot lately, but it still stands for something."

She turned to Annie. "He needs you. You won't be sorry to be his wife."

"But I *can't* marry him," Annie said. She glanced over her shoulder at Fitz, who was standing in the shadows by the door, and then it was back to Robert. "I mean no offense, Laird Cameron, but I have no affection for you. Keep the dowry. I don't want it. During the past weeks I've found out I can live without funds and little suffer the inconvenience."

She hesitated. "Well, maybe a little, but I'll grow used to it in no time a'tall."

"Thank you," said Robert with a courtly bow. "But your father has no' gained the wealth he has by being a poor man of business. He sent his money in the belief you would be the lady of Thistledown. It must be returned."

Annie started to protest, Robert tried to forestall her, Meagan put in her opinion, and even William, ever the attorney, attempted to arbitrate, all speaking at once and none listening to what the others said.

"Whisht!"

Fitz stepped from the shadows into the middle of the fray, and all argument ceased.

349

Evelyn Rogers

"You're all in a fine fret," he said, "and over nothing of consequence."

The babble took up again. He snapped his fingers and quiet returned. Everyone regarded him with degrees of surprise, no one more so than Annie. Over the past hour he'd taken on a stature that gave him both presence and dignity, little like the woebegone youth Meagan had observed on the Glasgow dock. Whatever he had been before, today he was a man, and not one to be ignored.

She caught Janet's eye. The housekeeper winked, a small smile tugging at her usually serious lips. Meagan felt a small tingle in the vicinity of her heart; she wondered if it might signify the beginning of hope.

She promptly tamped it down.

"Robert Cameron," Fitz said, "you must keep the money as an investment in the land. I've a feeling you'll be able to repay it afore long."

"Possibly," said Robert. "But I've been in conference with a banker who doesna share your conviction."

"He little knows what I know. You have me to serve as guarantor. Once Annie and I are wed."

"Oh, Fitz," said Annie, "have you been out in the sun too long? You've turned looby on me."

The young man's eyes were for only her. "I've no' been truthful wi' you, lass. I'm nephew to the sheriff, 'tis true, and son of his only sister, Sophia. But I'm also son to Humphrey, Earl of Sutherland, one of the wealthiest men in all of northern Scotland. Only son, I must add, and heir to his title, though I'll no' use it as he has done. He likes to put on airs, 'tis true enough, staying in London much o' the time, joining the Highland Society there, wanting me t' do the same."

"You'll be an earl?" Annie said, her green eyes

wide as a pair of verdant Highland pools.

"One day. Do you think your father will mind?"

"Bloody hell no," Tully interjected. "He'll be dancing a jig when he hears."

"Do you mind?" Fitz asked Annie. "I love you, and that's for sure."

She looked down, suddenly shy. "If we can go roaming about the countryside as we did, I've little in the way of objection."

He took her by the hand. "Then come wi' me, lass. We've plans to make." So saying, he led her from the kirk, leaving all to stand and watch.

Leaving Meagan to feel Robert's very knowing gaze on her. She'd made so many pronouncements the last half hour that she didn't know what to say, or even what to feel. Her head whirled, her heart pounded, and she felt a ridiculously strong urge to cry.

In desperation she turned to William. "I don't know if the incantation works the other way—"

"Then I'll find out."

Before she could object, he sat back on the pew, eyes closed, and whispered the magic phrase three times.

A haze formed, and when it cleared he was gone.

"Oh, my," Meagan said, hand to her heart, and in the background she heard Ermengarde gasp. Colin muttered something more substantial, as did Tully. Janet and Robert said not a word, and Jamie just gawked openmouthed, his eyes wide on her.

She sat on the pew and waved her hand where William had been. The air felt warmer there, but otherwise there was no sign he had ever come for her.

Now it was her turn. She opened her mouth. No

sound emerged. And then the mist returned and, with a wave of dizziness that overtook them all, William appeared beside her once again.

"Damn!" he said. "That's some experience. It takes something out of a man. One more time is about all I've got in me."

She touched his sleeve. He felt very, very real, and she jumped to her feet. How could she feel trapped when she had two centuries from which to choose? She must be daft and looby and crazy as a loon.

"What a strange place," said William. "It needs some study. If it's all the same to you, Meagan, I'm not so sure I want to leave again right away. Certainly if I've only the return journey left."

She stared at him. But he was looking at Ermengarde, who was looking back at him.

"Then 'tis settled," Colin said, "though I've need of an explanation, Coz."

Nothing is settled! she wanted to shout. But when she tried to tell them exactly that, all she could do was give way to tears. With a shake of her head in Robert's direction, she ran from the chapel as fast as her shaky legs would go.

Robert found her on the second floor of the castle ruins, the place where they had made such hot, sweet love so many days ago. She was weeping into her hands, but he made no attempt to be silent, and when she heard him she brushed the tears away and looked up with that all-too-familiar stubborn expression on her face.

Her hiccough took away from the solemnity of her gaze. "I never expected a happy ending."

"Dinna you want it?"

"I—" She shook her head and looked toward the jagged stone wall.

The Forever Bride

"'Tis time for the truth, Meagan. Did you mean what you said about wanting to leave?"

"It was a great exit line," she said, blinking away another few tears, "but now that William wants to stay, I've got no real reason to go. So what do I do without the exit?"

A more forlorn expression he'd never seen on her face. She looked around her, settling her gaze on a stone gargoyle that mocked them from amidst the rocks. When she glanced sideways at him, he caught the hint of a devilish light in her eyes.

"You have a husband for guidance. I'll show you what t' do."

He took her in his arms and kissed her. He wanted the kiss to be gentle, but all the fears of losing her came upon him again and he held her close, as if he would pull her inside him and keep her from running away.

The kiss was long and thorough, with a pair of tongues getting involved, and he knew if he didn't cease such a pursuit they would be making love in the ruins once again.

With more reluctance than she could ever ken, he lifted his lips from hers, but he did not cease his embrace.

"I love you," he said.

"I love you," she said.

"I had begun t' doubt I'd hear the words. You're mine, lass, the same as I am yours. My forever bride, for sure. I must warn you, though. We'll be making love more than once a year."

She smiled up at him, nestling close. "Robert," she said, with the sauciness back in her voice, "have you so quickly forgotten the hours we spent in bed at the inn? More than once a year? With you doing the loving, once a night will hardly be enough."

353

Epilogue

Standing by the door to the keep, Meagan eyed with pride and a sense of accomplishment the work that was taking place on Thistledown Castle. In the ten years since her arrival, the outer walls had been restored and the roof begun, monumental tasks to her way of thinking, considering the lack of heavy machinery to do the work.

Everything must be painstakingly done, but perhaps that was why the results were so satisfying.

Robert had been in no hurry to finish the task, choosing instead to make sure that his land and his people flourished.

His wife certainly did. Three children, two boys and a girl, and another baby on the way. She rather thought that after this one she would bring up the subject of eighteenth-century birth control.

A handsome young lad rode through the gate and onto the grounds. Solidly built, his skin dark, his hair the color of gold, he waved in greeting.

"Jamie," she said, returning the wave. "How goes it?"

"It goes well," he said, dropping to the ground

beside her. "We've twice the sheep t' shear than last spring. The wool will bring a tidy price at the mills."

"With the population of Buscar-Ban growing, you'll need the extra funds."

She thought of the village as she'd first seen it, and she thought of it now, the cottages repaired, the yards cleared of debris, and, best of all, the glint of pride back in the eyes of its people.

Thanks to William. Before he left for the twentieth century, she'd signed papers turning over her savings to the New York Historical Society for restoration work, and he had given her the engagement ring. She'd used the surprisingly large amount received from its sale to finance the rebuilding of Buscar-Ban. Jamie had worked hard, even though he had no family still there. When he turned eighteen she had put him in charge of the fields. Gradually he'd taken over every facet of the town's revival.

And he had a girlfriend, too, though he did not care to be asked about her, except to admit she did exist.

Robert talked to him about attending Glasgow University, and he had not said no to the idea. Meagan had hopes he would eventually agree, but she'd learned that in dealing with Scots, it was best not to push too much.

She had made one request, and all had agreed to comply. Not a single word must be said about what had happened in the pew, nor of what they'd learned about who she really was.

"And who are we t' tell?" Colin had asked. "They'd call us looby, or a bunch of drunken Camerons."

How things had changed since her arrival. All across Cameron land there was a sense of prosperity and a knowledge that though the work of raising stock and tending fields was hard, it brought with it more than adequate rewards.

Janet came up behind her. Of all the people she'd met at the keep, Janet had changed the least. Ermengarde had married the blacksmith, Colin had found himself a wife in Glasgow, Fitz and Annie were off on a sailing ship for somewhere in the east, but with Janet there was little change. Sometimes she visited her son and his family on their farm, but she always returned to her own duties, saying she was needed at the keep.

And she was.

When Robert slipped back to his arrogant ways, she put him down without Meagan's needing to say a word.

She kept Meagan in her place, too, reminding her of all she had gained by staying in her new-found time.

Meagan didn't need to be told, but she let her say it anyway.

There were three people she did not know about: Edgar Gunn, Fergus Munro, and William. All were in America, but one was separated by more than two hundred years.

She fervently wished they all got exactly what they deserved. Only in William's case did that mean an ending as happy as hers. Somehow she knew that he'd found happiness. He'd certainly found it for a while here in Scotland with Ermengarde.

"Our laird has need of ye," Janet said.

Her eyes drifted upward toward the high keep window across from the bedchamber door.

Meagan patted the brooch at her throat, and then her stomach. The pregnancy was not yet showing, but Robert knew of her condition. And he very definitely approved.

"We've nary a child t' resemble you, lass," he'd said when she told him. "I've need of a black haired bairn to balance our brood."

Meagan rather liked the children as they were— coppertops, she called them, a fairer version of their dad.

She found Robert standing in the middle of the bedchamber, his hands behind his back. There were flecks of gray at his temples now, but his body was just as erect as it had ever been, and his eyes just as steady.

Best of all, he was even better in bed, though she'd thought that impossible when she agreed to stay as his wife.

"Do you know what day this is?" he asked.

"Our anniversary."

"And tomorrow?"

"I'd rather not think of it."

"A birthday is nothing to bring you shame."

"This one brings another decade."

"You've held up well."

"Like smoked ham."

"Better. Like fine wine."

"What's behind your back?"

"A gift."

She tried to reach behind him, but he backed away.

"I don't need a gift." She heard the slam of the door to the tower and the laughter of children. The tower was their special place, where they slept and where they played. She liked it because it kept them close.

"They're my gift," she said. "The children and you."

"Then I'll keep this for myself. In truth, 'tis really mine."

"Can I at least see it?"

"For a kiss."

She willingly paid the price.

He pulled out a framed picture, or at least that was what she thought it was at first when she could see only the back.

He turned it around. In the center of the frame, pinned carefully to a background of black velvet, was the pair of panties she'd worn when first they'd met.

"Robert, you rascal."

"I've ever been so."

"I'd forgotten about them years ago. Where have you kept them?"

"In hiding for this day. Ten years past, I found them as intriguing as anything I ever laid eyes on. I've little changed my mind."

"I don't have anything for you," she said.

"That's no' the truth. You've everything for me, lass. Your life, my life, the bairns. I'd be in a sorry state wi'out you."

"Now that you mention it—"

"Whisht. Kiss me afore I pass out from the need of the taste of your lips."

"What a liar."

"Aye."

She kissed him anyway. It was a long, long while—forever, it seemed—before they left the room.

Author's Note

Readers and writers of time-travel romance novels understand the special challenges and rewards of the genre. We've got the best of both worlds: a contemporary protagonist complete with twentieth-century sensibilities and hangups and a historical protagonist who comes with a set of problems and beliefs from some time period in the past.

The Forever Bride, my first full-length time-travel, was both a joy and a test. Meagan and Robert come from such different worlds, yet they have the same values, a love of family and home. My favorite scene was when she tried to explain twentieth-century advertising to him, especially the concept of credit cards. If you have a favorite, let me know.

My next book for Leisure, *Texas Crystal,* will be on the bookshelves this summer.

Please write me at the following address:

8039 Callaghan Road, Suite 102
San Antonio, TX 78230
URL: http://www.nainc.com/rogers

TIMESWEPT

Don't miss these passionate time-travel romances, in which modern-day heroines fulfill their hearts' desires with men from different eras.

Reflections In Time by Elizabeth Crane. When practical-minded Renata O'Neal submits to hypnosis to cure her insomnia, she never expects to wake up in 1880s Louisiana—or in love with fiery Nathan Blue. But vicious secrets and Victorian sensibilities threaten to keep Renata and Nathan apart...until Renata vows that nothing will separate her from the most deliciously alluring man of any century.

_52089-3 $4.99 US/$6.99 CAN

Apollo's Fault by Miriam Raftery. Taylor James's wrinkled Shar-Pei puppy, Apollo, will lead her on the romantic adventure of a lifetime. One minute Taylor and Apollo are in modern-day San Francisco, and the next thing she knows, the lovely historian finds herself facing the terror of California's most infamous earthquake—and a love so monumental it threatens to shake the foundations of her world.

_52084-2 $4.99 US/$6.99 CAN

Dorchester Publishing Co., Inc.
65 Commerce Road
Stamford, CT 06902

Please add $1.75 for shipping and handling for the first book and $.50 for each book thereafter. NY, NYC, PA and CT residents, please add appropriate sales tax. No cash, stamps, or C.O.D.s. All orders shipped within 6 weeks via postal service book rate. Canadian orders require $2.00 extra postage and must be paid in U.S. dollars through a U.S. banking facility.

Name_____
Address_____
City _____ State _____ Zip _____
I have enclosed $_____in payment for the checked book(s).
Payment <u>must</u> accompany all orders.☐ Please send a free catalog.

FOREVER & A DAY

VICTORIA CHANCELLOR

When Linda O'Rourke returns to her grandmother's South Carolina beach house, it is for a quiet summer of tying up loose ends. And although the lovely dwelling charms her, she can't help but remember the evil presence that threatened her there so many years ago. Plagued by her fear, and tormented by visions of a virile Englishman tempting her with his every caress, she is unprepared for reality in the form of the mysterious and handsome Gifford Knight. His kisses evoke memories of the man in her dreams, but his sensual demands are all too real. Linda longs to surrender to Giff's masterful touch, but is it a safe haven she finds in his arms, or the beginning of her worst nightmare?

__52063-X $5.50 US/$7.50 CAN

BITTERROOT

VICTORIA CHANCELLOR

Bestselling Author Of *Forever & A Day*

In the Wyoming Territory—a land both breathtaking and
brutal—bitterroots grow every summer for a brief time.
Therapist Rebecca Hartford has never seen such a plant—
until she is swept back to the days of Indian medicine men,
feuding ranchers, and her pioneer forebears. Nor has she
ever known a man as dark, menacing, and devastatingly
handsome as Sloan Travers. Sloan hides a tormented past,
and Rebecca vows to use her professional skills to help the
former Union soldier, even though she longs to succumb to
personal desire. But when a mysterious shaman warns
Rebecca that her sojourn in the Old West will last only as
long as the bitterroot blooms, she can only pray that her love
for Sloan is strong enough to span the ages....

_52087-7 $5.50 US/$7.50 CAN

Rejar

DARA JOY

Lord Byron thinks he's a scream, the fashionable matrons titter behind their fans at a glimpse of his hard form, and nobody knows where he came from. His startling eyes—one gold, one blue—promise a wicked passion, and his voice almost seems to purr. There is only one thing a woman thinks of when looking at a man like that. *Sex.* And there is only one woman he seems to want. *Lilac.* In her wildest dreams she never guesses that bringing a stray cat into her home will soon have her stroking the most wanted man in 1811 London....

__52178-4 $5.99 US/$6.99 CAN

Anne Avery, Phoebe Conn, Sandra Hill, & Dara Jo

WHERE DREAMS COME TRUE...

Do you ever awaken from a dream so delicious you can't
bear for it to end? Do you ever gaze into the eyes of a love
and wish he could see your secret desires? Do you ever read
the words of a stranger and feel your heart and soul respond?
Then come to a place created especially for you by four of
the most sensuous romance authors writing today—a place
where you can explore your wildest fantasies and fulfill your
deepest longings....

_4052-2 $5.99 US/$6.99 CAN

Big Bad Wolf by Linda Jones. Big and wide and strong, Wolf Trevelyan's shoulders are just right for his powerful physique—and Molly Kincaid wonders what his arms would feel like wrapped tightly around her. Molly knows she should be scared of the dark stranger. She's been warned of Wolf's questionable past. But there's something compelling in his gaze, something tantalizing in his touch—something about Wolf that leaves Molly willing to throw caution, and her grandmother's concerns, to the wind to see if love won't find the best way home.

___52179-2 $5.50 US/$6.50 CAN

The Emperor's New Clothes by Victoria Alexander. Cardsharp Ophelia Kendrake is mistaken for the Countess of Bridgewater and plans to strip Dead End, Wyoming, of its fortunes before escaping into the sunset. But the free-spirited beauty almost swallows her script when she meets Tyler Matthews, the town's virile young mayor. Tyler simply wants to settle down and enjoy the simplicity of ranching. But his aunt and uncle are set on making a silk purse out of Dead End, and Tyler is going to be the new mayor. It's a job he accepts with little relish—until he catches a glimpse of the village's newest visitor.

___52159-8 $5.50 US/$6.50 CAN

Dorchester Publishing Co., Inc.
65 Commerce Road
Stamford, CT 06902

Please add $1.75 for shipping and handling for the first book and $.50 for each book thereafter. NY, NYC, PA and CT residents, please add appropriate sales tax. No cash, stamps, or C.O.D.s. All orders shipped within 6 weeks via postal service book rate. Canadian orders require $2.00 extra postage and must be paid in U.S. dollars through a U.S. banking facility.

Name _____
Address _____
City _____ State _____ Zip _____
I have enclosed $_____ in payment for the checked book(s).
Payment <u>must</u> accompany all orders. ☐ Please send a free catalog.